IT SHOULD HAVE BEEN YOU

Laura Ashley Gallagher

Visit www.lauraashleygallagher.com to read more about Laura Ashley and her upcoming releases. You can sign up for her newsletter so that you're always first to hear about her new releases, updates and exclusives. You can also find her on Facebook, Instagram, and TikTok.

Please note: There are topics in this book that some readers may find distressing. You can find the list of content warnings on www.lauraashleygallagher.com/books

DEDICATION

For the woman who fought to find the light in her darkness and went on to become the light in everyone else's.

This one is for you.

This is for my sister.

You light up my life.

ONE

Ten years ago

BETH

"I thought when you said we were going to spend the day together, it meant food and lots of wine, not needles," I groan, resisting as my sister, Kim, tugs at my wrist, dragging me towards the tattoo shop. "I'm not even getting the tattoo. Why do I have to go with you?"

"Because you're my sister, and we haven't spent time together in forever." She pinches my cheeks like I'm a child. "And you take amazing photographs. I'm going to look hot with this tattoo. I need pictures for when I'm old and saggy, so my grandkids know what a badass their grandma was."

"You don't even want kids."

"And?"

I try to dig my heels farther into the concrete, but it's no use. She's too strong.

Damn yoga.

"We haven't spent time together because we're both busy with work, and you're too busy banging Derek."

"Eric," she corrects, rolling her eyes. "And we broke up."

Surprised, I come to a halt. "You did? When? We live together, and

1

you never said a thing."

Running a hand through her dark blonde bob, Kim sighs. "It was only three days ago. It's fine. I don't want to talk about it. I just really want to get this amazing tattoo." She pouts and rests her hands on my shoulders. "Please, Bethany Rose," she pleads, fluttering her lashes.

"Using my full name, isn't going to gain you any brownie points. You remind me of Mom."

Kim visibly pales. "Take it back. That's the most horrible thing you've ever said to me."

My mother is the only one to ever use my full name. It sounds proper around her group of fake friends at the country club.

What she doesn't tell her friends in the country club is that she left both Kim and me with our respective fathers when we were just toddlers. Her idea of being a mother is checking in once every six months. Thank God our dad's got along and saw the benefit of sisters having a relationship.

"Sorry. That was a low blow." Being compared to our mother is about the worst insult anyone can ever conjure.

"It's Logan-fucking-King. Do you know how long I've waited to get an appointment with him?"

"Two years," we say in unison because she's talked about it enough for me to know that this is a big deal.

"Everyone who is anyone has gotten inked by him. A-list celebs, rock stars, movie stars, even politicians."

"Politicians?" I raise an eyebrow.

"Apparently half the Senate has a tramp stamp. The point is this is a cancellation. Eric had to pull some big strings just to get me this appointment, and I might want to chop off his balls right now and feed them to him for breakfast, but I won't let my personal grudge get in the way of something I've wanted for so long. And… and…" she stutters, this situation getting the better of her vocabulary. "You're up and leaving me on Sunday for God knows how long."

"Eight months," I remind her.

"Exactly, I want to spend time with you, but I also really want this tattoo. Please don't make me choose." She presses her hands together in prayer.

"Fine. You could get a gig on Broadway with monologues like that."

Giddy, she kisses my cheek. "I know. Now come on."

I really hate needles. The thought of sitting there watching as it drags over her skin, makes me shudder, but I know she's wanted this forever, and if the roles were reversed, she would do it for me.

I huff, rolling my shoulders as I crane my neck back and eye the black painted shop with "King Tattoo Studio" in gold block writing.

Stepping inside, I'm immediately captivated by the warmly decorated interior. I don't know what I was expecting, but it wasn't this. High ceilings with wooden beams, a black-painted wall adorned with pictures of people getting tattoos—some recognizable faces from magazines and movies. Kim was right about this guy. He's in every picture, but his face is always obscured by his concentration on the task at hand. The shop exudes a sense of luxury with its lush leathers and dark wood furnishings. A high desk stands to the right, against a red brick wall.

Kim bounces on her heels, pulling on the sleeve of my denim jacket. "I can't believe we're actually here."

I force a tight smile as the nausea begins to build. This is a terrible idea. I passed out during a vaccine in high school.

I send up a silent prayer that tonight won't be a repeat. How embarrassing.

My eyes drink in every inch and naturally fall to the booths at the back of the shop. It's quiet. I expected the buzzing of needles, but apart from the low bass of some music playing over the hidden speakers and someone rustling with papers behind the reception desk, there's not a sound.

"Why is it so quiet?"

"I was squeezed in on a favor. It's closed," Kim explains.

Approaching the high desk, we're greeted by a young woman with white platinum hair and amazing black ink crawling up her neck before disappearing behind her hairline.

"You must be Kim. Eric's girl, right?" she asks, a thin smile on her lips.

"That's me," Kim replies, omitting the part about their recent break up.

The woman introduces herself while typing something into her computer. "I'm Cindy."

Kim looks at me with narrowed eyes.

Cindy?

Her name suits her as much as Bethany Rose suits me—which is not at all.

3

Still hunched over, Cindy glances at me over her rimmed glasses. "And you must be… nervous?"

"Can you relax?" Kim whispers, embarrassed. "This is Bethany Rose."

I don't bother correcting her. She's doing it to get on my nerves.

"Whatever, Mom," I breathe.

I groan when she nudges my ribs.

"Bethany Rose," Cindy acknowledges, peering at me with a gaze that lingers a moment too long. "Well, I'll let Logan know you're here."

"Actually, I really need to use the restroom." Kim bounces back and forth on her heels. "Will you be okay on your own?"

I nod. "Unless someone comes at me with a needle, I'm sure I'll still be standing when you get back."

She rolls her eyes and follows Cindy.

Seizing the opportunity, I venture further into the studio, my gaze scanning the endless awards and black-and-white photographs on the walls. I recognize some faces, but one photo catches my attention—a picture of three men, one of whom I've recently seen in a magazine.

Jaxson King. He's the lead singer of an up-and-coming band. Apart from a shared last name, I'm assuming all three men are related. Their lips tilt into the same small grin for the picture, hair almost inky black with the bone structure only seen in magazines. Standing shoulder to shoulder, it's a wall I'd have no problem running into.

Brothers. It's the only explanation.

Some people get lucky with their genes.

It's not until someone clears their throat that I realize I've lost myself in a world of my own, captivated by a photograph of three strange men, creating stories for them in my head.

I spin around, the camera hanging from my neck lifting with the force. When I open my mouth to say something, only air comes out, and I'm left with a gaping hole in my face.

Holy shit, he's huge.

I immediately recognize him from the picture, but I underestimated his size when they were all standing together. He smooths his fingers over his short beard, but even under the kept facial hair I see his full lips lift, revealing straight, white teeth, and a smile I wasn't expecting. His arms are heavily inked, and I trace their outline until it cuts off where his T-shirt skims his bicep.

"I-I… hi." It's the only word I can summon, and it still comes out more husky than my voice ever is.

He laughs, a deep sound that emanates from his throat, and dips his chin in greeting before taking a step forward. "Kim, right? First time?"

He scans my visible skin, and goosebumps dance over my flesh wherever his gaze lingers.

"Kim needed to pee." *Really, Beth?* "I'm her sister."

Another step.

I feel like he's sniffing out his prey.

"You're scared of needles," he states matter-of-factly.

My eyes widen. "How did you know that?"

"Experience. I can smell the fear a mile away."

I tilt my head back to meet his jade eyes, thick brows, straight nose, and even under the dark beard I can see the outline of a sharp jaw. If I were ever to get a tattoo, I'd happily let someone poke needles in me to draw his sculpted face on my skin.

I urge my thirsty eyes to stay on his because I know everything south of his face is equally as carved. My gaze falls but only for a split second, and sweet baby Jesus, what does he do for those shoulders? Carry his clients while he inks them?

"You're a photographer?" There's light amusement in his features, almost boyish, then he smirks and it's all man.

Realizing what he means, I blush. "Oh. No, I just carry this thing around as a fashion statement."

A thick brow lifts, and with the sound of his deep chuckle, I finally leave out a long breath. "I'm sorry. Please don't listen to a word I say tonight. You're right. I'm not good with needles. They make me nervous, and when I'm nervous I ramble. It's not the needles exactly. It's more the thoughts of the needles, and I work myself into a frenzy. This is the last place I should be."

"I see what you mean about the rambling."

My cheeks heat like I've been sitting too close to a fire.

Taking pity on me, he finally says, "Why don't you take a seat?"

I nod, stepping around him, but when I finally get past his mammoth frame, I see the booth and the equipment set up on his tray.

I feel it immediately—the tingles in my cheeks and the blood rushing away from my face, pooling at my feet.

Don't pass out.

Do not pass out.

5

I must sway because his tight grip is on my elbow, steadying me again. My mouth dries as I lift my gaze to look at him, and I'm not sure exactly if my reason for being dizzy is just the tattoo anymore. My hands tingle, pins and needles fluttering from the heat of his touch and radiating to my fingertips.

A frown draws his features tight, and as his eyes rake over my body, I shudder. Instinctively, I wrap my arms around myself, grateful for my denim jacket so he can't see the goosebumps dancing over my skin.

His eyes—deep green with specs of dark brown—are glossy in the second it takes for him to make sure I'm okay again. He swallows. I swallow harder.

He's still touching me.

Why is he still touching me?

We both look at his hand wrapped around my elbow like it's the only energy source in the room.

He drops his arm, his fingers flexing like he's been burned, and I swear I still feel his touch like it's branded there.

Slightly humiliated from my dizzy spell, I sway on my feet—this time on purpose—to distract myself while fidgeting with the camera between my hands.

"You good?" His tone is gravelly, coming from deep in his throat. I decide I like it. Fuck, I think I love it. A voice of all sin and a bite of playfulness.

Mom warned me about men like this.

Good thing I never listen to my mother.

I blink, then blink again because I've obviously lost all ability to use my vocal cords.

"Bethany Rose?" Kim's singsong voice breaks my trance. When did she come back out here? "You good, babe?"

"Yeah." I swallow the break in my voice. "I'm good now. Sorry, like I said, needles aren't my thing."

"And you decided a tattoo studio was a good place to spend your evening?"

I scowl, feeling heat rush up my neck because he's right. This was a stupid idea, but I don't think he's interested in hearing I just want to be a loyal sister.

"Take a seat…" His eyes linger on my face, and I'm not sure if he can't remember my name or if he's realizing it doesn't suit me. "Bethany Rose," he finishes, and I know the latter of my conclusions to be correct. "And try not to pass out."

I laugh, but it's too loud.

I think I'm still dizzy. It's the only excuse as to why I've lost all sensibility because of a man. Granted, the spice and headiness of his scent is clouding my vision. And he's standing so close, I can feel the heat of his body. But I've literally had men inside me and I haven't felt this off-kilter.

"And try to relax. I don't bite… often." He winks and walks away as if that comment didn't just make my knees wobble.

Kim finally introduces herself, with an obvious attempt at flirting. I stand awkwardly by, feeling a mix of amusement and envy at her confidence.

Why is she talking like her throat hurts?

She throws me a look that says, "Shut up", and goes back to biting her lip.

"We should get started. I have your design ready."

Kim's shoulders slump forward when her charms fall flat.

He takes his seat as Kim hikes up her tank top to just below her breasts. He doesn't even flinch. Most college guys would be drooling and dealing with a painful erection at the sight of my sister's under-boob.

She's got great boobs.

But I bet Logan King is used to tattooing all parts of people's bodies.

I want to ask him. It's on the tip of my tongue, but I think better of it. Imagining needles near my most intimate parts is doing little to ease the rocking in my stomach.

"Do you mind if she takes some pictures?" Kim asks.

Logan's gaze flickers to me, and I hold my breath, waiting for his response. "As long as it doesn't involve me spending the night in the emergency department, she can go crazy with that camera."

"I'll do my best," I promise, acutely aware that we could very well end up in the emergency room.

Cindy emerges from the back, zipping up her coat and slinging her bag over her shoulder. "You girls all set before I take off? Can I get you something to drink?"

"I'm good, thanks," I reply.

She gives Logan's shoulder a friendly squeeze. "Okay, boss man. Don't forget your brothers are coming in an hour. You need to finish

Archer's back piece."

He slips on black rubber gloves and side-eyes Cindy. "How could I forget?"

"Anything else you need?"

"Actually—"

"I was just being nice, Logan. You're supposed to say, 'You already do enough for me, Cindy. Why don't you go and enjoy your Friday night?'"

I laugh under my breath.

This time he completely turns to face her, an indent between his brow from the frown he's casting. It's mean and sexy as hell. Nobody should be gorgeous while scowling.

"See you tomorrow, Cindy."

She blows him a kiss. "Thanks, boss man."

"And Cindy," he calls before she leaves. She spins around. "Enjoy your night. And be careful."

She rolls her eyes but smiles. "Whatever, Dad." She waves and disappears into the night.

I leave Logan to get on with his work while I take photos from a distance. Attempting to step closer, my head spins, so I retreat, staying far enough away and positioning myself on the side of Logan where I can't see what he's doing to my sister.

When I think I can finally do it, I roll my shoulders back and swallow the fear bubbling in my throat.

It's just a needle.

He's not going to stab me with it.

I hope.

I close my eyes and brace myself by gripping the side of the bed. The buzzing makes my mouth water, and my gag reflex proves to be as weak as ever.

Just fucking do it.

I open my eyes and see spots of blood on Kim's skin.

Then everything goes black.

∞∞∞∞∞

When me and Kim were young and spent our weekends sleeping over at each other's houses, it never went as smoothly as we always promised. We were sisters with only a two-year age gap, and after the love fest of not seeing each other all week ended, we fought… over everything.

She's older than me, and thought she knew better.

When I stole her clothes one too many times, she always made the same threat: "Have you ever woken up with a crowd around you?"

She was all talk and has yet to knock me out.

But as my eyes flutter open, it's painful. The light from above seems too bright.

"You've finally done it, haven't you?" I croak. "You've knocked me out."

I hear her nervous laugh and a warm palm on my leg. "If I knocked you out, you'd know about it."

When my vision adjusts, I see there really is a crowd around me.

Thank you, Lord, for giving me such a beautiful crowd.

"Hey, pretty girl. Welcome back." A deep voice startles me, causing me to jolt upright, but a firm hand on my shoulder eases me back down, a glass of water in his other hand. "Take your time."

Logan King.

I remember now.

The sight of the needle piercing Kim's skin, the tiny droplets of blood, and then… nothing. I wince as a wave of nausea washes over me.

Momentarily ignoring the other people around me, I ask, "What happened?"

"You passed out," Logan says, his voice teasing.

Embarrassment floods me. Of course I did. In front of a man who is probably used to women throwing themselves at him, I had to go and faint. I groan and bury my face in my hands.

"It happens more than you think," he reassures. "You sure you don't want a tattoo of your own now?"

I shake my head, the room spinning slightly. "I think I've had enough excitement for one night."

Accepting Logan's hand on my back as support, I sit up, and when I do the embarrassment washes over me.

"How long was I out?"

"Just a few seconds. A real damsel in distress, you fell right into Logan's lap," Kim answers.

I shake my head.

Don't tell me anything else. I don't want to know. Better still, kill me, and put me out of my misery.

"But then you sat down and just kind of… fell asleep."

Horrified, my eyes bulge. "Fell asleep?"

"I knew you were working too hard."

I finally find the courage to look around.

Last I remember, there were only three of us here.

I take a head count.

Six people.

Jesus, Beth.

When the ground doesn't open, I raise mortified eyes, and finally greet my beautiful crowd. "Hi, and sorry."

A young woman shoves her way to my side. She takes a seat next to me. Her smile is warm and makes me feel marginally better. Pulling her long, ebony hair back from her shoulders, she pats my thigh. "Don't worry about it. You're not the first, and you're far from the last to pass out here. I'm Molly." Her eyes are blue, startling so.

"Bethany Rose, these are my brothers, Jaxson and Archer." The men I've already seen but only in the picture flash a heart racing smile at me. "And this is Eden." I can't see her face because she's hidden behind the wall that is the King brothers, but I see a glimpse of roaring red hair peek out through the gap in their shoulders. She waves her hand in the air. "Hey."

"Nice to kind of meet you, Eden."

"Embarrassed?" Kim bites her lip, trying to stifle the laughter.

"Thoroughly… Wait. Is your tattoo finished?"

Christ, I hope it is.

"All done." She lifts her shirt to show a string of butterflies along her ribcage covered in clear film.

"I didn't even get the photos you wanted."

"We have plenty of time for photos."

I glare at her. We always had lots of time for photos. I didn't need to be here, passed out on a strangely comfortable couch.

Her phone buzzes for what seems like the fifth time since I woke. "What is it?"

She shakes her head dismissively. "It's nothing."

Jaxson peers over her shoulder. "It's a guy called Eric. He says he's sorry for what he did, and can they meet up?"

The brothers share a look. "Booty call," they say in unison.

"Hey!" Kim protests, getting to her feet. "That's just fucking rude.

And you shouldn't be reading other people's texts."

"You shouldn't open them in view of everyone if you don't want them to be read," Jaxson fights back.

He's wearing an ACDC T-shirt. "I like your T-shirt." I point, falling back on the couch.

"I like your face… Ouch." He bends forward after receiving a hard elbow to his ribs from Eden. With him nursing his new injury, I finally get a look at her face. Green, almond shaped eyes shoot me a wink as she shrugs, the sprinkle of cute freckles dance across her nose.

Kim's phone pings again. A frustrated growl leaves her lips, but this time there's no lingering excitement in her brown pools. They're the same as mine. She can't hide anything from me.

"Shit," she groans, blowing out a long breath. "It's the hospital. They're short staff and want me to go in. I totally forgot I made myself available this weekend."

I tug at her T-shirt because my legs are still a little wobbly to stand. "You should go."

"What? No way. I'm not leaving you here. We had plans."

"You're a nurse. Your job is more important. Seriously, go." I see her indecision, but there's no decision to be made, and all I want to do is go home and forget this night ever happened.

"Shit, sorry, sis. Are you okay to walk?"

I stand, but my knees shake so I sit again. "You can go ahead. I'm going to grab a bite to eat first anyway." I lift my handbag. "I'll be fine. I have my book."

Her tongue pokes out, her eyebrows doing something funny that always has me on high alert. She glances around at my very beautiful crowd, who have now, thankfully, taken a step back. "She reads porn."

I gasp, opening my mouth for a comeback, but Molly gets there before me. "Me too."

"Yep," Archer agrees. I was wondering if he spoke. "I can confirm." He leans over and kisses her. "We've got a toddler to prove it."

Oh.

I hope my books don't do that to me.

Never.

My vibrator can't get me pregnant.

I giggle to myself, earning a confused look from my crowd, and an amused smirk from Logan. I tilt my head, narrowing my eyes. He mirrors me before winking like he knows exactly what I'm thinking.

Then I'm thrown sideways, right into Jaxson's arms as he plops himself on the couch. He's built like a tank; he shouldn't do that.

I quickly adjust myself, but not before he pulls me back and looks at Kim. "Yeah, big sis, you should go. She's good here."

Offended, Kim crosses her arms. "How do you know I'm the older one?"

"I don't. Lucky guess. I'll take care of her." He smirks and wraps his arms around my back, earning a glare so intense from Logan, Jaxson releases me so I can right myself.

He's cute.

Dangerous, but cute.

Kim huffs, but she's holding onto that phone like it's about to detonate. "That doesn't make me feel any better."

Eden steps forward, not once taking her eyes from Jaxson. I swear, he cowers a little before she slaps the back of his head. She's hands on, and I can't say I'm opposed. "She'll be fine. We'll make sure she's okay before she leaves."

"Yeah, she's good here," Molly adds, squeezing my hand.

She's a hugger. I just know it.

Kim hums and haws, but in the end, it doesn't take too much more convincing for her to leave.

I have no intention of staying. I'm leaving the second my legs allow me to stand without wobbling.

When Kim finally leaves, I sip my water, and ignore the eyes on me from above. Logan crouches again, and my eyes immediately find his. "You good, pretty girl?"

It's the second time he's called me that tonight, and now I'm unsure why my body is tingling.

I try to swallow but my mouth is too dry. "I'm good."

"Because I need to finish my brother's tattoo, and—"

I cut him off, waving my hand. "I won't faint a second time."

Unconvinced, he simply leans his elbows on his thighs. It makes him larger. I need him smaller. He's consuming too much of my air.

"I don't faint twice. It's a thing," I explain. "When I see a needle, I faint once, and I'm good after. I'm sure there's a name for it, but I don't know what it is. Besides, I'm leaving, and you can—"

"You're nervous again, Bethany Rose."

I purse my lips. "You're not wrong, Logan King."

"Stay until you feel better, okay?"

I nod, too transfixed on the muscles in his jaw flexing.

All these men are dangerous.

I look down to make sure my panties aren't already on the floor.

A little damp maybe, but still where they're supposed to be.

With a gentle smile and a dip of his chin, he stands and resumes his work. Archer removes his T-shirt and throws his legs over the chair, his arms draping over the back of it.

A hit of cologne erupts through my senses, and my head lulls to the side to find Jaxson still sitting there.

He grins at me, and I feel like I've become his next meal.

"I saw you on a magazine," I say to distract myself more than him. His smile grows impossibly wider. "That's a big deal."

There's a collective groan.

"Please don't feed his ego. He's hardly able to keep his head upright since the band got signed," Eden says.

"In that case," I say, facing him again, "Your music is shit." It's not. I've listened to their new single enough times to know every word.

"I like you." Eden laughs before turning to Jaxson. "You, not so much."

He winks at her, sitting back in the chair. "You love it, baby."

For a moment, I wonder if they're together, but then she scowls at him before baring her teeth. If they are together, they're either a passionate couple or currently in the middle of an argument. Either way, the tension rolls off them, and I can't be the only one to feel it.

The minutes tick by and everyone falls into easy chatter as I sit and observe, refusing the offer of a beer. I don't look over at Logan again, and I do my best to block out the sound of the gun buzzing as I sip my water.

I need to get out of here.

Okay legs, please work. Do your job.

Pressing my hand on my thigh, I finally lift myself from the couch, grateful when my limbs seem stronger. My gaze sweeps around the room. Anywhere but what Logan is doing to his brother's back.

The worst part? Logan's work looks amazing. It's art. An art form I would love to partake in if it didn't mean passing out.

All eyes fall on me.

Not Logan, though.

Nope. He's concentrating on his work, and yet, I can't help wanting a final look at those eyes.

Setting my glass down, I hook my thumb over my shoulder. "I'm going to go. Nice meeting you all."

Logan's voice pipes up from where he sits. "You okay getting home?"

"I live close by," I explain, my embarrassment surfacing again to eat me alive.

"Need someone to get you home safe?" Jaxson's lips lift into a panty-melting grin as a collective "For fuck's sake," rings out from everyone. But I don't think he's asking for my benefit. His eyes keep darting toward Eden, who's sipping a beer on the other side while playing DJ from a laptop.

"You're a pig, Jaxson," she says, her attention still on the screen.

Logan finally stops what he's doing to spin around in his chair. The glare in his eyes resembles that of a disapproving father. "Okay, what the fuck is going on with you two?"

"Ask your brother," Eden says with so much bite, I feel the sting.

This is awkward.

"You two are best friends, and Jaxson, you go on tour next week. Do us all a favor and get your shit together before then."

"Hear, hear," Molly agrees.

Then all hell breaks loose, a choir of voices arguing back and forth.

Okay, I'm out.

Not my circus and all that.

I mutter another goodbye, but they don't hear me.

TWO

The smell of baking coming from the kitchen is heavenly to my slightly hungover senses as I make my way down the hallway of our two-bedroom apartment.

I may or may not have drowned away the embarrassment of passing out during Kim's tattoo last night. After rushing out of there as if my ass was on fire, I got home, popped open a bottle of wine, and drank the first half straight from the bottle. It was that kind of night.

Kim is wiggling her ass when I enter the kitchen, dancing to her eighties playlist blasting from the speakers. She takes a tray of brownies from the oven and replaces it with another.

Oblivious to being watched, she talks to the cakes like she's given birth to them herself. "You are going to be delicious."

My sister is weird.

"You really need more sleep."

Startled, she jerks back, managing to balance the brownies on the tray before placing them on the counter.

"What the hell, Beth? You scared the shit out of me."

I stifle my laugh, grabbing the orange juice from the fridge, and pouring a glass. "Why are you baking? It's nine in the morning."

She shrugs. "Couldn't sleep."

"You've just come off a week of night shifts."

She usually has no problem sleeping after a grueling shift.

She fiddles with the towel before wiping a drop of batter from the counter.

She does it again.

And again.

Then she performs the ultimate tell—she tucks her hair behind her ear, tilts her head, and puckers her lips.

"Okay, what's going on?"

She shakes her head. "Nothing."

Still no eye contact.

"You are such a bad liar. Out with it."

Nothing but a lip chewed half to death.

"Kim, I swear I will fight you for answers. What is—"

"I slept with Damon."

I grip the sides of the chair, her confession almost knocking me off the edge. My eyes must be so wide they're on the verge of popping out of my head.

"Damon?"

She nods with her eyes closed and shifts from one foot to the other. A timer dings somewhere. We both ignore it. Some things are more important than brownies.

Very little, but some things.

"As in Damon with the massive—"

She cuts me off by letting out something resembling a moan.

"The priest? Our neighbor? That Damon?"

Her lips bite together, and I'm not sure if the scrunch of her eyes is embarrassment or a sense of victory.

She's been crushing on him since we moved here.

"What about Eric?"

I blink, unmoving, wondering what I have to do to make my life a fraction as interesting as hers. Truth is, there's been little to no action in my life since I graduated and started my internship at the law firm. That combined with being a photographer for events, my schedule has consisted of sleep, eat, work.

Wash, rinse, repeat.

"Rebound?" It's more of a question than a statement.

Damon isn't a real priest. He's not even a pretend priest. It's the nickname we gave him because our walls are thin, and we hear every woman he has in there. They call for God so often we're convinced he's performing exorcisms or very violent confessions. And we only know about Damon's massive penis because the women like to scream about it. I would be curious to find out if they're exaggerating, but he

16

also likes to wear grey sweatpants while running… loose sweatpants.

Those women are not exaggerating.

"When?" I ask, still trying to process.

"When I got home after my shift late last night, but I guess it was early this morning. He wanted to see my tattoo."

"Did you tattoo your vagina while I was passed out?" We're both stuttering in an octave above our normal tone. "Oh my God."

Her face flushes red. "I called for our Lord and Savior too. I'm one of those girls now." We stare at each other before bursting into a fit of laughter. "And Beth," she says, wiping tears from her cheeks. "It's not confessions he does in there."

"No shit."

"Although, he's so good with that baton, I would have confessed to a murder from before I was born."

A baton?

I'm still in shock, trying to untangle my tongue to form words. "You're a beast. You come home from a shift at the emergency room to go a round with Damon."

She holds up three fingers.

"Kim!"

"I know. I know. My thighs are killing me, and I'm probably a walking STD."

She grabs a cooled cake from the wire rack and stuffs the entire thing in her mouth.

"You used protection, right?"

She rolls her eyes, obviously insulted. "I was horny, not stupid."

"Fair enough."

Quick to deflect, she asks. "You're not working, are you?"

"No. My last photography booking was last weekend. London tomorrow, remember?"

She grimaces. "Don't remind me."

I feel her eyes on my back as I grab my camera from the table in the hallway and place it in my bag. Her unspoken words are louder than anything she says out loud.

I keep my eyes on the bag when I say, "Spit it out. You'll give yourself an ulcer if you swallow it."

"I'm just worried, that's all. You're going to be in London for eight months."

"It's work."

Concern washes over her features. "Sisterly instinct, I guess."

A shiver crawls down my spine. "About what?"

"I don't know."

I grab her hands and pull her into a tight hug. "It's eight months. I'm only doing it because it will be good on my law-school application. I'll be home before you know it."

She smiles, but it doesn't reach her eyes. She seems unconvinced, but there's not much more I can do to reassure her off-kilter spidey senses. Pulling away, I press my thumbs to either side of her mouth, right where our matching dimples are. "Smile. You had sex with a priest last night."

I swear her cheeks burn my fingers. "Stop it."

We jump as three knocks sound at the front door.

Strange.

Visitors need to be buzzed in. You can't just call to our apartment unless… "I bet he knocked with his baton."

Poor Kim almost buckles as I take off towards the door.

Bingo.

The priest.

His wet hair is sleeked back from his face, looking more brown than blond when wet.

"Damon," I greet, trying not to make it obvious that he stuck it in my sister just hours ago, but I fail miserably.

"Beth," he says, unsure. "Is your sister home?"

I chew my lip between my teeth. I can practically hear her hyperventilating. "Let me check."

Wide, terror-stricken eyes greet me when I return with a shit-eating grin on my face.

"Why didn't you tell him I wasn't here?"

"Because you are."

She points to the door like an insistent toddler. "Go out there right now and tell him I'm sleeping."

I grab my coat and bag, biting my lips together to smother another laugh. "Can't do that."

I swear she stomps her foot. "Why not?"

"Because you're a grown ass woman, and he's our neighbor. I leave tomorrow and won't be able to act as a buffer between you two. You'll eventually have to answer the door yourself and face him. Better sooner than later."

"I prefer later."

"Maybe he wants rounds four, five, and six."

I don't know how someone can pale and blush at the same time, but my sister masters it. "Christ, Beth, I'm going to need an ice bath before any of that again."

Another knock on the front door. "I can hear you in there."

"Yeah, well, we can hear you every weekend," I shout back. I must remind Kim to teach me CPR because she's on the verge of needing it. "Just go and talk to him. Do something else. You don't have to have sex with him. Go for coffee, talk, or whatever it is people do on a date."

She gawks at me like I've grown another head. "A date?"

"Call it whatever you like. I gotta go." I grab a brownie from a container. "I have an art class to get to."

"I don't know why you sign up for those, you've always been really bad at drawing."

"Thanks, sis."

She eyes the brownie in my hand. "You're going to eat one of those?"

Seriously, that's what she's concerned about?

Before I can respond, she shakes her head, waving me off with a tight smile. "Never mind. Enjoy the brownie and your art class. Make sure you tell me *all* about it."

"Okay…" I drawl, suddenly confused.

She walks me to the door, but I exit before I'm dragged into their awkward silence.

As the elevator doors slide open, I cast them one final look. "Nice sweats, Damon." I wink, eyeing what's not hiding beneath the material. "And stay out of my room, you horny teenagers."

The elevator doors close as Damon erupts into laughter and Kim throws her head in her hands.

THREE

Art class is full, a stream of people enter into the brightly lit room, and an elderly man named Norris sits beside me. He introduces himself when I arrive.

I stuff the last of the brownie into my mouth without thinking it through and shake his hand. But now my mouth is too full, and I can't speak.

My cheeks flame.

He crosses his arms over his belly, one foot still resting on the floor with the other on the bar of the stool, and chuckles. It's hoarse and warm. It reminds me of my grandfather's laughter.

As I take my seat, I swallow the last of the brownie and wash it down with a hefty cup of embarrassment.

"I'm Beth." I finally smile, hoping there isn't pieces of chocolate in my teeth.

"Nice to meet you." He then proceeds to wipe the corner of his mouth with a knowing smirk.

It takes me a long moment to realize he is telling me to wipe my mouth.

I do with a nervous laugh and wait for the embarrassment to surface but it doesn't. I'm oddly relaxed for someone who just dragged their heels ten blocks.

I glance around. Spaced out in a semi-circle, the people already here are getting their supplies ready, rolling them out neatly on the high table next to their stools. I do the same as I turn back to Norris.

"First time?"

He fiddles with a single pencil between his fingers. "No, no. Cassie, the art teacher, is my daughter, and I come to her classes when she's busy. Her mother died ten years ago. She thinks it's a way for me to get out of the house, but really, I just want to see my daughter."

That might be the sweetest thing I've ever heard.

He continues before I can reply, "I like the painting classes. I've never been to one of these." He waves a hand towards the small, round stage in the center of the room where a stool and a white sheet are placed.

"Me neither," I tell him. "Photography is my thing, and to be honest, I'm not very good at art, but I like it, even if I struggle to draw a stick man."

He laughs before leaning a little closer and whispers, "This drawing naked people thing..." I smother the laugh bubbling in my throat. "It's weird, an old man showing up to draw a naked young woman. My Sylvie would have had me hung, drawn, and quartered if she were still alive."

"What convinced you?"

"It's a man for today's class."

Cassie strides into the room then, clapping her hands twice to draw our attention, but I remain looking at Norris for a minute and how his eyes fill with nothing but pride.

It reminds me of how my dad used to look at me and all the times I took it for granted. It makes me want to tell Cassie to cherish it.

She clears her throat and smiles a megawatt smile. Her black curls are piled on top of her head in a bun, and the tunic she wears over her black leggings is loose. With her height and those cheekbones, she looks more like a runway model.

"Thank you all for coming. It's lovely to see some familiar faces. We have a special guest tonight. It's his first time being a portrait model, and I want you to be encouraging." Her lips twitch as she fights the giggle trapped in her throat.

A sudden, unwelcome urge to burst out laughing for her bubbles up inside me, instead escaping as a deep hum through my nose.

Did I just make that sound?

"Everyone, you might already know his face, but today's unwilling body is Logan King."

21

It takes every ounce of strength to stay upright on the stool as excited whispers ripple through the crowd around me.

I'm still stuck to my chair, wondering how the fuck this man has appeared in my life twice in twenty-four hours. I wasn't supposed to see him again. That wasn't the plan after I passed out on his lap.

Breathe, Beth. It will be over soon.

There's the briefest warm contact on my shoulder, a slight breeze in my hair, and then he steps onto the stage fully clothed.

Fire.

That's all I feel in my body and the hottest flames lick right between my legs.

Why am I horny right now?

Avoiding all eye contact, I push my chair so I can hide behind my canvas, but the chair is noisy and scrapes along the floor like nails on a chalkboard. Thankfully, everyone is too enamored by the Viking that just entered the art gallery to notice what I'm doing.

Head tucked to my chest, I turn to Norris, offering an apologetic smile.

"He's an old friend of my Cassie," Norris explains like my body isn't dying to turn itself inside out.

"Does he do this often?" I whisper as Cassie makes a joke about… fuck if I know. I can't breathe.

Do I have to see this man naked?

On second thought, that's not a bad idea.

But to draw him? There's not one single person in this room that can do him justice.

Norris scoffs. "Logan? Never. He lost a bet with my girl."

What kind of bet?

Another forceful laugh escapes my lips.

I need to get some control of myself.

How will I ever manage in a court room?

I throw a silent prayer to my father.

Sorry, Daddy, your girl is going to be a shit lawyer.

Risking a peek around my canvas, Cassie claps her hands together, obviously amused by Logan's predicament.

"Ready?" she asks him, smirking.

He scowls at her with a loud growl. I know that face. It's how he looked at me last night.

Total caveman.

It could be five seconds or five hours before he removes the leather jacket and his T-shirt. I wait with bated breath for the rest to come off, but it never does.

Well, that's disappointing.

But holy mother of all the holy people.

The man is carved to perfection. Thick, muscular thighs strain against his black jeans, the deep V leading to so many abs I'm pretty sure I could wash my clothes on them, and those shoulders are even more spectacular without the material of his T-shirt hiding them away.

Cassie sighs. "This is as naked as we're going to get Logan today so do your best. Focus on his tattoos. Create art within art."

What?

I'm so out of my depth.

She tries to position him in a pose, but he always falls back to resting his elbows on his thighs, looking like he would rather walk across hot coals than be here.

"Are you going to take any of my guidance?" Cassie asks, tilting her head at him.

He doesn't look up as he grunts. "You're lucky I'm here".

I've been too busy peeking over my canvas to notice everyone else has already begun drawing. Cassie spouts off something about the ridges of his muscles and how to draw them, and another thing about anatomy—I think. But I've been sitting here with my mouth hanging open and engulfed by a warmth spreading further than just between my thighs. I shouldn't be drawing him. I want to photograph him.

"Ready?" I jump as Cassie appears at my side like a ghost, scaring what life I have left in me. She winks at me as if to say, "I know, girl."

We share a smile before she floats away, and I fumble to grab a pencil.

That's when it happens. The pencil simply rolls away from me and hits the floor, bouncing once, twice, three times, and then rolls right to the stage. I slide off my stool, bending to pick it up, all the while trying to hide behind my hair.

It's no use. My spine stiffens, and a shock roots itself at the base, radiating to my fingertips. Heart racing, I look up to see his eyes are already on me.

Why is he so beautiful?

Handsome doesn't seem like enough of a word to describe Logan King.

Everything about him is somewhere in between. His jade eyes have a hint of boyish mischief but are also so masculine they make me want to run in the opposite direction. His full beard is neither long nor short, the facial hair somewhere between well-kept and scruffy. The tick of his jaw is stuck in a constant state of pissed off and intrigued. His black hair is short at the sides, but there's plenty on top to feel through my fingers and tug.

Christ, Beth.

What has gotten into me?

A fire erupts deep in my belly because one thing is for certain, the man with his eyes locked on me is absolutely lethal.

I gulp to moisten my dry mouth. The heat of his stare has me sizzled from head to foot. His nostrils flare, his hands balling into fists earning him a warning from Cassie to stay still. Then ever so slowly, one side of his mouth lifts to a barely-there smile. It's not comforting. I feel like vulnerable prey, and it hits me right where it intended to… Square in the ovaries.

A smile shouldn't have this amount of power, especially with a man I don't know.

Something's wrong with me today.

And as if a lightbulb goes off in my head, the realization hits me, and everything makes sense. My fuzzy brain, the limbs feeling like lead, the giggles I've managed to suppress until this moment because all hell breaks loose in my head, and I laugh so hard I really do snort this time.

"Is everything okay?" Cassie asks, sounding concerned while a fiery gaze remains on me, his frown unaffected.

I choose not to talk, knowing from experience that when I'm stoned and hit by a fit of giggles, it won't stop until I tire myself out or hunger strikes. So, I abandon the pencils, manage to murmur a "I'm so sorry" through my fit of laughter, grab my bag, and make a hasty exit.

Damn Kim and her brownies.

FOUR

Food is glorious.

My stomach grumbles even as I stuff a mouth full of pancakes down my throat. I've never been this hungry and food has never tasted so good. I'm going to kill my sister for allowing me to eat that brownie, but I need to be mad to commit murder, and right now, I'm downright giddy.

There's a food coma incoming, but I can't find the strength to stop as I wash down the syrup with my second cup of coffee.

When I feel eyes on me from a judgmental woman across the diner, I finally realize I probably look like a pig and put the fork down. Her brows knit together before she shakes her head.

"You should eat a brownie," I tell her, giggling to myself. I'm surprised she doesn't stand and usher her children out of the diner and away from the indulgent crazy lady.

I laugh again. It's too loud and more eyes turn my way. I bite my lip and sink farther into the chair while removing my phone from my bag to text my traitorous sister.

Me: Never trusting anything you make. Ever.

Kim: What I wouldn't do to see you stoned right now.

Me: It's disgusting. I can't stop eating.

Kim: Everything tastes amazing, right?

Me: It's better than sex.

Kim: You need to have more sex.

Me: You're not wrong.

Kim: It's your last weekend here for eight months. Go get laid. You won't even have to see them again.

Me: I'm ordering more pancakes, then I'm going home to sleep. How did things go with the priest?

Kim: HA! The most boring stoned person ever. He brought me for breakfast. I feel like this is weird. Is it weird?

Me: Stop freaking out. It's not weird. Go with it.

Kim: OK. Love you. See you later... I think.

Me: Such a minx. Love you too.

I grab another fork full of food. Judgy lady with the evil eyes be damned.

"You."

The deep rasp of his voice startles me enough that the phone flies out of my hand and a lump of food lodges in my throat.

Please don't choke right now.

I swallow quickly, thankful when the food clears from my airways.

Cheeks flaming red, I tilt my head back to look at my guest, towering over me with the same power he exuded last night. There's an amused arch of his brow before he rubs the smirk away with his thumb. I follow the motion too intently. I blame my sister's brownie for thinking he looks edible.

"Me?" I giggle and quickly bite my lips together. Clearing my throat, I sit straight. "Yes, it's me."

"The runner."

I pout, but he's right, and I'm sure if I weren't stoned, I would be embarrassed. "The runner," I agree, wiping my mouth with the napkin. "Sorry about that, and in my defense, I said goodbye last night."

He eyes the table of food. "Weed makes you hungry, huh?"

"Hush." I glance around to make sure nobody heard. "I have no idea what you're talking about."

"Bullshit. You're flying high right now, Bethany Rose."

Everything in me goes to mush. I've never loved my name as much as I do when it's said with the timbre in his voice.

I still don't correct him because it's the first time I've ever liked my full name.

I'm so weird.

And high.

So, so high.

Fighting the nervous laugh bubbling in my throat, I focus on anything but him.

"I didn't smoke weed."

Really? That's what I go with?

He chuckles and slips into the seat across the table.

He's holding a coffee to go.

Why isn't he going?

Why is he sitting?

"It's in the eyes," he says.

He's right. I caught sight of my reflection on my way here, and I looked like I just woke up.

"Fine, but you should know, I didn't mean to get stoned."

"No?"

"No. My sister baked brownies and never told me they were *special* brownies. I'm sorry I laughed. Just know I wasn't laughing at you." I search for words that won't come and finally settle with the only explanation I have. "The brownie."

He spins his cup between his large hands and shrugs broad shoulders. "What were you doing there?"

Isn't it obvious?

"I like art. I'm not much good at drawing, but I'm a tryer."

He tilts his head like I'm an abstract painting he's trying to figure out. "You like art, but you just admitted you can't draw?"

"Uh, huh."

"Do you paint? Sculpt?"

"Nope. I'm an observer who would very much like to be good at art, so I keep trying new things, but I'm not. I'm shit. I take photographs because, to me, art is everywhere."

That inherent curiosity I was born with burns in my stomach, so I reach into my backpack and hand over the photo album. If anything, it will stop him from studying me so intently.

Interest twinkles in those emerald eyes.

I push it toward him. "Go ahead."

I never show this to anyone. I'm always too nervous of what they'll think.

It must be the brownie.

Without saying a word, he opens to the first page. His eyes linger there for an endless minute before he flips to the next picture. Then another. And another.

His eyes roam from the pages to me and back again.

"Never mind," I breathe, suddenly regretting ever showing him the damn thing. I reach out to grab it. "It's ridiculous. You don't have to look at those."

He backs away, taking the photo album with him. "I'm looking." His fingers gently trace the images. "These are good. Really good."

A sense of pride swells in my chest. "Thank you."

"This one." He spins the photo album around, showing me a bride on her wedding day. It's the typical shot from behind, her chin to her shoulder. Her smile is beautiful, but it's not the focus of the shot. Her dress is backless and there's a scar between her shoulder blades and running the length of her spine. "She's beautiful, but her face, or even her dress isn't your focus. You caught the light just right. My eyes are immediately drawn to her scar. What's the story?"

Because there's always a story.

"I shot this wedding last year. It's a side hustle. Pays the bills." And I happen to love it. "Anyway, the bride had surgery for scoliosis when she was a teenager. Her dress was a statement. She wasn't ashamed of the scar or what she'd been through. I thought her attitude was inspiring. Some people hide their scars for whatever reason, some embrace them." I glance up at him. "Some tattoo over them. There's no right or wrong answer, but each one tells a story. That's what I love about photography. An entire story is told in one snapshot of time."

"So, people are your thing?"

"My thing?"

"Your inspiration, your focus, your passion," he explains.

I've never really noticed, but now he's pointed it out, I guess he's right.

"My father bought me my first camera when I was four. I'm sure it got on his nerves how I always had it in his face. I guess it took off from there. Then he bought me my first professional camera two years ago, right before he died. I don't photograph amazing skyscrapers or mind-bending graffiti or warzones." I flip the album to the last page, ignoring how I'm blurting my life story at him. "Like I said, everything has a story, even a skyscraper, but the man sitting in front of that building—he was a stockbroker and had a Scotch every night with dinner. Then that one Scotch turned into two, then three, then four. Then it was one during his lunch break. Before he knew it, he was hiding a bottle in the drawer of his desk. You get where I'm going.

"He lost his job five years ago. His wife left him and took the kids. He thought he had nothing to live for and gave up, found himself on the streets watching men in suits go about their day, grab their expensive coffee, and spend a day at work like he used to. That's the story I'm interested in."

He rubs his bearded jawline between his thumb and index finger. "You got all that from a single photograph?"

I drop my head and laugh. "No. I sat and spoke to the guy, and he told me. But I love watching people. I love looking at a photograph of somebody I don't know and creating a life for them. Call it active imagination."

"It's why you're sitting at a table by the window."

I smile. "Exactly." I spin the photo album back around. "Even without knowing his story, it's in his eyes. Here, look." His face is weather beaten, his once youthful features now embellished with fine lines and wrinkles, but... "He has the prettiest brown eyes, and he wears every minute of his life in them." He doesn't speak, and I'm too nervous to stop. "How many people pass him out because they don't see him? He's invisible. And those who bother to look, they don't see the story in those eyes. They see how he looks now, because most people refuse to look past the end of their own noses. He deserves to be seen. Everyone does. I wanted to take a nice picture of him. After all, a good picture can make your day. A bad one can ruin your week."

He nods slowly, that deep laugh floating across the table until I smile so wide it hurts.

At least the weed makes my rambling a little more coherent.

I think.

"What age are you?"

"Don't you know it's rude to ask a woman her age?" I tease, attempting to mask my own intrigue.

He shrugs, it's confident and sexy. Who knew a shrug could be all those things? "But here I am, asking anyway."

"I'm twenty-two."

His brows lift, a glimmer of surprise in his eyes. "You're awful in tune for twenty-two."

I wave my hand, attempting nonchalance. "My father always told me I'm an old soul."

A hint of a smile tugs at his lips—at least I think it's a smile. "I'm inclined to believe him. You talk about your father a lot."

"He influenced me a lot." I pause, wanting to shift the focus. "My turn. What age are you?"

"Twenty-nine," he answers without any hesitation.

"That's impressive."

"My age is impressive?"

I shake my head. "I was just thinking you're twenty-nine and have your own studio. From what I've gathered, you're pretty good. It's impressive, is all."

"Pretty good?" For the first time he flashes me a full smile and my returning smile falters because holy shit.

It's beautiful.

Trying to play it cool, I shrug. "Meh. I guess you're okay." The artwork displayed in his studio says different.

When I look up to meet his eyes, he's already staring, studying me like he did my photographs. The heat of his stare is scalding.

"And your thing is tattoos. How long have you been doing that?"

"Since I was a teenager."

He crosses his arms and leans on the table. I find myself doing the same. He's all spice and leather, rough but with sharp edges.

"Who taught you?"

"Lots of people."

That's it. That's all he's giving me.

I think about asking him what's been bugging me since the art class. It's on the tip of my tongue before I swallow the words.

"Say it," he prompts.

"Say what?"

"Whatever you want to. Stop biting your tongue."

I give in with a sigh. "I heard at the art class you were there because you lost a bet. I was wondering what the bet was."

Something dark glitters in his eyes, the knowing curl of his lips making my cheeks heat.

Oh.

Oh.

It was that type of bet. "You and Cassie, huh?"

He shakes his head.

I'm not sure if his intention is to evade my questions and confuse me but I'm thoroughly confused. "Have you ever?"

I don't know why I'm so insistent in knowing his relationship with the art teacher. It's none of my business.

What the hell is wrong with me today?

I should want him to leave. My high is dwindling, and I'm exhausted, but I'm genuinely curious.

"A long time ago. She's an old college friend."

"Did you go to college to become a tattoo artist?"

Shut up, Beth.

Shut. Up.

"Business."

That makes sense, I guess, considering he owns one.

I pick at the now cold bacon on my plate just to keep my hands moving and my eyes from focusing on anything but how the muscles in his bicep strain when he grabs the back of his neck.

My stomach lurches. I'm finally full.

"You look like you should ride a motorcycle." My filter is broken today, it's the only explanation.

"I do."

Of course he does.

I chew my lip between my teeth.

As he folds his arms over his chest and sits back, his knee brushes mine under the table as he shifts. It's the briefest touch. It shouldn't make my skin burn or cause our eyes to lock from the heat of it, but it does.

Gaze narrowed on me; I'm pinned to my seat. I wait with bated breath for him to speak. He needs to say something because I've swallowed my syrup coated tongue.

31

A smirk curls on the corner of his mouth. "What are you doing today?"

My head snaps back so quick, I'm sure I hear it crack.

I can't think of a single thing. "Nothing."

"You got your camera with you?"

"Always."

"I'd like to hire you."

"Hire me?"

"You are a photographer."

I nod, more confused than ever.

"It just so happens I'm in need of one. Up for the job?"

"You don't even know how much I charge."

"Don't care."

I swallow. Hard. "What is it because if it has anything to do with tattoos then I think we both know that's a bad idea?"

"I gathered that last night when your ass was in my lap."

Logan King knows what my ass feels like.

Never in the history of time have I burned so hot.

"Don't worry. I'll ease you into it."

It takes everything to hold back the moan wanting to escape.

My voice cracks, every word shaky. "Ease me into what?"

When the waitress comes to the table, offering a refill of my coffee, I feel like someone popped the bubble we were in.

I refuse the offer, suddenly nauseous with a sugar headache. "No, thanks. I'm good."

She dips her chin, her attention quickly averted. "How're you doing, Logan?"

"Can't complain. How are the kids?"

She rolls her eyes and laughs. "Driving me crazy, but I wouldn't have it any other way."

"Be sure to have Kyle come in for that work experience over the summer."

She squeezes his shoulder, her smile warm. She can't hide the attraction, and who the hell can blame her?

"Sure will." She saunters away with a sway of her hips.

I expect his gaze to follow but it remains on me. I don't know why it makes my heart beat a little faster.

"Sleep with her too?" I blurt because my brain malfunctions.

No answer, but he winks at me as he stands. Grabbing his wallet from his back pocket, he tosses too many bills on the table.

"I don't need you to pay for my food. I mean, it's a lot."

"But here I am, paying for it anyway." I'm about to argue when he cuts in. "It's the least I can do."

"For what? I'm the one who ran out of your class."

"For making my day interesting."

Oh, sweet baby Jesus. I made his day interesting. I need to eat Kim's brownies more often.

I hiccup.

Maybe not.

He drinks the last of his coffee, and I watch, oddly satisfied by how his throat moves when he swallows.

He tips his head. "Coming, pretty girl?"

Careful, Logan, I'm swooning.

He still hasn't told me what we're doing, but everything in me is screaming to just do it.

"You're not going to tie me down and tattoo me, are you?"

His mouth falls open, but quickly snaps shut. "Fucking hell, no, I'm not tying you down."

What a shame.

"My brothers will be there. Not everyone will be strangers."

My eyes flit back and forth from the street to Logan, but I'm already standing and slipping on my denim jacket.

"Your family, huh? That's the second time I've met them. This is moving a little quickly. You could at least take me on a date first."

Another dark chuckle and a shiver races down my spine. "I just paid for your pancakes, consider yourself romanced."

"You're a terrible date, Logan. I expect wonderful things for our second."

He's still laughing when he reaches out and pulls my hair free from where it's trapped in my coat. I freeze, waiting for him to realize what he did, but nothing. Zilch. He simply steps away. "Are you coming?"

I don't know if it's the weed, the opportunity to take more photos, or the want to stay with him a little while longer—especially when I get to see him work, but a smile creeps in, and I nod like an enthusiastic toddler. "Why not."

I leave tomorrow and I haven't had anything resembling fun in a very long time.

He holds the door open when we step outside before passing me and going to the motorcycle parked out front. He unhooks a helmet from the side and turns back to me expectantly.

"No fucking way." My feet stick to the path, fear racing through my veins. "Sorry, Logan. You'll have to find another photographer. No can do. Nope. I am not getting on that thing."

Feeling my fear intensify, I instinctively grab the shoulder straps of my backpack, as if they can anchor me to the ground.

"It's perfectly safe," he says like he can hear my thoughts.

"I don't think so. It's a death trap."

He opens his arms wide. "I'm still here."

Yes, you are, you glorious, insane creature.

The blood drains from my face and pools at my feet. "I can walk. Your shop isn't far."

"What are you so scared of?"

You. I'm scared of you, and how I'm seriously thinking about getting on the back of your death trap.

"Come on." He tilts his head with a wink. "I'll keep you safe."

Something warm flutters in my stomach.

I'm certifiably insane because my feet are moving toward him of their own accord.

He says, "Good girl," and a slow wink has me melting all the way to my toes.

He throws his leg over, turning the key until the engine roars to life, the sound resonating in my chest.

Licking my dry lips, I straddle the seat until my front is flush with his back. He's warm and the muscles under my hands are rigid as I slide them around his waist and cling to his T-shirt.

He gives my hands a reassuring squeeze. "Ready?" he asks, looking over his shoulder.

Three deep breaths later, I nod, grip him a little tighter, and agree.

"I'm ready."

∞∞∞∞

Ten minutes later, Logan turns the corner to his shop.

My thirsty eyes drink in the sight as it comes into view.

Rows of motorcycles line the street. Smoke billows from food stalls, music blasts from a speaker somewhere. People laugh and dance, their loud chatter filling the air around us. The smell of food, leather, and engine fumes mix with the city air. Children queue at the ice-cream truck, some lick it from where it's melting down their hand in the summer heat.

And bikers.

Lots and lots of bikers.

Most are covered in tattoos. Some wear leather vests over their T-shirts even as the sun blasts blistering heat from the sky. A patch on their back reads, *The Kingsmen*.

This is nothing short of a street party.

A hairy street party, but a street party.

Directly in front of the studio, Logan turns into an empty space.

He looks over his shoulder at me, amusement in his dark green eyes.

"You'll need to let go of me if you want to get off the bike, pretty girl."

Blushing and grateful he can't see it under the helmet, my knuckles are white and stiff when I finally release my grip.

I remove the helmet and get off with shaky legs.

"What is this?"

He stands, but it's too close. The scent of spice and leather is intoxicating. He doesn't back away. I don't think I want him to.

His size is intimidating, his shoulders blocking the view of what's going on behind him, or maybe I just don't care when he's standing so close.

"What does it look like?"

I swallow before licking dry lips. His eyes fall. My heart drops into my stomach.

"A party?" I answer, still unsure.

"Then it's a party."

I lean a little closer, unsure if I should ask this question. Will it get me killed?

"Bethany Rose?" he prompts when I don't say anything.

There's no sign of a patch on his clothing. "Are you part of a gang?"

Those full lips threaten an actual smile under his beard, but it could be just a twitch. I'm not sure.

"A gang?"

I look around to prove my point. There are men here that look scarier than Logan.

"I'm not in a gang. If I was do you think we would be having a party with a police station a block away?"

I shrug. "I don't know how gangs work. How else would you close off an entire street?"

"A permit," he deadpans.

My mouth falls open. "Like a gang permit?"

He throws his head back and laughs.

A real laugh.

It's like a punch to the gut, but I find myself laughing with him.

In the next breath, he grabs my hand. Our fingers interlock and tingles dance over the skin.

Glancing down at me, his lips thin before his eyes fall to our connected hands. It's hardly long enough to notice, but I notice.

"Come on." He tugs the hand he's holding.

My hand.

He's holding my hand.

We're only walking a couple of feet to the shop. Why is he holding my hand?

His name reverberates among us, accompanied by firm slaps on the back—an age-old greeting employed by men as a substitute for the potentially awkward alternative of simply saying hello.

"Ain't you gonna introduce us to your girl, King?"

His grip tightens on me.

"How about you keep your eyes on something else, Ace?"

The man he called Ace shoots me a friendly wink as Logan finally stops to greet everyone. I try to step away to give him some space, but his hand comes around my waist, keeping me planted at his side. "This is Bethany Rose." It comes out in more of a mumble. "She's our photographer."

"Don't we already have one of those coming?" Someone pipes up… from somewhere.

I look to Logan for answers, but all I get in return is a blank stare.

"Not anymore."

What does that mean?

An older man steps forward and reaches out his hand to me. Wrinkles set deeper as his mouth widens. There are only flecks of black left in his grey hair, an impressive physique hidden under a white T-shirt and leather vest. "Please excuse my nephew's rudeness, darlin'. I'm Skip."

"Nice to meet you."

Ace is the next to shake my hand, a wicked smile plastered on his lips before he runs his fingers through messy blonde hair.

Very Sons of Anarchy.

Very mouth-watering.

People continue to introduce themselves, others don't. Some look at me with what I think is curiosity. Maybe it's suspicion.

Logan ends whatever conversation he's having with a dip of his chin and takes my hand again. "I need to get inside. And for fuck's sake, when she comes around taking photos, leave her alone. Maybe some of you might even smile."

"Now why wouldn't we smile for a beautiful lady?" Another wink from Ace.

Another growl from Logan.

There's too much testosterone here. So, when he pulls me through the crowd and into the shop, I follow.

With so many people inside, it looks different. A buzz vibrates in the air.

All eyes fall to Logan again. He has that effect on people.

It's a big shop. We should blend in with the crowd, but people notice when he enters.

Briefly, I catch sight of the poster on the wall. I saw a similar one outside, but I couldn't get a proper look when I was caged in by cavemen.

"A Heart for Evie."

The face of a little girl—I'm assuming is Evie—is beneath the words, her dark hair falling in loose curls around her shoulders. She's only a toddler. Her eyes are as blue as the dress she's wearing, but my heart breaks when I notice the oxygen tube in her nose.

I look at Logan and back at the picture.

They have to be related.

Does he have kids?

"You okay?" he asks.

I don't realize I've stopped walking until Logan speaks. My fingers are cramping from how hard I'm squeezing his hand.

His eyes follow what I'm looking at. He smiles, but it's too sad. "My niece, Evie," he explains. "Beautiful, isn't she?"

"She is. What happened to her?"

"She was born with a rare heart condition. It was diagnosed right

37

after her birth. Doctors said she probably wouldn't survive the first surgery, but she proved them wrong and survived many since."

Pride shines in his eyes.

I'm almost afraid to ask. "Is there a cure?"

"No." His pride quickly fades into something resembling fear. "But everyone is here today for her. I think it gives Archer and Molly hope, and we focus on that. We focus on the hope."

I can only imagine if it were my child, I would cling onto hope wherever I could find it.

I clear the emotion clogging my throat, then ask, "And what is today exactly?

I get why he wanted me to take photographs, but I still don't know what this is.

"People get inked with the small heart tattoo, and instead of paying, they make a donation."

"That's amazing."

He tugs at my hand. "Let's start easing you into this."

Now I know what he meant back at the diner.

If I'm here as the photographer, that means taking pictures of people getting tattoos which means I will need to be around needles, which means given what today is for, I can't be a baby and pass out at the sight of one.

With that in mind, I remind myself of a little girl who has probably been poked with more than her fair share of needles. I roll my shoulders back, swallow the saliva pooling in my mouth, and close my eyes.

Because if I can't see it, it's not there.

We stop.

Logan drops my hand, only to replace his touch with his heat at my back.

His breath sweeps across my neck. "Plan on taking pictures with your eyes closed?"

I peek through one eye. I'm grateful for all the commotion here because no one is paying attention to me.

Well, apart from Logan and Archer.

Archer's eyes dart between us. "The fainter? Really?"

"I'm a runner too apparently."

Logan side eyes me. "She's our photographer."

Archer's brows pull together. "I thought we had one of those."

"Why does everyone keep saying that? I don't want to step on anyone's toes."

"You're not," Logan clips.

There's some kind of silent conversation happening between the brothers.

Archer finally smiles. "You're good. Thanks for doing this."

Logan shoves a bottle of water in my hand and pulls an extra stool over to his booth. "Sit and keep drinking that. Let me know if you feel like you're going to pass out and I will stop. You'll get used to it."

I open the bottle and take a swig before he pries it from my mouth.

"Sip it," he demands, putting the cap back on and handing it to me.

Hands shaking, I reluctantly sit on the stool he's provided. When I look around, there's three other tattoo artists here, including Archer and the girl I recognize as Cindy from last night.

"Which one of you fuckers is first?" she asks, holding out her arms.

Why did I agree to this?

It's going to be so embarrassing if I pass out again.

But I remind myself I leave in less than twenty-four hours, and I won't have to see these people again.

"Ready?" Logan grabs my chair and yanks me closer before pushing his hands into black rubber gloves.

I don't agree with words because I'm afraid to open my mouth. I nod instead. It feels like the safer option.

Two minutes later, a man sits down opposite us.

He introduces himself, but I immediately forget his name.

"I need my hands."

I look down to see my nails digging into Logan's arm. That's going to leave a mark.

I pull away and fiddle with the water bottle on my lap.

Satisfied, he dips the gun. It comes to life with a buzz.

Holy shit.

I grip Logan's thigh because he said he needs his hands, and I need to hold onto something.

"You gonna let me take you to dinner first?"

He laughs under his breath, but when I look down, my hand is awfully close to the bulge in his jeans.

I'm going to pass out for another reason.

"Just do it," I urge, my hand remaining exactly where it is.

He smirks at me. "Not what a man wants to hear."

39

"Unless you want me passed out on your lap again, I suggest getting a move on."

"Wasn't that bad," he says with a shrug before pressing the needle against the nameless man's skin.

My head spins.

I tighten my grip on Logan.

He hisses, but when he stares over at me, I don't think it's from pain.

Scorching emerald eyes scan my face for one, two, three seconds, keeping me stuck to my chair.

Dragging his gaze away, he gets to work, and I, by some miracle, don't pass out. I find myself watching Logan rather than watching what he's doing.

It helps.

It does little for the somersaults happening low in my belly, but I don't faint.

He's three tattoos in before I remember why I'm here and take the camera from my bag to capture some shots.

When I finally stand, I'm steady.

"Good girl," he praises, and those somersaults slide right between my legs.

"I didn't faint."

"You didn't faint," both he and Archer confirm with a laugh.

Ten minutes later and I'm a pro, needles be damned.

They could almost poke me with one.

My mouth waters.

Maybe we're not there yet.

I go from station to station, keeping out of people's personal space while I take shots of everything that's happening.

I rest my hand on Logan's shoulder. I don't want to startle him with that thing in his hand. "I'm going to head outside."

"Are you okay?"

"Yeah, I'm good. I just want to get pictures of what's going on."

"Bethany Rose," he calls out just as I'm about to leave.

I spin around, a stupid smile already plastered on my face.

His gaze remains locked with mine, but it might as well be everywhere. He wipes another grin away with his thumb.

I want to cut off that thumb.

But there's no mistaking the slightest tilt of his lips as he shakes his head. "Nothing, pretty girl. Just looking."

FIVE

Present day

BETH

"Why is there a For Sale sign in your lawn?" Kim greets me with wide eyes, her hand resting on the handle of her suitcase.

I pull her into a hug. "It's good to see you too, sis." I reach out and take the suitcase, heaving as I pull it inside. It weighs a ton. "Is Damon in there?"

"Beth, why the hell is that sign in your garden?"

I forgot I needed to tell her… on purpose.

Leaving her suitcase in the hallway, I grab her hand and drag her through the living room. "Coffee?"

There are boxes everywhere. I bought the boxes months ago, but they've been hidden away.

Out of sight, out of mind.

Now I have no other choice but to deal with it.

The boxes are empty. Taking them out of the closet was enough for one day.

"Beth, what the fu—" I clamp my hand over her mouth.

"Isabel is napping, but Hannah is in the kitchen so watch your language. The landlord is selling the house. I've been trying not to have a panic attack since yesterday. I'm so happy you're here. I've missed you. I want to spend time with my sister, but I have thirty days to get out of this house and find a new one with two children. I'm having lunch with our mother today. Our mother, Kim. That's enough to send me over the edge, but now I have a house to pack, I'm going to a damn art exhibition this week, because God knows an art exhibition is exactly what I need right now, and I have a meeting tomorrow to sell a company. Oh, and... And..." I stutter, that panic attack beginning to rear its ugly head again. "I'm having lunch with our mother today. Did I already say that? I have no idea what I'm doing. I'm a mess. My life is a mess. So, I need you to not be a mess. I need you to tell me everything is going to be fine, even if it's a lie."

She grabs me by the shoulders and jerks me. "Damn it. Pull yourself together. Everything is going to be fine."

I inhale and hold it before blowing out a long breath. "Thank you for lying to me."

"No problem. I'm here for a week. We'll get it worked out together."

Now it's her turn to take my hand and pull me into the kitchen. After hugging Hannah and smothering her with kisses, Kim pulls out the chair and pushes me down to sit.

"Relax. I'll make coffee. We'll work it out."

"Mom is stressed because we have to move house," Hannah says, her eyes never leaving the page she's coloring. For eight, she's as sharp as a tack. "It's not a bad thing. I don't like this house. The back yard is too small. I can't even play soccer out there. Can we have a big back yard in our new house?"

"I'll add it to the list, honey." I take a crayon and begin coloring the other page. "Where do you think we should go?" I ask.

She puts her crayon down. Scrunching her nose, she looks up at the ceiling. She's thinking. I know because that's how I look when I'm thinking.

"We should move in with Kim and Damon."

Kim puffs out her cheeks and we both shake our heads.

That's definitely not the answer.

Handing me a cup of coffee, Kim crouches and takes Hannah's hand. "You are more than welcome to stay with me any time. You know that. But me and your mom can't live together."

"Why?"

My sweet, innocent baby.

"Because we'd end up killing each other, sweetie," Kim answers honestly.

She's not wrong.

I love my sister with every fiber of my body, but there are times when those same fibers want to strangle her.

"But can't we live closer to you?"

Kim turns to me. "It's not a bad idea."

"You live in the middle of nowhere. We need civilization. And Hannah, Kim lives two hours away. If we move closer to her, it means you will need to move to a different school."

"Good. I hate my school."

My mouth falls open in shock. "Since when?"

She lifts her shoulders. "Since forever."

I pull her from her chair and into my lap, guilt making my stomach churn. She never said a word. "Why do you hate your school?"

I want her to give an obvious answer. The simple one. I want her to say she hates school for no reason like so many other children, but she doesn't.

"When we lived with all the other moms, their kids were like me."

Like me.

She sees herself differently and it breaks my heart.

"You still have all those friends. We meet with them every week."

"I know. School is just different, I guess."

I kiss the top of her head. "I'm sorry, baby girl."

"It's okay, Mom."

It's not okay.

None of this is okay.

"Private schools," Kim says into her coffee. "You pay a small mortgage for an education and that's how she's treated."

I cast her a warning look.

Not now.

Private school was my husband's idea. He went to private school, and he insisted his children would too.

I don't remember having a say. Probably because I didn't.

Even in death, he made sure her schooling was paid for.

"Kids are assholes, Hannah."

44

"Kim!"

"What?" she mumbles around the cookie she stuffed in her mouth.

"But I'm a kid, Auntie Kim."

"Oh, sweetie, you're different. You're my niece. You could never be an asshole. You're a powerful woman."

Hannah's eyes slide between us. "Me and Isabel are going to be weird sisters like you, aren't we?"

"Absolutely," we answer together.

Her dimples are on full display when she smiles. "I'm going to read my book." She kisses my cheek and stands. Conversation over. She's returning to her natural habitat.

I wait until she's out of the room to throw my head in my hands, feeling tears sting the back of my eyes. "I didn't know. How did I not know my child hated school?"

"It happens. I hated school too. Kids are cruel. Besides, it's summer break next week. That gives you time to get out of here. Find somewhere you actually want to live. Treat it as a trial run. A long vacation if you will."

"I will not. I don't have time for a three-month vacation. Like I said, if we move, Hannah needs a new school, and I need to go back to work which means I will need childcare for Isabel. We can't live where you live. Your nearest neighbor is a herd of cattle."

She rolls her eyes. "But you can run around naked without anyone catching you."

Finally, I laugh, but it hurts my cheeks. Every muscle in my body is tense.

"You've sold the shares of the firm. You don't need to work."

It wasn't that much, and the money is for the girls. I'll use some for a house until I get on my feet, but I don't want it."

"You earned that money. You deserve it."

I earned it?

What a strange way to earn money.

"I need to go back to work."

It was out of my hands for so long. I didn't have a choice but to stay at home.

I have a choice now.

I have no idea what I want to do yet, but I know I need to do something.

"It's a good idea, you know. Moving closer to you. It makes sense."

I can tell she's trying to contain the excitement while she sips her coffee. "It does. There are some small towns close by. Good schools. Not sure about jobs, but you could look into it. Pine Falls is just thirty minutes from my house. It's beautiful and busy. Lots of tourists so there's got to be work there."

"I know it. I remember it from my photography days. Lots of people go there to get married."

I've never had any shoots there, but I've seen pictures and Kim is right, it's beautiful. Picturesque with a mountain backdrop.

"I can look online when you're gone. See if anything is available that suits."

"Thanks, Kim."

I'm pretty sure this day is already getting on top of me, so I go to the sink and toss the rest of my coffee in the sink. Coffee isn't helping my spiraling anxiety, so I clean dishes I've already cleaned.

Kim joins me, not saying a word as she picks up the towel and dries. I glance at her from the corner of my eye and hate when I see the sympathy shining.

I already know what she's about to say.

"Don't, Kim."

"You're tired," she says.

"I'm always tired."

"No, you're really tired. You've got that look in your eyes again. Are you still going to therapy?"

Frustrated, I press my hands against the sink and drop my head. I don't want to have this conversation.

She's worried.

I get it.

But I can't do this. Not now.

"Yes, once every fortnight."

"Beth—"

"Stop," I cut her off. "I love that you're here and that you're helping. I appreciate you more than I can say, but I need to get this week over with."

"You're scared," she states because she knows me. I might have lost her a long time, but she knows me just like I know her.

"I'm terrified," I admit not daring to look at her and confirm all her suspicions.

I don't sleep and when I do, nightmares haunt me. I find it hard to breathe for no reason. I zoned out in a queue yesterday as memories raced through my mind. The man standing behind me touched my shoulder to see if I was okay and I flinched. Not a small one either. I almost jumped out of my shoes. He looked at me like I was crazy.

Maybe I am.

Maybe that's the answer to everything.

I'm crazy.

I'll get it together again. I always do.

I have to.

Her tone is softer when she rests her head on my shoulder. "Tell me."

This is going to sound stupid because it is stupid. "I've never chosen where to live before. I went from living with my father to living with you when I was in college. My apartment in London was chosen by the firm. Someone organized for me to stay here. It was done for me. Then there's…" I swallow the acid rising in my throat.

"He who shall not be named?"

I hate when a chill runs down my spine, but I refuse to give his name more power than it deserves. "My husband. You can say his name."

"I fucking hate his name," she snaps, each word coated in venom. "I hate him. I hate that he kept us apart. I hate what he did to you. He was a monster."

"Yeah, well, he was a monster that made all the decisions. What if I get this wrong? What if leaving is a bad idea?"

My heart is pounding, and a bead of sweat runs down my back. If I don't get it together, I won't be able to breathe.

She takes my hand and squeezes. "It's okay to be scared. But you never wanted to live in the city. We both know that. Do something you want to do for a change. If it doesn't work out, it doesn't work out."

She makes it sound so easy, simple.

When none of this is either of those things.

"I hate to break it to you, but you have a lunch date with mother dearest right now, and if you don't leave soon, you're going to be late."

I throw my head back with a groan. "Jesus fucking Christ. Kill me," I beg, not completely sure I'm joking. "It would be easier than sitting through lunch with that woman."

She rolls her shoulders straight and pouts, her lips stiff. I know

47

exactly what she's doing. "Honestly, dear," she mocks in my mother's voice. "You always find something to complain about. Now please brush your hair. Be presentable. Always be presentable, Bethany Rose. You don't want to miss the opportunity to marry a rich man and leave your children behind."

We laugh because it's sad.

"You sure you don't want to come? When is the last time you saw her?"

"Just after you moved to London, and I would rather pull my eyelashes out than sit at a table with her. But I'm curious. I want to know what she wants."

I don't want to go either, but I can give her an hour of my time. I wish I had Kim's strength because she cut ties a long time ago. There's barely a thread keeping me and my mother's relationship together, but I can't seem to sever it. I should. I know I should. She's not healthy.

But unlike Kim, I didn't have the luxury of moving out of state. I married into a powerful family with a good name. My mother clung to me like a lifeline over those years.

I wanted to do the same, but I'm afraid my mother allowed me to drown.

When my marriage went to shit, she was the only one I had, so I told her. I bled out with her in front of me.

Her advice: "No marriage is perfect, Beth. Women make sacrifices. You need to stand straight and get on with it."

It's hard to stand straight with broken ribs.

"Now go." Kim nudges me. "I'll stay here with the children and keep away from the wicked witch."

SIX

I wonder if everyone breaks out in a sweat when going to visit their mother because, although my visits are rare, this pounding heart always accompanies them.

I knew something was wrong when she called me yesterday and asked me to come for lunch. My mother has avoided her children since we were in diapers. And she asked for just me. Not the kids. I would be insulted if I didn't know her so well.

I wouldn't have brought the girls anyway. Having spent my life around her, I know there's only so long she can keep her negativity concealed in her chest before she releases her talons and digs. The girls don't need that.

The gates open before I have a chance to fully stop the car at the intercom.

I stare at the upstate Victorian mansion and do what I always do when I come here. I try to conjure childhood memories I don't have. I imagine a different world where my mother is so excited to see me, she's already outside and standing on the steps before I get out of the car.

But I'm not in that world. I'm in this one where the house brings nothing but nerves, and I see only bricks and water surrounded by well landscaped lawns.

It's a far cry from how I grew up with my father in our two-bedroom apartment. We struggled, but he hid it well. It got easier when

I got older, and he got a promotion in the firm he worked for. We survived and we were happy. I was loved beyond belief by at least one of my parents.

Inhaling a steadying breath, I give myself the once over in the rear-view mirror. The less I give her to pick apart the better.

It takes a long minute of me throwing my head back and cursing into thin air to finally get out of the car.

Why did I even agree to this?

I know why, because curiosity killed the cat and when my mother texted this morning to remind me of this lunch, she ended the text with kisses. I almost passed out from shock and an uneasiness settled in my stomach. It's remained that way ever since.

The front door swings open before I can knock.

Hair tied back in a tight bun, her grey eyes have more wrinkles since the last time I was here, but they're no less warm. She claps her hands together, standing at least four inches smaller than my five seven.

"Oh, sweet girl." Rita pulls me into her embrace. I was never here long enough to really get to know her, but she was always kind to me when I was a child. She pulls back and cups my face. "You just get more beautiful."

I squeeze her shoulder and smile. "I get older, but it's so good to see you."

She swipes her hand through the air. "Nonsense. You've still got your daddy's eyes."

"Thank Christ for that," I mutter under my breath.

She peeks over my shoulder, her chest visibly deflating. "No girls today?"

It's on the tip of my tongue to tell her they weren't invited, but I choose to say, "They were tired."

This is a house kids should be able to run riot in, but having children play here would have my mother popping Xanax like her favorite candy.

"You need to show me some pictures before you leave."

I can't help but grin. "Of course."

"They're in the dining room, but your mom is in the kitchen. She wants to speak with you first."

My eyes narrow.

Something is off. I'm surprised to hear my mother even knows where her kitchen is.

50

Before Rita can usher me away, I take her hand and inspect the hallway for prying eyes. When I'm sure we're alone, I lower my voice. "Is she sick?"

"What?"

"My mother. Is she dying?"

I hate being caught off guard so if it's that, I would like a heads up.

Her lips thin before she shakes her head and blesses herself with the sign of the cross. "No. Not at all. Your mother is as healthy as a horse."

My laugh comes out in a mystified huff. "Huh, today just keeps getting stranger." Something dawns on me then. "You said *they*. Who are *they*?"

Her gaze averts to the round table holding a giant vase in the middle of the hallway. "You should go on in now. She knows you're here. You don't want to keep her waiting."

That uneasy knot flips in my stomach, making my chest feel tight, but I won't press her. I don't sign her paycheck, and her loyalty isn't to me.

Time to get this over with.

With an understanding dip of my chin, I walk away.

"Beth," she calls with an undeniable crack in her voice. When I turn, her eyes are glossy. "You're a strong girl. Hold onto that strength today."

And with that, she walks away, leaving me with a pounding heart and the urge to run.

My mother is observing the new chef when I enter the kitchen. At least I think he's new. I haven't been here in a long time.

"You look pale, dear."

She's used that one before. It was justified then, but she hasn't taken her eyes off the man sautéing onions long enough to know how I look.

I can see why.

He can't be much older than me, and beautiful.

That poor, poor man.

When she doesn't bother to introduce us, I give him a sympathetic wave. He flashes me a smile before getting back to his work.

"Good to see you too, mother. Where's David? Your husband."

"Away on business." She sips from her wine glass.

"Starting early, I see."

This earns me her signature glare. "Don't start, Bethany Rose."

Contorting her perfectly made-up face, she tucks a blonde strand behind her ear. I can admit my mother is beautiful even if her face is frozen in place. It's not from Botox injections or fillers. Nothing like that. She never shows emotion to have fine lines and wrinkles.

Her powder blue pantsuit is tailored perfectly to her slim frame. She's always looked like this. Even after giving birth to two children, which she reminded me three days after I gave birth to Hannah. I was nursing a newborn, wearing something resembling an adult diaper. My hair was greasy, my feet were swollen, and I still looked nine months pregnant. So, in other words, I looked like someone who just had a baby. But my mother chose that moment to ask when I could start working out again or I'd always have *that pouch*.

"Would you like a glass?" she asks, refilling her own.

"No. I'm driving, and I need to get home to the girls."

She's still transfixed on what the chef is doing when she asks, "How are the children?"

Cold.

Unfeeling.

That's my mother.

"The *children* are fine."

"Good. We should go into the dining room." Finally meeting my eyes, she tilts her head. She's scrutinizing me, and I suddenly feel like I'm under an x-ray.

When she runs manicured fingers through the ends of my hair, I know it's a touch that should be affectionate coming from a mother, but the act rings hollow.

I can't shake the feeling she's up to something.

"Why am I here?"

She doesn't answer. Instead, she walks away and beckons me with a tilt of her chin.

I suppose I'm just doing as I'm told today.

I smooth down my navy summer dress and follow.

The dining room screams money. It even smells of it. There are twenty chairs around a table that only ever sits two. It's lonely here.

But the table is meticulously set. The cutlery is polished. The marble is without a scratch despite it being older than me.

It's none of those things that make my heart drop into my stomach.

It's the people sitting at the table that make me want to run in the opposite direction.

My footsteps halt as the swinging door crashes into my back, pushing me further into the room.

Familiar eyes meet mine.

My blood cools, the music dims, and the betrayal is like a knife straight to the chest.

"Hello, Beth." I never realized how much my husband sounded like his father until this moment.

"We were hoping we could speak to you." My mother-in-law, Camilla, stands from where she sits at her husband's side. When she takes a step in my direction, I take one back. She was always kind to me—as kind as anyone can be in that family. I mean, she advised me on what concealer works best after her son put bruises on my face.

Camilla's hands are trembling at her side, and I hate when I recognize a small piece of myself in there. It's the faraway look. The look when you want to be anywhere else but where you are. You become robotic. Your limbs move. You smile when you should. You might even answer some questions when asked. But you are somewhere else entirely in your head.

In your head you can escape.

"Please, sit down, Beth." Jared nods towards an empty chair.

I don't want to sit. I want to run, but my legs have turned to lead.

The knife twists when I look at my mother, but her expression is blank, and her eyes never meet mine.

"What have you done?" I whisper, my lungs burning for air.

"There's things you need to discuss with your family," she insists.

"My family?"

"Don't be difficult. Sit and we will speak."

"I am not sitting down." With a ragged breath, I close my eyes and pray for some composure. "What do you want?"

"How are the girls?" Camilla asks, her chin quivering.

I laugh when I want to scream. I look around the room but there's no answer in the walls. "How are the girls?"

They haven't set eyes on Hannah in two years, and they've never met Isabel. Even when I was married to their son, they only saw the girls at family gatherings.

He wasn't brought up in the warmest environment, but that's not a surprise.

A knot forms in my stomach, and I want to be sick.

But I can't let my anger get to me. I knew something was going on

53

before I came today.

Despite the fear turning my blood to acid, I force a smile and say, "They're good. Happy."

She seems content with the answer.

"I need to get back to them."

Jared's finger taps against the table.

Tap. Tap. Tap.

"The business," he says.

"What about it?"

"What are you doing with it? It's been two years."

I try to hide the flinch of shock. They haven't heard.

Lie and get out of here.

"I haven't decided."

"We think it's in everyone's best interests if you keep it. The partners will essentially maintain control, and you will take home a monthly salary for the privilege of having your name on the door." His lips are tilted in a smile, but it's not warm. "Robert worked hard for that firm. We want to keep it in the family."

I can't do that. I'll be tied to them forever.

I flinch when my mother touches my shoulder as she sips from her glass of wine in the other hand. "It will be good for you. The girls are getting older. You can finally go to law school."

Older? Isabel only turned two.

"When you're done, you can take Robert's position at the firm," Jared adds.

Did they concoct this plan together? My own mother? Whatever idea I had of her actually having a heart, evaporates.

And I finally cut the last thread.

I don't want to be tied to her any more than I want to be tied to Rob's family.

"Sounds like it's all planned out," I say, my voice strained around the lump in my throat.

"The girls can stay with us while you're studying. Not full time, of course. But during the day," Jared adds.

I try to bite my tongue. I really do, but the anger finally erupts.

I've had enough.

"No," I snap. "I'm not going back to law school. I'm selling the shares of the business because your son is nothing but a stain on my life. He's a ghost that haunts me in death just as much as he did when

54

he was alive. I don't want any part of it. And as for my children, they will not be staying with you. Now or ever. You already raised one monster." A heavy tear threatens to fall but I wipe it away before it can. They don't get to see me cry. "The girls don't know who you are. Hannah hardly remembers you. You've never even met Isabel."

With all eyes on me, the room falls into silence.

They don't fight me on seeing the girls and that breaks my heart a little for them.

But they don't argue with me about the business either and that scares me more than anything.

Jared finally stands. He's a little shorter than his son, but no less intimidating. "Have you spoken to any reporters?"

"Reporters?"

Lie, Beth.

It's not a lie exactly. I've only responded to an email from one, and in it, I told him to leave me alone.

"I haven't spoken to anyone. Why?"

My husband's death isn't news anymore. They held a small funeral so the press couldn't report that his wife and kids weren't in attendance. We were insignificant, but Rob's status as the son of a high-profile judge garnered some media attention, especially given the swirling rumors of his father's potential nomination to the Supreme Court.

I was never even mentioned. Named only as *The Wife*. No photos. Nothing.

I'm sure Jared pulled some strings to keep the circumstances surrounding my husband's death out of the news.

But there's always one.

Journalists aren't journalists for nothing. They can smell when something is rotten. Buried stories will eventually come to light.

But for once, I agree with my father-in-law. This story can't come out because this story isn't about my husband. It's about me. It's about how I suffered at his hands.

I'll be another headline and the judge will be disgraced for all of five minutes until everyone forgets, while I'll walk around with something akin to a scarlet letter on my chest.

"You should know there's someone sniffing around. I don't know what they want or what they know, but they can't run a story without corroboration. It's best if you don't speak to them."

That's not a suggestion.

It's a warning.

Like I said, I forgot how much my father-in-law's voice reminds me of my husband's.

I nod because my tongue is getting tangled around everything I want to say.

"Good because I'm delighted to hear that my grandchildren are happy. I would hate to hear of their mother grieving so much for her husband that she can't take care of them anymore. Of course, if that were to happen, they would always have a place in our home."

My arms fall to my sides. The room sways. I reach out to grab the chair because my knees can't support my weight anymore.

I was wrong.

That's a threat.

I was brought here to be reminded of his influence, of how easily he can pull the rug from under my life. He can take my girls.

"Understood?"

I chew my lip to stop my teeth from chattering. "Understood."

"Well, that's settled then."

Just like that.

The bad guys win again.

I know what this is. They didn't fight me on keeping the company because in their twisted minds, I'm allowed to do what I want with it in exchange for my silence.

I want to be sick.

I should be used to it… being silenced. But it's still a bitter pill to swallow.

I'll swallow it over and over again if it means my children are safe.

"Is that it?"

He dismisses me with a wave and a firm nod that makes me want to curl up in a ball.

"I need to get back to the girls."

I don't look at anyone before I leave. If my mother opens her mouth, I won't be held responsible for my actions.

Someone calls my name, but I ignore it. I just want to get home.

My legs wobble as I run down the steps toward my car.

"Bethany Rose, come back inside."

I turn around to see my mother standing on the top step. It's like I imagined in my little fantasy. Except she's not welcoming me home.

She's here to drag me into the depths of hell or chastise me for running from it.

Out of everything that has happened today, her betrayal cuts the deepest because I'm a mother too. I know what it feels like. Knowing what she has done makes me want to claw at my flesh.

"What's it like, Mom?" The tears finally fall, and I let them. "To not want to protect your children. To stand aside while they bleed in every way a person can."

I swear there's a flash of guilt before it disappears. She squares her shoulders and pulls at the hem of her blazer, righting herself.

"How dare you? I gave you everything growing up."

I almost tumble down the remaining steps.

"Everything? Are you that delusional? You gave me nothing but issues not even a therapist can sort through. Dad gave me everything. He was there. He picked me up when I fell. For my first period, he was the one that went out and bought me everything I needed. My first broken heart, he was there to mend it. He never would have stood by and let what happened in there today happen."

"Are you blaming me for your marriage too?"

The audacity of this woman.

I shake my head and scrub the tears away with the back of my hand. "No. Marrying Rob was my choice. But if dad were alive, and if he saw bruises on my body, he wouldn't have told me that every marriage has its struggles. He would have fought tooth and nail to get me out of there."

She gives me nothing but a stony stare.

I don't know why I'm surprised.

"But I guess I should thank you." Her eyes widen in surprise. "For teaching me everything a mother shouldn't be."

She stands there, mute and unfeeling when I turn my back. She remains like that as I get in the car and drive away.

Her silence is deafening.

It's in her silence, I finally break.

SEVEN

My heels are the loudest thing I've ever heard as they clink against the marble tiles of the lobby. Tiles that are so perfectly polished I can see my reflection in them.

That has a sexual harassment suit written all over it.

Blowing out a steadying breath, I right myself as my heels continue to pound.

Jake is waiting by the elevators, standing tall in his signature custom suit. I wonder if that man wears a suit to bed.

"Hey," I say.

"Ready?"

No warm smile or friendly hug from the man that has become more like an older brother to me in the last two years. Today he's wearing his business face. Dark chocolate hair styled to perfection; his mouth is set into a hard line. The man exudes confidence without even trying.

Thankfully, he's on my side today.

The elevator doors open as I square my shoulders and ignore the sweat breaking out at the nape of my neck.

"I think so."

He holds the elevator door while keeping his stare on me. "I'm going to ask you again. Are you ready?"

I take a deep breath knowing once I'm inside that elevator there's no backing out. Ellison & Smith law firm is on the third floor.

"I'm ready," I tell him as we both step inside the elevator.

The doors close, and the air escapes my lungs in quiet gasps.

"Okay, I might be a little nervous," I admit, not daring to look at him. I feel crazy. I don't need to see it reflected in his eyes when he looks at me.

"Nerves are good."

They don't feel good to me.

"Aren't you nervous?" I ask.

A sidelong glance is my only answer.

Right, Jake doesn't get nervous.

"You're here as a means to an end. Stay strong in there."

"Okay." But I think I shake my head.

"You've got vomit on your sweater," he points out as casually as if he were buying a pair of shoes and not about to walk into one of the biggest meetings of my life.

I understand these kinds of meetings are child's play to him, but to me, it's everything.

I haven't set foot in this place in over two years. My memories here are nothing but nightmares now.

Panicking, I look down at my red blouse to see a small stain on the collar. How did he even notice that?

I sniff it.

He grimaces.

"It's not vomit. It's Isabel's breakfast. And are you quoting an Eminem song?"

"No, but it's a good song."

I lick my thumb and do my best to remove the stain. It's no use so I pull my hair over my shoulders to hide it.

Ironic, considering today I'm trying to rid myself of the biggest stain of all.

"This is your fiancé's fault," I tell him.

"How is this Claire's fault?"

"She arrived early this morning to bring Hannah to school so I could get ready for this. You know what she gave my kids for breakfast?"

Finally, I see a hint of a smile on his face. "Let me guess: chocolate ice-cream?"

My mouth falls open. "You gave her the ice-cream for the girls, didn't you?"

Nothing but a shrug.

"The joke's going to be on you when the girls come to their Uncle Jake to pay for their dentist bills."

He doesn't get a chance to respond because the doors slide open and take all the oxygen from my lungs.

The carpet is a different color than it used to be. It's the first thing I notice. My heels sink into it as we step onto the floor.

Audrey, my lawyer, greets us with a handshake and some friendly chit-chat about how everything is going to be fine, and I don't need to speak if I don't want to. Honestly, I tune her out because I'm here. I'm standing here in this building.

If I turn left and walk down the hall I would be outside his office.

But I can't because a young woman with a fake smile is guiding us to the board room on the opposite side.

Handshakes are exchanged. "Mrs. Ellison, it's good to see you again."

Eye contact filled with pity and a touch of loathing is cast my way from the men on the other side of the table. Lawyers fiddle with their folders. An intern takes the minutes of the meeting at the end of the table. Drinks are offered. I try to keep my breakfast down.

Someone says, "Let's get this over with." I think it's Jake.

I close my eyes and zone out.

The voices around the board room table are muffled, negotiating business I should be involved in, but I can't get past the way the familiar smell in this building is making my pulse race beneath my clammy skin.

When I close my eyes, I can almost smell him. It's like he's still here, haunting the floors. I'm half expecting him to open the door in his tailored suit and take a seat across from me.

He would flash me that million-dollar smile that always held a warning only I could see.

I count backwards from ten and remind myself he's not here.

He's dead.

He's gone and he isn't coming back.

But why do I still feel his whispers over my shoulder, following me, doubting me?

Haunting me.

"Beth?" Audrey's voice breaks my intense stare on the clock. "Does all of that sound good to you?"

I glance between my lawyer and the sheets of paper stacked neatly on the table. Across from me, I feel two pairs of searing eyes assessing my every move. Eyes filled with pity, questions, regrets.

I've already looked over the contract. This meeting is merely a formality to get everything signed off.

My husband left me with a lot of things, most of which you can no longer see—memories, a mind unable to trust even the smallest decision because he made so many for me, internal bruises that will never fully heal, scars that my clothes hide.

But as his wife, I was also left with shares in his law firm. It has taken me two years to decide what to do with them. A small part of me wanted to keep them.

I had ambitions. I once wanted to be just like the men sitting across from me. In fact, one of the men refusing to meet my eyes is Mathew Smith, and before he and Rob opened their own firm, I interned for him. He believed in me enough that he offered to transfer my internship to their newly opened London office for the experience.

It's been ten years, and the experience I have can't be found in here, textbooks, or even in a courtroom.

He shipped me off and right into the hands of a monster.

I was beyond saving the minute I walked into Robert Ellison's office. He was successful, gorgeous, and also my boss, which should have made him off limits.

I soon learned that rules didn't apply to men like Rob, and he mentored me in a lot more than law.

The second I set eyes on him, a tingle erupted at the base of my spine—something primal. Something I foolishly mistook for attraction.

The attraction was there, no doubt, but that vibration in my very core, I now know was my fight or flight instinct. But I was distracted prey. He hunted, he captured, he devoured.

He took me under his wing because he said he saw something special in me.

What he really saw was weakness.

He saw how easily I would bend and contort my beliefs, my gut instincts, my intuition, and my trust in myself because I thought he knew better. I fell in love halfway across the world in a building very similar to this one. I'm pretty sure I also got pregnant there.

My eight months in London turned into eight years of hell.

By the time we returned home, I was a shell of the ambitious young

61

woman that got on that plane.

I returned with a ring on my finger and a three-year-old.

After I left him for the first time, he found me and swore he was going to change. And he did until he put another child in my belly.

I take responsibility for my weakness, for my inability to see beneath the mask he wore even when I knew what lay beneath.

I refuse to carry the burden of how he manipulated it and used it until I was nothing more than an echo of my former self.

The people in this room may not be able to see what he did to me for so many years, but they know. They probably always knew and decided to turn the other way because 'boys will be boys', and their buddy was a little rougher than most, but I was probably into it.

I wasn't.

"Beth?" Audrey repeats, dragging me out of the dark shadows until I sit straight and shake the tremble from my hands.

"Everything's fine," I agree.

"Beth, we really suggest you think about this. We can give you more time." Mathew interlocks his fingers and leans forward. He's the one that saw something in me.

I wonder what he sees now.

I do my best to keep my tone steady when I say, "I've had all the time I need."

"You can address me from here on out, gentlemen. I am your new partner after all." There's no denying the hint of satisfaction in Jake's voice. He flashes a smile of encouragement from his seat next to mine.

If someone had told me three years ago that one of the closest people in the world to me would be Jake and his soon-to-be wife, I would have laughed in their face and poured myself a stiff drink.

In another world our paths would never collide.

Another world isn't as screwed up as this one.

Jake shares a history with my husband that not even I will ever fully comprehend. All I know is when I first approached him for help, he was in the early stages of building a women's shelter for domestic abuse survivors. No questions asked, he and his fiancé, Claire, were there for me every step of the way. I spent almost a year at the shelter. I gave birth to my youngest daughter there.

I owe them my life.

I owe them my children's lives.

Though, they find it difficult to even accept a thank you, no matter how hard I try.

I could have sold my shares back to the partners, but my trust has been shattered, and I don't know the first thing about brokering a deal of this magnitude. When I went to Jake for advice, his offer was generous and, most importantly, trustworthy.

"Beth," Mathew implores once again.

Jake is fast to cut in. "I will not repeat myself. Do not address her again." He's a force to be reckoned with, his frame as intimidating as his voice, and the men all but curl back into their chairs.

I don't need to be involved in this meeting. Not in practical terms. I don't bring anything of value to the table, and they won't change my mind. But at the same time, I *needed* to be here. I wanted to face them one last time and prove to myself I still have the strength. That the fire still burns in my belly. It's not as bright as it once was, but it's there, simmering in the background.

It just needs a little air.

"Mrs. Ellison and I have come to our own arrangement and payment has already been transferred," Jake goes on, but I find my mind wandering again as he speaks.

The money doesn't matter. I've struggled since leaving Rob, but I survived. My girls are happy.

We're safe.

Today is for them. It's to make sure their future is secure. The majority of the sale will go into a bank account until they're adults. What's left will give us the opportunity to start over.

"Beth, before we leave today, on behalf of myself and the entire firm, we would like to once again express our condolences on the passing of Robert. He is truly missed around here."

The laugh that leaves my mouth is humorless and doesn't sound like me. "Tragic?"

This is a joke, right?

My reaction shocks the room. Maybe it's the years of feeling threatened into silence, or all the words I've had to swallow, but they finally slip past my defenses and boil over. If my hands weren't trembling, I might notice the color drain from their faces. Rob took all my sympathy with him the day he died.

Shame.

I'd know it anywhere.

I've seen it in my own eyes enough.

I stand on shaky legs but force myself upright. "Like Mr. Williams has already said, you no longer have any need to address me."

Their mouths are still hanging open when I turn and leave. My heart is beating so hard against my chest I feel it in my throat.

Jake and Audrey follow closely behind. He squeezes my arm. "Proud of you."

The lump in my throat has stolen my voice, so I offer a watery smile.

I ignore the various eyes on me as we leave. I'm nothing more than their dead boss's wife. Something to fill their lunch time gossip.

I roll my shoulders back, trying my best to ease the knot in my neck.

I'm angry at him today. So angry.

Daily, I try to avoid evidence of the stains he left, but today it's hard. I'm in his building, with his business partners and employees. I'm surrounded in the scent of these offices—it's how his suit smelled when he came home from work, wrapping me in it when strong arms came around my waist while I was cooking.

I hate this confusion. I hate the good memories. I hate remembering the things I loved about him. Things I craved. Things that became so few so quickly.

I hate myself for those unwelcomed memories.

I don't want the good memories to creep in like water over a raging fire. It dilutes the indignation and makes my mind muggy.

I need to be angry at him, or better still, I need to feel nothing at all.

Clarity. I just need some clarity.

But clarity will have to wait. Audrey rests a reassuring hand on my arm and tilts her head in the direction of the boardroom we left.

Mathew strides towards us, head slightly down, eyes anywhere but on me, yet he's walking this way.

"Beth, can I have a minute?"

I tense, digging my nails into my palm.

Jake looks me over, scanning my face for any signs of panic. I'm petrified, but I school my features like a professional, indifference dripping in my gaze.

"I'll wait," he offers, looking between me and Mathew.

"No." I smile, not knowing why I'm agreeing to speak with him. "Thanks, Jake." I need to do this on my own.

He's hesitant before he leaves, a silent warning in the glare he leaves burning in the side of Mathew's face before he gets on the elevator with Audrey.

I think he takes all the oxygen with him.

Mathew stuffs his hands in his pockets, shifting on his feet. It's unusual to see a man with such unapologetic confidence to be nervous. What could he possibly have to say?

His wife was once a friend. He was Rob's best friend.

I haven't heard from either of them in two years.

"Mathew," I say. "I need to get back to the girls."

"Right, I'm sorry. I just wanted to see how you're doing."

"How I'm doing," I blurt, stunned, because it's the last question I expected him to ask. These people really are just book smart. Zero common sense. It takes every ounce of my power not to laugh in his face, but instead, I say, "I'm fine."

He wipes his thumb over his chin. "I'm sorry we haven't stayed in touch."

"I really need to get back to the girls." I press the button for the elevator, wishing the ground would open instead. The stares our way become more intense, burning holes in me like bullets.

"We're clearing out his office tomorrow. I wondered if you wanted to go in there, or what we should do with his stuff?"

My head spins. "You haven't cleared out his office?" It's a stupid question, but it's been two years.

"We weren't sure what you were going to do with his shares, and we didn't know if you would want anything in there."

I think about it: going in there, pressing my palms to his desk. But he's already in everything I do, every step I take, in each breath. He's in my daughter's hazel eyes.

His ghost is suffocating enough.

My pulse echoes behind my ears, and fear makes my hands tremble. My legs twitch with the need to run in the opposite direction. I shouldn't go there. I should leave. There's nothing for me here.

I shouldn't do this, but I do. I put one foot in front of the other and into the mouth of the dragon. There's a part of me that wants to face it, face him, even when he won't be there. I need to know his ghost won't kill me.

Mathew opens the door, and I'm tossed back in time. I'm shaking so much my teeth chatter.

"I'll give you a minute." I hear him say, but my eyes are still closed.

When I open them, I'm back. He's not here, and there's a pinch in my chest. It's foreign. Unwelcomed. It's not for the loss of him. It's for the loss of who I thought he was going to be when I stepped inside an office like this for the first time.

There are no dust particles in the air despite the time it's been unoccupied. It's surprisingly clean. His desk is polished, the blue skies reflecting against it from the floor to ceiling windows.

I hold my breath and take a large step inside.

It smells… different.

His cologne no longer lingers in the air. The floors are freshly vacuumed, every picture frame centered to perfection.

I round his desk. There's a photo of all of us, and a single picture of me. I look happy. We were on vacation, and it was our first day at the beach. My hair is blowing in my face, my swimsuit hidden beneath a cover-up. The large sunglasses are hiding the fading bruise around my left eye.

"You can't be in here."

My head snaps up to see a young woman I recognize standing in the doorway, her hand already on the door handle. Her face drops when she sees me, her mouth falling open.

"Beth?" she breathes, steadying herself on her feet. "I'm so sorry. I didn't know it was you. Forget I was here." She attempts to rush away.

"Charlie."

She stops and drops her head. I can't blame her for not wanting to face me.

She followed him here from London, and I knew it.

I was such a fool.

Old habits take hold, and no matter how hard I try to fight it, bitterness clogs my throat. I drink her in like I've done so many times before. I memorized her so I could stand in front of the mirror and compare everything she had to what I didn't. Black hair cut in a sharp angle. Her eyes are a deep grey. There's no c-section pouch under her skirt.

She's beautiful and despite her having slept with my husband, I always liked her.

He betrayed me, not Charlie.

But for years I was jealous of her because he gave her all his passion and she took it. I was left with scraps and scars.

I'm surprised when the bitterness falls away and I feel nothing. Maybe a little pity, but I bat that away too because I hate when people pity me. She deserves the same consideration.

I'm sure she was trapped in his web. And me and Charlie… we weren't the only ones.

When she steps inside, her perfume is familiar. It clung to his clothes most nights. But I'm not angry with her. I fell for his charms too.

Her eyes water, her bottom lip wobbling as she drinks in the office. Her memories replay on her face just like mine. The difference between Charlie and me? She's mourning.

I take a step towards her. "Can I ask you something?"

Swallowing back her nerves, she dips her head and agrees.

"Was he kind to you?"

A single tear falls to her cheek. "Yes."

"He didn't hurt you?"

"No."

Relieved that we don't share all our painful memories, I take one last look around, roll my shoulders back, and silently say goodbye to everything that could have been.

"Can you pass on a message to Mathew?"

"Of course."

"Tell him to burn everything in here. Rob's things can rot in hell with him."

EIGHT

I texted Kim to let her know I would be home soon. I'm sure she's chomping at the bit to find out how everything went down.

She will be the anger to my hurt.

Right now, I need to walk.

I need a couple of minutes to walk among strangers, to get lost in the distraction.

I need to numb.

Despite the angry clouds in the distance, the sun is still shining in the summer heat. But when heavy drops of rain begin to fall again, I raise my umbrella and keep walking.

I've always loved the rain.

It feels cleansing.

I walk for twenty minutes, my feet leading the way as my thoughts drift in and out of memories.

Some good.

Some horrifying.

That's when I see it.

King Tattoo Studio.

I'd say I don't know why I came here, but I do.

I've passed that studio over the years, always hoping for a glimpse of the man inside it, but never brave enough to go in.

Not again.

It's like walking by a crime scene while hoping I bump into the only witness. The last man to see the old me alive.

I lean against the wall and look over, laughing at myself.

It's stupid to still think about him. But for some reason, my mind always returned to him throughout the years. It helped me to survive because after only one night, I didn't know enough, and I could easily create the life I wish he had.

I remember how I laughed that night, a laugh that hasn't sounded the same since. I smiled until my cheeks hurt. I still remember his hand on the small of my back as he moved me in from the road just to keep me safe from the passing cars.

I took a mental photograph of him so long ago, and I went to it when I needed to escape.

It's no different today as I take a deep breath and force myself to walk away.

I start to wonder if things would have been different if he had just... I don't finish the thought. There's no point in dwelling. It won't change things.

He was a stranger to me then even if I convinced myself otherwise.

I take one final look back before I leave and wonder the same thing I've wondered in my darkest moments.

I wonder what Logan King is doing.

NINE

~~Dear Diary,~~
~~Journal,~~
~~Day One,~~
~~This feels stupid.~~
I don't know exactly why I'm doing this, but here I am. I need to document everything going forward, and everything I remember. I can't stay here in this house, and he won't let me leave. The only way to fight him is with evidence.

I think writing things down and taking photographs will help.

I'm not sure when all of this happened. I'm sure it began with words, but I don't remember when. I'll start from where I do remember, from where things started feeling wrong.

Fuck it, here it goes...

I was dressed in a black off-shoulder gown. A delicate diamond necklace glinted on my skin under the harsh light of our bathroom, but it was the bold red lipstick that was my crowning glory. I chose the shade meticulously, a fiery crimson. It was a big night. I wanted to look my best.

As I inspected my reflection, I traced my fingers over my lips, the lipstick smooth and unmarred. Stepping out of the bathroom, my gaze sought out Rob, eager to see his reaction.

He was seated on the bed, his attention glued to the documents spread out on the blanket. The sound of my heels drew his eyes, and they raked over me, taking in my attire. I waited for his praise, the compliment that would validate my efforts.

But instead of the admiration I expected, a frown creased his forehead, his gaze landing heavily on my lips.

In an instant, my confidence deflated, replaced by a chill of dread. He rose from the bed, strode toward me, and before I could react, his hand was on my face. His thumb pressed into my lower lip, his hand gripping my face as he smeared the crimson shade onto my cheek.

My tears dripped onto his hand.

He didn't notice.

"Take it off," he ordered, his voice hard and uncompromising. "You look like a whore."

∞∞∞

"You look pretty, Mom."

I try to hide my reaction as I'm pulled back to reality. Instead, I focus on the cinnamon eyes of my daughter in the mirror's reflection, and smile, because she deserves all my smiles.

"Hey, baby. Thank you."

She walks to where I sit at the vanity unit, tossing her hair over her shoulder before grabbing the ends again to knot them around her fingers. It's a habit she picked up when she was only a baby. I think I would mourn it if she stopped.

"I like your makeup. Can you do mine?"

When did she grow up? And why did it happen so fast? She's still only eight, but I remember the day she was born like it was yesterday. I remember how she felt when I held her for the first time.

I wish I had never let her go because there's a knowing glint in her eye now that I wish she didn't have.

Plastering another forced smile on my face, I kiss her cheek before running my fingers through my freshly curled hair. "I can't right now. Tomorrow night?"

She nods, the most beautiful smile warming my heart. "Sure." She's quickly distracted by the tube still in my hand. "That's a nice color. You should wear it."

I gulp back the nerves as I set the red lipstick back on the vanity with trembling hands. One lipstick and I become a nervous mess. I thought today could be the day I wear it again. I'm facing demons and proving to the world that I can do everything on my own.

I'll just have to do it without red lipstick.

I offer my hand, and she takes it. "How about some ice-cream before I leave?"

Downstairs, Kim is leaning over the kitchen sink, her phone to her ear. "Okay, babe. See you in a couple of days… Love you too… Okay, I'll tell them… Love you… Bye." Her eyes rake over every inch of me. "Holy shit, you look hot. Sorry about the language, Hannah."

Hannah shrugs like it's nothing. I try to keep my language to a minimum, but sometimes my thoughts don't stay in my head.

"It's okay. She's right, Mom. You look awesome."

Uncomfortable, I wipe imaginary wrinkles from the satin material. I can't remember the last time I wore a dress like this.

"Thank you," I murmur.

Hannah releases my hand to open the freezer and grabs her favorite chocolate ice-cream.

It's chocolate brownie.

Me and Kim share a knowing look.

She helps Hannah while I slip my feet into heels that are too high and expertly ignore the boxes waiting to be packed in the living room.

"You really do look beautiful. I need to get the name of that concealer. I almost can't see the bags under your eyes," Kim teases.

I glare at her.

"I'm joking. Don't want you to think I'm going soft."

"Believe me, I could never think that." I kiss the top of Hannah's head. "Have a good night with Kim."

"You too, Mom. And try to relax," she suggests, sounding older than her years.

"Good advice."

She takes her bowl of ice-cream and disappears into the living room.

"Why the long face?" Kim asks.

"I feel guilty." A lump forms in my throat, but I swallow it. If I cry, I won't stop. And Kim wasn't wrong. This concealer is amazing. I can't ruin it. "I've never left them at night before."

I trust two people with my children, Kim and Claire. On the rare occasion I need to leave them, it's for two hours tops.

"Exactly. This is the first time ever. How often do you get away longer than to use the toilet?"

I think about it and shrug. "They like to chat with me when I'm on the toilet."

"You can't even piss in peace? You need this night more than I thought. Everyone needs their own space."

"They're my kids," I fight back.

"And they'll still be your kids in the morning." Kim grabs my long black coat from the rack and holds it up for me to slip my arms inside. "After the day you've had, you need a drink or five. It's a charity art exhibition, not a week in Barbados."

I smile. "Now that would be nice."

Grinning—probably because she's a step closer to getting me out of the house—she kisses my cheek. "It's only for a couple of hours. You wanted to do this. And you said yourself you need to start stepping out on your own." She tucks her fingers under my chin and tips my head back. "And do it with this held high."

"You're sure you don't mind babysitting?"

It's my last-ditch attempt to stay home. I wait for any hesitation on her part so I can kick off my heels and curl up on the sofa with Hannah.

"Beth," she starts, releasing a stuttered breath. "I missed out on so many years with the girls." There's no blame in her voice, not for me at least, only sadness tinged with regret. "I want to soak up every minute."

"Okay." I pull her into a hug. "I love you."

"Love you. Now go. You could meet your future husband tonight, who knows?"

I give her a sideways glance, waiting for her to realize how crazy she sounds. Then we both burst into laughter.

TEN

The low bass of music muffles the voices around the art gallery. My heart is beating in sync, bashing against my chest in a steady rhythm. Blood gushes behind my ears as I wipe my clammy hands against the black satin of my dress. I wish I had worn my hair up because sweat breaks out on the nape of my neck.

I need air, but I can't leave yet because I'm trying to blend in.

The red light that shrouds the room plays across the floors and ceilings in slow motion while the twinkle from a disco ball caresses the white walls. It's unusual for the lighting at an art exhibition to be so dim. Yet, there's something sensual about it. It gives me a place to shrink away inside the dark corners.

The artwork is displayed on the rows of walls, a single light hanging over each piece and illuminating it for the guests streaming by to admire.

I take another step inside, plucking a glass of champagne from a waiter as he strolls by.

Slowly, I work my way into the center of the room.

These events aren't new to me, but I feel like I've stepped into the deepest part of the ocean with no shore in sight. It feels foreign, irritating. My new skin doesn't fit in here. It brings back too many emotions of the way I used to feel. The constant eyes on me no matter where I went. The reinforcing hand on the small of my back, always seen as a gesture of affection but spoke a thousand violent words. This place reminds me of how I had to evaluate who I spoke to and how I acted if I did.

Eyes.

Eyes always on me.

I halt my steps as I drain the glass, catching sight of a familiar painting. A woman with long flowing hair nurses an infant. Their skin is painted an array of colors like a cross-stitch blanket. The adoration in one simple look is undeniable. I lean an inch closer, studying the strokes, so fine some would mistake it for a photograph.

'Sold' is stamped right beside the artist's name.

Cassie Emmels.

She's come a long way from teaching art classes at any gallery that would give her the time of day. I haven't seen her since I left ten years ago, and although I choose to ignore the painful tug in the center of my chest when I think of that day, an unusual sense of pride swells there.

In the next breath there are arms around my shoulders, pulling me into a tight hug. "You made it." Claire beams as I squeeze her in return.

My cheeks are flushed when she pulls away, and it could have more to do with the champagne rather than the heat in here.

"I'm so proud of you for coming," she says, tears swimming in her eyes as the glare from the disco ball floats over her face.

"Oh, Jesus, don't cry again." Jake appears at her side, rolling his eyes with a smirk as he wraps an arm around her waist and leans in to kiss me on the cheek.

She sniffles. "Shut up."

Tumbler in hand, he gestures toward the painting. "Like this one?" he asks, his eyes narrowing on me.

I look away to hide the truth from shining through. "It's beautiful."

"It's sold."

His eyes are boring a hole in the side of my face. "I can see that."

"Someone bought it today," he continues. I know by the probing tone of his voice he's figured me out, but I don't say a word.

"Is that so?"

"What's going on with you two?" Claire asks.

He tucks a strand of her hair behind her ear with more love than I've witnessed in my entire life. Individually, they're the most beautiful people in the room. As a couple, they're devastating.

He smiles at her before looking back at me with imploring eyes. "It was sold before the exhibition. Someone saw it on the website, called up, and bought it."

"Holy shit!" Claire holds her hand over her mouth. "Who?"

"Anonymous," Jake says casually.

"Well, it won't stay anonymous when it's hanging in someone's living room."

"That's the thing. It was donated back to the shelter." He's talking to his fiancé, but his eyes remain on me.

I simply offer a soft smile. I know he won't out me. I owe them both more than I can ever put into words, and he wouldn't accept the donation if he knew it was coming from me. It was my way of giving back to a place that dragged me out of the darkest depths. The women there shared their oxygen so I could breathe a little easier.

I would give them more if I could. God knows they deserve it.

It's the only reason I'm here. I'm here on behalf of all the women at the shelter who can't come to these events because the men who inflicted their pain are still breathing.

These events aren't a part of who I am anymore. I don't think they ever were. I squeezed into a mold that I never truly fit.

Besides, the painting will look beautiful hanging in the shelter. It's nurturing, it gives hope when there's very little to be found. And it gives me a sense of satisfaction knowing money from my husband's business—a business he worked so hard for—is going towards a women's shelter.

Jake dips his chin, resignation in the chaste wink and nod. I'll never admit to it, and he doesn't push, radiating reassurance like Jake always does.

My secret is safe with him.

"That's amazing," Claire mutters, tilting her head as she examines the painting, still none the wiser.

Jake is quickly drawn away by other guests, his company in high demand.

Claire links her arm with mine. "I fucking hate these events."

"Can't wait to see your wedding," I say, knowing it makes her break out in a cold sweat.

She groans and changes the subject. "How are my girls doing?" Her eyes shine with warmth.

Hannah and Isabel might not have a father, but they have enough mothers to go round.

"Good. Kim has them tonight. Isabel was already snoring when I left."

Rolling her eyes, she laughs into her glass. "Isn't she always? She's the laziest kid in the world."

"Don't jinx me. Hannah still doesn't sleep through the night. The gods might have given me my second child to test how strong my heart is, but she sleeps like the dead. I pick my battles."

"And the move? Now that everything is finalized on the business end, have you found a place yet?"

"Nope." Thinking of the pile of boxes stacked in my living room, I feel anxiety spiraling in my chest, but I manage to swallow it down. "I'm hoping to move closer to Kim, but apparently houses are hard to come by. I'll be lucky to find a shed."

She averts her gaze, chewing her lip between her teeth. "I might have something... or someone that can help."

"Claire, I warned you. You've helped me enough."

"And you've helped me. You're my friend. Isn't that what friends do for each other? Let me introduce you?"

I guess it can't hurt, and I'm running out of options... fast. I mumble my agreement while I drain my glass, letting the burn settle in my chest.

"I'm going to cry like a baby when you leave."

"You'll find any excuse to cry."

She sighs, smiling despite the tears I know she's fighting. "I'm so glad you're here."

I rest my head against hers as we simply stand, not caring that people have to step around us.

"Always," I whisper.

We remain silent for endless minutes, allowing my heart to calm to a regular beat. It's like she knows I need the stillness. I guess she would. There are bonds much deeper than words, much deeper than skin or blood. They run deep in the marrow of our bones.

Although we've only been friends for two years, she's the closest thing to family—aside from Kim—that the girls and I have.

With the girls on my mind, I slip my phone from my bag, trying to hide the obvious glare of the light it emits at my side, but Kim has beat me to it.

Kim: Girls are good. Me and Hannah are watching a movie.

Isabel is still sleeping. Try to enjoy yourself.

I feel a fraction of the tightness in my shoulders ease, but I'm still far from relaxed.

"Mrs. Ellison?"

My head snaps up.

Claire's grip tightens on my elbow, standing straight at my side like a tiger ready to protect her cubs.

And I love her for it.

I vaguely recognize the couple staring back at me with wide eyes. He's tall and stocky. In his sixties, maybe? The lady at his side is slender, and were his hand not possessively placed on her lower back, I'd guess she was his daughter.

"Hello," is all I can muster because for the life of me I can't remember their names.

Your husband would know, a voice echoes in the back of my head.

Of course he would, but my husband is dead.

"How are you doing?" the blonde asks, the golden shimmer of her dress hugs every curve, her smile sympathetic but genuine.

He, on the other hand, looks at me like I've committed a crime and he's the only one not falling for my act.

I should be used to that look by now, but I'm not made of stone.

Instead, I plaster the fake half-smile I've mastered. "I'm good, thank you."

"We were so sorry to hear of Robert's passing. So sad for the family."

I nod, slow and steady, my eyes averting to the floor.

I can't do this.

I knew there was a chance someone might recognize me, not just because of my husband, but the family I married into. The Ellisons are a prominent name and ties run deep. Although, I knew none of the family would be here tonight—they wouldn't be welcome—not at a charity event for the shelter their daughter-in-law ran to when their son broke one too many of her bones, but I knew someone would recognize me. Especially when there's been whispers of me selling his shares.

The man scrutinizes me again, the eyes behind his glasses like an x-ray, trying his best to figure me out, to see what I'm hiding.

If only he knew.

The half-truths they've heard are nursery rhymes compared to the horror movies playing in my head.

I clear my throat and reach for another glass of champagne.

"Thank you, but if you'll excuse me," I say, making an abrupt exit that leaves them gaping.

Claire squeezes my hand, winks at me, and takes over like a pro.

I dash for the doors at the back of the room, grateful when it leads straight to a large and scarcely occupied balcony.

The city lights don't bring me comfort like I wish they did. They shine down on me like judgmental glares. I down the champagne and rest my hands on the metal railing. Closing my eyes, I inhale a steadying breath.

I need to get out of this city... for good. I'm suffocating.

My lungs are burning, desperate for some reprieve. I focus on the cool evening air on my skin until my spine straightens.

There's someone watching me.

I can feel it.

I spin around expecting to see someone there.

Nothing.

A couple mutter a greeting as they pass me and step back inside. A man farther down the balcony is smoking a cigarette and sipping a brown liquid from his tumbler, his eyes focused on his phone, but not on me.

Am I going crazy now, too? Paranoid?

I check the time on my phone. Thirty minutes and I can leave. I can do thirty minutes.

I lift my head as I begin to walk back... and boom.

I'm almost rocked off my feet when my chest comes crashing into a navy shirt.

"I'm so sorry," I gasp, jerking away to find a pair of apologetic grey eyes.

"It was my fault," he stutters, grabbing my elbow to steady me.

My fight or flight instinct takes over and I glance around to see we're alone.

Breathe, Beth. He's not going to hurt you.

I notice a large camera and a press badge hanging from a lanyard around his neck.

A reporter.

"I don't want any photos." I smile, hoping he'll see me as shy and drop it.

"Oh…" He looks down at the camera and back at me as if he forgot it was even there. "No photos."

I cross my arms over my chest, trying to gather heat to my bones and hating the unease that's beginning to peek its ugly head in my stomach.

"I need to get back inside."

When I try to sneak around him, he steps out of my way, but grabs my elbow. It doesn't hurt. It's not even threatening, but I flinch.

I don't like being touched.

I spin to look at him. "Who are you?"

"My name is Benjamin Sullivan. I'm a reporter. I'm currently working on a story for The Times."

My blood cools, and it takes all my power to stay steady on my feet. I know that name which means he knows exactly who I am.

I tip my head back a fraction, determined to take Kim's advice and hold it high.

"I've responded to your emails. I have nothing to say."

He nods, but I can tell he's not giving up. "I understand this is difficult. But this story is running, and we would love to get your side. A short comment? I really think having your voice on this will help so many survivors."

I try to bite my tongue, but it misses, and the words spill out. "Don't give me that bullshit. I've met enough survivors—a lot of them my friends—to know this has nothing to do with helping us."

His brows almost hit his hairline. "So, you *are* a survivor?"

Shit.

I've said too much.

"I already told you I have nothing to say."

I try to turn away, but he barricades me in. Not physically, but his next statement makes me stick to the railing.

"We have proof of the abuse you suffered at the hands of your husband."

My mouth falls open as the air leaves my body, but I school my features and stand straight.

"What abuse?"

He doesn't even respond. There's been rumors, I know that much, but nothing concrete.

After Jared's warning yesterday, I know I need to get this man out of my face and keep my mouth shut.

I hate being backed into a corner. If there ever comes a time when I want to share my story, it won't be for the public, and it will be on my own terms.

"This is useless. You're chasing a story that doesn't exist anymore. My husband is dead."

Finally, he drops the sympathetic act. "Suicide, right? He took your daughter—"

"That's enough. Whatever you want to drag up about my husband, go ahead, but leave my children out of this." My blood drains from my body and pools at my feet. Fighting the bile rising in my throat, I blink the sting away from my eyes. "Have you spoken to my husband's family?" I ask only because they fought to keep that part of the story out of the headlines and succeeded—until now it would seem.

My husband's suicide may not be news anymore, but my daughter's involvement is. With the mention of her, I feel the steel barrier come down between us because fuck him. I will go to the ends of this Earth to protect my baby.

"Tried to, yes. But we don't need them. We have sources close to the family. Is it true that you stayed at Guiding Light Women's Shelter before and after your husband's death?" He doesn't give me the opportunity to respond. "Is that why you're here tonight?"

I stay silent, and the bastard keeps going.

"On the day your husband died, you were in the hospital after giving birth to your youngest daughter, and your eldest daughter was in the care of the manager of that shelter." He unfolds a piece of paper in his hand. I don't know if he's doing it for dramatic effect or just being an asshole, but he doesn't read it because we both know who managed the shelter, and she's right inside those double doors. "Claire Russell."

Fuck. Fuck. Fuck.

How does he know these details?

"You're barking up the wrong tree. You do realize who funded that shelter? You're at his event."

He shakes his head, keeping his voice as calm as the moment he approached me. "Jake Williams, CEO of JW Media and soon to be married to the same Claire Russell I speak of."

This guy has balls, I'll give him that much. Jake will hit the roof when he realizes this is being investigated, and he'll probably turn murderous when he finds out Claire was mentioned.

As if reading my mind, he answers my unasked question. "Miss Russell's name will never be mentioned, and Jake Williams has no power over what we print."

"What's your angle here?"

"The Ellison family are a powerful family."

As if I don't know that.

"Our angle, Mrs. Ellison, is corruption within the justice system."

I scoff a laugh and roll my eyes. "That's hardly news."

"It is when a judge gives preferential treatment to his son. Your husband was never prosecuted because of the family he was born into. Doesn't that make you angry?"

Of course it makes me angry. It haunts my sleep, but I left this behind. I don't want to relive my past. I shouldn't have to.

He slips his hand into his pocket and pulls out a business card. I leave it resting in the air between us.

"If you ever feel like talking, please contact me."

"And if you ever have actual proof, please come back to me."

His hand is on my arm again, his eyes soft and imploring.

I might think Benjamin is a nice guy if he wasn't trying to shed light on the parts of my past I buried deepest.

"We do have proof." He grimaces, sympathy I don't want radiates from him as every second ticks by and he's still touching me.

I study him, unsure if he's telling the truth. He must be lying. There is no proof. Anything of mine is long gone. Rob made sure of it before he put a gun to his head.

"Please get your hands off me." My voice breaks, and if he feels the tremble in my hands, he doesn't react to it.

"It's best if you tell us your side before people make their own assumptions."

He's still touching me. It's featherlight but there. The air releases from my lungs and won't come back.

"Please—"

"If she has to ask you again to remove your hands, I'll remove them for you. So, I suggest you do it while the bones are still intact."

Benjamin quickly steps away, and my eyes snap to the man standing at his back—hands in his suit pocket, the briefest glimpse of a tattoo peeking over the white collar. I know his eyes are emerald green because I somehow committed them to memory all those years ago.

But the dark specks are all that are showing now. My chest tightens until it hurts. The city lights merge into a single blur. The distant sirens become a muted echo, and the cool air feels like a blistering inferno on my skin.

No. No. No.

"If you want to talk—" Benjamin tries to say, but he sounds lightyears away.

Jade eyes remain locked with mine, but he's not speaking to me. "Don't fucking look at her."

The man is as intimidating as he is gorgeous. He's lethal and just as I remember.

He hasn't changed. Not one bit.

I hold my breath as he dips his chin and says, "Bethany Rose."

Oh God.

Panic coils around my belly, the vague bass of voices beginning to dim.

He remembers me.

I wondered over the years if he would.

I've thought about him. Some days it was an obsession. A comfort to look back on the girl I was that night and know he was the last one to see her. That's how he remembered me, and it was a solace I clung to every time I looked in the mirror and could no longer find her.

But now he knows.

He must know.

He knows what my husband did—the man I met not even twenty-four hours after spending a night with him. A night of laughter and stolen glances. The last night I felt truly safe.

My safety.

Now the idea of safety and the place I went to in my mind when the rest of me was vulnerable and on the verge of breaking is staring back at me as if I've come back from the dead.

When he repeats my name, it resonates, driving into me with so much force the air is knocked from my lungs.

I'm dreaming. This can't be real. I've slipped back into my own head, so desperate to escape reality, I've summoned him in my mind.

I close my eyes, pinch the skin on my wrist, and count backwards from ten. But when I open them again, he's still there, looking at me as though I've lost my damn mind.

It takes an eternity before I finally fill my lungs to say his name.

"Logan."

ELEVEN

Ten years ago

LOGAN

"You know if you stare at her anymore, she's going to stick to where she's standing." Skip slaps my shoulder before pulling off his T-shirt and sitting with his back to me.

"Fuck off, Skip."

"Our little Logan is smitten," he singsongs, then almost chokes because he smokes two packs a day and the man can't string a sentence together without needing to breathe after every word.

"Little? I've been taller than you since I was thirteen. Now shut the fuck up so I can ink you."

He chuckles and the sound makes my blood boil.

Thankfully, the shop is too loud with other people for anyone to hear what he said.

I prepare the patch of skin, dip the tattoo gun in the ink, and get to work, willing my eyes to stay focused.

I don't get distracted.

Ever.

But the ultimate distraction is currently laughing at something

Jaxson said with her hand on the counter and the other holding her stomach, tears spilling from her big brown eyes.

She should be laughing with Jaxson. He's younger. I remind myself of that when I feel the bubble of jealousy curdling in my veins.

Her laugh is throaty and full of mischief.

Bethany Rose.

That name doesn't suit her. It's too prim, too polished, too childish.

The only thing polished about Bethany Rose is the blonde locks curled around her shoulders. Everything else is a contradiction. Like she's not sure who she is. Her blue dress, hugging her waist, falls to mid-thigh and has fucking daisies on it, but there's nothing colorful about the black leather Doc Martens on her feet. Her wrist is full of bracelets that make too much noise, and her smile is far from innocent. I should know, I've been staring at it all day.

She sways on her feet, making her dress whoosh back and forth around her tanned thighs.

Eyes on her face, Logan.

Fuck. Her face is no better.

It's not until her eyes find mine from the other side of the shop that I realize the gun isn't buzzing.

I'm looking at her.

Distraction.

She should have the word tattooed on her forehead.

Her lips curl on one side like she knows exactly what I'm thinking.

She's mischievous.

Dangerous.

Her eyes fall to the floor, a blush creeping to her cheeks.

Another contradiction.

She's going to be the most intoxicating type of woman in the world if I'm not careful.

I was worried about bringing her here. She was high and too fucking young.

I have no idea why I even brought her. We didn't need a photographer. There's some journalist here taking photos for a news article. Yet I couldn't leave that diner without her. I kept thinking about how she would look on the back of my bike.

That's where I should have left it: in my imagination because the minute she hopped on the back and wrapped her hands around my waist, my cock became painfully hard.

There's a glow of curiosity in everything she does, and it's too much to refuse. I remember feeling that way—eager to learn everything about what I loved.

Her voice pipes up from my side. "Mind if I sit?"

I clench my fists.

Skip hisses.

Good enough for the old bastard.

"Sure," I grit, not looking at her. I need a shower and my cock in my fist just to wash her away. "Don't pass out."

"I'm good. I promise." I can hear her smile.

How do you hear someone smile?

"Move your chair up here, darlin'. I want to get a better look at you." Skip motions with his hand.

Another sexy as hell laugh from Bethany Rose.

My cock twitches in my jeans.

I want to throw everyone out of this shop just to show her exactly what her laugh does to me. How the tilt of her lips and blush to her cheeks doesn't go unnoticed when she looks my way. I want to wrap my hand around her throat, watch her eyes grow wide, and feel how wet she is between her legs while her moans fall from her full lips.

I don't want anyone else to hear that laugh.

It's mine.

What the fuck is wrong with me?

I've got this weird as hell *I saw her first thing* going on. We're not fucking children. I can't call dibs on her, but I can't help the want to claim her... just for today.

I take a deep breath which is a bad idea because the air around me is completely her.

Still grinning, she stands at the other side of the bed. "Good enough for you?" she asks, lifting the camera and taking some pictures.

"Perfect. I can see why my nephew can't take his eyes off you."

I'm a professional.

I'm a professional.

I'm a professional.

When I look up, her eyes lock with mine, her cheeks already flushed.

"He can't, huh?"

"All day."

"Interesting." She bites away the smile curling on her lips.

87

"Didn't I tell you to shut the fuck up, Skip? Leave the girl alone. Bethany Rose, get over here and sit your ass down."

"Gotta go, Skip. The boss is getting grumpy." She winks at him and takes a seat.

"I raised that boy. He was born frowning, darlin'."

"Stop moving," I warn him. "You good?" I ask, glancing up at her.

She nods, not taking her eyes off the half-finished tattoo on Skip's back. "I'm good."

The hours blend until the sun is beginning to set outside the shop. Everyone is still as rowdy as ever and the donations keep coming long after we finish.

There's pride in Archer's eyes when he looks around and sees the same heart tattoo on everyone. My baby brother did good.

Bethany Rose got up and mingled a couple of times, using that smile to coax people into some photos. By the end of the day, I've seen some of the angriest men smile for her. She checked in every so often, taking her seat by my side to watch.

"I'm impressed," Archer tells her when she takes a seat again and swivels in the chair. "You remained on two feet."

"It was fun. This is amazing, Archer. Your little girl is going to be so proud of her dad."

The smile he flashes is genuine, but the fear remains behind his eyes. The fear that our very special girl might not always be here. It guts me. I can't imagine what it does to him and Molly.

But we won't go there.

Not today.

"Is she here today? I didn't see her or Molly."

"Molly only came for the night to make sure everything was set up, but she went home to Evie this morning. It's not good for her to be around so many people. Too much risk of infection."

"I get it."

I wink at Archer when she's not looking and nod towards the bed. "You're turn, pretty girl."

Now I think she's going to pass out.

She looks to Archer for help, but he only shrugs.

"I'm so sorry. I… I really can't," she stutters, her face turning a worrying shade of white.

She looks petrified.

Archer squeezes her shoulder, finally putting her out of her misery.

"He's fucking with you."

With her hand on her heart, she leans over and leaves out a long breath. "Thank God." Reaching for her bag, she pulls out her purse and grabs more than she needs to. She said her photography pays the bills. I'm pretty sure she's giving money she can't afford.

"I'm meant to be paying you, remember?"

"Oh, please don't insult me. I'm not charging you for this. It's a great cause, and I had fun."

Archer nods, the emotion on his face reflecting mine. "I appreciate it."

"Have you got any other photos of your daughter?"

He pulls his wallet from his pocket and opens it to a picture of Evie. Her dark hair curls around her face, her blue eyes prominent against her fair skin.

Bethany Rose pulls that face women always pull around babies. "She's so beautiful."

"Yeah," he agrees. "She gets it from her mother."

She hands him back the wallet and holds up her camera before turning to me. "Have you got a computer I can upload these onto?"

Her eyes are glossy, tears threatening to fall.

"Sure. The office is in the back."

She stands and pulls Archer into a hug, whispering something I don't catch. He nods, returning her warm smile.

"It was good to meet you. Tell Molly I say hi."

"Will do. Thanks for today."

She squeezes his arm before disappearing down the hallway and into my office.

I don't realize I'm staring after her until Archer breaks me out of my Bethany Rose-induced trance.

"Brother, don't fuck with this one. I like her."

"You're as bad as Skip. Nothing's going on."

"Yeah?"

"Yeah."

"Tell your face that."

I need to tell my cock first.

"Where's Jaxson?" I ask, choosing to ignore his comment. "I haven't seen him in a while."

"Who knows. I don't know what's going on with him lately."

I'm going to need to talk to him before he sets off.

He's always had a good head on his shoulders, but his mind tends to spiral to darker places. He's smart. Too smart for his own good sometimes. And it would be a lie if I said the little shit doesn't make me lose sleep.

I usually trust he'll turn to Eden if he's having a hard time, but something's off with them lately.

I decide that's tomorrow's problem. There's not much I can do for him tonight. He probably won't listen to me anyway. He rarely does.

"Thanks for everything, brother. I'm going to get home to the girls."

I stand to hug him. "I'll be back next week. I might kidnap that beautiful niece of mine so you can finally take your wife out."

"Thanks, man. That sounds great."

"Be careful driving home. It will be dark soon."

He rolls his eyes like he did when he was a child. "I will, Dad," he jokes, grabbing his coat and keys.

He's too young for the weight he carries so visibly on his shoulders. I'm not his father, but he's nine years younger than me, and when our father couldn't be bothered to stick around for longer than five minutes, and our mother was too busy shooting up into bruises my father left her, I felt protective over him and Jaxson. I did my best for them until Skip and his wife took us in after our mother died. But I can't take his pain away. I'm not a father. It drove them crazy when I tried to act like one over the years, but I still don't know what he's going through.

They had Evie young, they married young, yet they're going through more than some couples do in a lifetime.

And I've yet to see them without a smile.

It's cruel.

If I could take a fraction of his pain, I would lay myself down and volunteer, but I can't. And that realization goes down like a lead balloon.

Another problem for tomorrow.

"Logan!" Jaxson shouts from the front of the shop.

There he is.

Even from this distance, I can see that his eyes are glossy, and sweat is forming across his brow. He's drunk. I don't even want to know how. There wasn't any alcohol here today. Fuck, I hope it's just alcohol. "Me and the guys are playing a set down in Frankie's Bar.

Everyone's comin'. You in?"

"Since when are you playing in Frankie's?"

"Since five minutes ago. He would be an idiot to refuse the Savage Saints our last small gig before we go global."

Cocky little shit, but there's a dull throb blooming behind my eyes, and I'm in no mood to argue with him.

"Sure," I agree with a sigh.

"Bring the leggy blonde, won't you?" he says with a sly smirk.

"Bethany Rose."

He looks around like I'm speaking to someone else. "Who?"

"Her fucking name, Jaxson. Her name is Bethany Rose. Don't make me beat some respect into you."

He scoffs. "Like you're one to talk."

This time when he disappears, he doesn't come back.

Jaw tight with tension, I walk to my office and stand still at the doorway. She doesn't notice me yet, and I can't help but take in her effortless beauty and the way she bites her lip in concentration. All those problems for tomorrow are quickly forgotten.

She has this way of brightening up a room, even one filled with ink and needles.

As I approach her, she finally looks up and gives me a warm, slightly embarrassed smile.

"I don't have my usual photo editing software, so I had to make do with the basics."

I lean over the desk, pressing my hands on the cool surface, as I study the photos she's captured. Just like the ones in the album she showed me earlier, she has a keen eye for detail.

"These are incredible."

She doesn't fight the grin. "Thanks. I really enjoyed it."

Realizing I'm probably too close and one sniff of hair away from becoming a creep, I take a step back. She's stirring something in me, and I don't like it. She's younger, and I'm sure we come from different worlds.

Then she starts to gather her things, and everything warning me to stay away is wrestling with the unexplainable need to keep her close.

Just not too close.

I can do that.

When she stands, it's definitely too close.

I expect her to take a step away when I don't, but nothing. Brown pools slide up to meet my eyes.

"Thanks for today." She does this weird punch thing on my arm. I see when she immediately regrets it.

Pulling her out of her misery, I finally say, "Everyone is heading to a bar down the street. Jaxson's band is playing."

She stares up at me, unblinking, but remains mute.

"Would you like to come?" I say slowly, fighting my own smile as her mouth begins to part.

Composing herself, her lips turn into a smirk. "Are you asking me out?"

This isn't what this is, and it's far from what I meant. "No."

She picks up her bag from the floor and packs away her camera. "Because this feels like a date."

"How does this feel like a date?"

She shrugs. "I mean you bought me dinner—"

"I bought you pancakes. That was breakfast."

"I've met your family... twice. And now you're asking me to a bar for some drinks and music and dancing... with your friends."

I'm sure I'm gawking at her like a wild animal. "How the hell did you get all that from me asking if you want to join *everyone* at the bar?"

Another shrug before she winks at me. "So, no dancing?"

"I don't dance."

Her eyes rake me in from head to toe and back again, clearly amused. "Hmm. That's a shame."

I can't tell if she's teasing or if she's still high. "Did Jaxson give you something?"

"Yeah, a belly ache from laughing."

She walks away, only turning back at the office door. "You coming?"

My head is spinning.

"Coming where?"

She tilts her head like she feels sorry for me.

And that makes me want to punish her for it.

"The bar. On our *not* date." I resist the urge to chew the inside of my jaw just to stop from smiling before she adds, "I'm not missing out on seeing the Savage Saints live... And Logan?"

"What?"

"You should smile more often."

I roll my eyes and frown.

Her smile only grows wider.

TWELVE

As I push open the door to the bar, I survey the room, taking in the sea of people packed tightly together. My eyes settle on the stage in the corner, being loaded with the band's equipment. The bar is already jam packed.

Bethany Rose tugs at my arm, shouting over the crowd. "How did you do that?"

"Do what?" I ask, looking down to see her eyes wandering to every corner before falling back on me.

"The line is a mile long out there. You just nodded at the doormen, and they parted like the red sea."

"They know me."

She opens her mouth, but quickly snaps it shut again, eyeing me like I've performed magic.

"Let's go," I urge, already growing annoyed with the rowdy groups swarming like flies.

This isn't my scene. I prefer a quiet bar, a cold beer, and for no one to speak to me. Being around this many people—drunk people—makes me itchy.

I grab her hand, feeling how small it is in mine. She tenses like she did earlier but doesn't let go. Pulling her to my side, I guide her through the crowd. She's lucky I do because she's not even watching where she's going, wide eyes darting everywhere. She's an accident waiting to happen.

I know the rest of the guys are here somewhere, but I saw the way Ace looked at her. I don't have a problem admitting I'm a selfish bastard. I want to keep her a while longer.

Reaching the bar, I pull her in front of me, resting my arms on the counter at either side and caging her against it. Hands can begin to wander in crowds like this—other men's hands—and I don't feel like fighting tonight.

She came here with me. She's my responsibility.

Tilting her head back against my chest, she rolls her eyes.

I lean close to her ear to ask, "What do you want to drink?"

"Um." She chews her bottom lip between her teeth, assessing her options.

"Are you always so indecisive? It's a drink. Choose one. You don't like it. Choose another." In the mirror behind the bar, I see her rolling her eyes again. "If you do that anymore, they're going to roll out of your head. Choose a drink."

Our eyes lock in the mirror and despite the frown, the corners of her lips shake with a threatening smile. She stills when I reach around her body, press my thumb to her chin, and pull her lip away from the hold of her bite.

She glares.

It's fucking beautiful.

"Just a beer," she says, her breath sweeping across my wrist before I let go.

Looking up, I see a very familiar platinum blonde bartender traipsing our way.

For fuck's sake. Am I to introduce Bethany Rose to every woman I've slept with?

It's in this moment, I curse myself for not paying closer attention when the bartender told me her name. Didn't really need it when I had that platinum ponytail wrapped around my fist.

Smile fixed in place, she throws a towel over her shoulder. "Logan King," she says slowly. "What can I get for you, handsome?"

I almost grunt in response. I don't do small talk and I'm definitely not in the mood for it. "Two beers."

Looking up at me under hooded lids, she leans close. "You never called."

"I never wanted to."

It's cutting, but I need to stop this now because all I can pay attention to is how Bethany Rose is bristling against my chest, and I can already feel her eyes boring a hole in my face. She's clearly not a fan of my reply.

Platinum taps the counter and winks. She sounds confident when she says, "Until next time. For now, two beers."

Bethany Rose is practically heaving; her cheeks red and her tiny hands balled into fists.

After paying, I grab a stool and pull it to her side. "Sit. You're going to combust."

Crossing her arms, she does everything but stomp her feet.

"What?"

"That was rude," she finally lets out.

She sits anyway when I nudge the stool closer. Her outburst is more adorable than scary, but I'll let her have her way.

"What was rude?"

"The way you spoke to her." Another flush. "You two obviously…" She struggles to find the right words, the heat rising up her neck as she does.

I suddenly want to see her squirm.

Leaning in, my lips graze the shell of her ear. "Fucked?"

A small noise escapes before she straightens. "Yes. You didn't need to be so harsh."

"Why are you offended on her behalf?" I look back over at the bartender. She has her head thrown back as she laughs. "She looks fine to me."

"That's not the point. You were mean."

"Mean?" I chuckle. "Would you prefer if I lied to her? I never planned on calling her. I don't plan on seeing her again."

And you're right fucking here.

My ultimate distraction.

"Have you got any sisters?"

"One."

"What age is she?"

"Eleven," I answer, blowing out a breath because I know exactly where she's going with this and a knot forms in my stomach.

"You have an eleven-year-old sister?" She looks like she's trying to solve a complicated math equation.

"Long story. Keep up, pretty girl. You were about to school me. Don't get distracted now."

"Right." She shakes her head, turning serious. "When she's older, how would you like—"

"A lot older," I cut in.

"Okay, caveman, a lot older. How would you like if some guy treated her like that?"

I'd kill him.

Simple.

"I know to you it was a one-time thing, but maybe think about being a little nicer next time you bump into a woman you've slept with. There are other ways of letting her down. Who knows? That night might have meant something to her."

I cock a brow. "And who said it didn't mean something to me?" It didn't, but I haven't watched anything more fascinating than her mouth move in a very long time. I want to keep her talking.

She crosses her arms over her chest. "What's her name?"

"What?"

"Her name, Logan? What is it?"

Fuck.

She's got me by the balls on that one and the shit-eating grin on her face tells me she knows it.

Platinum's return is a welcome distraction this time. She slides two cold beers toward me, still smiling. "What brings you in tonight?"

I hand one to Bethany Rose before taking a swig of mine and holding it up. "Beer and music."

She leans over the bar, her cleavage on full display. "Well, if you want some company, you know where to find me," she purrs before walking away.

Bethany Rose downs a mouthful of beer before slamming it on the bar, her eyes crawling after the bartender on the other side. "I take back every word. She doesn't know who I am. What if this really was a date?"

"It's not a date."

She ignores me. "She doesn't know who I am to you, and she still throws herself at you. Gotta give it to her for taking her shot, though… Stop looking at me like that."

"Like what?"

"Like you're about to eat me."

She has no idea.

There's heat in her eyes when the lights go down. A loud strum of a guitar and the band begins. No introduction. That's Jaxson. He didn't get into music to talk, and he rarely does.

Going by the screaming crowd, it works.

Eyes wide, Bethany Rose squeals and spins around in her chair.

I sit back and watch because this part never gets old, listening to Jaxson sing and seeing how everyone reacts to him. I bought him his first guitar for his tenth birthday. I barely had two cents to my name, so it was an old acoustic I found in a second-hand store, but he loved it. He taught himself until he finally convinced Skip to allow him to go to lessons.

Pure fucking pride. It's all I feel.

This is their last gig like this with such an intimate crowd. He's about to take on the world.

I haven't heard this song before, but it's good.

Bethany Rose is practically standing on the stool when the song comes to a close, her beer long forgotten as she sways back and forth.

Then the crowd erupts when the band break into a cover of *Mr. Brightside* by *The Killers*. With the familiar guitar opening, the crowd goes feral and she's one of them.

"I can't stay sitting for this one." She's bouncing when she looks over at me. "Come on. Don't be a bore."

"I'm not dancing, or whatever the fuck they're doing." It looks like a migraine waiting to happen.

"My feet belong on that floor. See ya later, Grandpa."

Not caring that she's on her own, she quickly melts into the crowd and goes wild.

Throwing her head back, her dark blonde waves fall down her back as her dress swishes against her thighs, her feet stomping in her black boots.

I drain the last of my beer to quench my parched throat and order another. I'll need more if I'm to resist the urge to touch her for another hour.

One song rolls into another. She comes back once to take a swig of her drink, laughing as she wipes a sheen of sweat from her brow. "They're so good."

Like a magnet, my eyes follow her back to the dance floor. When I force my gaze away, it's fucking painful.

Platinum shoots me another wink.

Jesus Christ.

The room is pulsating with the rhythmic beat of the music, and the air is thick as Bethany Rose sways.

There are eyes on her, and not just mine.

The surge of raw possessiveness hits me square in the chest. A possessiveness I have no right or reason to feel.

With a clenched jaw, I force myself to stare at the label of the beer bottle when Ace approaches me. Elbows on the bar, he's facing away, and I know exactly what he's looking at.

I want to rip his eyeballs from his head.

He raises a brow and leans in, trying to be heard over the music. "What's the story with you two?" he asks, his eyes never leaving the floor.

Never leaving *her*.

My hand clenches around the bottle.

I hesitate, feeling an inexplicable desire to keep her away from him. But knowing there is nothing between us, I reluctantly reply, "There's no story."

His eyes light up, a sly grin at the edges of his mouth. "Cool. So, you won't mind if—"

"Have at it," I grit out.

If she wants Ace, it's not my place to interfere.

But as he walks away, my blood boils. Thinking of him getting close to her twists my insides. I try to drown the fire burning in my chest with more alcohol, but it does little to ease the weight that has settled heavily in my chest.

She laughs at something he says, his mouth so close to her skin, I want to rip his tongue from his throat. Then her expression changes, her laughter turns into a scowl, and she looks over at me, anger flashing in her eyes.

And... she's off, storming towards me so fiercely, that this time, she might be a little scary.

Cheeks flushed with indignation, her palm slams down on the counter. "Have at it? Really?"

I glare over at Ace who merely shrugs an apology, holding his hands up.

Bastard.

Bethany Rose snaps her fingers in my face. "You're an asshole."

"Tell me something I don't know, sweetheart."

"Screw you."

Don't laugh.

Do not laugh.

I fucking laugh, and I swear, if her face turns a deeper shade of red, she'll combust into flames.

I throw my head back to look at the ceiling, only because I need a second to get the smirk off my face before she slaps it off.

Three seconds later, her fingers are snapping in my face again. "I'm talking to you."

I don't think it through, and it's done in my next breath, but I wrap my arm around her waist and pin her to my chest.

Now I'm angry, and I know she isn't this pissed off about nothing. She didn't want me to let Ace near her, and by how her breath hitches and her eyes roll when I squeeze her tighter, I know exactly why.

She wants me just as much as I want her.

I pinch her chin between my fingers and tilt her head back to look at me. "Snap your fingers at me again, and I'll put you over my knee and spank some manners into you."

A mixture of fear and heat blend and pool in her features as her curves become molten against my body.

It takes all of five seconds—I know because I count each one—before she stiffens, presses her hands to my chest and pushes away.

"I am not some little girl. And again, screw you."

I can't help but admire her fight. Admire it and want to fuck it out of her. She's made me into an indecisive mess today.

She shakes her head, grabs her bag, and with a final glare, storms toward the exit.

"First quarrel?" Skip asks, laughing under his breath. I didn't even notice him standing there, and I don't bother to pay him any attention now because I'm too focused on the woman growing further away with each step she takes.

As the door slams shut behind her, I'm left standing here, the stupid grin still plastered on my face and a knot in my stomach.

I drain the last of my beer, torn between staying where I am and going after her.

It would be the sensible thing to do to let her go. She's young. She's having a temper tantrum.

"Fuck it," I hiss.

I was never sensible. No point in starting now.

There are echoes of my name behind me as I push through the

100

crowd and go after her.

The moment I step outside, I scan the street.

A rumble of thunder in the distance means I don't have long before the sky opens.

Great.

My eyes shift to the streetlight, and there she is, standing under the faint glow, her shoulders hunched, arms crossed, typing furiously on her phone.

Was it that bad?

She looked hurt when she left. I don't know what gets on my nerves more, the fact that I was the one to hurt her or that it bothers me so much.

Catching me coming toward her, she rolls her eyes and continues her little tantrum, walking away from me.

"Bethany Rose," I call, but her steps only become more determined. "Wait... Goddamn it. Can you stop?"

Digging her heels into the path, she spins around and almost crashes into my chest. Despite the hands I place on her arms to steady her, her eyes are murderous. "Will you stop calling me that?"

"Stop calling you what?"

"Bethany Rose."

"It's your name, isn't it?"

She blows out a forceful breath, puffing her cheeks. "No, I mean, yes, it is. Never mind, I'm mad at you."

"I didn't notice." Eyes flaring, she attempts to turn away again, but not before I can grab her arm. "I shouldn't have said what I said in there. I'm sorry."

Her mouth softens slightly, but it's not enough.

"It's fine. I should go anyway."

And I should let her. That's exactly what I should do.

Guess what?

I don't.

"You sure do like running away."

Her hands twitch at her sides, and I'm sure she's about to slap me, but she doesn't. Instead, she stands straight and cocks her head. "You know what, you're right. Why should I leave? I want to dance. I'm going to dance."

Storming back toward the bar, the crowd in line make their objections known. "She just left. Get back in line," someone shouts.

101

She pins them with a glare so intense, I feel it. Then she gives them the finger before turning to me and giving me the same.

Seems fair.

Once inside, I grab her arm and pull her onto the floor, making sure to find a corner cloaked in shadows while I lean back. I don't feel like watching someone else with their hands on her.

She heaves, but I see how her eyes dart from mine to my mouth. "What are you doing?"

"You want to dance, then dance."

"Right here?" She glances around, a blush creeping over her cheeks as if she only now realized the position I've put her in.

"Yep," I say, popping the 'p'. "Impress me, pretty girl."

For a moment, her gaze holds mine. Then she blinks, and I see nothing but challenge. With a sultry smile, she steps closer, her fingers grazing against my chest.

She rolls her hips to the beat of the bass, her hands trailing up my chest until they wrap around my neck. Her body moves in a sinuous rhythm, every sway, every turn designed to draw me in, hold me captive. Her gaze never leaves mine, challenging me to look away, to break this connection. But I can't. I won't.

The song shifts, the beat becoming more intense, and her movements match it. And with every move, every sway, I find myself drawn deeper into her, my pulse matching the throb of the music.

Every cell in my body screams for me to reach out, to pull her close, to claim her.

As she spins, the swing of her hips is like a hypnotic rhythm that draws me in, and when she grinds against me, heat rushes through my body. I reach out, my fingers digging into her hips to pull her closer, making sure she feels exactly what she's doing to me.

Her breath hitches as I lean in, my lips brushing against the shell of her ear. "You're playing with fire," I murmur, the vibrations from my words making her shudder.

She laughs, a soft sound that dances over my skin, making me want more. "You said you couldn't dance."

I give her hips a slight squeeze. "I said I don't, not that I can't."

The surprise in her eyes morphs into a daring glint as she continues swaying against me, her moves growing bolder, more intoxicating.

I rock with her, hidden away where there's no prying eyes.

She smirks at me over her shoulder.

My ultimate fucking distraction.

THIRTEEN

Present day

LOGAN

I'm nursing a tumbler of whiskey, the strong notes of the aging spirit coating my throat, when a familiar, sweet perfume wafts towards me, cutting through the scent of the liquor.

"Well, if it isn't my could-have-been-husband."

Glancing up from my glass, I see Emily approach, her signature grin accentuated by the scarlet lipstick she always wears.

"Seeing you in a suit... I'm wondering why we didn't get married."

I laugh under my breath before I kiss her cheek. The sight of her brings back memories, but it doesn't cause regret. We made the right decision.

"It was my inability to separate laundry. Tragic, really."

"Yeah, I did have a penchant for wearing rose-tinted outfits for a month straight," she retorts, her eyes gleaming with shared amusement.

She's dressed in a form-fitting, sleek red dress which I'm sure is designer. A testament to her successful career as a model.

My eyes slide to the rock she's sporting on her ring finger.

"Congratulations."

I heard she was engaged again but hadn't had the chance to congratulate her.

She twirls the ring around. She looks happy, and she deserves it.

Squeezing my arm, she winks, "He doesn't quite pull off a suit like you."

"Yeah?" I scoff, finishing my drink. "Bet you say that to all of your ex-fiancés."

"Ah, but you're my favorite."

Taking another drink, I ask, "What are you doing here, Em?"

"Just passing through," she explains. "I have a few photoshoots in the city, thought I might as well stop by. Wasn't expecting to see you here. I heard you're a small-town boy again." She shakes her head. "Never thought I'd see the day Logan King moved back to Pine Falls."

I lean back, the cool glass of whiskey settling in my palm. I always lived in the city, expanding the business to open studios across the country. It was a life shaped on relentless work, filled with long hours and sleepless nights, consumed by the need to succeed. And it worked. But I had always planned on moving back to Pine Falls, settling down, getting married, and having some kids. Not exactly in that order, but something close to it. I tried to pull back over the years, but work was all I knew. I buried myself in the business. It took me places I only ever imagined in my wildest dreams. I was grateful for it. I'm still grateful every fucking day. It's a far cry from how I grew up.

But in the haze of building my own empire, time turned traitor. Before I realized, years had slipped through my fingers, with those dreams losing their footing on my priority list.

Then life as I knew it got turned on its head, and I realized all those things, even the business, didn't really matter. Not in the grand scheme of things.

When everything went to shit and tragedy hit our family, I knew where I needed to be.

It was time to go home.

I opened another studio there, wondering why I hadn't done it sooner.

Now small-town Pine Falls sees a regular inflow of paparazzi for the celebrities who fly in to get inked by me.

I draw a deep breath, feeling a familiar sting in my chest, the memory of the painful past making its presence felt.

"It was time to go home." That's all there is to it.

A flash of sorrow crosses her eyes, and I know there's a thousand memories playing in her head. She was there. She knows.

"I hear you. It always calls us back." She holds up her ring finger. "I'm going home to get married."

That surprises me. Emily marrying back home? "The Plaza couldn't cut it for you?"

With an exaggerated eye roll and a coy grin, she replies, "Pine Falls has something The Plaza will never have."

I raise an eyebrow, resting my elbows back on the bar as a knowing smirk curls on my lips.

She catches my eye, and then, in perfect unison, we both say, "Jed's Deep-Fried Twinkies!"

The shared memory prompts laughter from both of us. It's a ridiculous contrast—comparing The Plaza with a deep-fried delicacy from a small-town fair.

Emily continues to speak, but my attention is suddenly yanked from her words.

Across the crowded room, in a sea of glittering gowns and sharp tuxedos… it's her.

The sight is like a punch to the gut.

Dressed in a simple yet elegant dress, her hair is back from her shoulders, revealing the graceful curve of her neck, her eyes as bright as I remember.

Emily's voice is a distant blur because my eyes are trained on the woman walking into the center of the room. Even from here, I see the fear on her face, but when she steps fully into the light, my breath catches.

Bethany Rose.

With just the sight of her, I go tumbling back in time.

Slowly, she scans the room, turning so her eyes lock with mine. I know she can't see me from where I'm cloaked in shadow, but I still feel the gravity of her stare. The red light floating over the room shrouds her for a second. She squints and steps back, hiding herself.

Instinctively, I take a step forward.

Then those full lips lift into a smile, the accompanying dimples etching grooves into her cheeks.

Fuck me.

That's the knockout punch.

I take another step, but Jake and Claire beat me to it.

"Logan, are you even listening to me?" Emily laughs, resting her hand on my arm.

I'm not.

I haven't heard a word she's said.

I shake my head, attempting to put pieces together that don't fit. Jake has been my friend since college, and I've never heard him mention her. Looking at her, laughing alongside Claire in the heart of the gallery, sharing a private moment, I realize they are far more than acquaintances.

The two women are friends.

I've been around Jake and Claire enough, but I've never set eyes on Bethany Rose again since that night all those years ago.

"Ah," Emily purrs, following my line of sight. "She's stunning. Need a wing woman?"

"No," I snap, immediately regretting it. "Sorry. Thought I spotted a familiar face."

"Is it a ghost? Because you look like you've seen one."

I think I have.

Forcing my eyes away, I turn back to Emily.

Maybe I'm wrong. It's been a decade. I probably shouldn't recognize her, not to the extent I do—every detail memorized.

It's agonizing minutes of conversation I can't keep track of before I finally let my gaze drift again. More people I recognize make their way toward me. I shake hands, nod when I think I'm supposed to, yet my focus stays stubbornly attached to the elusive figure on the other side of the gallery.

When I glance over for the last time, she's taking determined strides toward the balcony. I take a deep breath, telling myself to let it be. To let her go.

And I do… for all of two minutes.

I need to know if it's her.

With a mumbled excuse, I walk away, making my way through the crowd until I reach the doors.

And then there's no denying it's her.

But gone is the warmth in her eyes.

I recognize the man with his hand on her arm, only because I saw him earlier taking pictures with a press badge around his neck.

I can't hear him, but her… I hear every word.

Her eyes widen, fear slicing through them like lightning. The sound of her pleas reaches my ears, her voice strained. "Please get your hands off me."

I wait for him to let go, but he doesn't. He still has his hand wrapped around her elbow.

A wave of fury surges, hot and blinding. The fear on her face is all too familiar—a chilling echo of the fear I witnessed too often in my mother's eyes. It sets my jaw, tightens my fists. My vision narrows, the background noise fades, and my focus zeroes in on the two of them. I take a step out.

"It's best if you tell us your side before people make their own assumptions."

Stupid bastard is still touching her.

"Please—"

Another step, and it takes all my power to stuff my hands in my pockets to stop myself from ripping him away. "If she has to ask you again to remove your hands, I'll remove them for you. So, I suggest you do it while the bones are still intact."

I keep my eyes on her, the shock in hers confirming what I already knew.

"If you want to talk—" he tries to say, but I cut him off, not once taking my eyes off her. I couldn't if I tried.

"Don't fucking look at her."

He mumbles some curses as he walks away.

Good choice.

I take a moment to drink her in before I say, "Bethany Rose."

The color drains from her face as she meets my stare with wide eyes. Her silence leaves me doubting myself, her body still, unmoving.

"Logan." My name slips out from her lips like a strained prayer.

She echoes it a couple more times, each utterance sounding like a question she doesn't want the answer to.

She lifts a shaky finger. "Please don't call me that. Bethany Rose. People call me Beth... just Beth."

I arch a brow at the sudden heat in her voice. "Alright."

I anticipated a hint of recognition, a spark of familiarity, perhaps. But the haunted look in her eyes, the way she's watching me as if I were a ghost, that was not on the list of things I expected.

I don't know why I followed her, but the compulsion was as irresistible as a flame to a moth.

"I'm sorry." Her smile, as shaky and unsure as her words, breaks the silence. "I just didn't expect to see you. It's been… a long time."

"It has been. You okay?" I ask, nodding toward the reporter making his way back inside. "He seemed… determined."

She shakes her head, her gaze skittish as it darts around the balcony. "It's nothing."

"Oh, good! You two have met already," Claire's voice cuts through the air, her heels clacking against the tiles as she joins us. Beth freezes, her eyes slipping from mine.

I curse under my breath. "Claire—"

"Beth, this is Logan, Jake's friend." She continues, seemingly oblivious to the tension, "He might be able to help you find a place. He's got some properties. He provides houses for some of the other women…" She stops, finally catching up as her eyes volley between us. "What's going on?"

My mind reels, as my hands ball into fists in my pocket. Jake's vague request earlier when he came to see me at the studio and asked if I could help a 'friend'.

It was her.

The woman in front of me looking as if she has just seen a ghost.

Brows drawn, I spin to look at Claire, who's looking at me like I should have some answers. I have nothing but questions swirling in my head.

My gaze returns to Beth, if only to check I didn't imagine her. Her face is ashen, her fingers trembling as they knot at her waist.

"You two know each other?" Claire asks.

We both answer at the same time, "No."

Because that's the truth of it.

Beth tries to explain, "We met a long time ago. Before…" she trails off, her eyes glazing over. "I'm sorry." As she mutters an excuse, she stumbles backward, distancing herself from us both. Her eyes, wide and vulnerable, settle on the doors leading back inside. "I just need a minute."

"Wait…" Claire begins, her voice laced with concern. But Beth has already turned, her satin dress billowing out around her as she makes a hasty retreat. The sight of her fleeing resonates somewhere inside me, stirring a strange and unsettling feeling of desperation.

I shouldn't follow her. I know I shouldn't.

Then why the fuck am I?

It was the familiar look of terror in her eyes that has my legs moving.

"Logan!" Claire's voice cuts through the turmoil of my thoughts, sharp as a knife, but it barely registers. I hear her talk into the air as I leave. "What the hell is happening?"

Instead, my gaze is locked on the door that Beth disappeared through.

She didn't just walk away; she ran.

Ran away from me.

The bitter taste of regret spreads in my mouth, and I swallow it down. It doesn't belong here. Not now.

What the fuck am I doing?

I ask myself that over and over again as I usher my way through the crowd. I don't chase after women... Ever.

Except her.

This scene feels all too familiar.

Jake stops me before I can leave, his hand clamped around my forearm. His eyes, normally cool and collected, dart anxiously between me and the door I was about to leave through.

"What just happened?"

"Where is she?" I ask, my impatience flaring. The image of her frightened eyes still burns behind my own, fueling my urgency.

"You know her?"

I don't know how to explain it, so I don't. "When you came to me today and asked if I could help a friend with a house, was it for her?"

His silence is the answer.

I clench my jaw, grinding my teeth so hard that I'm surprised one doesn't crack. I don't know if I want the answer to the question I'm about to ask, but something in me needs to know. "Is she staying at the shelter?"

He stares at me, a sudden understanding washing over his face. He doesn't reply, but he doesn't need to.

"Listen, man, I'm just asking for a nod. That's all I need."

With a frustrated groan, he gives a reluctant dip of chin, allowing me to proceed as we step away from the crowd.

"Is she staying at the shelter?"

He shakes his head, but its fear coating my veins, not relief.

"Has she ever stayed there?"

His slow nod in response sends a chill crawling up my spine.

When I try to step away, he speaks up. "She was married to Rob Ellison."

Jesus fucking Christ.

I had known that Ellison's wife had sought refuge in the shelter a couple of years ago. I had known that the bastard torched his house before taking his own life. Most of this, by some miracle, had stayed out of the press.

But the pieces hadn't fallen into place until now. How could they? My stomach lurches as the realization dawns on me.

It was her.

I understand Jake's worry, his protectiveness. His dedication to the women at the shelter is a cornerstone of who he is, a trait I've come to deeply respect.

It's one of the reasons we teamed up in the first place. When these women found the strength to leave the shelter, they needed somewhere safe to rebuild their lives. I purchased several properties throughout the city for them to occupy… a majority of them did. I had a reliable network of people who could keep a vigilant eye on them, ensuring that the men they escaped from weren't creating any further disruption. But I never had any direct contact.

This was the deal. The line that was drawn. And I never crossed it. Not until now.

"You mentioned earlier that her landlord is putting the house on the market?" I question, my brow furrowing as I try to piece together the puzzle.

He offers another nod in affirmation.

"So, she isn't living in one of mine," I conclude aloud, feeling a strange mix of relief and frustration.

Without another word, I turn to leave.

"For fuck's sake, Logan, wait—" Jake starts, but I'm already walking away.

Barreling down the grand staircase of the historic Blackstone Art Gallery, the evening air hits me hard, a cool contrast to the stuffy atmosphere inside.

It takes a long minute to find her, but when I do, I blow out a breath.

Standing under the yellow wash of a streetlamp, she's trying to flag down a passing cab. She doesn't see me, her gaze focused on the busy road, her determination evident in the set of her jaw.

She bounces on her heels, hurling a string of curses when a cab fails to stop.

I pause for a moment, watching her. There's a strange sense of déjà vu, a call back to a time when things were simpler, when the two of us had too many dreams and too few cares. The sight of her conjures up a flood of memories, each one painted with a bitter-sweet tinge of nostalgia, and I can't help the smile that tugs at the corner of my mouth.

With a shake of my head, I stroll towards her, slipping my hands into my pockets as I lean in.

"You running from me again, pretty girl?"

FOURTEEN

BETH

There's got to be thousands of taxis in this godforsaken city, but not one will stop for me. Swearing under my breath, I drop my hand as another yellow cab ignores my existence.

Is anything going to go my way tonight?

Feeling the burn in my feet, I'm reminded of how fast I rushed out of there, of who I was running from.

My phone buzzes in my bag. A quick glance tells me it's Claire, but I can't get into this right now. Instead, I shoot her a text to let her know I'll call her tomorrow.

It's as I put my phone away, I feel a prickle dancing along my spine, my skin breaking out in goosebumps, and it has nothing to do with the evening chill.

"Running from me again, pretty girl?"

The breath leaves my lungs in a whoosh.

A simple sentence, and I go back in time.

Spinning around, I find myself staring into a pair of piercing eyes.

He's dressed in a sharp, dark suit that accentuates the breadth of his shoulders and the lean lines of his body. His midnight hair is tousled in a deliberately disheveled way. God, he's beautiful, and with a slight twitch of his lips, my breath catches in my throat.

"You followed me?" I breathe. "Why?"

He shrugs, his eyes never leaving mine. "You ran."

Heat crawls up my neck. "I didn't run," I correct him before looking down at my feet. "I can't run in heels."

With his deep chuckle, some awkwardness slips away.

Surveying the busy street once more, the reality that I won't be catching a cab anytime soon starts to sink in, so I take a deep breath, roll my shoulders back, and plaster a friendly smile on my face. Time to take back a sliver of my dignity.

"Let me start this again. I was in a little bit of shock last time," I say, extending my hand. He looks down at it with an arched brow. "Shake my hand."

He does, engulfing mine.

I remind myself to breathe. Breathing is good.

"Oh my God, Logan. It's been a long time. How are you?"

The corners of his eyes crinkle as he grins. It's the only indication that this man's body has experienced ten years since we last met.

"Considering I've just chased after a beautiful woman that I haven't seen in a decade, I'd say the night has gotten a hell of a lot more interesting than it was."

I drop my hand, only because his compliment seems genuine, and I feel... uncomfortable.

His smile softens, as do his eyes, and I swear, if I look hard enough, I'll see sympathy in there.

"How have you been... Beth?" he asks, hesitating like he's adjusting to the name.

That's a loaded question, but I give him the stranger's answer because he's no more than that. "Good. I'd be better if I could get a cab." I try and fail to hail another. "Want to help?" I ask, turning back to him. I'm getting desperate.

He stares back at the building we just came from before his hands slide into his pocket. The motion somehow makes him seem bigger. "You'll be half the night trying to get a taxi here. Let me drive you home," he offers, almost too casually. This meeting obviously isn't having the same effect on his nervous system as it is mine.

"I can't." I shake my head, feeling my heart beat bruising rhythms against my chest. A car is too small of a space to share with him. I won't be able to contain the emotions on the verge of boiling over.

"Besides," I add with a smile, the old memory resurfacing, "Last I remember, you liked to ride around on one of those death traps. A Harley and this dress won't work."

He leans in slightly, enough for me to get a whiff of his heavenly cologne. "Believe it or not, I also drive a car."

"I really can't. I mean, I don't even know you. Not really."

He's not offended, his features impassive. "Don't you?"

Yep, here goes my brain misfiring because I'm truly considering it. That old curiosity is breaking out of its shell to bite me in the ass.

When I don't speak, he says, "Plan on standing here in the rain?" His gaze lifts from me to scan the night sky.

"It's not raining."

"No, but it's going to… any minute now."

Sure enough, when I follow his gaze, the night is clear, but a distant rumble of thunder rolls across the sky.

My protests are rendered moot.

I can't get a cab, and I would rather suffer in Logan's car than go back inside.

Folding my arms over my chest, I tip my head back to look at him. "Is this your thing?"

"What?"

"Giving random women rides home."

His gaze heats my skin. "Tonight it is," he says, his voice lowered in a tone that has me inching toward him.

A palpable tension brews, stretching out and enveloping us. I'm torn between stepping back or stepping closer. It's an odd feeling. So much time has passed, yet here we are, as if the past decade never happened.

But it did. It's why I'm on the sidewalk trying to hail a cab.

And it's with that thought my chest tightens.

I trusted him enough ten years ago to get on the back of his bike, what's so different now?

Me.

I'm different.

Seeing him only serves as a reminder of the girl I once was, and for just a little while, I would like to be her again.

With a resigned sigh, I look up at him, my decision made. "Lead the way."

Dipping his chin, he gestures for me to follow. The impending storm and the man standing next to me—both seem equally unpredictable, but I find myself stepping into the chaos, if only to remember what it feels like for a couple of minutes.

I trail behind him as the wind rustles. The earlier clear sky has been replaced by dark clouds rolling in.

Logan, a few paces ahead of me, opens the door of a sleek, black, very expensive, very new, Range Rover. With a shaky smile, I slide into the passenger seat, the soft leather plush beneath me. As I buckle up, he closes the door, rounding the car to the driver's side before slipping into the seat with an ease that's disarmingly comfortable.

He catches me watching him, and a lopsided grin plays on his lips. It stirs something in my belly. I'm not sure if it's nerves or the need to vomit, but I decide to ignore it.

A tense silence follows as he drives away and into the city streets.

Despite the warm air wafting through the car, a chill snakes its way up my spine. I attempt to shake it off, but my hand trembles slightly, betraying my attempts at keeping calm.

How am I supposed to keep calm?

I'm in his car.

Universe, I am not okay.

I mumble my address, afraid to say anything else.

His gaze flickers to me as he maneuvers around a tight corner.

"You're shaking," he observes, his voice a deep timbre that somehow stirs even more butterflies in my stomach.

"I'm a little cold."

He quirks an eyebrow, not quite buying it, but he doesn't challenge me.

"This is crazy, isn't it?" I finally voice out, breaking the thick silence that's been hanging between us. "Us, meeting like this."

He nods, pulling his focus away from the road to look at me, his eyes piercing in the dim light. Then they're gone, back on the road. "Jake's been my friend for twenty years," he murmurs, a note of disbelief threading through his words. "Twenty years, and I haven't met you again until tonight."

He wouldn't have seen me again. How would he? I've been far too comfortable in the shadows.

He shifts in his seat, his grip on the steering wheel turning his knuckles white.

He knows.

Choosing to quell the awkwardness, I tell him, "I spent some time at the shelter."

There it is. It's out there.

No flinch. No shock.

The breath he exhales only confirms he was already privy to that information. "Fuck. I'm sorry, Beth."

"Don't be. It's life." And I don't need his pity. "Did you know?"

"About you?" I nod. "No. Not until tonight."

Since he's Jake's friend, I need to ask. "Did you know my husband?"

"I only knew *of* him." That speaks volumes. "And I definitely didn't know you were his wife." I'm not sure if there's sadness or anger in his words, but there's a hint of something deeper lurking beneath the surface. "I left the city a couple of years ago. Went back to my hometown."

"Do you still have the studio?" I only ask so I don't sound like a complete stalker.

"Yeah. How about you? You been back in the city all these years?"

I shake my head, trying to keep the memories from breaking free. "I stayed in London. We moved back when my oldest daughter was four."

"Daughter?" He flashes me a heart stopping smile before wiping it away with his thumb.

"Two of them." I glance at his left hand. No wedding ring. "How about you? Any kids?"

"Haven't been lucky enough."

As he navigates through the city, I can't help but steal glances at him, the way his jaw is set, his shoulders relaxed against the seat. It brings a keen sense of awareness—of his proximity, his presence.

As we approach my neighborhood, I sit straight. "Take the next right. It's the third house on the left."

When he parks out front, he gets out first, rounding the car just as I open the door. He extends his hand, and I take it, easing out of the car. A hot blush creeps up my neck. This chivalry is not something I've come across too often lately.

He doesn't have to walk me to the door, but he's already doing it, and I don't have the words to stop him.

I'm convinced when I wake in the morning this will all be a very strange dream.

His eyes flicker to the 'For Sale' sign posted in the lawn.

"Your house is for sale."

Well, he's good with the obvious.

It hits me then. I was in such a rush to get out of the gallery, I hardly heard a word Claire said, or they didn't sink in until now. Logan... the houses... Claire wanting to introduce me to someone. He's the friend she was talking about.

What is my life and how the fuck did I end up here?

"I don't plan on staying in the city. I need..." The right word eludes me, but he seems to understand.

"An escape," he finishes.

Not the word I would have chosen, but he's right. I'm running. I've been doing a pretty good job of that these past few years.

This time, I don't feel guilty about it. I need to run... for my girls and my sanity, from reporters determined to dredge up a past I'm fighting to bury.

I grip my clutch bag, needing to stay grounded. "Something like that," I whisper.

Is this it? Do we just say goodbye again and that's it for another ten years?

I wish I knew what to say. I wish he wasn't looking at me like he's trying to figure me out—or worse, like he already has.

"Thanks for the lift home." I cringe inwardly. "I better get inside..."

"I might have it." He runs a hand through his hair, shifting on his feet.

Confused, I simply blink at him. "Have what?"

"The escape." My throat closes. "Fuck, I can't believe I'm doing this," he mutters, and I'm sure I wasn't meant to hear that part. "If the escape you're looking for is two hours north, in a small, but busy town." He's saying it like he can't believe the words are coming out of his own mouth.

"Logan, that's..." *Amazing... Exactly what I'm looking for... Thank you.* All of those would be great replies, but fear has me rooted in place. He arrived tonight like he appeared from thin air and now he's offering me somewhere to live.

"Why would you do that?" I meant it when I said we don't know each other. He doesn't owe me anything.

I watch as his throat bobs on a swallow before those eyes implore mine. "It's what I do for…" he trails off, jaw clenched.

"For who?"

"For women at the shelter. I've got some houses they use."

I look back at my house. "This isn't yours, is it?"

Please don't say yes.

"No."

I blow out a relieved breath.

"Jake asked if I could help a friend. A friend of Jake's is a friend of mine," he adds. "And I know what it's like to need a fresh start."

I open my mouth to respond when the front door swings open, revealing Kim in her pink fluffy bathrobe. "What are you doing ho… Holy shit." Her eyes fall to Logan and almost fall out of her head. "I know you? I do. I know you." She looks at me. "That's Logan King."

I've noticed.

He simply raises his hand in a casual salute, as if this is a normal occurrence. Poor Kim looks bewildered.

"What… What's happening right now?"

"Logan is a friend of Jake's," I explain, practically crawling out of my skin. "He gave me a ride home."

Her eyebrows almost reach her hairline, getting her message across without having to say it.

Oh, did he now?

"And offering her a house," Logan adds smoothly, an amused smile dancing on his lips.

I glare at him.

He chuckles.

Kim slaps my arm.

It hurts.

"She needs one of those." She points to that damn sign. "Her house is for sale." Why is everyone so obsessed about my living situation? "Where?"

"A town called Pine Falls."

Well, shit, he didn't say it was there.

The mention of the town adds another layer of shock to Kim's face, if that's possible.

I can't help but interject, my gaze flickering between my sister and Logan. "And I was about to refuse. It's very kind, but I can't."

Her mouth falls open. I resist the urge to stick my fingers in there and laugh to myself. "What is wrong with you? This is exactly what you've been looking for. We spoke about Pine Fall, remember? Because it's so close to where I live. Or have you come down with amnesia?"

Shut up, Kim.

Shut. Up.

She continues, "You know Pine Falls is only thirty minutes from me, right?" Grabbing my arm, she takes a deep breath, and turns to Logan. "If you'll excuse us for a moment."

Before I can protest, she drags me inside, shutting the door behind us. Instantly, she rounds on me.

"I'm just dying to get into why *he's* standing on your doorstep right now. But let's focus on the immediate crisis. What the hell is wrong with you? You need to go see that house."

"What I need is for you to calm down."

She prods a finger at my forehead. "No, you need to wake up. You ever hear of that story about the man that got caught in the flood?"

"Seriously? You're going to do this right now?"

She ignores me. "A boat comes along, offers help. But the man refuses, claiming God will save him. Same story with a helicopter later on…" She's totally mutilating this story. "The poor fucker dies, and when he gets to heaven, he says, 'God, why didn't you save me?', and God says, 'What do you mean? I sent you a boat and a helicopter.'"

I roll my eyes, acutely aware of our audience standing on the other side of this door.

"He's your boat."

When she sees my lips twitch, she throws her head back in a frustrated groan, pushing me out of the way to open the door again. Her scowl swiftly morphs into a beaming smile.

"Sorry about that," she says, leaning against the door.

Logan shrugs those broad shoulders. "I'd much rather be a helicopter."

I hold a hand over my mouth as she glares at us both. "For heaven's sake. Here." She hands him her phone. "Put your number in there. Once I've knocked some sense into my dear sister, she'll contact you to view the house."

"Kim!"

She shoots me a warning look. "Nope, you don't get to object right now. You're desperate."

"I'm not desperate—"

She silences me with a finger to my lips.

Logan simply looks on with amusement as he stores his number in Kim's phone and hands it back to her.

I'm slightly jealous it's not my phone.

"I'll be in the city for a couple of days if you have any questions." He tips his head, and I know he's about to leave. "Goodnight, ladies."

As he walks away, I can't help but feel like I just let my boat—or helicopter—sail away.

That old feeling bubbles in my stomach. My gut is screaming at me, but I haven't been able to trust it in a long time.

I think of the two little people sleeping upstairs, and not knowing where they'll rest their head in a matter of weeks is enough for me to step forward.

Am I doing this?

Oh, God, I really am.

"Logan, wait." He turns, and those eyes are enough to take my next breath. "I think I need a boat."

FIFTEEN

The sun is shining down on us as we drive into Pine Falls. The road winds through a picturesque landscape that seems like it's been pulled straight from a postcard. The colors of summer paint the scenery with vibrant hues; wildflowers in full bloom create a patchwork quilt of yellows, blues, and reds along the roadside. The air is filled with the sweet scent of blossoming trees, and I crack open the window to let it in.

I glance at Kim, who hasn't stopped nattering since she got in the car. I don't even think she's noticed my lack of replies.

She reaches over and squeezes my thigh. "You're going to love it here."

"Hold your horses. I haven't agreed to move yet."

She ignores me.

As we enter the small-town, the charm is evident in every detail. The main street is lined with cobblestone sidewalks and wrought-iron lampposts, each adorned with hanging flower baskets. We pass a bar called Molly's advertising live music on a chalk board outside, and the aroma from the café next door is mouth-watering as I slow down and take everything in.

And there it is, staring me in the face. Daunting me, daring me to go further.

King Ink.

I notice the slight change of name from the city shop, but the font in the sign is still the same, as are the black and gold colors of the exteriors.

"I told you it was beautiful here." Kim sighs, resting her head back against the seat, oblivious to my heart climbing into my throat until I swallow it back down when I finally drive past the shop.

I knew this place was popular with tourists, I just didn't expect it to be so—I don't know—busy.

"Okay, I'll admit, it's gorgeous," I say, trying to keep the nerves out of my voice. "A fresh start? I'm still not sure."

Kim rolls her eyes. "Oh, come on. It's not like you're moving to a haunted house."

I check the mirror to make sure the girls are still sleeping in the back before I say, "Yeah, well, my life has been like a horror movie lately, so you never know."

"You've got this. You, me, Hannah, and Isabel. We've got this."

God, I love her.

As the car drives away from the town, the road begins to incline and wind its way up the mountain. The scenery quickly changes from the town to towering trees and rolling hills. The air grows cooler and fresher, filled with the sweet scent of pine and earth.

After a few minutes, we reach a narrow road that leads off to the right. It paves through forest land, with trees crowding on either side. The light dapples as my heart begins to expand out of my chest, my knuckles white as they grip the steering wheel. But soon the forest opens up to reveal two, almost identical farmhouses standing on a large piece of land. I can tell they've been recently renovated, but still have that charming look of a bygone era. With wraparound porches, white railings, and large white shutters, the only difference between the houses is the color of the doors. One is red and the other is black.

"It's beautiful," I whisper, more to myself than Kim.

Regardless, she gives my shoulder a comforting squeeze. "This is it. I know it. And hey, if things get too boring, you can always join the knitting club."

I laugh, feeling the tension ease. "A knitting club, huh? Who knew I could be such a wild child?"

"Always living on the edge," she teases, and despite my anxiety, we both burst into laughter.

As we pull into the driveway, I glance back at the girls sleeping in their car seats. Hannah's chestnut hair frames her face, and Isabel's cheeks are flushed with the warmth of sleep. The sudden stop jolts them both awake.

"Are we there yet?" Hannah asks, rubbing the sleep from her eyes.

"Yep, we're here, sweetheart," I reply, forcing a smile despite the ever-churning knot in my stomach.

Isabel lets out a loud yawn and stretches her tiny hands over her head. "House," she mumbles, not seeming the slightest bit fazed as she rests her head back again.

Stepping out of the car, I take Isabel from her seat. The moment her feet touch the ground, she starts toddling around, exploring her new surroundings with wide eyes.

"Look, Izzy!" Hannah calls out, pointing to the lake far off in the distance.

Too good to be true. It's the only thing I can think of and mentally curse myself for it.

Kim nudges my arm and tilts her head towards the house with the black door. At first, it's only a silhouette—broad shoulders almost filling the doorway, and so tall, I know how much I need to tip my head back when he's close.

The man whose memory has been tucked away somewhere deep inside me for the past ten years.

His boots hit the steps with a thud, and my thirsty eyes drink in every step.

"I'm going to explore with the girls," I hear Kim say.

I think I make a sound of agreement. I can't be sure.

As he makes his way toward me, the sun catches his raven hair and the tense jaw I can somehow see even under his beard. He's wearing black jeans and a simple white T-shirt that shows every contour of muscle. He exudes a casual confidence that seems so effortless.

His eyes meet mine, and his lips curl into a warm smile.

If I didn't know any better, I would say he's nervous too.

But I know better.

And Logan King doesn't strike me as a man that gets nervous over anything.

"You made it," he says, his voice rich and smooth.

"I did."

He takes a step closer. It's instinct when I take one back, and I hate it because all I really want to do is drown in the musky scent of his cologne. I want to go back in time to a night when I didn't know better.

His hands slide into his pockets, the black ink on his arms seeming more vibrant in the afternoon sun.

I clear my throat, trying to find my voice. "Is this it?"

He has shades covering his eyes, but I wish I could see them. "This is it."

My heart thumps in my chest as I take in the two houses, the rolling hills, the surrounding greenery, and the path of blossom tree petals blowing at my feet.

I love blossom trees.

My mind is playing tricks on me because this place feels familiar, but that's impossible because I've never been here.

"You okay?" he asks, breaking my train of thought.

"Yeah, just… taking it all in."

"Mom!" Hannah squeals, rushing towards us, her face bright red. She skids to a stop, her chest heaving from her sprint.

"What is it?"

Her excitement is infectious, and I can't help but smile as she takes a deep breath and announces, "There's a pool back there!"

My eyes snap to Logan.

"Don't worry, it's got a steel cover. Completely safe. It's on my side of the yard, but you're more than welcome to use it."

Funny how he calls it a yard. It makes as much sense as calling a football field a yard.

"Awesome! Auntie Kim," she roars, running back, "We're allowed to use the pool.

"Well, not today," I call after her, but she's already gone. Then my brain finally catches up, and I swear, my heart stutters in my chest. "Wait. *Your* side of the yard?"

He tips his head toward the house with the black door. "This one's mine."

I'm going to hyperventilate.

Neighbors.

With Logan.

"You live here?"

"Who did you think lived here?"

"I don't know."

Not you.

The air becomes thick, struggling to fill my burning lungs. I'm not sure if having Logan as a neighbor terrifies me or if I just don't want to accept the unexpected comfort my mind feels.

The warm smile he offers fills my chest with a strange sense of relief. "Let me show you around."

oooooo

"It's really beautiful here," I say.

He hands me a bottle of water as he steps out onto the deck of his house. I feel his curious eyes on me as I open the bottle and take a sip of the icy water, deciding to keep my gaze forward.

His shoulder brushes against mine, and I wish he would step away. Not that I don't like the contact, but I shouldn't.

Male touch is foreign to me, especially one so innocent.

"Thanks for letting us visit."

"Is this all it is then? A visit?" He shifts his weight in his boots, hands delving into the pockets of his jeans. His gaze drifts to the grass. Over the top of his sunglasses, the shades of green reflect off the lenses.

Mulling over his question, I let it stew for a long minute. I wait for the panic to take hold, for the anxiety to wrap around my throat so I know that this is a terrible idea. But then I look at the girls picking daisies in the grass, giggling together. Hannah's smile is so big, it stretches across the open land until it plants itself on my face.

I didn't get any of those nasty feelings inside the house. I don't get them around Logan either. It feels like my childhood home—safe and warm, like nothing can harm us inside those four walls. It's our bubble.

I search for more reasons, not trusting the zing of excitement in my gut. We'll be on this land with Logan. Just two houses, side by side, two completely different stories.

But neighbors don't have to be best friends, and I'm sure he works a lot.

But what about when he's not working? Specifically, the nights when he's home. Does he want the sounds of two little girls seeping through his windows as he kisses his hot date goodbye?

I'm making assumptions, but it just seems odd.

"You could have anybody live here. Why choose me and my two kids? We're not quiet, and we come with some craziness."

"Good," he says, not faltering. "I grew up not far from here, and my niece used to come here a lot."

"Used to?"

There's no denying the flash of pain on his face.

A Heart for Evie.

Oh, no.

"Logan, I'm so sorry. When?"

"Two years ago." He looks away and clears his throat, covering his pain so easily before he continues, "You're right. It's beautiful here, but it's been missing something. It needs their imagination. We see a large space covered in grass, and a lake beyond the trees. We see what's in front of us. They see another world. They bring everything in their minds to life."

I swallow the sticky lump in my throat, fighting the sting behind my eyes. He's right. I mean, they're already so lost in their own world, and it's amazing.

A beautiful escape.

For all of us.

Do I take the risk and jump, close my eyes and hope for a safe landing?

I chew my lip between my teeth, my skin tingling with elation, and a touch of intensity from the heat of his stare.

We need a fresh start, and it needs to be somewhere. Why not here?

And yet, I can't commit with my whole heart. Not yet. "Can I take a trial run? Say three months?"

"If that's what you want."

I don't know what I want. That's the point.

"I have one condition."

He cocks a thick brow before swiping the glasses off his face, so our eyes meet for the first time today, and it's like a gut punch. I remember that, although his features are now all sharp edges and sculpted to perfection, there used to be a boyish charm to his smile.

Not today.

"Okay?" he drawls, turning so the toes of our shoes are only inches away.

"I want you to increase the rent."

Eyes wide, it takes a second before a deep chuckle vibrates in his chest. Then his smile falls when he realizes I'm being serious.

"You're kidding?"

"Nope."

"Why the hell would you want me to increase the rent?"

"Because Jake and Claire have already done enough for me. I can't accept anything more."

He wipes the hint of a grin off his lips with his thumb. "Beyond recommending you, Jake and Claire have nothing to do with how much I'm asking for the rent."

I lean into my hip, assessing him.

"Then why don't you ask for more money? This is a beautiful town with tourists all year round. I'm sure you could make a small fortune with this place." I wave a hand towards the house, already willing my mouth to shut the hell up. I don't want to talk him out of letting us move here. I love it. Yet I keep yapping as if there's grease preventing my jaw from shutting. "Isn't this a popular place for weddings?" It is. I even saw a sign on the way into town that said, 'Voted most scenic town for weddings.' "I mean look at it. Couples would love to get married here."

"I see you still ramble when you're nervous."

Now I stop talking, my mouth flapping open and shut like a fish.

I laugh to distract from the burn in my cheeks as he continues, "I don't want tourists here. It's more trouble than it's worth… Take the house or not. It's no skin off my back, but it's yours if you want it." A long second passes before he lowers his voice and says, "You'll be safe here."

My safety.

I rub my hands together, and when I laugh this time, it's not to hide embarrassment, but it's excitement bubbling over. I can do this. We can make a life here.

"Girls," I call out to them. They're still smiling when they look up at me. "What do you think about living here?"

Their cheers are all the confirmation I need.

SIXTEEN

LOGAN

It's far too fucking early on a Sunday morning to hear banging on my door. I close my eyes and pray for it to go away.

No such luck.

I'd know that knock anywhere.

Cora.

It's as if she taps the Hail Mary every time she drops by.

Groaning, I rise from the bed, muscles still stiff from sleep. Missy, the world's laziest golden retriever, huffs a bark before looking at me and going back to sleep.

I pet her head. "Remind me to never rely on you if there's an intruder."

The taps on the door begin again, growing more impatient.

"Alright. Alright. I'm on my way," I shout, grabbing last night's jeans and a fresh T-shirt.

She's still tapping her knuckles against the glass when I open the front door. "Morning, darling. I didn't wake you, did I?" She smiles, pushing past me into the hall and disappearing into the kitchen.

My uncle, Skip, shrugs and mumbles, "At least you don't have to be married to her. You know how she is."

A fucking thorn in my side is what she is. She's been living in my ear since I moved back.

But she's holding a fresh batch of her chocolate chip cookies, and the smell has my stomach grumbling. I paw at the foil, but she's quick to slap my hand away. "They're not for you. They're for the children."

"Sorry, I released the slave children in my basement last week. You're late."

She makes the sign of the cross with her free hand. "Sweet Mother of God." Even after all these years, she still slips into her Irish accent. "Honestly, Logan. Did I not raise you right at all?"

I kiss her on the top of her head. "You raised me just right. I fucked up all on my own. Now why are you coming into my house at…" I glance at the clock on the wall. "Nine in the morning with cookies, if they're not for me?"

"Your new neighbor. She has children, doesn't she?"

I nod as the TV blasts from the living room, last night's game playing on repeat. Skip is already engrossed.

"Make yourself at home."

"Will do. Thanks, son."

Sarcasm isn't his strong suit.

"So," Cora urges, tapping the toe of her shoe against the floor. "Aren't you going to introduce me?"

"Now?"

"Yes, now. I want to meet the woman you deemed good enough to live here. That house has been finished for two years and you haven't entertained a single interest from anyone."

"It's not about deeming anyone 'good enough'—" I begin, but she cuts me off with a wave of her hand.

"No, no, don't even start with that. You've been picky about who moves in there and you know it."

I don't want to admit it, but she's not wrong.

It had been standing there, finished but empty, for two years. Initially, my plan had been to sell both houses after I'd finished renovations, but when Evie passed and I moved back home, it felt like the house, this land, was calling me back. It felt wrong to sell, to let someone else claim what felt like a piece of me. Yet, the other house has remained unoccupied.

Until now.

When Beth came into the picture, looking as if she had walked out of one of my distant dreams and into reality, her eyes seemed to echo with a familiar sense of being lost, of feeling trapped.

I remember that feeling.

The offer for her to live here was out of my mouth before I could think it through. Once the words slipped out, there was no taking them back. And now she's here, living right next door.

Fuck. Me.

Cora's impatient tap on my arm snaps me back to reality. She pops a hand on her hip, glaring up at me under raised brows. It's that stern look that still makes me nervous. I'm almost forty years old and she still scares me half to death.

Blowing out an exasperated breath, I grab a glass of water while wishing it was something stronger.

"Don't you think it's a bit early? And she only moved in yesterday," I try to argue, but I'm cut short by pounding on the double doors.

"Loggie?" Chubby handprints mark the glass before a button nose is squished against it, a tongue sticking out.

Isabel started calling me that yesterday and it looks like it's stuck.

"Skip, quick," Cora calls, finally dropping the cookies on the counter. "Will you look at her? Isn't she beautiful?"

Confused, I open the doors to a mop of curls and a smile as bright as the morning sun. "Loggie," she beams with the cutest stomp of her feet, but she's quick to forget me when she sees new people.

She marches past me.

What is it with the women around here?

But I find my lips turning upward despite the bombardment of a toddler. She's on a mission, and nobody is going to stop her.

I watch as Cora melts on the spot, her eyes becoming soft before she crouches. "Good morning, sweetheart. You are just the cutest."

"Morning, Miss Isabel. Where's your momma?" I ask.

"I'm here. I'm here." Covered in a light sheen of sweat, Beth comes running up the steps. Her face is flushed when her eyes finally meet mine, a sheepish smile spreading on her full lips. "Logan, I am so sorry. She's a runner, and for two, she's freakishly fast." With one foot inside, she catches Isabel before she runs again and scoops the escape artist into her arms with her brows drawn tight. Then Isabel kisses her cheek and I watch Beth forget why she was angry. "You can't go around disrupting Logan's morning, Izzy."

Cora waves her hand dismissively. "Oh, she's fine. He wasn't doing

131

anything important."

Just sleeping on my only day off.

For the second time this morning, Cora pushes past me, eyes on Isabel like she's the best thing she's ever seen. "I'm Cora, Logan's aunt. This is Skip."

Beth waves at him. "We've met."

"I'll be honest, darlin', I can't remember what I ate for breakfast."

Cora glares at him. "It's so lovely to meet you, Bethany Rose."

Beth can't hide the surprise in her eyes when she glances at me.

Yeah, I've told them about you.

"Please call me Beth. And it's great to meet you. I'm sorry about this little one."

Isabel mumbles something incoherent, but Beth understands her like they've created their own language. "We'll play soon, baby girl."

"How are you settling in, dear?"

She blows her hair from her clammy face and tugs at her over-sized T-shirt. "Getting there. Living out of boxes, and this one keeps me from doing any task for more than five minutes, but yeah, getting there."

I flinch when I receive the sting of Cora's slap on my chest. "Why aren't you helping?"

"Oh," Beth stutters.

I fucking tried. Hard. I unloaded her boxes yesterday, but having me in the house made her tense, so when she thanked me and demanded she could do the rest herself, I left.

"He offered," Beth continues. "I appreciate it, but I'll get through it."

Cora grabs the tray of cookies and squares her shoulders. "Nonsense, honey. We help our own around here."

She's gone, marching towards next door, and taking Beth's protest with her.

Archer appears at the doorway with Molly close behind. "I brought breakfast."

My house has become a community center hosting a meet and greet with my new neighbor.

"Bring it with you," Cora calls, her voice growing distant with every word. "We're all hands-on deck today. Let's go."

"I'm sorry," Beth mouths.

I'm the one that should be apologizing, but best she gets used to it

132

around here if she intends on staying.

"Beth," Archer drawls, standing closer and pinching Isabel's cheek. "You haven't changed."

"I'm surprised you even remember me, and you obviously need your eyes tested." Her lips tilt. It's beautiful. "It's good to see you again."

I don't see Molly coming closer, but her arms are around Beth in the next breath.

She's a hugger.

After her initial surprise, Beth wraps her free arm around Molly.

"Of course we remember you. We have some of those pictures you took hanging in our living room. And his eyesight is just fine. You're as beautiful as I remember, and passed it down to this little one, it would seem." Eyes heavy, Molly curls Isabel's wild hair around her finger.

Isabel tries to bite it.

We're going to need a pen for this one.

Archer pokes his head out to see the final sight of Cora before she disappears. I can already hear boxes being moved when she screams, "Come on, Skip."

He sighs and leaves, knowing his life is easier when he does as he's told.

Archer cocks a brow. "What's she doing?"

"We're helping Beth unpack."

Molly rolls her sleeves up and wraps her arm around Beth, guiding her out of the house like they've been best friends for years. "Many hands make light work. I'll give Eden a call."

"You really don't have to," I hear Beth say.

"I really do."

Archer is still holding a tray wrapped in paper from Molly's café. "At least you brought food I'm allowed to eat."

There's a giggle when I hear, "Work now. Eat later."

My head falls back with a laugh when I realize it's Beth's voice drifting back into the kitchen.

"You're going to fit in just fine."

SEVENTEEN

BETH

I'm standing in the middle of a room once filled with dozens of cardboard boxes, all taped up and marked in black marker, every piece of our lives categorized into words. But now, the room has a different story to tell. The walls bear framed photos of the girls, memories embedded in prints. Although, I can't help but wish Hannah's baby pictures were up there.

Logan stands in the entryway, leaning on the door frame with a satisfied smirk. Missy, the most beautiful golden retriever, takes her rightful place at his side, wagging her tail. The man spent the day lifting furniture and hauling boxes, and there's not a bead of sweat to be seen.

"So, you're officially one of us," he announces, crossing his arms over his chest.

I shake my head, still in disbelief. "I didn't know there was a membership card, but I guess moving day is as good a rite of passage as any."

He laughs, a deep sound that echoes throughout the otherwise silent room. "Cora has practically taken ownership of the girls, and Molly's all set to hire you for the coffee shop."

"Eden offered me a job at her hair salon, but I'm afraid I'm not much good at highlights, so I'm headed for the coffee shop."

When I asked earlier if they knew anywhere that was hiring, Molly was quick to ask if I ever waited a table. I had, but it's been years. She smiled and offered me some work in her café on the spot. Childcare wasn't a worry because Logan wasn't wrong: in a matter of hours, Cora has all but adopted my children. She used to run a daycare in town, but retired last year and misses it dearly. She made me feel like I would be doing her a favor by looking after the girls while I work.

My throat went dry, and the agreement got stuck in my throat. Thinking about leaving the girls with someone else makes me anxious, but this is the fresh start I wanted, and it's being offered to me without much effort on my part. How could I refuse?

Noticing me pale, Logan says, "Don't be afraid to tell them no."

I could, but I won't because this is why I'm here. I need to be out of my comfort zone. It's everything I wanted, and it's terrifying.

He must see something in the look I shoot him because he barks a laugh, nodding like I'm about to enter a club I don't know about.

"It's a cult, isn't it?" I deadpan.

He brushes his thumb against my chin. It's a playful gesture but my skin still burns. "It's so much worse."

When we step outside, the sun begins to cast long, slanting shadows across the yard, and that's when I spot Hannah. She's on the grass, playing with a soccer ball, her every move full of intent and focus. She's in her own little world, oblivious to the dwindling day and our watchful eyes.

"She's a beauty," Cora says, standing beside me on the porch.

She really is.

I watch as she makes a run for it, kicking the ball with all her might, but it goes astray, her aim off. She stops, her shoulders slumping with disappointment clear on her face. It pulls on my heartstrings so much I almost go to her.

But before I can, Logan steps forward. "Mind if I give it a try?" They exchange a few words I can't hear before he playfully tackles the ball away. Her eyes light up before she runs after him.

It only takes a minute until Archer joins, and before I know it, there's teams established.

The sight fills me with a warmth that blooms from my chest. Even Isabel, with her chubby little hands, claps and bounces in my arms, her giggles only making me laugh harder.

"Should we give it a go?"

"Go, Momma," she insists, almost jumping out of my arms.

I step onto the grass. "Looks like I'm missing all the fun."

Logan throws me a challenging look, kicking the ball towards me. I catch it easily, and for a moment, all eyes are on me.

Should I disappoint them now and admit that's as far as my soccer skills go?

I'm shit.

"Come at me, King," I taunt, even as I move to block his next move. I'm surprised I get that far because Isabel is still laughing her little head off in my arms.

The grumble of his laugh is my only warning before he's darting around me, taking advantage of my distraction. It's a blur of movement, followed by the sounds of the ball hitting the makeshift goal.

"Cheater!" I accuse.

"Eater!" Isabel agrees, pout on full display.

He raises his hands before bowing. "That's how it's done."

Asshole.

But I love a challenge.

"Get him, Mom," Hannah encourages.

"I will, baby. Don't worry."

Eden is at my side, taking Isabel from my arms. "How about we let Mommy go crazy?" She leans in and whispers, "Get him, girl."

"Hope you're good at keeping your balls, King," I warn, the edge of my mouth curving.

"I am, but something tells me you're going to like kicking them."

"Absolutely."

Maybe it's the atmosphere, or maybe it's the idea of my girls watching, but the next thing I know, I'm stealing the ball, dribbling it past him, and landing it in the goal.

Logan's mouth falls open with a groan. "Where did that come from?"

"Guess you're not the only one with tricks up their sleeve."

Hannah immediately demands a rematch.

I gasp for air. "Sure, just let me collect my lungs. I left them around here somewhere."

While I'm catching my breath, everybody else takes their turn with the ball. Molly, surprisingly enough, shows some impressive soccer skills, blocking Archer's attempt at a goal by diving across the grass. Even Cora kicks the ball a few times, but with each one she lets out a high-pitched laugh that has her out of the game for a minute each time.

"Again," Hannah insists, nudging the ball towards me.

I wipe my brow, feeling sweat trail down my back. "You sure you don't want to go one on one with Logan?" I ask, jerking my thumb in his direction. He's sprawled out on the grass, hands behind his head, a lazy grin on his face.

She scrunches her nose. "You can do it, Mom."

I can't, but thanks, baby.

"You're up," Logan calls, cocking a challenging brow my way.

It's still not too late to kick him in the most valuable balls he has.

As if reading my mind, he quickly gets to his feet, ready to challenge me.

"Here goes nothing," I mutter, wiping my hands on my shorts. I square up to him, holding my gaze.

"May the best woman win." He winks.

The game resumes.

Hannah runs in to take over with only a little help from me.

By the time the sun begins to lower in the sky, painting everything in a wash of golden light, I'm spent. Breathing heavily, I flop down on the grass beside Logan.

"You okay there, champ?" he teases, nudging me with his shoulder.

"Never been better," I reply between breaths. "You?"

"I'll survive. You've got quite a kick. Should have taken up soccer."

I chuckle. "Maybe in another life."

"Logan!" Hannah calls. I'm grateful it's not my name. "Time for penalties."

I wink at him, too exhausted to move. "Gotta save the legs for the next match."

"Sure," he says, getting to his feet while his eyes drop to below my waistline. "Gotta save those legs."

EIGHTEEN

LOGAN

Today is one of those days where I wish I could shut my eyes and erase everything. I tried to make it go faster, but no matter how hard I worked, even doing the admin I've been putting off for weeks, the day still ended with having to check in on my brother just to see if he's holding it together for his daughter's birthday. Her second one away from us. The gaping hole she left in my chest is only getting bigger. I miss hearing her laugh around here. I miss her smiley face. I miss picking her up and spinning her around until she almost vomited.

Fuck, I just miss her.

I'm barely standing today. I can only imagine that Archer and Molly are finding it difficult to breathe.

Archer kept himself busy at the bar, standing tall and putting on a brave face when he didn't need to. He's my baby brother and he's hurting, and it's fucking killing me. I expected him to spend the day with Molly, but she was planting new flowers at Evie's grave.

My hand tightens around my beer bottle.

What kind of a fucked-up world do we live in when a young mother isn't spending her daughter's birthday throwing a princess themed party and reliving the day she gave birth? Instead, she's only left with memories and goddamn pansies.

I've noticed the distance between Molly and Archer. Those kids have taken on the world together, and the cracks are starting to show. But who can blame them when these are the cards they've been dealt? There will always be something missing.

Evie is part of every breath they take. How can the air in their lungs ever be pure without her?

I know my world definitely feels a couple shades darker without her in it.

God, I miss that kid.

I gulp the last of the beer from the bottle and lean back in the chair, moving my neck back and forth to ease the tension. The sun is setting over the water—Evie's favorite part of the day. She always insisted we sit on the deck when she stayed just to watch the sun set.

"Happy birthday, baby girl. I miss you every day."

I swallow the painful lump in my throat before shooting a text to my brother and Molly. They might be going through a difficult time right now, but I still love Molly like a sister. I've known that kid most of her life.

They'll get through whatever it is. They have to.

The breeze picks up and a very familiar sweet scent wafts over me.

"Want some company?"

I peer over at Beth standing with her arms crossed, shielding herself from the evening chill. She tucks a wild strand of blonde hair behind her ear and smiles.

Still fucking breath-taking.

"Sure. Want a beer?"

"Thanks," she agrees, taking a seat in the deck chair next to mine.

She wasn't home with the girls when I arrived from work. They've only been here two weeks, and I've already grown accustomed to the sounds of playing on the land.

I shouldn't. It's dangerous.

But here I am anyway.

I glance back at the house, and all is still quiet. "Where are the girls?"

"They're staying with my sister for the weekend."

A ball of jealousy burns in my gut remembering when Evie used to stay with me. "Being an aunt or uncle sure has its privileges."

She smiles but it doesn't reach her eyes. "We lost touch for a while. She's been back in my life for about two years, and she's amazing with the girls. They love her."

There's a flicker of emotion washing over her features before it's gone.

I don't say anything, but I feel myself leaning forward, hoping she'll continue. I have some sick want to claw under the flesh of this woman and see what's underneath. Or maybe I'm just desperate for the distraction today.

Her fingers nervously tap against the beer bottle, and I can almost see how she curls in on herself. Anything to make herself smaller. I don't want to tell her there's no point. She's too beautiful and oozes something that just makes me want to get closer. Beth's attempt to blend in only makes her stand out.

Something tells me she would hate hearing that.

When she starts speaking again, I immediately find my eyes drawn to her like I can pull out her words. "We were close growing up, but…" She stalls, shaking her head. "Life, I guess."

By that, I'm certain she means her husband.

She gets lost for a long second before she changes the subject. "What are you doing out here?"

My chest deflates, the same hole screaming at me. "It's Evie's birthday, and she loved to watch the sun set."

"Logan," she breathes, brown eyes wide. "I'm so sorry. I didn't realize." She places the bottle on the grass. "I should go. I didn't mean to impose."

"Stay." I reach out my hand and place it on her arm. Touching her still makes a zing of electricity tingle over my fingertips like it did all those years ago.

I think she can see in my eyes the fragile thread I'm clinging to, the only thing keeping me together today.

She nods. "You must miss her."

"Every minute," I agree, the knot in my chest threatening to kill me. "I know you're starting at the café, but there's a law firm in town. You ever thought about going back to work in law?"

Her beer stalls mid-way to her full lips, and I regret asking because watching her drink is oddly satisfying. "I never started."

"Isn't that why you left?"

She looks away, taking a long breath. "I quit when I got pregnant with Hannah. I stayed home. I was needed as a mother, and I loved every second." That part she says with a warm smile. It's the next statement that leaves a bitter taste in my mouth. "We got married shortly after I found out I was pregnant, and Rob needed to stay in London. I wasn't just needed as a mother anymore. I was needed as a wife."

She doesn't say it, but I read between the lines. She wasn't allowed back to college.

"But come on." She laughs, and her change of tone knocks me back. "I would have made a shitty lawyer. I can't even win an argument with my toddler." She's trying to keep it light, but I see the hollowness in her eyes as she dodges the memories invading while she sits here with me.

Her smile falters.

I mourn it.

"Ever think of going back?"

"No. You were right. It didn't suit me."

My back straightens so fast, I'm sure I hear it crack. "When did I say that?"

"When we first met."

I bark a laugh. "I'm an asshole. You shouldn't have listened to me."

She shrugs. "You were right. Law wasn't for me."

"Do you still take photographs?"

An amused grin dances on her full lips. "How much do you remember?"

"Enough."

Biting her lip, she tries to smother the smile, but it's too wide.

It's too fucking beautiful, too.

"Yeah, I still take photographs."

There's something about her tone, a finality. She doesn't want to talk about it, so instead we both relax with a sigh and watch the sun set in silence.

Neither of us ever feel the need to speak as we sip our beer. The air chills as the sky darkens, the moon reflecting on the still water of the lake.

"It's beautiful," she whispers mostly to herself.

I look at her.

With her here, the sun, moon, and stars aren't so fucking obvious in the sky.

"Yeah," I breathe. "Beautiful."

All day, I'm wishing for time to speed up. An hour with her and I want it to slow down.

Choosing to stay in the silence, we both stand. I collect the empty beer bottles before we head back.

It's not the first time I've seen Beth home, and I know I only live next door, but I suddenly wish she lived on the other side of town just to keep her close. The day has left a dull ache in the chambers of my heart, but she naturally brings a comfort I'll never find at the bottom of a bottle.

She halts at the first step and gazes up at me under long lashes.

"Thanks, Logan. Goodnight."

I'm not sure what's she's thanking me for, but if I brought her just an ounce of the peace she brought me then I'll happily accept it.

She dips her chin, climbs the steps, and disappears inside the house. I wait until I hear the door lock and the first light to switch on before leaving.

NINETEEN

First days.

I'm having many first days since I arrived in Pine Falls, but this one feels like my first day at school. It's the hum of nerves swishing in my belly. I wasn't this nervous starting my internship.

I haven't worked since I had Hannah, and I haven't waited tables in even longer. But I'm here, doing this.

Today is just another first. After today, it won't be a first anymore.

Before getting out of the car, I check my phone. No missed calls from Cora which is reassuring. The girls ran off with a spring in their step when I dropped them off. Hannah didn't even hesitate when she let go of my hand.

I tried not to cry.

I succeeded until I got in my car.

But this is good.

It's good for them.

It's good for me.

It's just another first for all of us.

When I exit the car and stand outside the café, the air is fresh, if not a little chilly. Like those minutes in the morning when the dew still

143

clings to the grass and the heat hasn't reached the ground yet.

The door to the café opens with a ding. A couple exit with coffee cups in hand. The man stands aside, holding the door open for me. I thank him and step inside.

The café opens at eight. It's ten minutes past, and the place is already filling with people for breakfast.

Booths line the wall on the far side, tables in the center and a row of stools are tucked in under the counter. Nobody occupies those just yet.

The smell of coffee has my mouth watering.

I don't realize how long I've been standing here, drinking in everything, until someone blocks my view. "Can I help you with anything?" Her smile is familiar and warm, the green of her eyes haunting against her ebony hair. She pulls an order book from the pocket of her apron.

"I'm looking for Molly."

"Beth?"

"That's me," I say. It's half a question because I have no idea who this girl is.

"He told me you were beautiful," she says as she rubs her hand up and down my arm. "I'm sorry I didn't get a chance to meet you before now. I only got home yesterday, and I left early this morning. But I've heard so much about you."

My blinking and gaping mouth must give me away.

She laughs. "I'm Maria."

Logan's sister.

I knew I recognized that smile.

"I should have known. It's lovely to meet you."

"My mother hasn't stopped talking about those girls since you arrived. Thank you for letting her look after them. You have no idea how much she's missed taking care of kids."

"I think they're just as happy to get a break from me. They left my side without a second look this morning." I swear that sounded a little bitter.

"You're starting today, right?" she asks.

"I'm going to try. I didn't know you worked here."

"Just for the summer months when I'm home from college. When I'm not here, I work some shifts next door at Molly's—the bar, I mean."

"I was wondering what the connection was."

"Archer owns it." And named it after his wife. That's adorable. "You open that door at the back and you're in the bar. Sometimes Archer comes through that way." She grabs my hand. "Come on, Molly is in the kitchen. I'll show you around on our way." Behind the counter, she grabs an apron and hands it to me. "There's a room in the back where you can leave your stuff."

She pulls her phone out of her apron and checks the time. "We've got about twenty minutes before this place gets crowded."

"This isn't crowded?"

Almost every table is already full.

She laughs in a way that says, "Just you wait and see."

When she pushes the door open and we step into the kitchen, steam rises from a pot, grease sizzles in a frying pan, and my stomach growls at me.

It smells like heaven.

She introduces me to the cooks, Marty and Joleen. She tells me they're married and not to pay any attention when one threatens to stab the other.

I'm still not sure if she's joking.

A door off the main kitchen leads to a smaller one. All stainless steel, large ovens and flour.

So much flour.

"If you're looking for Molly, she's usually in here. She does all the baking. We're in the middle of wedding season, so you take your life in your hands coming in here. She's been known to throw things."

That makes me laugh. "Molly?"

"Don't let the innocent smile fool you. She's feisty."

Molly is scooping batter into cupcake trays when we go in. What looks like a wedding cake is sitting on the counter waiting to be iced.

"You made it into the battlefield, huh?" Molly calls from across the room. She's armed with a spatula, a smear of what seems to be chocolate glaze on her cheek.

Maria shoots me a sidelong glance, her eyes twinkling with mischief. "She just calls it a battlefield because she once fought a croissant and lost."

"A very stale, very stubborn croissant," Molly counters without missing a beat.

I wave my hands. "I'm neutral when it comes to croissants."

Molly laughs, "Good. Get yourself an apron and go to war."

∞∞∞∞

"So, what's a city girl like you doing here?" Ace leans against the counter after settling his bill with a hefty tip.

It seems like all the ghosts of that night ten years ago are living right here in Pine Falls.

The day's relentless stream of customers has battered my walls of reserve. The locals, eager to know the woman now living next door to Logan, are a force of nature with their prying questions.

I did learn something from what felt like a day of interviews. Logan finished renovating the house I'm living in a couple of years ago. He's had interest from just about everybody—locals, tourists, outside buyers, but he never let anyone move in. It's a little flattering, but also sad if I think about it too much because he felt sorry enough for me to let me move in there.

I prefer to take the flattery.

"The tourists flock here, sure," Ace continues. "But a city slicker moving to our town? You're either seeking a slow-paced retirement or you're on the run."

City-slicker?

I was anything but.

His words ricochet around my brain as I grapple for a suitable response, eventually offering a noncommittal smile.

"I guess we're all running from something," he concedes.

I think he had blond hair once, but now it's tightly shaved in a buzz cut. His biker attire seems oddly out of place in this rustic café. My gaze inadvertently falls to the embroidered patch on his leather vest.

The Kingsmen.

I was curious then. I'm curious now.

"So, what do you do exactly? In the crew, I mean?" I question, gesturing to the patch. A group of them had piled into the café twenty minutes ago, looking every bit as intimidating as the outlaw motorcycle clubs I've seen in movies.

Ace chuckles. "The Kingsmen aren't what they used to be," he explains. "Mostly just a group of friends who enjoy a good ride now

146

and then."

I study him, not completely sure that's the full truth. "And what were they? Before you all became a group of friends."

He leans in like I'm about to be let in on a secret. I find myself doing the same, eager to soak up everything he tells me.

With a devilish smirk, he whispers, "Outlaws."

I stand back and roll my eyes. I should have known I wasn't going to get a straight answer to a question like that.

"Don't worry, we're law-abiding citizens now." He winks at me, and I hope he doesn't notice the blush creeping to my cheeks.

Molly comes to my rescue, casting a skeptical glance over the counter. "Or they've just gotten better at keeping their shady shit under the radar."

Now that is interesting. Molly's insight seems more in line with what I suspected.

She turns to me, giving Ace the finger without looking at him. "Skip and my father founded The Kingsmen before I was born. They liked to… let's just say… bend the law a little. Skip *stepped* back when the boys came to live here." She says it in a way that makes me think Skip didn't step back as much as he let it seem.

Ace groans. "You gonna let her in on all club secrets?"

"What? A secret a quick Google search or a chat with Betty the Busybody won't tell her?"

When Molly told me Ace was her brother, I didn't quite see the resemblance… until now. With both of them practically growling at each other, there's no denying they share blood, probably spilled some too.

"Why did Skip step back?"

"He had a family to look after. It's a dangerous business to be in." When she looks back at Ace, I see nothing but worry.

"Which is why we're just a group of friends," Ace adds with another wink.

It's on the tip of my tongue to ask. I could broach the subject with Logan, but now that I'm here and already talking about it. "Logan?"

"An occasional user of our services," Ace answers, not providing me with anything more.

What does that even mean?

This conversation feels like a labyrinth, each turn leading me deeper into the mystery.

Sensing I'm not going to get more out of this topic of conversation, I try to probe a little more into Ace. "What do you do when you're not running around with your hairy friends?"

"Hairy friends." He barks a laugh. "I run a garage with some of those hairy friends."

Molly breezes by him, ruffling his shaved head affectionately before readjusting a display. "And he's not just a grease monkey," she teases. "My brother here also happens to be a tech genius."

Ace laughs, a playful grin tugging at the corners of his mouth. He smiles more than any biker I've ever met—which I can count on one hand. "No, Moll, I just always have to hack back into your emails when you forget your passwords."

"You're a hacker?" The words slip out before I can stop them.

"Now that's a secret not even Google will tell you."

Just when I think I'm getting somewhere, Logan strides into the café, his arrival as impactful as a thunderstorm. A T-shirt clings to his muscular torso, and faded jeans fit him like they're tailored. The sight of him alone is enough to make my pulse spike, but it's the dark look in his eyes that makes my heart lurch.

Glaring from me to Ace, his gaze is so heavy and intent, I'm surprised it doesn't physically hurt.

"What are you doing?" He's looking at Ace, but I think the question is aimed at me.

"Getting a few club secrets," I answer lightly.

His glare deepens on Ace who simply shrugs, casts me another signature wink, and says, "See you around, Beth," before walking away.

I can't help but think back to what he said earlier. About Logan "using the services". I push down the nauseous feeling that stirs in my gut at the thought of what that might mean.

"What can I get for you?"

He shakes his head, his eyes sweeping me. "Nothing. How's your first day going?"

"Did you come in here to check in on me?"

"Call it neighborly."

He breaks my train of thought as I quickly grab a cloth to wipe the counter. It's just after three, so technically I'm finished for the day, but I need to keep my hands busy when I speak to him.

It's unnerving.

"Um… Good, thanks." I stumble over my words because he just

148

flashed me a smile that makes my breath lodge in my throat.

"The girls came to visit me at the studio earlier."

Cora said they would after they called by to see me. She was busy making plans for Hannah to meet the kids here that are her age.

"It'll be good for her. If you decide on staying, she will know the kids in her class when she starts school," or so Cora said.

I haven't been here long enough to know if this is permanent, but I'm grateful to her. Hannah needs kids her own age.

"Did I pass my fear of needles onto my children?"

"The opposite."

I narrow my eyes on him.

"Hannah may or may not now have a full sleeve of temporary tattoos."

"What?" I laugh.

"I said no, but…" He looks bewildered. "She does this thing with her eyes."

I bite my lips together. "It's her superpower."

"Superpower? How do you ever say no to her?"

"It's hard, but I've had plenty of practice."

His eyes soften a fraction as they meet mine.

I pull the apron from my waist and grab my bag, thanking Molly before I leave.

Logan insists on walking me to my car. I don't object.

"Any regrets about trading city life?"

"It's different here, but not a bad different."

A dip of his chin and his eyes rake me head to foot as I reach my car. I hope he doesn't do that again or I'll need to sit. My legs feel a little shaky when he's this close.

"Good to hear. And don't take any shit from that lot." I'm assuming he means The Kingsmen. "They're not as scary as they look."

"I figured," I reply. "And you?" It's out of my mouth before I can think about it. It must be the desperation I feel to know more about him, to understand what's going on beneath the inscrutable exterior. My conversation with Ace only intrigued me to him more.

"Me?"

It's not too late to back out.

And that's exactly what I do.

Casting my eyes anywhere but on him, I say, "It's nothing."

I decide my handbag is a good place to hide, so I root in there for my car keys.

"Oh, no you don't." The heat of his hand on my arm sends a shockwave through my body.

I shake my head. "It's nothing, honest."

"It's something. You're just too scared to say it."

"Ace said something about you using the services?" I immediately want to suck the words back in.

His brows furrow in confusion.

"Forget I brought it up. It's none of my business what you do…" I lower my voice. "Or who you do it with."

With one determined stride, he pins me to the car. My breath hitches, every molecule of air abandoning my lungs. His muscular form against mine is a wall of solid heat, his energy consuming. His proximity does more than just ignite my senses; it invades them, flooding me with the scent of him—a heady mix of leather, ink, and something inherently male. My pulse echoes in my ears, a rhythmic testament to the storm he's stirring within me. Each beat is a silent acknowledgment of his raw power.

"And what do you think these services are?" The menacing curl of his mouth is nothing compared to the molten heat in his stare.

He's going to make me say it, isn't he?

"Women?" I squeak, losing my voice somewhere between his body and the urge to squeeze my thighs together.

"I don't pay for sex," he clips, his hot breath sweeping a stray strand of hair from my face. "And we don't deal in women."

The *we* and not *they*, doesn't go unnoticed.

I swallow as he steps back, leaving only cool air in his place. I right myself, pulling at my shirt.

"It's not what you think," he says, the intensity of his gaze making it impossible to look away. "I do use the services, but not in the way you're imagining."

Ground, please open and swallow me.

"I've got a few guys that I trust on the payroll."

"Can I ask what for?"

He seems to ponder it for a long second before answering. "Security. You know some of the women at the shelter come to live in the houses I own?"

Not how I was expecting this to go, but I nod.

"Security is for them. To make sure they don't… get hassled."

150

"Oh." My mouth falls open. "And what if they do?"

"They don't." His answer is final, and I can see exactly why people would be scared of him, but I'm not.

Why?

I expect my mind to catch up, for the fear to run through my veins. I wait.

Nothing.

I don't fear him.

He jerks his chin. "Next time, just ask. Don't assume."

"I didn't…"

"You did."

He's right, and it's a cold reminder of how Rob left me with the inability to trust any man. I'm left to always assume the worst.

I can't deny the truth, even if it stings.

Guilt gnaws at me, but then the corner of his mouth tugs and my shoulders let go of the tension.

I open my mouth to apologize, but he holds up a hand. "Don't do that either. You've got kids. I would be more worried if you weren't concerned."

I snap my mouth closed again.

Speaking of kids. "I should go and collect them. They're probably driving Cora halfway up the wall by now."

"Those tattoos should wash off in about a week. Use olive oil if you want them gone faster."

"Ah, let her live on the wild side for a couple of days."

His returning smile is enough to make my heart slam in my chest.

I offer a wobbly smile in return before climbing into the driver's seat. It's only when I'm sure he's out of sight that I let out a long breath, pressing my hand to my wildly pounding heart. The flutter in my chest is not from the intensity of our conversation, but the lingering feeling of his body against mine.

It's as if I've just woken up from a deep sleep, every nerve ending sparking back to life.

Looking down at myself, I scoff. "Seriously, him? Now?"

Leave it to Logan to awaken my dormant libido.

TWENTY

"Mom, this sucks," Hannah moans, the side of her face pressed to the glass of the door as she peers out at the rain, looking more like someone from a pining country music video than an eight-year-old. "It's been raining all week."

"It 'ucks," Isabel agrees, kicking her toy car.

She climbs onto my lap where I've been sitting at the kitchen table, staring at the rain just as miserably as Hannah.

"I'm sorry it's raining, but there's not much your mom can do about that."

She frowns. "But I thought you had superpowers."

The lies mothers tell will always come back to bite us in the ass. "I do, but only super hearing, and sometimes I have eyes in the back of my head."

I get a sidelong glance that burns like a physical thing.

"Believe me, sweetheart, being stuck inside isn't what I want either."

I have two days off, and I'd love nothing more than to bundle them up in the car and drive somewhere. Anywhere I can have a coffee without Isabel trying to dunk her cookies into it. But there's a summer storm forecast, and although it's hours off, the sky over the mountains is progressively getting darker, an angry cloud moving slowly our way. The wind and rain have picked up in the last hour. I can't chance driving in that.

We've spent the morning painting and making art out of pasta shells, and the afternoon playing Monopoly when Isabel was down for her nap. Any other day, I might find it difficult to get Hannah's head out of her books, but today it's raining, so today she wants to go outside.

Isabel joins her sister cross-legged on the floor, staring out at the rain as if they can will it away.

When Isabel starts singing her favorite song, *It's Raining, It's Pouring*, Hannah joins in.

"Look, I think it's working, Isabel. Keep singing."

The rain is getting heavier, but I don't tell them that because seeing them sitting there together warms my heart.

It's five minutes before Hannah relents. "This sucks. I want to play with Missy."

I look over at Logan's. It's dull inside. No sign of life, but his truck and motorcycle are parked out front so I know he's home.

After I've tidied away after our lunch even I'm left restless and wondering what we can do.

"Okay, you two. No more long faces. Up you get."

The storm hasn't arrived yet. It's only rain.

Hannah is still giving me the stink eye when I grab our raincoats. "Shoes on."

Hannah looks down at her sister like I'm going crazy, and they need to find a way to sedate their mother.

"What are we doing?"

"Going outside."

Her eyes widen. "We'll get wet."

"And? You get wet when you go swimming, don't you? You want to play outside, let's play outside."

Scrambling, Hannah grabs her shoes while I put on Isabel's and slip her arms into her coat.

By the time we get outside, the wind has calmed.

Hannah stalls, eyeing the dark clouds overhead. Isabel takes off in a wobbly sprint and straight into a puddle, her giggle loud and straight from her belly. She doesn't have a care in the world.

Her lack of fear toward anything scares the life out of me sometimes, but I'll be damned if I ever suffocate it.

I grab Hannah's hand. "Come on, baby girl."

When she does, we take off in a run into the middle of the open land. Our hoods fly back with the speed, saturating our hair, but Hannah is laughing so hard, her legs have buckled. Our feet kick against the wet grass, sending water flying onto our clothes.

Hands wide at our sides, we tip our heads back, stick our tongues out to taste the rain and spin around. The clouds blur into one, the trees in my peripheral nothing but a green haze.

And we're happy.

Catching my bearings, I take a single moment to look down at the girls as they spin in circles and snap a quick picture on my phone. The back of my throat stings and a single tear falls, but they'll never see it as it washes away with the rain.

With my next breath, my lungs open up, my body loose and mind empty of everything other than this moment.

This is freedom.

This is happiness.

This is what I've always wanted.

The screen door to Logan's house flies open. Missy is hot on his heels as he stumbles down the steps while trying to get on his shoes. The look of pure horror on his face should worry me, but I know he saw the three of us out here like crazy people, and it takes all my strength to hold back the laugh.

"Missy!" The girls scream as they run toward their long-lost best friend. The dog shakes the water from her fur, splashing them.

Logan's eyes dart back and forth between me and the kids, and my heart swells when they're the first he goes to. Eyes squinted, he kneels so he's eye level with them.

"You girls get hurt? You were screaming." He's in nothing but jeans and a black T-shirt. The rain soaks through the material, sticking to every contoured muscle.

"No, silly. We're playing in the rain." Hannah stands with her arms by her side, the sleeves still a little long. We're all in matching yellow raincoats, and now I understand the horror on his face when he came down those steps. We look like something straight from a scary movie.

He looks up at me, brows drawn tight. It's similar to how he always looks at me. Like he's trying to dig inside and see what I'm hiding. Like he's doing his best to figure me out.

I bite my lips together, but a laugh bursts out of me. He looks far too serious for the fun we're having.

I shrug. "We got bored."

Is he mad?

Did we wake him from a nap?

Teasing, I pop my bottom lip. He's not going to ruin our fun. "Was the poor burly man having a snooze?"

Isabel closes her eyes and pretends to snore while Hannah mirrors my stance. "Poor Loggie." She pats his shoulder.

"Am I being ganged up on by a bunch of girls?" he feigns insult, scrunching his nose in disgust. Missy barks, and he's not teasing anymore when he turns to her. "Traitor."

Hannah crosses her arms over her chest, obviously offended and discovering her newfound feminism. "Girls are better anyway."

"I'm outnumbered here so I'm not about to disagree with you." Eyes scanning the three of us, they finally settle on me. "Burly, huh?"

I roll my eyes.

Just when I think he's about to stand and go back inside, he spins back to the girls and grabs them in his arms. They scream bloody murder as he attacks them with tickles. They fight to escape but lose. "You three almost gave me a heart attack."

"We're sorry, we're sorry," Hannah gasps until he finally grants them sweet relief.

Isabel, my little grump, stomps her feet, not impressed by the attack. She hates tickles.

He glares back at her, but there's a twitch at the corner of his mouth. It's ridiculous. He's still kneeling as the rain pours down with nothing protecting him from the elements. The drops drip from his hair, but if he notices, he doesn't show it.

"You mad at me, Isabelly?"

He smiles at her. That full smile that always makes it hard to pull my eyes away.

Give the kid a break.

She shakes her head. "Yes, Loggie." Then, with all her little mite, she swings her legs and kicks the excess water from the grass... right into his face.

I would correct her for it, but his face is priceless, and I end up standing there, biting my lip until it's raw, not trusting myself to speak.

Bemused, his eyes find mine again.

It's a warning.

My stomach drops.

"How about your mom? Does she have tickles?"

My mouth falls open and my skin prickles with anticipation.

"Yes," they scream at the same time as I say, "Absolutely not."

He stands, towering over me, an amused smirk keeping me rooted in place. I tip my head back, meeting his eyes.

"Is that so?"

The roof of my mouth feels like sandpaper. "Uh huh." I lick my lips, my heart stopping when his eyes drop and follow the movement.

Trapped.

I almost miss him reaching for me.

Almost.

Letting out a blood curdling scream, I take off on a sprint back towards our house, one burly man, two crazy children, and a dog right behind me.

I'm close.

So close.

Just a few more steps and I'll get inside.

I hate tickles almost as much as Isabel.

But I'm not close enough.

The air is knocked from my lungs when his arm wraps around my stomach and then his fingers are digging into my waist.

"Please stop," I half cry, half laugh so hard I can't breathe.

"No tickles, huh? You seem pretty ticklish to me." He chuckles, his laugh vibrating against my back, his breath hot on my neck.

It's not the only place I'm ticklish.

Hannah and Isabel join in on the torture. Even Missy rubs her nose on me.

Spent and out of air, my body crumbles. He doesn't let me go at first, even after I beg for mercy. Eventually, I'm sliding down his body until my ass hits the grass. It's cold, wet, and muddy, but the smile on my face is so big it hurts, and honestly, I don't care how dirty I am.

My bullies all share a high five, victorious.

He crouches with his elbows on his knees. The rain is getting heavier, washing over our faces in torrents.

"You lose, pretty girl."

I swipe my hands through the grass to splash him, but I'm far too exhausted to put any effort behind it.

"Wipe that grin off your face, King. I'll get back at you."

Standing, he reaches out his hand to help me up. I think about dragging him down here with me, but who am I fooling? He's huge.

"I'm looking forward to it." A slow wink and I melt all the way to my feet.

Leaning over, I rest my hands on my thighs, still feeling my lungs burn. "Your mom needs a rest. You've got five minutes." They scurry away to do more twirls while me and my ass seek refuge on the steps.

Logan joins me. We're both dripping wet, but neither of us seems to care. We share a smile and remain in a comfortable silence as we watch Hannah and Isabel having the time of their lives in the rain. We're sitting so close, our arms brush, and the heat from his body is enough to send goose bumps prickling along my flesh.

Five minutes later, the rain takes a brief respite, and a rainbow creeps out from behind the clouds.

"A rainbow! Mom, Logan, look!" Hannah points to the sky.

"I see it. It's beautiful."

There's a moment of silence before Logan speaks up. "You're doing good with those two."

I look over at him, the unexpected compliment making the back of my eyes sting. His gaze remains on the kids with a warm smile.

"Thanks. That means a lot."

It means the world.

I wonder every day if I'm doing enough. If our past has followed us. If it haunts us enough to affect our future. I worry about every decision. I worry if they get too much screen time, should they be eating more vegetables, will Hannah need braces, do they see me cry or believe me when I say I don't need as much sleep as everyone because like I said, moms have superpowers. I feel guilty on the days I lock myself in my room for just five minutes to breathe.

So hearing Logan say what he said makes a crack I didn't know I had fill in my chest.

I don't need recognition for being a mom. It's my job, and I love every minute, even the bad ones. But it's still good to hear it.

As if reading my thoughts, he squeezes my knee.

My chest tightens. In my best attempt to deflect from the tears threatening to fall, I say, "No more tickle attacks, or I'll set Isabel loose on you."

He barks a laugh. "She's feisty." He arches a brow. "I wonder where she gets it from?"

I point to my chest. "Me? You think she gets it from me? That kid does not get her attitude from me. I swear she was programmed with it from the day she was born."

His eyes linger on me.

Now it's my turn to laugh. "I guess I was pretty feisty."

"Not was."

I scrunch my nose. I'm practically fishing for compliments at this stage, but a girl's got to get them somewhere. "You think I still got it?"

His eyes turn to nothing but molten as they skim me head to foot and back again.

"You've still got it, pretty girl."

I feel the tips of my ears get hot before I clear my throat and stand. I'm not sure if it's to distract myself or him, but anything to ease the sudden throb between my legs. When he chuckles, I realize he knows exactly what I'm doing.

My reaction to him is no different than it was ten years ago. And he's criminally gorgeous. He knows exactly what he does to women. It's an unfair playing field.

"Girls, we gotta get changed." The sky is turning darker, making it feel more like late evening than afternoon. Thankfully, they both come without me having to bribe them. Missy rubs her head against my thigh until I pet her.

"Thanks for playing with us, Logan," Hannah says, wrapping her arms around his waist. It shocks us both. His eyes almost pop out of his head as they meet mine.

I want to curl up in a ball and cry.

She doesn't do that with anyone.

Not one to be left out, Isabel wraps her chubby hands around his leg.

His panic says he's worried about my reaction to this, like he's seeking permission to hug them back. I smile and dip my chin. With a harsh exhale, he kneels and wraps them up, and fuck if it doesn't make my blood gush hotter.

Ruffling his hands through their hair playfully, he says, "You girls have made this place brighter. Even in a storm." His final look is aimed towards me. My smile falters.

"You should come have dinner with us?" Hannah suggests. "Mom always makes too much."

"She's right. I do. You're more than welcome for dinner."

He looks down at the girls again before nodding in agreement.

"Give me an hour. I need to get these two washed first."

"Sure," he says. "See you in an hour." With a final sweep of my face, he dips his chin and walks away, calling Missy after him.

TWENTY-ONE

"Mom, you know what we should do?"

"Don't speak with your mouth full?" I suggest.

Hannah's mouth snaps shut before she holds up a finger. "Hold on," she mumbles.

At the same time, Isabel offers her spoon to Logan. He leans close and pretends to eat it while rubbing his stomach. "Yummy."

That must be the tenth time she's done it. If it annoys him, he doesn't show it. Instead, he picks up her spoon, fills it with more food and hollers, "Here comes the train." She opens her mouth wide and giggles.

My ovaries skip a beat.

I don't know why, but I always assumed he wouldn't like children.

Isabel offers more food, Logan pretends to eat it, then he feeds her.

I've told him that I'll take over, and that she's capable of feeding herself. She's just choosing not to. He demanded I sit and eat my dinner. I have to admit, it's nice to have a meal without getting covered with Isabel's. Now every time she drops her food, Missy is quick to lick it off the floor.

"I'm having her around every evening. She's making clean up a lot easier."

He rubs behind Missy's ears. "You won't find any shame with this one."

Isabel screams, demanding attention. "My turn, Loggie."

Hannah finally swallows her food, clears her throat, and sets her fork down. Crossing her arms, she leans them on the table.

I've entered her office.

"Go on," I prompt.

She blinks faster which means she's going to ask for something.

Strength, Beth.

You can say no.

"Me and Isabel spoke about this earlier." Although Isabel's speech is still incoherent to most, I think these two girls have created their own language, so I believe they've had a discussion. "Can we have a playhouse for outside? When it rains, we can go in there."

"Is that so?"

"That is so." She turns to Isabel. "Isn't it?"

An enthusiastic nod from Isabel. "So, Momma," she agrees.

Logan chuckles, eyes bouncing between the three of us. "Do they always team up like this?"

I give him a sidelong glance. "Welcome to my world."

"Logan, can you build us a playhouse?"

"Hannah!" I gasp, my fork clattering onto the plate.

There go her eyelashes fluttering over puppy dog eyes.

Poor Logan.

His face visibly softens.

He opens his mouth, but I stop him. "Don't answer that."

"I could—"

"No, you couldn't. Hannah, baby, let Logan eat his dinner. We'll talk about this tomorrow."

"I'm just saying." Her focus returns to the book she's reading while expertly finishing her meal. When I said Hannah's head is always in a book, I meant it. "I'll do all my chores for a month."

"How about you do your chores anyway?"

"Suppose but I'll clean my room."

My fork stills halfway to my mouth. She's still reading her book, taking in every word while arguing her case and eating.

She's already a better lawyer than I ever would have been.

"That's your *only* chore."

"Not true. You asked me to pick up Isabel's toys earlier when you were putting her down for a nap."

I look over at Logan. We share a smile.

"And did you do it?"

She didn't. There was a plot twist in her book.

"That's not the point."

I think she's determined to win by simply confusing me.

"We'll talk about a playhouse tomorrow after you clean your room in this real house."

Logan stares over at me while Isabel climbs into his arms. He hardly notices, holding her on his knee with ease. "She's only eight, right?"

"I'm eight and a half," Hannah is quick to correct.

I shake my head with a laugh. "The half is really important."

"What do you want to be when you grow up, Hannah?" he asks.

She doesn't miss a beat when she responds, "Someone who builds playhouses."

We both burst into laughter.

"She's quick."

I roll my eyes, but I can't help the smile. "Too quick."

She finally closes her book. "I want to be a librarian," she states matter-of-factly. She's been saying that since she first learned to read. "Mom always takes us to the library."

"So, you love soccer and books. Good to know."

"Uh huh." She nods, an orange tinge around her mouth from the pasta sauce. "They're my favorite things. Maybe I'll be a World Cup winning librarian."

His brows almost reach his hairline. "You know what, kid? I think you're gonna do it."

"Mom likes to read too, but her books always have people kissing on the front or men with tattoos like you." She pretends to gag.

I stare into my spaghetti while his eyes burn into the side of my face.

I stuff more food in my mouth, anything to avoid answering his unasked questions.

Thanks, Hannah.

"Do you read?" she asks.

"I can. Don't mean I like it."

Her eyes almost bulge out of her head.

Blasphemy.

"How can you not like to read?"

"Maybe you can recommend something?"

Her face lights up. "I'll be right back."

She's off like a shot.

I look at him from the corner of my eye only to be greeted with a shit-eating grin.

"Kissing books, huh?"

I chew the inside of my cheek.

"Just kissing?"

Heat rises up my neck.

I don't look at him because he will make me hot everywhere.

"Beth?"

With a deep breath, I finally lift my gaze to his. "Nope," I answer, reaching out to grab Isabel from his lap.

"Nope, what?"

"Not just kissing."

That smile gets impossibly wider.

It's intoxicating.

"Shut up. Eat your food."

His shoulders shake with a deep chuckle while I slowly die on the inside.

TWENTY-TWO

LOGAN

"You didn't have to do that." Beth leans against the counter as I rinse the plates and leave them to dry on the rack.

"You cooked, it's the least I could do. The girls asleep?"

She leaves out a long sigh. "Finally. Hannah fought it until the bitter end, but I think that final game of Snap took her out."

I laugh, still feeling the sting on the back of my hand. "She's violent."

"I like to call it healthy competition. Kim is coming to collect them in the morning. They're staying with her for the weekend."

She opens the fridge, pulls out a beer and hands it to me as I dry my hands on a towel.

"Beer?"

I was going to leave, but when she takes one for herself and clinks her bottle against mine, I know there's no way in hell I'm leaving, because I don't want to. At least I can admit that much.

She's changed too. It's only sweatpants and a top that falls loosely from one shoulder.

It's a fucking shoulder, and yet my eyes drink in how it leads to her slender neck.

I clear my throat and focus on something else.

There are new pictures hanging on the wall.

Those are good. I can focus on those.

It's a collage of the girls. They're recent pictures, all taken here. Simple, but shot with all the taste I remember Beth having.

For someone who loves photography, there are surprisingly few photos in the house. From what I can tell, all of them are recent.

Noticing where my eyes have landed, she takes a large gulp of her beer. "I shot those on my phone. A crime." She laughs, but it's forced and her eyes drift into the bottle. "I haven't got around to buying a new camera yet."

"What happened your old one?"

By the way her eyes snap to mine, I think I'm supposed to know the answer.

Realization hits me a second after the words leave my mouth.

You're a fucking idiot, Logan.

After she left her scumbag of a husband, her house was burned to the ground, no doubt with everything in it.

"Shit, I'm sorry."

She smiles. It's supposed to be reassuring. It's anything but.

"Don't worry about it. I lost all my photographs in the fire. Thank God for technology and clouds, hey?"

The mask falls for the briefest second. Like she's tired of holding it in place. Her eyes close, shielding herself from the blow of memories while trying to hide it from the rest of the world even when they're not looking.

But I'm looking.

And as fast as it fell, it's back in place.

She puts the bottle on the counter before pulling her hair back from her face and securing it with the hair tie around her wrist.

"Want to sit outside?" she asks.

"You're not tired?"

A blush rushes to her cheeks. It's fucking beautiful. "No."

"Come on then."

The storm has passed, but the trickle of rain still falls on the roof. We're covered on the porch as we take our seats and look at the moon dancing on the lake. The air is fresh, but still clings to the summer heat. Missy takes her place at my feet.

Beth curls her legs under herself. Her shoulders relax with a long breath. "God, I love it here."

"Good."

"Careful, I might never want to leave."

"I told you already, you're welcome to stay as long as you want."

Her thank you is a smile and dip of her chin. "So, tell me, what's going on in your life?"

"What's going on in my life? Business, that's what."

She sits straight. "Nobody likes a bore, Logan. My life revolves around two beautiful but crazy little girls, so my days consist of work, laundry, dinners, endless Lego—which should come with some industrial standard padding for your feet, by the way—bedtime routines, and constantly buying anti-aging creams that never work. I'm a wash, rinse, repeat kinda gal, so I'm going to need juicy details."

"Ain't you too young for those creams?"

"I'm thirty-two."

I blink at her.

"Oh, come on," she implores, leaning on the arm of her chair.

"Don't you have Molly and Eden for this kind of shit? They're your friends."

"And so are you."

Friend.

That word makes my next drink of beer taste bitter.

"Hot dates?"

I don't answer.

She grimaces. "Not-so-hot dates?"

"I'm not doing this with you, pretty girl."

She flutters her eyelashes with that shit-eating grin on her face. Now I know where Hannah gets it from.

I'm not known for holding my tongue, but I find myself doing it around Beth.

But she asked. I'll answer.

"I met a beautiful woman six weeks ago. Well, that's not true, we met before, but I bumped into her again recently."

Her mouth falls open. "Oh, do tell."

I take a long drink before crossing my ankle over my leg.

"She's sexy as hell, funny, smart, has great t—"

She holds out her hand, offended on behalf of women everywhere. "Logan King, do not finish that sentence."

"Great teeth." I keep going.

She throws her head back and laughs, loud and free.

I'm addicted to the sound the second I hear it.

"Okay, so what's the problem? I mean she has great teeth." She wipes a tear from the corner of her eye.

"She's my neighbor."

The beer she just drank threatens to come spilling out of her mouth, but her hand flies to her face to stop it. It still doesn't hide from how red her cheeks have become.

"See my problem?"

She nods, but even as she clears her throat, her mouth still tilts into the most breath-taking grin. "So do you take women's panties off, or do they just melt?"

"I prefer to take them off. The melting is a hazard."

"I can see why."

"How are yours doing?"

"Third degree burns over here."

We clink our beers together.

Silent for a long minute, she rests her head on her hand and stares. I'm not sure if the beer is getting to her, but her eyes are glossy.

"Sexy, huh?"

"Are you fishing for compliments?"

She shrugs making the material of her sweater fall farther down her arm.

Eyes on her face.

"You said it."

"I said sexy as hell, and I meant it."

She glances at her watch. "I'll have you back at the same time every night for my ego boost."

Why hasn't someone been telling her this every fucking day?

Silence ensues. A comfortable silence.

It dawns on me that I've never been able to sit in silence with anyone besides myself...and Missy.

"What's the dream?" she finally asks, her eyes still focused on the lake. "What's your dream?"

"This," I answer honestly. "This is the dream. All I've ever wanted is peace, and I've found it here. I didn't have the best start. Shitty parents under shitty circumstances but find me someone that didn't have one of those things. Not everyone is as lucky as I've been, and I know that. I'm grateful for it. I might not have everything, but I have enough."

There's a mutual understanding when our eyes connect.

Something stabs me in the chest.

I had chances of more. I had opportunities to have everything I planned to have: a successful business with a wife and kids to come home to.

None of it felt natural.

"What's the dream?" I return the question.

"This," she says with a sip of her beer. "The girls are happy here and—"

"What's *your* dream?" I cut her off because I know the girls are her world and I respect the hell out of that, but she deserves dreams too. "You said it yourself, the girls are happy, so what makes *you* happy? When you imagine everything you want to do for you, what is it?"

Her smile falters, and for once she lets it. "You know it's been a long time since anybody asked me that."

"Well, I'm asking now."

Those whiskey eyes become bright as she thinks, lost in her own world. For a minute, I'm convinced she won't answer, but then she finally speaks. "I want my own studio... God, that sounds stupid."

"What do you want to do in this studio?" I'm desperate for more of her answers, anything she's willing to give. I'm here to pick up every crumb.

Chewing her bottom lip between her teeth, I watch her get lost in the endless dreams, in the opportunities, in her future. "Women. I want to photograph women. So many look in the mirror and see scars that are visible and the ones that aren't. I want to photograph them so they can see their true story through a lens. So they can see themselves how others see them. I think I just want them to know that they're seen."

The sight of tears she won't let fall has my hand clenching around the bottle.

"Beth." Watery brown pools meet mine. "I wish you could see what I see."

"Sexy as hell, huh?" It's her attempt to lighten the mood.

It doesn't work.

"Strong and fucking beautiful. If you ever need to know what you look like through the eyes of someone else, it's that."

She blows out a breath through a sniffle before rubbing the top of

Missy's head. "You hear that, girl? He can't take it back now." She holds up her empty bottle. "Beer?"

I shouldn't. I should leave because if she keeps looking at me like that, I'm going to go stir crazy. When she senses the protest coming from my mouth, she says, "I'm not ready to sleep yet."

How am I supposed to ever deny this woman of anything?

I nod and her smile is worth the torture of sitting here.

When she returns, she reaches out to hand me the bottle.

It's like slow motion. I watch her watching the bottle fall before it bounces once, twice, and then explodes to a thousand tiny pieces.

It's my fault. I didn't grasp it in time.

My first instinct is to move her out of the way. She's not wearing any shoes, but her face turns a haunting shade of white and the light in her eyes disappears.

"Shit. Mind your feet."

But she's not listening.

"I... I... I'm so sorry. I'll get it."

Lifeless, her knees bend and collapse until she falls onto the shards of glass, the beer soaking through her grey sweatpants.

"Stop, it was an accident," I tell her.

She's somewhere else.

In her eyes is the reflection of a woman I've seen before. A broken woman. A woman long gone. In her eyes, I see my own mother. Though I bet she never passed out with a needle still in her arm in front of her kids, I still see the trauma a man can inflict with his bare hands.

"Beth," I call, grabbing her by the shoulders, getting her to her feet and out of the way so she doesn't get glass in her feet. And fuck me, but she flinches away from my touch.

"I'm sorry," she repeats like a prayer.

I've lost her.

A punch to the gut would be easier to deal with.

"Beth," I shout, trying my best to knock her out of her trance. "Bethany Rose."

Her eyes finally snap to mine. She's trembling everywhere. I swear her lips have turned blue.

"Look at me," I plead, my heart bleeding out with hers.

"You should go."

"What?"

"Please go, Logan." A heavy tear falls from the corner of her eye. "I need you to go. Please go."

When I don't move, she shoves at my chest. "Just fucking go." A sob rips from her throat.

Is this what she needs?

Why don't I know what to do?

But I'm already taking backward steps, my eyes never leaving her. She doesn't even register that I'm still close when she falls to her knees again, trembling hands attempting to clean the glass.

Fuck this.

I'm not leaving her.

She can fight me about it tomorrow.

Cursing under my breath, I wrap my arms around her waist. When I pick her up from the floor, she locks onto my body with a guttural cry.

"I'm sorry."

"Oh, baby, don't be sorry. It was an accident, you hear me? It was just an accident." I try to sooth her as I carry her inside.

Setting her on the counter I inspect her body for any wounds but thankfully, the small cuts on her palms are superficial.

Coming back to reality, her head falls into her hands.

Carefully, I remove them. She doesn't need to hide from me.

"It was an accident," I repeat, drying her tears with my palms. "An accident that was my fault. It's just glass. It can be cleaned." Bewildered and crying with an agony I've never heard before, I press a kiss to her palms. "You're safe here. The girls are sleeping upstairs. They're safe. I promise *you* are safe." I repeat those words until it finally soaks in. Her breathing calms, but the silent cries are only proof of how well her mask fits.

Her fingers curl into my chest, pulling at my T-shirt. I think a part of her is trying to convince herself she's not back there.

I press my hands to her shoulders to gather heat to her trembling body before tracing my fingers along her neck and finally cupping her face. When she doesn't flinch, I release a slow breath.

"What do you need?"

Eyes filled with tears slowly lift as her hand comes up to cover mine. With a fractured exhale, she leans into my touch.

"This," she whispers.

I think she needs to know another's touch won't hurt her.

When I finally wrap my arms around her body and hold her close, she breaks.

No apologies because I don't want them.

She's hurting with a pain so raw that I feel it.

But she's here, and I want to keep her here, in my arms.

She can break here.

After all, even the most broken things can be put back together.

TWENTY-THREE

"Logan, to what do I owe the pleasure?" Claire chirps when she answers the phone.

"What happened to her, Claire?" I almost snap.

I had tried to collect my thoughts before making this phone call. I tried sleeping on it, but that only ended in me tossing and turning until I finally relented and went for a run at five a.m. Then, I saw a light switch on next door, and I knew she couldn't sleep either. It took everything in me not to put one foot in front of the other and go to her.

My blood has been boiling, and nothing is cooling it down.

I can't face Beth again until I get this under control, and I've convinced myself that the only way to do that is to understand.

When I finally peeled myself away from her, her eyes were swollen from crying. But after taking a deep breath, she scrubbed the flesh of her palms over her face, and the tears were gone. She acted as though it never happened.

Claire sighs. "Logan—"

"I know. I fucking know I'm not supposed to ask, and I know you can't tell me, but I'm going out of my mind. My imagination is running riot," I say, my patience wearing thin. "It's driving me crazy."

"Is she okay? What happened?"

No, she's not. Nothing about what I saw last night was okay.

"I don't even know how to answer that. She dropped a glass last night, and it was like the life left her body. She was shaking. Couldn't fucking speak. It was like she wasn't even there."

Another silence before she clears her throat. "That can be normal."

"Normal?" I shout, but my jaw locks in anger, and it comes out as a frustrated growl. "That wasn't normal."

Her voice is sullen when she admits, "You know I can't share details. It's unethical, it's not my story to tell, and I don't even work with the shelter anymore. What I can tell you isn't going to be what you want to hear, but it will be the truth. Whatever you're imagining, she went through worse."

"Fuck," I grit, slamming my fist into the punching bag. I came home during lunch hour just to burn off the excess rage.

"Can you tell me exactly what happened?"

"We had dinner. She put the girls to bed. We had a beer. She handed me one. It fell and broke. That's it."

"You had dinner?"

"What's that got to do with anything?"

"Were the girls there?"

"Yes."

There's hushed chatter before she's back. "Sorry, I had to put you on speaker. Did she invite you to dinner?"

"No, I fucking barged in there and demanded one."

"Friend or not, King, lower your fucking voice when you're speaking to my wife." That explains the whispering.

It's on the tip of my tongue to remind Jake that she's not yet his wife, but then I remember why I'm like a raging bull this morning. If I heard someone snapping at Beth, I'd snap their neck.

And she's not even mine.

What is she doing to me?

"Fuck, you're right. Sorry, Claire."

"You're worried. I get it. Now, put your penises away, gentlemen. The point I was getting to is that she invited you for dinner."

Please hurry up and get to that point.

"Do you and Beth spend a lot of time together?"

"She's my neighbor."

I can almost see her rolling her eyes.

"Beth doesn't trust people, especially men. And definitely not with her girls."

"Claire, I know you said you had a point to make, but I'm failing to

173

see it."

"She trusts you," she answers quickly. "And from what I'm hearing, she's trusting you with the girls. That's a big deal."

I feel a pinch in my chest when I think of Hannah standing on my porch with her soccer ball under her arm on the evenings I'm home, or how Isabel likes to stick her face to my doors and scream, "Loggie" until I answer.

And how all at once I realize those kids have become a highlight in my days.

"Do you know what you're doing, man?" Jake finally speaks.

I decide honesty is the best policy because I'm truly lost. "No fucking idea."

"Nobody does," he mutters.

I'm not sure if that's supposed to make me feel better.

Claire speaks again. "Don't focus too much on her reaction last night. That's something Beth will have to process on her own. Be there for her. Speak to her like a normal human. Don't treat her differently because of it. She'll tell you if she wants to. And she might never speak about it. You have to accept that you might never know. Both are okay."

"Both are okay," I repeat under my breath, doing my best to convince myself because none of this feels okay.

"There's a reason she's trusting you. Focus on that. And please, don't abuse it."

The memory of her curled up last night haunts me when I close my eyes. "Never."

"I need to ask because she's my friend. Is there something going on with you two? Something romantic?"

"We're friends." I hate that word with a passion when it comes to Beth, but as much as it feels like poison on my lips, I'll accept it. Being friends with her is enough.

When did I become so desperate just to be a woman's friend?

She's going to be the one that kills me. I'm sure of it.

"I'll choose to believe that, because Logan?"

"Claire?"

"Hurt her, and I'll break your balls."

TWENTY-FOUR

BETH

He's drinking more. He blames the caseload at work.

I think he will find any excuse.

His idea of being a father is merely dropping into the nursery to see his sleeping daughter, kiss her on the forehead, and walk away again. I wonder if he remembers the last time he saw her with her eyes open.

I was cleaning dishes in the sink from a dinner he didn't eat when his hands came around my waist.

I shivered.

It's not like it used to be.

Nothing is.

His flowers used to come when he thought about me. Then they were an apology. Now the flowers don't exist anymore.

What's the point in apologizing when you're just going to have to do it all again next week?

He pressed his lips to my neck. I tilted my head to get away from him, but he saw it as an invitation. Gripping the edge of the sink, I closed my eyes and begged for him to leave me alone.

Drink more and sleep.

It's hard to feel desirable to a man who reminds me I still haven't lost the baby weight.

He pressed into me again, and the erection digging into my lower back made me grit my teeth.

He didn't smell like himself.

He certainly didn't smell like me.

He smelled like her.

Like sex and not a lot of shame.

God bless his stamina.

I pulled away, drying my hands on the towel as I said, "Nice perfume."

He didn't even act surprised. Not a flinch of regret or any hint he was going to deny it.

At least he spared me that much.

"Don't be fucking difficult, Beth."

I reminded myself to close my mouth, hating the sharp sting right to the chest. But that sting was like an arrow and that arrow exploded. I was too distracted by the pain his lack of remorse caused to watch my mouth.

"I'm being difficult? You're the one coming home late smelling like another woman's perfume."

He turned away, choosing to refill his tumbler rather than argue with me.

There was no passion left in his gaze. No heat in his stare. There was only a quiet disdain when he looked at me. It made me want to claw at my flesh.

I tried. I tried to make the marriage work for two years. I did everything he asked, tore myself inside out just to please him.

"I want to go home. You promised we could go home when Hannah was born."

"We don't always get what we want, now do we, sweetheart? It's business, and you're my wife. Your job is to smile when appropriate, and to support your husband. The husband that gets up every morning to work for this lovely house you have over your head."

His words hit me like bullets.

I don't want a nice house when the relationship occupying it is poisonous.

Swallowing back the bile in my throat, I finally opened my mouth. I wasn't planning on doing it tonight, but I couldn't stand there and watch him looking at me… or not looking at me.

"I want a divorce."

The glass stilled mid-way to his mouth. Then he threw his head back and laughed. It was loud and sent an icy chill down my spine. His knuckles turned white, tightening around the glass a split second before it came flying toward me and smashed to pieces against the wall, inches away from my face.

I was in too much shock to feel the tears streaking my cheeks as I stared at the sharp shards lying at my feet.

I didn't get a chance to react before I felt his hand around my throat, pressing me to the wall. I could feel my face turn red, my eyes draining of life. He's taller than me so I stood on my toes to ease some of the pressure.

It didn't work.

"You stupid bitch. You don't get to leave me. You don't get a divorce," he said, spittle hitting my face as his rage took hold.

I gasped, desperate for air, but his hand only tightened its grip.

"Rob," I cried. "Please."

But he didn't hear me. "If you even think about leaving, you'll never see Hannah again."

Fear made my body rigid.

He wouldn't, would he?

As if reading my mind, he said, "You married a good lawyer, babe. I'm one of the best. You don't get to walk away. You're my wife. You're mine." With a bruising jerk, my head snapped against the wall. The edges of my vision turned black just before he released me. I folded in on myself, sucking in painful breaths.

"Look at me." He pinched my chin between his fingers and tipped my head back. I couldn't see him through the tears in my eyes. "Walk out that door, Beth. I dare you."

I don't know why I did it. Why my stubborn mouth wouldn't stay closed, but when it opened, I immediately wanted it to shut again.

"Fuck you." My voice was hoarse but carried so much hatred.

That's when it happened: the fist to the side of my face. The blow was so severe, so unexpected, I was knocked off my feet. The taste of copper pooling in my mouth was nothing compared to my hands landing in the broken glass.

A jagged edge lodged into the flesh of my wrist, painting the skin crimson.

Crouching, he grabbed a piece of glass before dragging it across my ankle until the flesh sliced open and blood poured to the floor. "When you bleed, you bleed for me." He grabbed the hair at the back of my head. "You'll fucking regret this. Now be a good wife and clean up the mess you've created."

I didn't register the pain. It was nothing compared to the hammering in my chest as he walked away and left me with blood dripping from my wounds.

Trembling, my teeth chattered, but I got to work.

I was the good wife.

I cleaned the mess.

I went to bed, curled up, and cried silently because I didn't want him to hear.

I convinced myself it was the workload.

He's stressed.

He loves me.

He didn't mean to hurt me.

I thought of an escape plan and then remembered how ridiculous it sounded.

I'm here alone.

I don't speak to my sister because he doesn't like Kim. He said she interferes too much.

She always pointed out how unhappy I was when she called.

Last night wasn't the first time he hit me.

Something in me knows it won't be the last.

This morning, when I woke, he brought me breakfast in bed, and an apology in the form of roses.

∞∞∞∞

"Miss?"

My eyes snap away from the box of roses to the man carrying them. Where did I go?

I blink and Logan is at the man's side, staring at me with too much concern, scrutinizing every inch of my face.

"I can take those," he offers.

"It's fine." I wave him off. Rolling my shoulders back, I plaster a smile on my face and force myself to feel the heat in my bones, to recognize I'm in the café and not in a bedroom from years ago, and to finally find the power in my limbs to reach out and take the box of flowers. "I've got it."

Hardly able to keep eye contact with Logan for more than a second, I take the box and sign my name to the delivery docket. Ignoring the eyes burning holes in my back, I take the flowers into the kitchen where Molly is icing some cupcakes. A five-tier wedding cake looks like it's defying the laws of physics.

"It's a topsy turby cake," she explains as I eye the confusing masterpiece.

"It's mind boggling is what it is. I'm assuming these are the flowers for it."

She laughs and takes the box from me before getting to work on assembling the flowers down each tier.

"You're an artist."

178

"Thank you." Hands on her hips, she stands back and proudly admires her work. "You can go. The lunch time rush is over. Maria can finish up."

Fear clogs my throat. I'm more scared than relieved because I know when I leave this kitchen, a six foot three Viking will be waiting for me on the other side of the door.

Embarrassment eats me alive from the inside out.

How do I even explain myself?

"I can stay."

She squeezes my shoulder. "See you tomorrow."

I untie my apron, grab my bag, and say a silent prayer that Logan needed to go back to work.

No such luck.

I decide it's best if I get there first. "Can I speak to you for a minute?"

Why does he look as scared as I feel?

I exit through the back door and into the alley. If I break down, I don't want the entire town to know about it.

The door closes and I finally turn, knowing what I say next could send him running miles in the opposite direction.

I can almost feel my baggage weighing me down.

"Beth—" he says as I speak, "About last night—"

It's enough to ease the tension, if only briefly.

I chew my lip so hard I'm sure I've made it bleed. "I'm sorry about last night. You must think I'm crazy."

No more words come out. He doesn't give me a chance because his hands come up, grab my shoulders, and pull me into an embrace so tight I think he can gather all the broken pieces and mold them back into one.

A stuttered breath escapes me when he releases his grip a fraction.

I don't want him to.

"Fuck, I hope this is okay."

My answer is wrapping my arms around his waist. His muscles tense under my touch.

It reminds me of being on his bike all those years ago.

His lips press a reassuring kiss to the top of my head and with it, I release a fractured breath. My shoulders fall, the muscles still tender from how tense I've been.

"I'm sorry," I try to say against his chest, but he only squeezes a little tighter.

He doesn't want my apologies.

After a long minute, but not long enough, he pulls away before pressing his thumb to my cheek as if wiping away a tear that isn't there.

"You don't need to explain yourself to me. Never. All I need to know is that you're okay."

Shit, now I think I'm going to cry.

Who knew this giant of a man was just all mush on the inside?

"I am. I promise."

He finally grants me the sight of one of those full smiles, the ones that always seem to make my heart beat a little faster.

"The girls are staying with Kim tonight, right?"

My mouth goes dry. "Yes. I need to pick them up, get their things ready, and drop them off. She'll bring them back in the morning." Why I felt the need to tell him all that, I'll never know.

He makes me nervous. The type of nervous that has my heart pounding behind my ears and south of my pelvis.

"Okay." Okay? "I need to go into the city today. I have a client."

Disappointment washes over me like freezing water.

I wanted a chance to sit on the porch again, have a beer and talk. I wanted the chance to show him I'm not always like I was last night.

But that wouldn't be the whole truth. I would be lying to both of us if I said it was.

I can't help how my body reacts in certain situations. I accepted that a long time ago. If he can't handle that, so be it. It is what it is.

Even if I hate what it is.

Does he want what I want, or is he leaving to avoid that exact situation?

Maybe he's seeing someone in the city.

I'm too scared to ask.

I remind myself that we're neighbors, and it shouldn't bother me.

But it does.

It bothers me so much.

"Come on. I'll walk you to your car." He spins me around and places his hand on the small of my back.

I shiver.

Lost in my own thoughts, I take a step back. Everything is muggy. Lines are being crossed. I need to cut ties now before the pull is too strong.

It's the only way to save myself.

We are just neighbors.

My voice cracks when I say, "It's fine. I'm sure I'll be safe walking the thirty seconds to my car." When he tries to protest, I hold up a hand and sigh. "Logan, please."

Please see that I can't do this right now.

I can't have him touching me.

Because he *can* touch me.

It's not a touch I hide from, and it scares me half to death.

Concern forms a dent between his brows, but with a resigned breath, he steps back.

One step and it feels like miles.

I have no idea what I'm doing.

"I'll see you before you go?" I ask.

"I'll be home in an hour."

Home.

My heart constricts in my chest.

With a watery smile, I turn and walk to my car.

Alone.

TWENTY-FIVE

"Pajamas, change of clothes, more clothes, cuddly toys," I whisper to myself through the checklist and hope I'm not forgetting anything.

"Goal!" Hannah screams from outside.

I walk to the porch and see Logan has returned from work. He has Isabel on his shoulders as he plays soccer with Hannah.

My earlier inner dramatics have subsided considerably, but my poor heart—it doesn't stand a chance.

Seeing me, he puts Isabel down and whispers something to Hannah. They both come running into the house.

"What are you two doing?"

"We're getting our coats."

"Wait, we're not ready to go yet," I trail off. They're already gone.

With a bag in hand, Logan passes me and goes straight to the kitchen. When I try to peek at what he has, he nudges me away and places the bag on the table.

"What's going on?"

"The girls are staying with your sister tonight, right?"

"Yes," I say slowly, unsure where he's going with this.

"I'll drop them off. It's on my way into the city."

"You don't have to—"

"And you are going to relax. If you'll have her, Missy will keep you company for the night. She hates the city."

Missy lets out a half-hearted bark before laying down at my feet.

Same, girl.

"Of course."

He pulls a bottle of wine from the bag. "I don't know shit about wine, but Archer assures me this one is good." A brown paper bag follows. "Tacos. I seem to remember you liking those. And these." He lays three books on the counter. "I have it on good authority from both Molly and the lady at the bookstore that these are disgustingly filthy."

I've gone into shock.

"Beth?"

"You went to the bookstore and bought these?"

He laughs under his breath as he grabs the bottle of white wine and puts it in the fridge.

"I did," he says like it's nothing.

I asked Rob once to buy me tampons and he glared at me in disgust.

"For me?"

I can tell I look ridiculous, unmoving with my mouth hanging open as I do nothing more than blink.

"For you," he agrees, tucking a strand of hair behind my ear. His touch is enough to snap me out of my stupor.

"You didn't have—"

"I did. Take a night. Relax, or..." He glances at the books on the counter before looking back at me with a smirk. "Do whatever it is you do when you read those books."

Heat.

Everywhere.

I clear my throat and look away, but there's no denying how my breathing is suddenly faster. "I read them for the plot."

"Sure you do, baby."

I throw my hands over my face and groan. "Thank you. This is amazing."

His brows pull together, and I swear I see a brief flash of anger. "It's a bottle of wine and some takeout."

But it's not. To me, it's so much more. He did it not wanting anything in return, and knowing he was thinking about me enough to do it has my blood running hot and a lump forming in my throat.

"Someday," he says pulling my lip from the hold of my bite with his thumb. "You're going to realize just how much you deserve."

Too soon, he steps away and smiles at me like I'm not melting all the way to my feet. A thumb across my cheek and he walks away.

"Gonna get Isabel's car seat and put it in my truck." He grabs my car keys from the table.

Still bewildered and downright turned on, I say, "I can do that; it can be difficult to install if you're not used to it."

"Just relax. I can manage a car seat."

Ten minutes later and we're all standing by the car—Missy included—watching Logan fight with the car seat.

I take a step forward. "Just let me…"

He holds up his hand, glancing over his shoulder with sweat on his brow. "I've got it."

Okay then.

Hannah looks up at me. "He doesn't have it, Mom."

"I know, sweetie, but it can take a little time for a man like Logan to ask for help."

Defeated and out of breath, he mutters what I'm sure are curses. I've seen him after working out and I can't remember him breathing this heavy.

"What kind of contraption is this? You know in my day we didn't even wear a seat belt."

"In your day? Okay, old man. Out of my way."

Under Logan's watchful eye, I get started. He takes in every movement. In less than a minute the seat is secured, and Isabel is climbing into it.

"Witchcraft," he whispers, hating that it got the better of him. "Next time. I'll get it next time."

He puts the girl's bags in the back and opens the door for Hannah. "In you get, princess."

"I'll see you tomorrow. Call me before you go to bed. Love you."

They both blow me kisses. I pretend to catch them and hold them to my heart.

Logan gawks at me. "You're not going to run after the car when I leave, are you?"

"No… I don't know… Maybe."

He rubs Missy between her ears, but she's had enough and wanders back into the house.

"You need anything, call me." He takes a breath. "If you want to talk, call me."

I know this is about last night. I scared him. I scared myself.

The corners of his mouth tilt upward into the most breath-taking smile. "You get a little hot and bothered reading your books, call me."

I slap his chest. "Perv."

"See you tomorrow, pretty girl."

He winks, climbs in the truck and drives away.

And just like that, they're gone.

Silence.

Nothing but the trees bristling in the wind.

With a grin that could split my face in half, I walk back to the house, bouncing up the steps because tonight, I've got wine and smut.

∞∞∞∞

A full belly, a bath, half a bottle of wine, and six of the sexiest scenes I've ever read later, I'm tipsy and my panties are rightfully wet.

Apparently, choking and being called a "Good girl" turns me on.

I'm feeling bold and pick up my phone from the coffee table. I stare at it for what seems like forever. My skin is clammy with nerves and my heart is pounding.

Missy looks at me from the end of the couch as if to say, "Just do it. Put us all out of our misery."

Kicking my feet, I unlock the phone and type out my text.

Me: You are buying all my books from now on. Disgustingly filthy doesn't quite cut it.

Delivered.

Read.

My head starts swirling with all my earlier fears.

He's hot and single. It's just after ten. He's probably out or has a woman in his bed.

He could even have her tied to it while he calls her a good girl.

Sweet divine.

I'm halfway to hyperventilating when the bubbles pop up on the screen.

It keeps going.

And nothing.

"Missy," I whisper, like anyone is listening. "This was a terrible idea."

The phone vibrates in my hand.

And it keeps vibrating.

He's calling me.

Not the plan, Logan.

"Missy," I whisper again. With her head on her paws, she hardly spares me a glance. "What do I do?"

I need to answer it. Of course I do.

"Hello." I'm still whispering.

"Why are you whispering?"

"I don't know. Why are you calling me?"

"Because you're turned on. I told you if you get hot and bothered to call me."

Oh, he was serious about that.

"Beth?"

"Yes?"

He chuckles. "You're not speaking."

I pour myself another glass of wine. "Sorry, I just thought…"

"You thought what?"

"I thought you might have company."

"I'm back at the loft. What kind of company did you think I had?"

I gulp a mouthful of wine. The situation calls for it. "A lady friend."

Lady friend?

The wine obviously turns me into an eighty-year-old woman named Mabel.

"Have you seen me with any of these… lady friends?"

I search my mind. I haven't. Not since I've moved here. I haven't seen him with a woman.

"No, but you can't honestly be saying you haven't slept with anyone since I moved in?"

There's silence for a minute. "That's exactly what I'm saying."

I close my eyes as it all sinks in and feel myself tumble a little further into him. "Logan…"

"Tell me about these books."

I've got a shit-eating grin on my face when I sit back and sip on my very delicious wine. "Next level. I think I have a praise kink."

Shut up, Beth.

I swear I hear a groan on the other end.

Shocked with myself, my legs stiffen, and I shoot upright. Pulling the phone away from my ear, I curse into the air.

The call ends.

I want to die.

I've scared him off.

But my self-loathing doesn't last long when the phone starts vibrating again. This time it's a video call.

You're killing me.

But I answer because I'm tipsy, and I'm desperate to see him.

That smug smirk is ready and waiting. My skin sets fire and he's not even here.

"I wanted to see that beautiful face when you tell me all about the *plot* in these books."

Relief washes over me. I grab the wine, taking the bottle and Logan to the kitchen to pick at some leftovers.

Placing the phone on the counter, I sit on the stool. "Okay so the first book—"

"You already read a book?"

"I'm on the second one. Don't judge."

Smiling, he shakes his head. "No judgement here. Come on. I've got my beer. I'm ready."

I hold up my wine glass and tip it towards the phone. "Cheers."

And we talk. I tell him all about my books. He notices when I squirm. I notice when his breathing comes a little heavier.

When neither of us want to say goodnight, we continue talking. We talk about everything and nothing.

We cringe about past relationships—none of the dark ones. I learn he almost got married once. It didn't work, but they're still friends, because of course they are. It's Logan.

He tells me Hannah is getting really good at soccer and how it makes his day when Isabel runs to him after work.

And I can only sit here, mesmerized by how he speaks about my children. I don't stop him because I can't.

As it turns out, praise isn't the only kink I have.

I have an entire Logan kink.

By midnight my eyes are closing.

"Go to bed," he tells me.

My nod is slow and takes effort.

"Now," he demands.

"So bossy."

"And take the phone so I know you didn't fall asleep in the

kitchen."

I roll my eyes but obey.

Missy follows close behind and takes her spot at the end of the bed while I climb in.

"See. I made it."

"Such a good fucking girl."

My mouth falls open.

"Goodnight, sweetheart."

The screen goes black.

TWENTY-SIX

"Mom," Hannah squeals at a pitch that can only be heard by dogs. "It's too cold." She dips one toe in the water and immediately comes running back.

"You gotta just jump in, sweetie. You've already been in. You know it's only cold for a second."

I woke this morning to a text from Logan telling me he opened the pool so we could use it to cool off on one of the hottest days of the year. We spent our morning in there, but after going back inside for snacks, Hannah decided she wanted to jump in on the deep end, which is why I'm here, trying to tackle a toddler and encourage Hannah to jump just like she wanted to.

She chews her lip right before the upper half of her body jerks forward like she's finally going to do it, but her feet remain planted to the ground.

She turns back to me, eyes wide. "What if I drown?"

Seriously, is she always this dramatic?

"You're a great swimmer, and I'm right here."

Isabel bounces on her heels, not hiding her growing frustration with her sister. "Jump, Hannah."

"Shut up, Isabel." Hannah pouts, crossing her arms.

This seemed like a great idea but now I have two sulking children, the sun beating on my back, and I'm ten seconds away from turning around and going back to our house.

"You cried because you wanted to jump," I remind her.

She did.

I wasn't keen on the idea, but she moaned until I relented.

"I do it." Isabel bounces forward with far too much confidence. I grab her before she makes a dive for it.

"Not you. You need to put your floaties on."

She growls at me like a dog.

Jesus fucking Christ, these kids.

"Can you come in with me? If I drown, you won't be able to save me from there."

I close my eyes and hold my breath for a beat. She's two feet away from me. If I reach out, I can hold her hand.

"I'm going in. I need to sort your sister first before she takes off." I swear, second children are born to test our patience. "You can do it."

Hannah drops her foot. At least she gets to her ankle this time before letting rip a blood-curdling scream.

Progress.

At this rate, we'll be in the water by tomorrow morning.

"Momma, I need to go potty." Isabel tugs at my leg.

For the love of all that is holy.

"Okay, honey. Hannah, you can't go in now. I need to bring your sister inside."

"But I really want to go in."

I'm going to cry.

"There's the ladies." Logan's voice startles me enough that I jump. "What's going on?"

"What are you doing home so early?"

His eyes lick over me, and I'm suddenly all too aware of how little I'm wearing. The blue one-piece leaves far too much of me exposed. It's already too hot out here. I don't need his hungry eyes devouring me. I'll dehydrate.

"The shop was quiet. The guys had it covered."

Something in my stomach makes a weird flip. I like to call it the flip of betrayal.

Clad in his signature black jeans and T-shirt, he looks as cool as a spring day, and not like the sun is baking us.

Blowing my hair from my face, relief instantly washes over me at the sight of him. I don't know what his plans are today, but he's about to be roped into helping me.

Hannah yelps at my side when Missy takes a dive into the pool, splashing all of us.

"See, baby, if Missy can do it, so can you."

"Are you calling me a dog?"

Desperate, I stare up at Logan as if he can help with a way out of this because my kids are proving to be impossible today.

"We're in crisis, King. We've already been in, but Hannah wanted to jump so we've been standing here for ten minutes waiting. In those ten minutes, she's developed the personality of a disgruntled teenager."

He throws his head back and laughs.

I frown.

Like second nature, he takes Isabel from where she's trying to wriggle out of my arms.

I stand, my back already beginning to burn from the blistering heat. In my rush to get out here, I forgot to put suncream on myself.

"Please, help a neighbor out."

I don't know if it's my flushed skin or the sweat beading down my face, but he takes pity on me.

"I need potty, Loggie."

He places Isabel back down and says, "Okay, baby girl. How about you go do that with your mom? I'll go change and help Hannah."

The man was sent from heaven, I'm sure of it.

"I can't do it," Hannah whines.

"We'll see about that. Don't hang around the pool on your own. Go inside with your mom, and when I get back, we'll do it together."

Head hanging between her shoulders, she mumbles, "Okay."

He ruffles his fingers through her hair as she passes. "That's my girl."

My girl.

I wait for him to react, but he doesn't.

Hannah's lips begin to lift, and my heart takes flight.

My girl.

Goddamn it, heart, stay in your lane.

Ten minutes later, we're all back outside, suncream freshly applied, and eager to get back in the damn water before we scald.

Logan is wearing navy swim shorts.

Let me repeat that.

Logan is wearing navy swim shorts.

Tattoos on full display, sweat trickles over his bicep and stomach.

He is glorious.

He takes Hannah's hand where they stand at the edge of the pool while me and Isabel cheer them on. But she's still not ready.

Take the leap, baby.

Jump.

He never forces her.

"I have an idea," Logan says as he walks away and seeks shelter under the cover of the trees. "I'm not going to let anything happen to you. You can trust me on that, okay?"

She nods.

"Here, let me prove it. Your mom can go first."

He winks at me and beckons me forward like that wink didn't make my knees a little wobbly.

Confused, I take the steps toward him. He spins me around, so my back is to his chest, and my ass is now on full view.

His breath sweeps across my neck, inducing a shiver even in the sweltering heat. "I'm amending the contract. If you want to live here, you have to wear this every fucking day."

Air gets trapped in my throat, and I need to cough to clear it. His chest vibrates with a low chuckle.

Today will be the day I die of heat stroke, and it has very little to do with the sun.

"Fall back," he instructs.

With those arms, I have no doubt he will catch me, but seriously?

"A trust fall?" I laugh nervously. "I haven't done one of those since I was a child."

"Do it, Mom." Hannah claps.

"Do you trust me?" he asks to my back, his voice husky.

I nod. "I think so."

"Good enough. Now fall."

This is stupid, but I'll do just about anything if it helps.

I cross my arms over my chest, close my eyes, and fall back.

Just as I suspected, I fall right into his arms. When I finally open my eyes and tip my head back, he's looking down at me.

"You caught me?"

"Wasn't that the plan?"

I guess so.

Hannah is next, and seeing her fall into his arms means more to me than anything else, because my little girl doesn't easily trust. A part of me always carried guilt for that because I'm afraid she learned it from me.

But he catches her. He's right there.

I make sure to grab my phone just to capture some photos.

She does it two more times, laughing her little ass off.

Isabel has her turn, and by the time we're finished, everyone is ready to jump in the water.

Sitting on the edge of the shallow end with Isabel on my lap, I cup water in my hand to splash her legs.

"You go, Hannah."

Isabel claps and screams something incoherent.

Hannah takes Logan's hand and stares up at him with so much adoration, it makes my heart swell in my chest.

He dips his chin. "Ready?"

She rolls her shoulders back. "Ready."

Hand in hand, they take a short run-up. They jump, soaring through the air without a care.

A lump forms in my throat.

My baby did it.

They swim to the surface.

"Well done, kid. I'm so proud of you." I notice when the pride gleams in his eyes because I've seen it in mine so many times.

I grab Isabel around the waist. "Our turn, my little daredevil."

We're in the shallow end, but I've no doubt she would jump on the other side just as quickly.

"Move your butt, ladies. What are you waiting for?" Logan laughs, lifting Hannah onto his shoulders.

As Logan and Hannah reach us, I kiss the top of Isabel's head, and we kick off the edge, right into his waiting arms.

TWENTY-SEVEN

LOGAN

Hannah comes tiptoeing into the kitchen with a lazy smile and red faced from the sun.

"What's up, kiddo?"

She shrugs, pulling herself onto the high stool at the breakfast counter. "Mom fell asleep with Isabel." She rests her head on her hands, exhausted from a day of play in the heat.

I open the refrigerator and grab two bottles of water, opening one and sliding it across the counter to Hannah. She rolls her eyes so hard I'm surprised they don't get stuck in the back of her head.

"I hate water."

"Stay hydrated, kid. It's hotter than ball—" I stop myself just in time. "Balloons out there," I quickly say.

Balloons?

Jesus, Logan.

I really need to get a grip on my language around these kids, and by the way Hannah pulls her brows together I know she's onto me.

She's too smart.

I tap my knuckles against the counter and stand straight. "I don't know about you, but I could eat. Want some lunch?"

She perks up. "Sure. What are you thinking?"

I glance around like food will appear from thin air. Knowing Beth fell asleep so easily makes something warm rush to my chest because I know she doesn't trust her daughters with just anyone, so I'm happy she knew Hannah was safe enough with me. But I also don't want to try my luck and drive somewhere for lunch. The last thing I want is to scare her half to death when she wakes and realizes Hannah is missing.

I open the refrigerator again, tapping my foot against the tiled floor and rove over the options but come up empty.

"When Mom doesn't know what to make for lunch, she makes peanut butter and jelly sandwiches."

I eye her. She's playing me.

Giggling, she holds up her hands before drawing an imaginary cross over her chest. "Honest, Logan. Cross my heart."

Is she fluttering her eyelashes?

"Fine." I give in, grabbing the bread, peanut butter, and jelly from the cupboard. I place them in the middle of the island. "But you're helping. I'm in charge of peanut butter. You can handle the jelly. We'll make enough for your mom and Isabel."

"Cool," she agrees, pulling slices of bread from the packet.

We work in silence for a minute, and I bite the inside of my jaw to stop from smiling. The concentration makes her brows pull together and a pout form on her lips. She looks just like her mother.

"Your mom must be tired, huh?"

She licks a dab of jelly from her finger and continues. "Isabel woke lots last night because it was too hot, and Mom doesn't sleep much anyway."

There's a pinch in my chest that I can't identify. "How come?" I try to make it sound easy as I continue spreading peanut butter on the bread before passing it to Hannah. It's not often she opens up. Hell, it's not often she talks to me. We practice soccer, but she never talks, so I don't want to push her.

"She always says moms don't need as much sleep as other people."

No, they need a hell of a lot more in my opinion.

Thinking of Beth roaming the house in the dark at night stirs something in me, making my stomach twist into uncomfortable knots. I suddenly want to know what keeps her up at night. What has her roaming this house with only her thoughts for company?

Hannah stretches on the stool, leaning toward me and beckoning me forward like I'm about to be let in on a top-class secret. "Logan," she whispers.

I press the palms of my hand into the counter. "Hannah?"

She assesses me for a long second. I can almost see the cogs turning in her head. She's weighing her ability to trust me.

Fall, kid. I'll catch you.

Finally, she presses her cheek to mine and speaks so low I hardly hear her. "I think my mom is a superhero."

I stifle a laugh and fall back on my heels, feigning surprise for her benefit.

A superhero.

My damn heart swells in my chest.

She sits back in the chair, continuing the task of making our sandwiches.

"A superhero? Really?"

Flustered, she drops the knife and glances in the direction of the stairs. "Hush. She'll hear you. She can't know that we know."

"Sorry," I say quietly, noticing how her cheeks flush just like Beth's. "Why do you think she's a superhero?"

I'm genuinely interested. I think every mother is a superhero, but Hannah isn't sharing my thought process, and I'm beginning to wonder if she thinks her mother is an Avenger.

She chews her lip between her teeth, rocking back and forth. She gives another check toward the stairs and when she's satisfied there's nobody there, she answers. "Well, superheroes protect people, right?"

I nod, taking the finished sandwiches and cutting them in half, remembering to cut the crusts off for Ms. Picky here. "Sure."

I hand her the bread and she takes a bite. "Good," she mumbles.

I grab my own sandwich. "Good," I agree.

Who knew peanut butter and jelly sandwiches could reduce a grown man to one-word sentences?

"Okay, back to why you think your mom is a superhero."

"She protects me and Isabel all the time. Just last week, she helped an old lady cross the street. And you know what? She always cooks enough dinner for you because she doesn't want you to be lonely."

I swallow, but it's forced, her confession causing my mouth to go dry.

I have a sudden urge to run and wake the sleeping woman upstairs, wrap her in my arms and remind her that what she does doesn't go

196

unnoticed. She would blush a bright red and act like it's nothing. Because Hannah is right. She's a protector, and she doesn't do it for the recognition. It's who she is.

A funny, sticky feeling lodges in my throat.

Hannah's mouth turns down, a somber shadow casting over a freshly freckled face. "Logan, can I ask you something?"

"Of course, kid."

Nervously, she nibbles her lip again and puts her sandwich down. I do the same.

This must be serious. We're both abandoning our food for whatever she's about to ask me.

"You're strong like a superhero."

A slow smile begins on the corner of my mouth, but I try to school my features to remain attentive.

She stays quiet for another moment, but I don't interrupt. "Mom is a superhero, but superheroes need someone to protect them too. Do you think you could protect my mom?"

The weight of her request almost knocks me back, but I clench my fists and remain still.

How much worry is floating around in this little girl's head to ask a question like that? I don't know many eight-year-olds so self-aware they put other's needs before their own.

And the question gnawing at me most, the one that clouds my vision in red: what has she seen? What does she remember? What was so bad that this brave, beautiful little girl needs someone to protect her mother?

I remember when I was her age. I spent hours imagining someone would come along and protect my mother, take us away from everything. I see so much of that kid in Hannah.

It takes all my power, but I shake the blood curdling thoughts and focus on what matters. She needs an answer and of all the people, she asked me. She took a tiny vulnerable part of herself and handed it to me to protect.

"I'll protect her."

Her eyebrows lift to her hairline like she was expecting me to refuse, and it's like a punch to the gut because she expects disappointment from outsiders. "You're up for the job?"

I chuckle, rustling my hand over the top of her hair. She groans her annoyance. "I'm up for the job, kid." I push her water into her hand.

"I'll protect all three of you crazy women. Now drink your water."

She pouts but obeys.

"What are you guys talking about?" Beth pads barefoot into the kitchen, yawning as she pulls her hair back into a ponytail.

"Nothing," me and Hannah reply together.

Beth halts, scrunching her eyes in suspicion. "Weird."

And for the umpteenth time today I have to remind myself to remove my eyes from the smooth skin of her long legs. She has shorts over the bathing suit now, but it's little help.

"We made peanut butter and jelly sandwiches, Mom."

Beth rubs her hands together and sits next to her daughter before plucking a sandwich from the plate, leaning on her elbows, and digging in. "Good," she mutters over a mouthful of bread.

I watch in silence as they both chat and laugh over their food. Beth gives me one of her rare, signature smiles—a sight so precious I want to capture it and hide it from the rest of the world. She dips her chin, conveying her thanks without uttering a word.

I shake my head.

Anytime.

Minutes later, we hear tiny feet pound downstairs and into the kitchen, a mop of crazy blonde curls falling around her face.

"Hello, sleepy head," Beth smiles, standing to greet her daughter, but the little traitor passes her and goes straight to me.

Beth crosses her arms, blinking rapidly. "Do I need to buy loyalty around here?"

"Hi, Loggie," Isabel says sleepily, her arms already outstretched for me to pick her up. When I do, she nuzzles her head into my neck, taking her time to fully wake.

"Hey, Isabelly."

Laughing in disbelief, Beth returns to her seat.

As we gather around the island and binge on peanut butter and jelly sandwiches, I remind myself of the promise I made to Hannah, a vow I made to myself: to protect these beautiful girls and their mother. The woman who began clawing her way into the depths of my soul ten years ago and remained there, waiting to take full bloom, to consume me.

Right here, in the kitchen, I silently make a vow.

I will burn down the world before I let one of them get hurt.

TWENTY-EIGHT

BETH

"I still can't believe you live next door to Logan King." Kim empties her bottle of beer, her eyes volleying back and forth like she's watching a tennis match as Logan sits on the chair with a sleeping Isabel on his chest. "I mean, look at him."

I stare at her with amusement as she sits back on her chair and sighs. "I am."

"Fuck," she groans.

"You're squirming, Kim."

She eyes me, her gaze falling to my lap. "Please. As if you're not. Get used to rubbing those thighs together."

A laugh burst out of me. "You're disgusting."

"I mean, he did this." Without shame, she pulls her sweater to below her breasts, displaying the ink he gave her all those years ago. Everyone is too busy playing soccer with Hannah to notice my sister exposing herself. "And his family? I want them to adopt me. You fit right in here. They obviously adore the girls, and don't get me started on Molly and Eden. Those two are my type of people."

She's right. They've made me feel nothing but welcome.

Kim arrived this morning to stay for the weekend and they've taken her in too. Cora and Skip insisted she come up to the house for a barbeque so everyone could meet her. I'm not surprised she slipped right in amongst everyone. That's just what they do. It's in their nature.

"Another beer, kid?" Skip nudges Kim and hands her a Bud Light before taking the empty.

She looks over at me, her eyes wide. She's falling in love with this family.

She smiles up at him and takes the beer. "I think I might love you, Skip."

Case in point.

He chuckles. "Well, you're welcome here anytime, darlin'. We want to keep this one around." He dips his chin toward me, and my chest fills with emotion.

When he walks away, Kim leans back in her chair. "Jesus, I love it here."

The sun is setting beyond the trees. Laughter filters from all corners as the smell of barbeque lingers in the air.

I glance over at Logan to see him cheering on Hannah as she shoots and scores in their makeshift goals, all the while rubbing a comforting hand on Isabel's back as she snores on his shoulder.

I know we agreed I'd stay for three months, but I don't want to leave. I don't want to leave Pine Falls. I don't want to leave this family. I don't want to leave the house that is quickly becoming a home.

But the truth is: if I leave, I think I would miss him most of all.

"You go, baby girl," I shout to Hannah as Eden and Molly lift her high and celebrate her goal.

She doesn't want to leave either. She said so just last night when she asked if she could go to school here.

For the first time in so long, I've found somewhere I can make a life. A real one. A happy one.

But I'll need to talk to Logan. I won't leave Pine Falls, but if we can stay at the house is ultimately his decision.

As if sensing me watching, he looks over at me, a ready smirk on his lips.

He dips his chin. It's always a silent question. "You good?"

I nod.

He winks and cradles Isabel.

My heart skips a beat.

She'd climbed up on his lap thirty minutes ago and his chest had been her pillow ever since.

I love that she felt comfortable enough to do it.

"There's no such thing as coincidence," Kim whispers at my side. When I turn to her, I see she's been watching our exchange.

"What do you call this then?"

Taking my hand, she squeezes love into my bones. It's a touch that screams an apology she always feels she needs to give, but the apology is mine. I lost her through no fault but my own. Rob might have tried to feed me lies about her, but I never believed it. I just never wanted her to get hurt too. And seeing me with him hurt her more.

"I don't know what this is yet, but it's too weird. It blows my mind." Mine too.

We remain in silence for long minutes, watching the world go by. Contentment.

It's the only word I have to describe how I feel.

Red-faced and exhausted, Hannah climbs onto my lap. I hate that her legs almost reach the ground. How much longer do I have like this?

I squeeze her tighter. "Having fun?"

"So much," she replies, breathless.

Equally as tired, Molly and Eden drag their feet to their chairs, laughing as they take a long gulp of their beers.

Eden turns to me and Kim. "Let's have a girl's night. Let's go out."

"Oh, girl's night," Molly agrees, her face lighting up. "There's a great band playing at the bar."

Archer kisses the top of her head. "You should, baby," he tells her, but her eyes fall to the grass. She recovers quickly, her lips tilting up into a smile.

I turn to Kim. "You should go."

"What? You too," Eden insists.

"I've got two kids to look after."

"They're more than welcome to stay the night here," Cora offers.

"You watch them all the time. I couldn't ask that of you."

"I'll watch them." All eyes fall to Logan. I think my eyes are so wide they'll pop out and roll to his feet.

"I can't expect you to babysit."

"Why not?"

"Yeah, why not?" Molly chimes in. "He used to watch Evie all the time."

"You should go out and have some fun, Mom." Hannah's eyes are already closing.

"You should go out and have some fun, Mom," Logan mocks, smiling at me. "I can handle these two. We both know Isabel will be asleep until morning and Hannah is already well on the way."

"Uh huh," she says through a yawn. "He's right."

"Really?"

Excitement bubbles in my stomach. The last time I went out was the night of the art exhibition and we all know how that went. I can't remember the last time I had a girls' night.

"Really. Go have some fun. You deserve it."

"Fuck," Kim mutters under her breath. "He just gets hotter."

"Um…" I'm racking my brain for all the reasons not to go. I can't find any. I look over at Kim's expectant gaze. She wants to go. Honestly, so do I.

"Come on. When is the last time we got to go out together?"

That confirms it then.

"Okay, I guess."

Molly and Eden holler while Kim wraps her arms around my shoulders with a squeal.

We hold our drinks up in toast. "Girl's night."

TWENTY-NINE

It's only eleven thirty when I hear Archer's truck pull into the driveway.
Molly's laugh booms long before I open the front door.

Archer has the window down when I step outside, sending silent
pleas from the driver seat. "They haven't shut up the entire drive
home."

I chuckle, not feeling the slightest bit sorry for him.

Molly, Kim, and Beth are so busy yapping, they don't even notice
me standing here.

"How was your night on babysitting duty?" he asks.

I roll my eyes. "I'm a pro, brother."

Stumbling out of the back seat, Beth and Kim wrap their arms
around each other.

"Best night ever," they agree.

Dragging her feet as she climbs the steps, Kim grabs my arms, her
eyes swirling. "Goodnight, Logan. I'm going to bed. I trust you'll take
care of my sister."

"Of course."

"You two make me nauseous but I love it."

She pulls off her heels and drops them at the bottom of the stairs with a thud.

Beth follows, but her footsteps are accompanied by an uncontrollable giggle. "I fucking hate high heels," she tries to whisper but she's far too loud.

"Beth!" Molly shouts from the car. When I look back, I see her leaning over Archer in the driver's seat. He shakes his head as he slaps her on the ass. "Stop it, Archer. I'm having a moment with Beth," she scolds.

Beth spins around, leaning against the door frame.

"You're the best," Molly whisper-yells, or at least she tries. She loses all sense of hearing when she's drunk.

Beth points at what I think is supposed to be Molly, but only certain limbs are working, and she falls back against my chest. "No, *you're* the best." Tilting her head back, her eyes are glassy when she explains, "Tequila."

"That will do it." I grab her shoulders to steady her.

Archer tries to get Molly back in her seat, securing her with the seat belt. He turns back as Molly blows kisses. "There's my favorite brother-in-law," she slurs.

"I bet you say that to all of us."

"Only to you and Jaxson."

"Trouble."

"And Beth." Molly hiccups. "You should take my brother up on his offer. He's really into you."

My blood freezes in my veins, my muscles tensing up. Jealousy, possessive and raw, grips me tight.

Beth's cheeks color instantly, her eyes wide with shock. She refuses to meet my gaze, her fingers nervously twisting the hem of her shirt.

Archer shoots me an apologetic smile before driving away.

The engine revs in the distance when I turn to Beth, trying to keep my expression unreadable. "What offer?"

She looks at me, her eyes clear despite the alcohol running through her veins. Her cheeks flush a deeper shade of pink. "Ace may or may not have asked me out."

My jaw clenches. "And what did you say?"

"I didn't say anything. I froze," she answers, the words spilling out in a nervous rush. "I'm not good in those situations."

"Do you want to go out with him?" I ask, my tone deceptively casual.

She eyes me for a moment, even drunk catching onto my jealousy. It does nothing but make her blush more. She bites her lips together and shakes her head. "No, I don't want to go out with him."

I let out a low growl of relief, still unsatisfied. "Did he touch you?" I'll fucking snap his neck.

Beth blinks at me, surprised by the question. The ensuing silence is far too long for my liking.

"Beth?" I ask again, my tone harder this time.

"No," she replies quickly. "We just talked. Ace is nice, but I'm not into him like that."

The tension eases out of my shoulders as I hold back a triumphant laugh.

There's not a man on this planet that wants to be seen as "Nice."

But it's not the time to react. Not now, when Beth's clearly uncomfortable, her embarrassment tangible. I school my features into an impassive mask, the sudden possessiveness in me struggling to maintain control.

Knowing I can sort a certain brother of Molly's tomorrow, I offer her a smile and watch as she releases a breath.

I cross my arms over my chest as she looks up from massaging her feet. Her curtain of dark blonde curls covers her face, but I can still see that perfect bright smile when she flashes it my way.

"Were the girls okay?"

"Not a peep."

That makes her smile.

"Loggie." She stands straight, pressing her back against the wall. "Everything is spinning, Loggie."

"God, woman, stop calling me that."

When she laughs, I feel like I've gone back in time to a random night ten years ago. She wasn't drunk then, but her laugh was the same. There's always caution when she smiles or laughs now. Like she's afraid to offer too much or have hope at being happy—even if it's only for a minute. But this laugh, the one that makes me want to touch her, comes from deep in her belly. Eyes closed; her shoulders vibrate.

It's carefree.

Beautiful.

She stops abruptly, her hand covering her mouth.

"Did you just vomit in your mouth?"

She gags. "No, but almost. I can't drink like I used to when I was twenty."

Taking her into the kitchen, I grab a bottle of water from the fridge and hand it to her. She glares at me, but she will thank me for it in the morning.

"Sip it," I warn.

She doesn't.

Through her gulps, she looks up at me. "I want to ask you something."

The flush in her cheeks makes me curious.

"Go for it."

Taking a deep breath, which I'm not sure is for courage or to stop herself from vomiting, she casts her eyes to the floor before saying, "I want to stay. We want to stay. Me and the girls…we want to stay here. Make Pine Falls our home. Hannah wants to go to school. They've made friends. So have I. It feels like home. This house feels like home." She looks up at me with her mouth open, but she closes it before she says what she really wants to say. "I totally understand if you had other plans with the house. We can find somewhere else… Forget it. This was stupid." She puts the cap back on the bottle before removing it again and taking another drink of water.

Something twists in my chest. She considers this home and that does weird fucking things to my insides.

I didn't have other plans for the house because I never thought of them leaving. I knew she wanted this to be a trial run, but I obviously put that to the back of my mind. Now just thinking of losing her, losing those girls, it makes my heart sink into my stomach.

Going to her, I spin her around in the stool so she's facing me and tilt her head back with my hand under her chin. She hiccups but smiles. "You don't want to leave?"

She shakes her head.

"Then you're not leaving."

"Really?"

"If you move out, I risk the chance of having quiet neighbors with just normal kids."

Her smile broadens as she rests a hand on my chest to steady herself. "That would be tragic, but I'm sure you would survive. You love kids."

"I love *your* kids." It's out of my mouth before I can think about it, but I don't regret it, because I do love those little rugrats. Not having them here wouldn't be the same.

"I think the feeling is—" *hiccup* "—mutual. And I love that you love my kids. Does that make sense?"

"Let's get you to bed."

"That's a good idea. Will you do me a favor?" She stands, clinging to my arms as she does.

"Anything."

She chews on her bottom lip and that flush rushes across her cheeks again.

"Beth?"

Her breath catches as I tuck the stray curls behind her ear.

"Uh huh?"

"You wanted to ask me something."

Blinking, she clears her throat. "Right. Can you remind me tomorrow that I've already asked if we could stay because I'm drunk, and I'll forget? I'll just end up embarrassing myself when I ask you again."

"Deal. Now bed."

Nodding, she stumbles away. I think she might be finally sick when she stalls, but instead, she spins around and wraps her arms around my waist. I swallow dryly, trying not to notice how the soft curves of her body fit perfectly against me, but that would be a fucking miracle.

"Thanks," she breathes against my chest. "For everything."

Her scent from whatever coconut infused shampoo she washes her hair with invades me.

"You don't need to thank me."

Still in my arms, she tilts her head back so I can see her eyes, and in them, I see a thousand unspoken words, an ocean of secrets I might never know, and a woman strong enough to do anything she sets her mind to—even if she doesn't see it herself yet.

There's no smile, only fire dances in the honey flecks of her whiskey-colored eyes. She bites her already abused lip between her teeth.

I want so much to replace her bite with mine. To know what she tastes like. To feel her on my tongue. To touch every inch of her.

Resisting her comes with needing a strength I never knew I possessed. And it's failing the longer she's in my arms.

"Go to bed, Beth."

Her chest rises and falls in synch with mine as our breaths release harshly, dancing between us.

"What if I don't want to?"

Christ.

Don't say that.

My fingers dig into her waist as I try to focus on anything but how hard I'm becoming.

Her mouth parts in a gasp.

She's drunk.

As much as I want her, I know she will regret it in this state. My only hope is she forgets all this by morning.

Releasing her to cup her face in my hands, I keep my eyes on hers, urging her to walk away. "Believe me, you want to go to bed."

"Why?"

"Because I *need* you to go to bed, baby."

She drops her hands and steps back, the cut of rejection playing so visibly on her face, and it stings like a bullet to the chest.

"I'm drunk." She nods in understanding. "I need to go to bed."

She's beautiful. The sexiest woman I've ever set eyes on, but we can't go there tonight.

I walk her to the stairs, not trusting myself to bring her to her room. I wait until she reaches the top step to open the front door.

"Goodnight, Logan," she whispers over her shoulder.

"Goodnight, pretty girl." I wink, wanting to see that smile just one more time tonight.

I feel like falling to my knees when her lips tilt and a quiet laugh escapes her throat before she disappears into her room.

THIRTY

"You okay, boss man? You seem a bit out of it today," Kyle's voice cuts through my reverie. He's leaning against the counter, brows furrowed.

"Fine," I grunt, not having the energy to force anything beyond that. "I've got business in the city later so I'm going to take off early." I don't. I'm just desperate to get away. Maybe a change of scenery will help. "You okay to cover here?"

"Sure." His eyes light up. "We've got a bachelorette party coming in soon. I'm sure me and the guys can accommodate them."

I shake my head. "For fuck's sake."

"Come on, man. A bachelorette party coming in for tattoos. You know they're up for making some bad decisions."

"I'm guessing you're the bad decision."

His smile is so wide it looks painful. "Bingo."

"Just keep your cocks in your pants until you close up, and don't get yourself in any trouble. I'm not having your mother in my ear."

"I can do that."

I don't know who he's trying to convince, but he's failing.

I took Kyle under my wing when he was just a teenager after he got himself in some trouble with the law. His mother worked in a diner not far from the studio in the city and needed someone to guide him. He's twenty-six, but I feel just as responsible for him now as I did when he was sixteen.

When I leave the shop, his tongue is practically wagging.

It's in the silence of my truck, I regret leaving. I need distraction. I need noise. Something to drown out the thoughts consuming me.

I look down to see my hands gripping the steering wheel before catching sight of my reflection in the rear-view mirror.

I look just as I feel—like shit.

"Get it together," I grit out before blasting the radio on and driving away.

But no matter how hard I try to drown it out, the darkness creeps in.

I haven't slept in days. Three days to be exact. Ever since Beth came home drunk and I had to send her to bed. Holding her, feeling her in my arms, almost knowing how she tastes, opened up more than wanting her—and fuck, did I want her. But it awakened something more terrifying.

I went to sleep that night still feeling every soft curve of her body in my arms, but when I woke, fear took its place. The nightmares have gripped me every night since, shaking me awake. A nightmare that's been haunting me for years, but it's different now, more real. I wake in a cold sweat, my heart pounding in my chest as I stumble from the bed and make a beeline for the bathroom where I lose the contents of my stomach.

When I stare at my reflection in the mirror, I see the same haunted eyes, the same tortured soul. It's not my face I see, but my father's, his sins etched into my own features. Work is a distraction, a way to keep the demons at bay, but today I can't focus on anything. The same phrase torments me like a broken record, a taunting reminder of my sleepless nights, "Like father, like son."

Shaking my head, I drive past the turn to home and keep driving. Last night was worse than most. I need to know the girls are safe.

I'm still on autopilot, too far gone in the depths of my own thoughts when I pull up to Skip and Cora's house.

There's always something special about coming home. Even if it's one I've been to countless times.

The smell: a distinct flowery potpourri Cora always insists lie in a bowl in the hallway, the baking of something different every day, and the pine from the trees surrounding this house. The wind chime that's been there since I first arrived at age fourteen, clanks in a breeze.

It's a home I rejected for so long, not wanting to believe this is where I belonged. I was a city boy, born and raised. The people inside this house were outsiders, no matter how hard they fought for me and my brothers over the years. I was strong headed. I didn't need them. I was doing a good job with the boys myself.

Fourteen-year-old me didn't realize that's not how it was supposed to be. It wasn't my job to bring them up, even if it's all I knew. It wasn't my job to pick my mother up from the floor and stay watch all night so she wouldn't die from an overdose. It wasn't my job to get in the middle when my father decided to drop by and win his argument with his fists.

I still remember the drive to Pine Falls after my mother's death. Skip and Cora were granted full custody. Not hard when the only living parent is nowhere to be found and doesn't show up to court.

I was enraged, quiet, and already planning my escape when we pulled up to the house. Cora tried to pry a sleeping Jaxson from my arms just to allow me to get out of the car, but I wouldn't let her.

I could do it by myself.

I didn't need them.

They were temporary, and I was determined to get us out of there as soon as possible.

But like most things in my life, it didn't work out to plan.

Weeks turned into months.

Cora was the mother mine failed to be, but I couldn't trust her. I thought she was faking it.

Jaxson was only four and soon fell in love with her. Before I knew it, he was calling her mom. Archer soon after. I wasn't mad at them for it. I was mad at Cora and Skip for being the parents mine couldn't be. I was mad at my mother for leaving us, for choosing the drug in her veins rather than the flesh and blood she gave birth to. I was beyond the point of being mad at my father.

Back then, being here, in this house, the only good thing I could see was that Archer and Jaxson were away from him.

The days blended into one, and I hated every second. Chaos followed me wherever I went. I made sure of it. My high school was close to kicking me out for my "unruly behavior". Girls were too many and studies too few. It wasn't hard considering I was the city boy who already had too many tattoos.

It's my biggest regret, the worry I put Skip and Cora through. They tried everything. They planned family nights—I never showed up.

They grounded me—I always found a way out. Weed in my pocket—I asked them if they wanted some. They showed me love—I rejected it.

I can't imagine the hell they were going through. A couple who never had kids of their own were suddenly thrown into a world of two little boys and a disgruntled teenager who felt like the world was out to get him.

They did everything parents should do, proving themselves every day that they weren't going anywhere.

I thought I knew better. I knew what they really were.

I didn't know a damn thing.

I was hurting and scared, desperate for relief. I wanted out.

I pushed them away because I didn't know what else to do. Survival was all I knew. I didn't know how to accept love and be taken care of. So, I did everything in my power to make them hate me just so they would send us back.

On my fifteenth birthday, after too many run-ins with the wrong crowd in town, I wrapped poorly made sandwiches in foil and stuffed them in a bag with a bottle of water. Then I took my brothers' hands and snuck them out of the house.

When Archer and Jaxson's legs grew tired, we sat under a tree and ate. I let Jaxson nap in my arms while Archer asked questions I didn't know the answers to. All I knew was that we needed to get away. We were doing fine before. We could do it again. We could do it on our own.

I didn't have a plan, but I was going to find one.

It felt like days before someone found us in the forest. In reality, we were less than a mile away from the house and only gone for three hours.

But it's Skip and Cora's face I remember most. The relief overshadowed any anger. Cora fell to her knees as the boys ran into her waiting arms. I remember her tears most of all. How, as she held the boys close, she looked up at me and smiled. It was shaky and her hand trembled when she reached out and grabbed mine.

I waited for the anger, for the punishment I surely deserved.

It never came. Instead, she squeezed my hand a little tighter.

Skip wrapped his hand around the back of my neck, unable to fight the tears as he pulled me close.

My body stiffened.

I had never seen a man cry.

Men weren't supposed to cry, right?

"You had us worried, son," he choked out.

Son?

There was a pinch in my chest, and the longer he held me, the more it hurt.

When he pulled away, I wiped a stray tear before he could see it.

He saw it, but he looked away because he knew what it meant to me. We both went on like it never happened.

I don't remember much in the weeks that followed. I didn't speak, thinking better of it. I put them through enough, and if I had to stay, it was best I stayed quiet. Skip gave me a job at the garage, working with some of the crew. I kept my head down and did my job.

He came down the stairs one morning and began loading the back of his truck with fishing rods and camping gear.

When he was done, he stood over me, wordless, until I finished slurping my cereal.

"What?" I grunted, feeling uneasy with his presence.

I was already taller than Skip, but there was always something intimidating about his presence. Maybe it was the fatherly nature, or maybe it was because he looked too much like my father. As brothers, their features were eerily similar, but Skip's eyes weren't as harsh, his face not as marred with years of self-inflicted abuse, his hair only peppered grey at the temples.

"Get dressed. We're going away for a few days."

The spoon clanked against the bowl before I crossed my arms over my chest. "I'm not going anywhere with you."

Pressing his fists against the table, he leaned forward, only a breath away from my face. "Oh, but you are, boy. I'm sick of looking at you mope around this house. Get up and get dressed."

Defiant, I dug the heels of my feet into the floor. "Isn't it your birthday tomorrow?" I asked, like he had suddenly forgotten. Why would he want to go anywhere with me on his birthday?

"It is, and I'm choosing to go fishing with my son."

"I'm not your son."

He ignored me. "Let's call it a man's weekend. You consider yourself a man, don't you? Or are you going to continue acting like a little boy with your temper tantrums and silent treatment?"

"If this is punishment for failing my classes, you can find someone else to go with. I don't give a fuck."

Another inch closer, and despite the long breath he let out, I could see his patience wearing thin. For some reason, I didn't want to see Skip reach the end of his tether.

"The classes you're failing on purpose? We both know you're punishing yourself enough for that. I don't need to do a damn thing. Now, move, boy. I'm done waiting."

For the first time, I realized how much he could see right through me, see beneath the mask I thought was perfectly placed.

I was failing my classes on purpose. I always worked hard despite everything that was going on at home. My education was supposed to be my way out. It was the only way I could make a life for Archer and Jaxson

But they didn't need me anymore.

Rage bubbled until my teeth clenched together.

I would like to think I argued some more, but I know I didn't. The timbre of his voice left no room for arguments.

It was the trip that changed it all for me, and I think I'll remember it as long as I live. I stayed silent most of the weekend, only mumbling a quiet "Happy Birthday" when he woke up the next morning.

He allowed me the silence which I was grateful for. Later, around the campfire, he took two bottles of beer from the cooler and handed me one. I gawked at it for what felt like forever.

"Best you do it in front of me than come home every weekend in the states you've been in."

There was that feeling again, the sting in my throat that his disappointment conjured, but I swallowed it down with the beer.

Elbows on my knees, I stared into the fire, watching the sparks fly into the air.

"Your mother loved camping."

My head snapped to where he was sitting on his chair, but he never looked at me, choosing to keep his focus on the flames.

"She was always a little wild. Like you, I guess."

On the inside, I was screaming for him to stop. Talking about her hurt, yet somehow, hearing about her before she became a shadow of her former self eased the burn.

"She always wanted to see the good in people even when they didn't deserve it. She always fought so hard to find the good in my brother. But people like that will only drag you into their darkness instead of allowing you to share the light." When he looked over at me, his eyes were glazed over, lost in thought somewhere I'd never know. "She was a good mother. She doted on you when you were born."

A sting prickled the back of my throat. Memories that seemed buried came back to life. It was only me and her for so long. My father was in prison. She was clean. And Skip was right, she did dote on me. I was a momma's boy, and I knew it.

Images of her singing like she had a tune and grabbing my hands just to dance in the middle of the kitchen. She did that a lot. Her crazy bedtime stories that never came from a book, but her own imagination. Sometimes, she got so invested, she acted out the scenes until my stomach ached from laughing.

When my father got out of prison, it all changed in an instant. He promised her the sun, moon, and stars. He blinded her with hopes for the future and visions only he could see.

He ruined her.

The beatings started long before Archer and Jaxson were born. With three children to look after, a husband that treated her no better than the dirt at the bottom of his shoe, and pain I will never understand, she wanted to numb.

So, she did.

She numbed until she couldn't feel.

She couldn't feel the love for her children, or the hope she always had.

She numbed until she took her final breath.

I found her after school, needle still in her vein. She was breathing but barely. Archer and Jaxson were down for a nap.

I'm thankful for that much.

After I called the ambulance, I turned her on her side just as they told me to, and I held her hand. I was so scared. I don't think I ever felt fear quite as potent.

So, when Skip turned to me and said, "She loved you, Logan. You did her proud," the anger I was holding onto opened like a dam.

"Then why the fuck did she leave us? She didn't give a shit about anything but her precious drugs. She had a choice, and she didn't choose me, she didn't choose us. She chose him. A fucking monster, and she chose a needle. Fuck her, Skip," my voice broke with his name, and I hated it. I hated myself for letting it show. "Fuck her."

"And what are you choosing, son?"

"What?"

"What are you choosing?" he repeated, turning toward me. "All this bullshit you're doing. You're trying to hide and it's only going to lead you down one path. The end of that path looks like this: you end up like your mother, or you end up like your father."

I flinched.

Turning out like my father was a worse outcome than death.

I could never lay my hands on someone I loved.

I wasn't him.

I couldn't be him.

But the fear always remained. "What if I'm more like him than I want to be?"

Skip shook his head. "You're nothing like him. There was a darkness in your father even when we were teenagers. He made his choices. He had every opportunity in the world, but he chose the path with no way back."

It's a path I was walking down.

"I look at the way you are with your brothers, and I wish I had that with mine." When he gets up, he takes a seat on the log beside me. "You did a great job with those boys. I'm not here to take your place, but it's time to focus on doing what you want to do. Sometimes I forget because you're already almost six foot and your shoulders are bigger than mine, but you're still only a kid. Archer and Jaxson already look up to you. Is this what you want them to see? Is this what you want them to become?"

Shame swirled thick in my stomach.

"Is it?"

"No," I breathed, swallowing the sticky lump in my throat.

"Be the big brother they need. Be the man they need. Show them all the things they could become." Hand on my shoulder, he squeezed reassurance into my bones. "Give me and Cora a chance. We love you like our own. Just give us a chance."

A chance.

I could do that.

I nodded and murmured an agreement I'm not sure he heard, but his shoulders relaxed as he reached for another beer.

And with one chance, everything changed. I got my life on track… for the most part.

What can I say, sometimes trouble finds me.

I was in college when Maria was born. There was a part of me that feared Skip and Cora having children of their own. I thought they might treat Archer and Jaxson differently for it.

Like everything else, it wasn't what I was expecting. Maria brought everyone closer.

I don't think she's so happy about it. I can't imagine having three protective older brothers is easy.

"Loggie." A small hand pounding against the window snaps me out of yet another trip down memory lane.

Isabel slams her chubby hands against the glass again, propped up on Maria's hip.

"Loggie, what are you doing in there?" Maria mocks.

I roll my eyes and get out before taking a giggling Isabel from her arms. Instantly, her head nuzzles into the crook of my neck, and my heart constricts in my chest.

I fill my burning lungs, and for the first time in days, I feel like I can breathe.

Now I just need to find the other one.

"Can't a man have a minute to himself?"

"You've been in there for ages just staring into space."

"Have you been watching me?"

"Yes," she admits before tickling Isabel. "What did we say about Loggie?"

Isabel points her finger and twirls it around her temple. "Loggie, crazy."

"Her mother is going to love you for that."

Maria shrugs and tucks her hair behind her ear. "Wait until we move onto swearing."

"Come on, Princess Isabel. Let's get you away from the bad influence."

"Hey," Maria calls, following us. "You taught me all the worst words."

"That's different."

"How?"

I don't know. "It just is. Where's Hannah?"

"Making a birdhouse with Dad. Why are you home so early anyway?"

When I enter the house, all those smells I've come to love waft through the air. I take a second to breathe it in.

217

Maria frowns, studying me. "What is with you?"

"I'm feeling a little reflective today."

"Old age will do that to you."

Barking a laugh, I nudge her forward. Isabel tries to pronounce Maria's name while telling me she's crazy.

The tables have turned.

"She's a brat, Izzy. Always has been."

"A brat you love," Maria shouts over her shoulder.

Cora almost drops her cup of coffee when I enter the kitchen. "You're here."

"I should think so. I drove."

"Why? Is something wrong?" Her face pales. "Oh, Jesus, who died?"

Maria turns from where her head is in the fridge. "Someone's dead? I knew there had to be something."

Puffing out my cheeks, I put Isabel down to play with her toys. "Nobody died."

"Logan, love?" she implores, wanting answers I don't have. "What's wrong? You're home early."

"Can't I finish early? Aren't those the perks of being a business owner?"

She tries to smile, but unlike Maria, she reads me like a book, and in her eyes, I see she's figured out motives I haven't yet.

Through the double doors, Hannah traipses in with her new birdhouse in hand. Her eyes widen and she flashes a smile that lights up the room. "Hey, Logan."

With one arm, she rests her head against me in a half-hug like she can sense I need it.

"Good job with the birdhouse."

She sways on her feet, a blush creeping to her cheeks. "Thanks. Skip kind of helped."

Good of her to give him credit.

"Speaking of Skip. Where is he?"

Cora smiles. "Checking the camping gear."

The year after our first fishing trip, we brought Jaxson and Archer along. It's become a tradition ever since. "It's not his birthday for another two weeks."

She waves her hand. "You know how excited he gets."

Hannah tugs at my sleeve. "Where have you been?"

Guilt churns in my stomach. "Sorry, kid. I've just been busy."

"We missed you."

We?

"I missed my favorite girls too," I say, forcing cheerfulness into my voice as I ruffle Hannah's hair. She immediately gives me a look that could kill.

No touching the hair.

"Ah, I see," I hear Cora mumble at my side.

I give her a sidelong glance, but she only laughs. "You see what?"

"Nothing, love. I see nothing."

We spend the next hour in their yard, the girls' laughter filling the air. It's the best distraction, their innocent joy momentarily pushing the nightmares to the back of my mind, but it doesn't take long for Cora to call me back into the kitchen. When I enter, she pulls out a chair and places a sandwich on the table.

"You're not eating," she says, goading me to argue with her.

I know better.

She takes a seat in the chair opposite and bores a hole in the side of my face with that stare of hers. It holds some kind of magic. I've always been sure of it. "You're getting attached."

"No offense, this is a good sandwich, but I don't feel myself getting emotionally involved with it."

She rolls her eyes and pushes the plate toward me. God forbid I stop eating. She's the reason I've needed to work out since I was sixteen. Food is her love language.

"You know that's not what I meant. You came home early to see the kids."

Arching a brow, I open my mouth to reply, but she simply points to the plate again. This is her way of telling me to shut up, eat, and listen.

"You did. No point arguing with me about it. I know you well enough. And don't get me started about the way you look at their mother."

I don't meet her eyes. Not because I can lie. I can't. But if I look at her, she will see exactly how true her words are. How Beth makes me feel like the ground has disappeared under my feet.

There's a long pause, and for a second, I think she wants an answer, but then she says, "Logan, you might almost be forty years old, but to me you'll always be that boy I took home when he was fourteen, and for the first time in so long, I see how scared you are."

Shifting in my chair, I finally risk looking at her. She takes my hand and squeezes. "You're not him, love. You're not your father."

How the fuck does she know these things?

There's a form of agony I buried long ago, but now it's jumping to the surface to twist in my gut. Her words hit a raw nerve always partially exposed.

"You're letting your fear get in the way of your happiness, of their happiness. You think people don't notice the atmosphere in the room when you and Beth are together? You would be wrong if you did. It's special. It's a feeling you grab hold of with both hands and don't let go of."

I don't answer her with the response she wants. I can't go there, not today. After the night I've had, it's too raw. Instead, I force a smile and wink at her.

"Well, I'm not letting anything get in the way of me and this sandwich. I might be getting attached after all." Another roll of her eyes. "Besides, I like to think I get my stubbornness from my mother. You know, the one who likes to feed me sandwiches when I'm not hungry."

Her lips turn up into a shaky smile as tears she can't fight brim in her eyes. Not one to show too many emotions, she stands and pats my shoulder. "My son, there's more of me in there than you know."

It's when I hear Beth's car in the driveway minutes later that my heart begins to pound again, beating bruising rhythms against my chest.

I had planned to leave before she got here.

I can't face her even when I know I need to. I need to know everything in my nightmares isn't real. I need to know her skin is unmarked by my touch.

The moment she walks through the door, the atmosphere shifts. Her presence like sunlight—warm, inviting, radiant—and the sight of her smile ignites the surge of want in me that's as bewildering as it is intense.

But then the fear comes knocking.

My eyes search her head to foot, and relief washes over me. She's not hurt. It takes all my power to stand and stay there without stepping closer for a better inspection.

When our eyes connect, her smile is replaced with something else—

a hint of concern, a subtle questioning.

Can she see it? Can she see the secrets, the parts of myself coming undone at the seams?

Am I doing what my father did and pulling her into my darkness?

"Hey, stranger," she says.

"Stranger?" Cora questions, her eyes darting between us.

"My neighbor hasn't been very neighborly. I haven't seen him in days." She's talking to Cora, but her eyes never leave mine as she studies me. When she speaks this time, I know it's just to me. "Where have you been?"

Her question hangs in the air, a simple inquiry that feels heavier than it should. I brush it off, responding with a half-truth. "I've been busy."

I fucking hate how awkward we suddenly become. We are never awkward.

I hate how her gaze softens on me, how she hides the subtle flinch from the icy tone in my voice.

Most of all, I hate how she feels miles away when it's only steps, and I could have her in my arms again.

I hate how I remember the way her body feels. How perfect the soft curve of her waist felt in my hand.

I hate how scared I am of it all.

"You okay?" she asks.

"I'm fine." But even as the words leave my lips, they feel hollow, a façade I'm desperately trying to uphold.

With a nod, she turns to Cora, and I find myself drinking in the sight of her. Her gentleness, her strength—they're qualities I admire, qualities that draw me to her. But she doesn't know the full truth about me. She doesn't know the darkness that lurks in my past, the ghosts that haunt me.

If she knew, would it change the way she looks at me, the way she smiles at me, the way she trusts me with her girls? She just asked to stay. Would she want to leave if she knew the truth?

Even as she speaks to Cora about how the girls' day went and how Hannah starts school soon, her eyes search mine, and it's like she can see right through me. I want to tell her, but I'm terrified—terrified of losing her, of seeing fear replace the warmth in her eyes.

I'm torn, caught between my fear of losing her and my fear of hurting her. And all the while, the echo of my nightmare lingers, a haunting reminder of the potential darkness within me.

I don't know much right now, but I know I need to get out of here.

"I'll be in the city for a couple of days," I tell her, my words are as much an escape for me as they are an explanation for her.

With a look of confusion, she steps aside to let me pass, but not before my knuckles brush against her fingers, burning my skin from the simple touch.

It's not nearly enough, but it will have to be. In this state, I can't trust myself to touch her at all.

As I leave, her voice follows me, a ghostly whisper in my ear. "Take care, Logan."

THIRTY-ONE

BETH

The cool breeze hits my face as I watch Logan through the window. His silhouette is outlined by the dim glow from the porch light, highlighting the intricate tattoos up his arms. He's shirtless, working on repairing his porch. A bead of sweat slides down his sculpted chest. I bite my lip, torn between this sight and the pressing ache in my heart.

It's been a week. A week since he looked at me for more than ten seconds or spoken more than "How are you?" before walking away.

He was in the city for three of those days, and when he's home, he still treats the girls like the world revolves around only them. But me? I'm being pushed out of the circle.

I know what it feels like to be held captive under the heat of his stare, but this week it's cold in the shadows, and it's driving me crazy.

There's a distance between us I can't place, a tension thicker than the humid summer air.

I wrap my cardigan tighter around my frame, taking a deep breath before I step outside. My heart pounds with every step I take towards him.

"Isn't it a bit late for D.I.Y?" My voice cuts through the silence of the night.

He glances over at me, his eyes shadowed. My obvious attempt to approach this conversation with lightness just washed away. "Did I wake the girls?"

I love how much he cares, but tonight, I need him to look at me.

I shake my head as I wrap my arms around myself. There's no heat in his eyes, and a chill creeps down my back. At the sight, he softens, almost putting the hammer down before changing his mind. Wordless, he continues hammering away at the loose piece of wood.

I swallow hard, twisting my hands together.

"Can we talk?"

"I'm busy, Beth," he says, his voice low and gruff.

"I can see that, but—"

"Go home." His words are icy, slicing through the air like a dagger.

I flinch, the sting of rejection gnawing at my chest. I search his face, trying to find an answer in his stern expression. "Did I do something wrong? Is this about the other night? I shouldn't have drunk so much—"

"Drink every damn night if you like."

He blows out a breath. I do too, if not to remember how to breathe, then to calm the pounding in my chest.

He turns away and picks up the hammer again. "It's not that."

I want to grab the hammer and tear the whole damn porch down.

My heart lurches at his dismissal, and as if on autopilot, I turn on my heels and start to head back. The knot in my stomach only grows until it takes root and spreads through my veins like poison. The ache in my heart echoes in my ears, each beat another reminder of the growing gap between us.

But I stop, my breath hitching as my feet plant themselves to the ground. As much as I pleaded with him before, he's never turned his back on me, doing his best to gather broken pieces and put them back together, even when I wished he wouldn't. Not because I didn't want him near, but I didn't want him to see. Pretending is exhausting. It takes work. And on those days when the pretending slips, it gives someone a chance to peek inside the darkest parts of your soul. The parts you paint over just to blend in. But beneath will always lie the truth.

It's exactly what I've seen in Logan this week. Tonight, he's exhausted from pretending.

Another long breath and I turn around again. This time if he wants me to go home, he can carry me. I sit down on the steps of his porch, folding my arms across my chest. I'm not going back until he speaks to me. I need to know what's going on before I go crazy.

I don't look at him, but I feel his eyes on me, the confusion, the frustration. Still, he remains silent. He's a fortress, a castle with its drawbridge up, and I'm left outside, trying to weather the storm.

He should know better.

I've been through worse and come out stronger. I can be as stubborn as he is when I want to be. I won't back down, not when I know he needs me, even if he can't admit it. I'll wait, wait until he's ready to let down his walls and let me in. Because that's what friends do, and Logan, whether he likes it or not, is my friend. I refuse to let him face his demons alone. Not when he's been holding my hand while I face mine.

I'm not letting go now.

Determined, I check the baby monitor before releasing a long, bored sigh. I know it's going to annoy him, but I need a reaction. I need emotion. I can work with that. I'm quite good at riddles.

"I told you I'm busy."

I shrug. "I heard you."

"I also said go home, Beth." His voice is harder this time, a sharp edge to his tone I've never heard before. But I'm not moving, not until I get answers.

"No," I state, defiant and firm. "I'm not going anywhere until we talk. You want to ice me out? Fine. Go ahead. We'll both freeze."

He clenches his jaw, looking at me as if I'm some puzzle he can't figure out. He drops his hammer onto the ground and strides over to me, looking every bit like the storm I know is brewing within him.

Another menacing step forward and he leans over me, putting his hands on the step at my sides, caging me in.

"Why can't you just do as you're told for once?" he growls, the frustration in his voice echoing in the silence around us.

"Because this is not you!" I shoot back.

"You don't know a damn thing about who I am."

"Then tell me. You're pushing me away, and I don't know why."

He ignores me, leaning in until my back presses against the edge of the step. "Are you afraid of me, Beth?" His voice booms out into the night. His dark eyes are filled with a torment I've never seen before.

My mouth falls open, my pulse beating so fast I'm sure he can hear it. "What?"

"Are. You. Afraid. Of. Me?"

Yes.

No.

All of the above.

But I'm not afraid of him in the way he expects, in whatever he's attempting to do. I'm afraid of how much my body betrays me when he's this close.

I can almost see his demons swimming to the surface and his fight to keep them buried. I look away, lip quivering because I need to break the intensity of his stare.

Just as fast, he grabs my chin between his fingers. It's in his gentle touch, I know he's not lost, and all of this is an act. It's a test he doesn't know he's giving. He wants to know if I'll run.

"Look at me."

I do while fighting the sting behind my eyes. I don't want him to confuse my tears. They're not for me. They're for him.

"Now answer me. Are you afraid?"

I swallow the lump in my throat and answer. "No. You won't hurt me." My voice doesn't break, but he does. The heat I know so well comes flooding back to his eyes. I try to press my hand to his chest, but he stands straight and runs a trembling hand over his face. When he turns away, a crack forms in my heart.

Don't turn away from me, Logan.

"You should be." His voice is barely audible.

"Why? Why should I be afraid of you?"

When he spins around, the wildness is back. I stand and step closer when I know he wants me to run.

"Because I'm just like him!" He roars, his chest heaving.

It takes all my strength to remain standing. "What are you talking about? Like who?"

If he says Rob, I might go crazy. I've learned to trust my judgement again, and Logan King is not about to shit all over it. I've learned when to be afraid. What signs to look for. I know when my gut screams at me until I want to be sick. He's nothing like Rob.

As if reading my thoughts, he says, "Maybe I'm not all that different."

"Stop it."

He keeps going until my hands shake at my sides. "Maybe it's in me. Ever think of that?"

"It's not," I demand, but my words stick to the lump in my throat. "You're nothing like him."

He tilts his head in that way that makes me want to slap him, like he feels sorry for me.

"Stop it, Logan."

He allows me to stew in the silence before he finally says, "I come from a man just like him. My father was an animal."

My breath leaves my lungs in a whoosh.

"And not just with my mother, with his kids too."

Oh, Logan.

I bite my lips together, keeping the words in because I need him to keep talking. Thankfully, he does.

"He was a monster. And after last week…" He stalls, a thousand words on the tip of his tongue. "Just having you and the girls here… You just deserve better." I try to take another step toward him, but he shakes his head, as if having me too close is his personal hell. "What if it's in me? Because sometimes I look in the mirror and all I see is him."

"It's not." I shake my head, tears welling in my eyes. The thought of Logan believing he's anything less than the incredible man I know he is… it breaks my heart. "You're nothing like him."

"How can you be so sure?" He challenges, his voice filled with a desperate sort of anguish.

"Because as much as you don't want to admit it, I know you. I've seen you with my girls. With me. You're nothing like what you think you are." There's tension across his broad chest, and I want nothing more than to reach out and ease it, but I don't because I don't think it's what he wants. "Why didn't you tell me?"

He lets out a humorless laugh under his breath. "Because I'm a selfish bastard."

"No—"

"I was scared of losing you."

"You thought telling me would make me leave?"

No words, but I see it in his eyes.

We're both petrified of each other. Petrified of falling into each other with no way out.

With a deep breath, he turns away from me again, his fingers tightening around the wooden beam he'd been working on.

I think he's about to go back to work, but then he says, "It's this dream." His voice drops so low, I barely hear the words. I tilt my head, trying to catch his gaze, but he's looking down at his hands, his brows furrowed. "I keep having this fucking dream."

I know what that's like.

"Tell me about it," I plead.

He looks so lost. Not like the strong, steady man I know him to be. He rubs his face, looking like he's aged a decade in a moment as his face pales.

"I keep having this nightmare about my mother and father. Maybe it's a memory. I don't know. But he's hitting her, and I'm screaming at him... but when I look again... it's you." He finally meets my gaze, his eyes wide with fear, and something resembling regret. "And when I look down there's blood everywhere. My father isn't there anymore, and there's blood on *my* hands. *Your* blood."

I take a step back, needing a moment to process.

But it's not fear that fills me. It's understanding, a horrifying understanding. Logan is afraid of himself. He's afraid there's a monster lurking in the parts of him he paints over. That's why he's been pushing me away.

The admission hangs heavy in the air between us, a haunting specter of a nightmare he fears could become reality. My heart aches for him, the man who sees a monster in his own reflection. I need to banish the fears, to dispel his illusions.

"Touch me," I tell him, my voice calm despite the turbulent emotions.

His eyes widen slightly, surprise flashing in their depths. He hesitates, his gaze darting from my face to my outstretched hand and back. "Beth—"

"Logan," I cut him off, keeping my hand steady, an open invitation. "Touch me."

He's still for a moment longer, his conflict palpable. Then, with a resigned sigh, he reaches out. It's feather-light, as though he's afraid any more pressure might cause harm.

With both our chests heaving, I hold his gaze, wanting him to see what's true.

My breath stutters when his other hand grazes my wrists before coming up to trace over my cheek.

"Your touch doesn't hurt me."

His eyes don't leave our connected hands, his expression one of deep concentration as if he's trying to memorize the sensation. The touch is so light, it's almost not there. But I can feel it, the warmth of his hand, the tremble on his fingers as he cups my face.

"Could you ever hurt me?" I ask.

His eyes finally snap to mine, and in them I see raw vulnerability. For a moment, he just looks. Then as if coming to some internal conclusion, he shakes his head.

It's a long second of forgetting how to breathe before he wraps his hand around the back of my neck and pulls me to him, pressing his head against mine. "Fuck, no. You hurt, I hurt."

I almost smile.

"You hurt, I hurt," I repeat. "You're not your father," I say again, my voice choked. He needs to understand it, to believe it as much as I do. "You're not a monster. You're a man with fears like any man, but you're a good man."

We both have souls that bear the marks of a brutal past, but they don't need to mark our futures.

"I'm not running." In my best attempt to dampen the thick air between us, I say, "I think I did enough of that when we first met."

It's a whisper against my skin when he says, "My runner."

"I'm not going anywhere. Just don't push me away. I missed you this week. I had so much leftovers."

We both laugh this time, and I feel his shoulders relax against my hands.

"I missed you too, pretty girl."

There he is.

We don't say anything else as he squeezes me a little tighter. It's a small, silent affirmation. Hopefully he let go of some demons tonight.

We don't speak about whatever this is, about whatever's happening between us. I think we're both too scared of that yet. Our steps are small, but they always seem to guide us closer together.

I don't know what we're doing or how we're going to deal with it. It's both uncertain and terrifying, but at least we're doing it together.

THIRTY-TWO

Once upon a time.

It's the beginning of every fairy tale. The same ones I lost myself in so many times when I was a little girl.

Those four words hold so much promise. You know it's just the beginning. Dark obstacles will creep up along the way, but seeing those four words means that you're on a journey to a happily ever after.

It's how everyone's story starts, isn't it?

We all begin with a "Once upon a time…"

My story does.

But I wasn't trapped in a tower somewhere in need of rescuing. I grew up loved and protected.

I was one of the lucky ones.

I was going to jump right to the happily ever after.

But those dark shadows linger. They don't make themselves known until it's too late and sometimes a knight in shining armor is simply a monster in disguise. A disease eager to dig its claws into an unsuspecting mind. To infect.

I look back at my once upon a time and wonder how I didn't see the villain in my story until it was too late.

He blinded me with the good, and my vision only cleared in the darkness.

He allowed me to see who he really was when the lights went off. That smile everyone adored—the one I adored—suddenly changed.

His pupils dilated, spreading out over irises until all I could see was black. I could see my future in those eyes. My punishment.

And in the second it would take him to change, I would rack my brain wondering what I did wrong that night. Did I smile at someone I shouldn't have? Did I smile for too long? Did I drink too much? But that was impossible because I wasn't allowed to drink. Maybe I didn't answer a question in the right way?

He's dead. I know it. They buried him, and he can't hurt me. But I can't escape the nightmares.

It's not every night, but sometimes, because living with it obviously wasn't punishment enough, I close my eyes and he's there, doling out kicks like he'll never tire, squeezing a hand around bruised ribs while I'm cooking dinner just to keep me in check, pinning me to the bed when I said no.

A tear leaks from the corner of my eye before lulling on my chin and falling onto my lap. I wipe it away to feel my cheeks are soaked.

I always find those are the saddest tears. Not the ones you can't breathe through or the ones you know are coming. It's these ones. The ones when you're trying to live, and they flow down your face without even knowing it. They don't consider that you're just trying to move on. That you're trying to numb.

I wish the girls were here. I wish they were jumping on my bed, smothering me with hugs and kisses because they fill the void.

Pulling my robe tighter around my waist, I shiver as the morning air seeps into my bones. I've always loved the summer chill, so I open the double doors in the kitchen and stare up at the trees as they sway in the gentle breeze.

Logan.

He's home.

He left two days ago for a fishing trip with his brothers and Skip for Skip's birthday. I'm surprised to see him home so early.

"What are you doing?"

Already unloading supplies from the truck, he merely spares me a quick glance and a half smirk before continuing where he left off. "Morning, pretty girl."

I wrap my robe tighter around my waist. "It's eight in the morning. Why are you back already? And what are you doing in my yard with... wood?"

He stills, barking a quiet laugh at my expense as heat rushes up my neck.

Morning wood.

Right.

He's a child.

"Technically," he pulls more supplies from the truck before running a hand through his hair, "It's my side of the yard."

I roll my eyes, crossing my arms over my chest because there's not enough heat in the sun yet, and I'm not wearing a bra.

"That doesn't answer my question."

"The girls are still at your sister's, right?"

It's eight in the morning. Of course they are.

I nod, eyeing him as he finally stands still to look at me.

"I'm building a playhouse before they get home."

I gawk at him. "Excuse me?"

"Hannah said she wanted a playhouse. I'm giving her one before she starts school next week. I thought it might take her mind off things."

Straightening my spine, my sleepy brain finally begins to catch up as my chest tightens. Hannah is naturally an anxious child. She's been worried about starting a new school, and the fact that Logan paid attention to it makes my heart swell.

"You're kidding?" His blank stare tells me he's not. "Just because she asked for a playhouse doesn't mean she can have one."

"Why not?"

"Why not? Seriously? This is crazy. You don't need to build a playhouse for my kids."

Slowly, he reaches out and rests his hands on my arms. "No offense here, but those kids are yours, and I'm sure you've had years to become immune to those eyes, but I haven't. I'll be lucky not to keel over next time Hannah flutters her eyelashes at me, or every time Isabel calls me Loggie. If they want a playhouse, I'm going to give them a damn playhouse."

My heart just expanded in my chest.

Who is this man?

Do I argue with him? Hug him? Cry?

"You're the craziest neighbor I've ever had."

His eyes fall from my face and dance over my robe, a smile pulling on the corner of his mouth the more he explores.

His eyes meet mine again. "Cold?"

I feel the first rush of heat expand over my neck and into my cheeks like the lick of a flame. The second rush of heat is much lower down.

It's the smirk.

I'm sure it has powers, seducing women with a simple yet wicked tilt of his lips.

I swallow the nerves bubbling in my throat. "A little," I admit. It's only half a lie. The full truth is that my body always surprises me with these reactions to him.

Only him.

I was sure I would never feel the rush of heat low in my belly ever again. Logan has once again proved me wrong.

Not that I'd ever act on it. He's my neighbor. He's my sexy as sin neighbor, but that's not the point. I know he said he hasn't been with anyone since I moved here, and honestly, I still don't know how to take that, but I've seen the way women's mouths fall open when they see him. His look alludes to a bad boy we all so desperately love, while his actions are kind, caring, soft.

Although, soft is never a word I'd use to describe Logan. Nope. This man is all hard planes and layers of muscle.

I blink away the fog, shaking the thoughts and pushing them to the farthest parts of my mind.

"You okay, pretty girl?" His eyes narrow on me, bringing me back to the present.

I rub the palms of my hands over my arms, gathering heat. "Yeah, sorry."

Noticing my sudden embarrassment, his brows lift slightly. "Go back to bed. I didn't mean to wake you."

"You didn't. I was awake."

His brows pull together, like he can tell my nightmares keep me awake, but he doesn't say anything.

"Want some breakfast?" I ask. It's the least I can do.

"I could eat."

"You can always eat."

His smile is enough to ward off the morning chill.

∞∞∞∞

By one o'clock, Skip and Archer were here to help finish the playhouse. I say playhouse lightly. At this stage I'm unsure if it's a playhouse or a small apartment. Either way, they've been out there for hours and are determined to finish it before the girls get home.

I called Kim earlier to tell her what's going on. She agreed to hold off on bringing the girls home for a few hours.

They finished just in time.

Kim makes sure to park out front, so the girls are none the wiser. I want to see their reactions, and as much as I want to be the one to show them, this isn't mine to give.

"Did you two have fun?"

"Yep," Hannah agrees, hugging me as Isabel climbs into my arms.

Kim wraps her arms around my shoulders. "I can't believe he's building them a playhouse," she whispers low enough so the girls won't hear.

I nod, my eyes wide, saying "I know" without saying it.

Keeping me close, she whispers, "Are you not turned on right now because I'm close to orgasm?"

I sigh. "Absolutely."

She gently slaps her palm against my cheek. "My poor sister."

"Ladies." Logan steps into the living room covered in sweat and sex appeal.

Kim steps forward and grabs his chin. "You are my favorite person right now."

"Happy to know." I think that's what he says, but she has his lips squished together.

Releasing him, she goes out back and takes out her phone to record.

Isabel wiggles out of my arms and climbs into Logan's just like she always does.

Hannah has a new soccer ball under her arm. "You wanna play later?"

"Of course, but your mom has something to show you first."

My heart swells because he wants to give me the credit.

I shake my head. This is his moment, and I can't wait to stand back and watch.

"There's a surprise out back for you, but Logan did everything."

Stepping forward, he takes my hand. "Okay, it was both of us."

It wasn't. It was all him.

But he wants me here in this moment.

And that's it.

We're a team for today.

I did nothing but make breakfast, and he won't acknowledge it. To him, I might as well have been out there building.

With Isabel in his arms, I hold Hannah's hand and take them outside.

When Hannah sees the playhouse, tears stream down her face. I cry while Logan coughs to clear the lump in his throat like I won't notice, but I do.

The girls climb inside.

And inside is a treasure trove.

A little table and little chairs. Two bean bags and some toys. A ladder leads to an upstairs compartment.

Hannah takes the lead and when she reaches the top, she stalls.

"Mom," she whispers, looking down at me.

"What is it, baby?"

"Books," she gasps.

When I join her at the top, my heart stops beating for what seems like forever.

Logan has laid blankets and cushions. A double tiered shelf lines the wall, and it features all her favorites. There's some I don't recognize, but I can tell they're all about soccer or superhero librarians.

"This is so cool. Thanks, Mom."

I take her hand and kiss it with tears coating my cheeks. "Thank Logan. He built all of this."

With the biggest smile I've ever seen, she almost pushes me down the ladder. I've never seen her this panicked. Isabel is too busy not knowing what is going on, but Hannah—she gets it.

She runs into his arms, and he's there waiting. Eyes closed, he squeezes her close to his chest.

Kim is crying, I'm crying, I think Skip is wiping a tear from his eye, and Archer is definitely crying.

Of all the people I can go to in this moment, I go to Archer because I'm sure if Logan had the chance, he would do all of this for Archer's little girl.

No words, I wrap my arms around his waist. Resting his head on mine, he pulls me close.

"They'll always have their Uncle Archer, you know that, right?" he says against my head.

I rest my hand against his chest and hug him. "I know. Thank you."

"Don't thank me. He's happy. I've never really seen him this happy."

I blow out a long breath as we stand and watch Hannah guide Logan into the playhouse to show him around like he's never seen it before.

Happiness.

It's the only word that comes to mind.

After a few minutes, Logan exits the playhouse and stands by my side. He replaces Archer because Hannah wants to show him around next.

"This is why we do it together," Logan says, holding me tight against his chest. I look up at him. "Because you made these beautiful kids, and I don't get these moments without you."

While wiping the tears with the flesh of my palms, he squeezes my waist a little tighter.

"Together?"

"Together," I agree.

THIRTY-THREE

Darkness engulfs the room as a sudden scream severs the silence. My heart lurches, the tranquility of sleep instantly replaced by an onslaught of adrenaline. Before I can fully react, I hear the pitter-patter of feet approaching, and the door to my room creaks open.

"Mom, are you sleeping?" The voice is soft, almost drowned out by the whispering wind outside.

"No, baby. What happened?" I ask, my voice heavy with the remnants of sleep.

Her cheeks glisten as she moves closer. Yet, instead of seeking the comfort of my embrace as she usually does after nightmares, she settles herself cross-legged on the bed.

Gingerly, I wipe away the tear tracks on her face, coaxing her to open up.

"Nightmare?"

She nods.

"Bad one?" I ask, my heart hammering against my chest as a familiar sense of dread starts to settle. "Do you want to tell me about it?"

"I was dreaming of daddy."

Her statement is simple, yet the implications hit me like a wave. I swallow the lump in my throat before I choke on it, my mind racing to process as I anticipate what comes next.

"Dreaming of dad isn't a bad thing." I force my voice to remain steady, offering her a comforting smile that hides the turmoil raging inside me.

I'm no longer tired.

"He told me he loved me and gave me a hug."

Fresh tears prickle in my eyes. I blink them away and pull her closer, pressing a kiss on her forehead. "He did love you. Very much."

Reaching for the glass of water on my nightstand, I encourage her to drink.

"What else did you dream about?"

"The fire," she whispers, and my heart sinks to the pit of my stomach.

Fire.

That word always brings back a rush of unwanted memories. Memories of him. Memories that stoke the embers of my resentment for him.

The nightmares have been sporadic over the last two years. They stopped in the months since we moved here… until tonight.

As her confession hangs in the air, I squeeze her hand, offering the only comfort I can. A soft sigh escapes my lips as I pull her into my arms, repeating, "You're safe," until we both believe it.

The morning is still hours away. There's still time to lull her back to sleep, to offer some respite from the terror of her dream.

"Want some warm milk to help you get back to sleep?"

With a nod, she agrees, and I gently slide off the bed.

The house is silent except for the faint hum of the refrigerator in the kitchen. I pour a small glass of milk, popping it in the microwave to warm. A light catches my eye from Logan's house. Clad in nothing but shorts, his fists beat against his punching bag over and over.

It looks like our house isn't the only one not welcoming sleep tonight.

Back in the bedroom, I find her waiting, her large eyes following my movements. I watch as she sips slowly, her eyelids drooping as the comforting warmth of the drink takes effect.

Her gaze falls to my ankle, her fingers reaching out to touch the silvery skin. "What happened?"

I chuckle, shaking my head. "You always ask about that scar."

She shrugs. "I like when you tell me."

Smiling, I prepare myself to lie to my baby girl again.

Is that why she always asks?

Can she see that the story I tell her isn't the whole truth?

Still, I won't let it take from the moment because it's moments like this I cherish most. Even if I have to lie, just a little, to protect her.

"Alright," I begin, settling back into the pillows with her head on my chest. "Do you remember how I got that scar?"

"You got it when you were learning how to ride a bike," she recites, her lips curving into a smile.

"Your grandpa was teaching me. I must've been about your age." I pause, letting the nostalgia wash over me. "And, well, let's just say I wasn't the most... graceful learner."

Hannah giggles through a yawn. "What happened?"

She must know this story by heart now, but I keep going anyway.

"Well, I was doing pretty good at first. But then..."

"Squirrel," we both say.

Her giggles intensify, easing the knot in my chest.

"It frightened me so much that I lost control of the bike. I fell right into a bush of thorns. That's how I got this scar."

I should feel guilty, but I don't. The truth is uglier.

The story is true. I did fall off my bike, but I escaped without scars. That scar on my ankle came much later.

"I can't believe you fell because of a squirrel."

"Yep," I confirm. "Scared me half to death."

Her laughter fills the room, her joy overshadowing the nightmare from earlier.

She started school last week and spends the next half hour in a sleepy ramble about the book they're reading in class. As her speech slurs into the silence, I hold her a little tighter, feeling her breathing even.

When I'm sure she's sleeping, I tuck her into my bed and kiss her flushed cheek before slipping out.

Tonight serves as a reminder of why I'm here, why I'm doing what I'm doing. For Hannah. For us.

∞∞∞∞

I sit alone on the porch steps in the pitch-black predawn, my fingers nervously tracing patterns into the wood. It's too quiet, too still, mirroring the ominous dread creeping in.

Footsteps crunch on the grass, pulling me from my spiraling thoughts. We might be the only people on this land, but it could be full, and I think I would still know when he's nearby. His steps are unhurried, steady, confident. It's that inherent tranquility that lends me some courage, easing the knot of tension in my gut.

"You're up early," he says, running his fingers through his wet hair.

"I could say the same for you."

He takes a seat next to me. "Couldn't sleep. Went for a run."

"It's not even 6 a.m."

"I like the quiet. Why are you awake, pretty girl?"

The nickname has a tingle fluttering low in my belly. I'm sure I look far from pretty at this hour. I can practically feel the bags under my eyes.

"Hannah had a nightmare," I admit as he eases back on the step, his presence a silent beacon in the shadowy night. He remains quiet as I continue, "She had a dream about her father... and the fire." My voice is barely audible, the words catching in my throat as I fight back tears.

He bristles next to me. "Fire? But I thought you weren't in the house when it burned down."

I look at him. "*I* wasn't." The confession is a mere whisper, a ghost of a sentence that carries the weight of a thousand unspoken horrors.

A tense silence envelops us, Logan seemingly at a loss for words. I can't blame him; there's a lot he doesn't know about me, about the demons from my past that continue to cast long shadows over my present.

"How much did Claire and Jake tell you about me?"

"Not a lot. I knew something happened two years ago. I knew how Rob died. I didn't know you were his wife." Something terrifying flashes in his eyes before it disappears. "I didn't ask for details. It's only my business if you want it to be."

With a deep breath, I turn away, fiddling with an imaginary string in my pajama top. I don't know why, but I can't look at him when I tell him.

And with the memories, the words tumble out, unfiltered, raw, and clawing at old wounds until I bleed.

"The day after I had Isabel, I was supposed to go back to the shelter, but there were some minor complications doctors wanted to keep an eye on," I begin. "Claire was looking after Hannah. I asked her to come to the hospital so Hannah could meet her baby sister. Rob found out. He tried to muscle his way into the hospital earlier that day, but security shut him down hard."

My eyes are trained to the ground, unable to meet Logan's gaze. I'm terrified of what I might see. "Once Claire and Hannah left, Rob was in the parking lot... waiting. I don't know, I think he thought I was coming home too. In some delusion, he thought he could bring his family home again. I remember holding Isabel and feeling so much love, but something else sank in my gut. And I knew... I just knew something wasn't right."

Swallowing back a sob, I push forward. "Thirty minutes later, there was a cop standing at the end of my bed. Claire and Hannah hadn't made it back to the shelter. Rob had taken her. She thought they were going for ice-cream."

I bite down on my lip hard enough to taste copper on my tongue. "I wasn't sure of a lot in my marriage, but I was sure of how much he loved his little girl. I didn't realize his selfishness was stronger. Something made him snap that day."

I find myself pinching the skin of my ring finger where a gold band once fit perfectly. I had the indent of the shape for months. Right now, I think I can still see it.

Dropping my hands to my lap, I stare at the grass and listen to the birdsong in the trees as the creatures come to life in the morning glow. I concentrate on that when I say, "She didn't see it because she was playing in her room, but he set the house on fire with her still inside."

His touch keeps me in the present as his thumb collects a tear from my cheek. "Jake and Claire got her out in time. She only remembers the smoke. She remembers she was scared, but she doesn't know the real story. She doesn't know how her father was willing to hurt her, to take her life. How he put a gun to his head and fired while letting the house burn down around him rather than face the consequences."

A wave of sorrow washes over me, my words coming out in broken fragments. "I failed her. All those years I tried to shield her from the man her father really was... a man who was supposed to protect her, not put her in harm's way. I left to keep her safe, and I couldn't even do that."

The words hang in the air, their true meaning doing little to set me free. Instead, it burrows into my veins, poisoning my blood. "There will come a day when she remembers more, when she starts asking questions. And when she does, how do I tell her? How do I explain to her what her father did, why I couldn't stop him?"

His answer is gentle even when there's so much anger setting his jaw tight. "You do what you've always done," he says, his words a soothing balm to my frayed nerves. "You love her. You guide her. And most importantly, you remind her every day that she's safe. The past doesn't define her, or you. Remember that."

"Is that what you did?"

I don't know why I ask or even if I have a right. It's a selfish thought, but I don't want to be alone here.

He gazes at me for a moment, his elbows on his thighs, as if considering his answer. Then he sighs and leans forward. "I suppose I didn't really have a choice," he finally says, a faint smile tugging at the corner of his mouth. It's a mouth I can't help but stare at. "You learn to adapt, to push through, to survive... because you have to. The alternative is slipping back into darkness."

"Where is your father now?" I venture, the question slipping out before I can think about it.

"Prison," he answers. "Drugs and assault. He's a real diamond, my father."

There's an intense sadness in his eyes that makes my heart ache for him. But then he blinks, and it's gone, replaced by that same calm resilience.

"Did you ever forgive him?" I've been told I need to forgive, but I'm finding it real hard right now.

Logan laughs, but it's humorless. He looks at me, and I'm trapped again in emerald eyes. "You know, I used to think it was about forgiveness. I used to think that if I could forgive him, then I could move on. Then I realized that's a lot of effort and focus on a man who doesn't deserve it. It wasn't about forgiveness. Not for me. It's not about him at all. It was about how I coped, how I chose to live my life despite everything."

His fingers drum softly on his knee as he continues. "We're all dealt a hand in life, some of us better than others. It's how we play the cards... that's what matters."

His words ring with such clarity, such conviction, it's as if I can feel my own strength growing. I draw in a deep breath as he traces the dried tears away with his thumb, cupping my face and drawing me until I'm breathless from just a simple touch.

With the first light of dawn playing hide and seek with the morning mist, we stay seated on the porch steps, cocooned in a comforting silence. Our shoulders brush slightly, grounding me, reminding me that he's here, willingly sharing this moment with me. I can't quite put my finger on it, but there's something about him that makes the shadows of the past a little less daunting, the present a little more bearable.

He finally breaks the silence, his voice low but gruff. "Beth, look at me."

His eyes, always heated and understanding, warm the chill that has seeped into my bones. It's in his gaze, he holds me captive.

"You didn't fail her. You did everything you could to protect her, and you still do. Don't ever doubt that."

His words chip away at the icy fortress of guilt I've built around myself, warming the numb parts of my soul.

"You're doing good."

I nod, swallowing past the lump in my throat. A silent acknowledgement of the painful yet necessary truth he's making me face. A meek smile tugs at the corners of my mouth, the first one since Hannah's nightmare.

THIRTY-FOUR

I had a dream about Logan.

In the dream, Logan was seated on his porch. His inked arms rested on either side of the chair, his confident posture drawing me in like a moth to a flame.

I boldly strode over, dream-me untethered by real-life inhibitions. His penetrating gaze traced my every move, the intensity of it setting my skin aflame. I slid onto the seat beside him, our bodies only inches apart.

He reached out, his large hand swallowing my smaller one. His touch was a lit match, igniting a fire within me that threatened to consume me whole. His scent, a heady mixture of musk and outdoors, invaded my senses, leaving me dizzy.

Suddenly, he was pulling me closer. His warm breath fanned across my face, his eyes locked onto mine with a look of raw desire that mirrored my own. His free hand traced the line of my jaw, his fingers threaded through my hair, pulling me in.

The kiss was seismic. It was heat and want, passion and intensity. His lips moved over mine, tasting of temptation and unspoken promises. He explored my mouth, each stroke of his tongue eliciting a moan from me.

In the dream, his hands roamed freely, touching places that had been starved of affection for far too long. His hands slipped under my shirt, his touch branding my skin as he traced my ribs, then lower, till his fingers rested at the hem of my jeans.

The dream Logan was a man unleashed. His eyes were dark as he whispered my name, his voice husky and laced with an insatiable need.

But then, the dream shifted. The warmth of Logan's touch disappeared, replaced by the cold reality of my loneliness. The remnants of the dream, the fiery memory of his touch and taste, lingered in my senses, reminding me of what I was desperately yearning for. It was a harsh awakening from the intense connection, leaving me wanting, craving for a reality where that connection was more than just in my head.

It's been a week, and I can't stop thinking about it.

A week of obsessing about my neighbor.

A man asked me out today. The first man in ten years, and I've hardly thought about it because my mind is flooded with Logan's calloused hand on my inner thigh. A touch that never even happened.

I knew it. The second I woke in a cold sweat, I knew I was done for.

I haven't felt anything for a man, in well, a really long time. It's pathetic. I haven't even been able to touch myself, but there was no ignoring the distinctive throb between my legs after I woke.

I'm not dead inside after all.

It doesn't help that I've been reading nothing but the smuttiest books since then. I'm going through them like I can rip the answers from the pages, but all they leave me with is a wetness between my legs and more dreams of a tattooed neighbor hovering over me.

I glance at the bookmarked page on the table. "You're not helping," I mutter to the book like it can answer me back.

I'm losing it.

A simple dream and all those feelings I thought were gone erupted in me until I could hardly catch my breath.

"Walls, Beth," I whisper to myself, dicing carrots smaller than I need them.

I'm an expert at building walls. I swore off men. I'm good at shutting things down. I did it just today when Ace asked me out on a date again during my shift at the café.

I did it while trying not to stutter and burning up from the inside out. I'm not denying it felt good to be wanted by someone, but it hit me with the force of an arctic truck—I wanted that someone to be Logan.

Ace was a sweetheart about it.

"You're going to let someone snap you up, and I hope they hold onto you," he said after we hugged away any awkwardness.

Just one more wall, a barrier, a fucking white picket fence. Anything to shut down this tsunami of unwelcomed desires.

One wall between me and Logan King.

That's all I need.

"Beth."

I jump, dropping the knife in the process as he appears at the threshold like he's been summoned by dirty thoughts alone.

"Are the girls here?"

"Isabel is down for a nap and Hannah is in the playhouse doing her homework."

He takes a step inside before dipping his chin. "Got a minute?"

And with just the sight of him, there goes my wall.

Brick by brick.

You're shitting all over my walls, Logan.

"Sure," I say, my voice sounding too high. I busy myself with adding the chopped vegetables to the pot. "What's up?"

"Tell me you didn't agree to go on a date with Ace fucking Blackwood today." His tone is strained.

It's only when he steps inside from out of the late afternoon sun that I see a faint darkness in his eyes, the clench of his jaw, and hands balled into fists.

I wipe my palms on the towel, not knowing why my heart has suddenly started racing in my chest.

There's something hungry in his gaze.

Something primal.

Something irresistible.

Walls.

I laugh to hide the nerves bubbling in my throat. "News sure does travel fast around here."

"Beth?"

There's a warning there. Not one that scares me, though it probably should. It's one that brings that same ache between my legs.

Why am I like this?

I swallow hard before answering. "He asked me out. I said no."

He takes another step forward, and I grip the counter at my back, needing something to keep me steady.

"Why?"

Why?

Why did I say no?

Because I had a sex dream.

Because he wasn't you.

But I don't say that because I'm not completely crazy. Not yet anyway.

"I don't think I date."

Really? That's my reply?

"You don't think you date?"

I chew my lip between my teeth to buy myself time.

What I said wasn't a lie, so I keep going. "Yes. I mean, I don't think I can, and I'm far from ready." I feel stupid, but there's no point in stopping now. That would be sensible. "I wouldn't even know what to do. I've never had a first date."

He simply stares at me with the muscles in his jaw still twitching. It's oddly fascinating to watch.

"You were married. Surely he took you on a date at some point. And weren't you in relationships before then?"

"Two not serious relationships. We were in college. Our dates consisted of hanging out with friends and ended in one of our beds."

His eyes flare.

"With Rob, our relationship started as a secret. Then we jumped straight to the pregnant part. Our first date was our wedding day. I never had the stereotypical first date." I smile at him. "Although I did have an almost first date with a tattoo artist once, but he turned out to be an asshole."

All tension leaves his body as he throws his head back and laughs. His eyes meet mine again, lighter now, but no less dangerous.

"That's a fucking tragedy. You deserve so many first dates."

I shrug, focusing on the water beginning to boil in the pot. "It is what it is. Want some dinner?"

The lift of his lips is enough to set my blood alight. He presses his hands against the counter, and I need to tear my eyes away from the bulging veins in his forearms.

"I can't. I need to go into the city for a couple of days. I've got some meetings and clients booked in."

I try and fail to hide the disappointment on my face. "Cool."

Cool?

"You been reading again?"

Both our gazes' zone in on the open book. It's turned upside down on the bookmarked page.

Thank the heavens for discreet covers.

But it's too late. He's already noticed the sheer panic on my face.

I dive for it.

He's quicker and grabs it before I can.

"Give me the book," I demand.

I'm hot.

Everywhere.

"Put the book down, Logan." I'm begging now. I'll happily beg.

With his shit-eating grin, I go from wanting to rip all his clothes off to wanting to kick him in the balls... after I rip his clothes off.

"You're blushing, Bethany Rose."

"I'm not, and don't call me that."

I take a step forward while he takes one back.

"Are you reading dirty books again?"

He's teasing me.

I hate it.

"Logan, put the book down."

My skin prickles like there's a bomb about to go off.

I swear the world spins in slow motion when I see him scanning the words. His eyes widen, and the tension returns to his shoulders.

Why couldn't he have opened one of my tamer books?

I'm pretty sure the hero was just tying the heroine's hands to the bed while he grabbed her throat and called her a "Good little slut."

"Oh, God." I hide my face with my hands, defeated. I wait for him to finish without looking at him.

I'm dying.

"You're into this?"

I still don't look at him, but his voice carries no judgement. He sounds curious, and dare I say it? Turned on?

"Look at me," he rasps, sending a shiver down my spine. I do, but I still want to stick my head in the boiling water. "Now answer me."

"Doesn't everyone like to be praised for their good work?" He steps closer as I throw my hands out. "I don't know. It's weird, isn't it?"

Another step.

"What is?"

"That I could be into..." I wave at the book in his hand. "That?"

248

Another step.

"Why is it weird?"

I swallow.

I'm sure he hears it because he's slowly getting closer, his frame beginning to crowd me until I can hardly breathe. If he touches me, I'm going to combust.

Shame I shouldn't feel rises to heat my cheeks. "After my past, I shouldn't be into that."

"That's fucking bullshit," he snaps, but he sounds more offended on my behalf.

"It's stupid. It's just a book. I don't know if I'm into it, and I don't need to know... Logan, please stop doing that."

That look is enough to make my legs give up on me.

I press my hand to his chest as he reaches me, feeling his heart pound and his muscles tense beneath my palm. My head tilts back to meet his eyes, and what I see has me holding back a moan. With a stare so heated I'm panting, my clothes feel heavy on my skin.

"Do you trust me?"

Nothing good ever comes of that sentence, but I nod because now I'm curious.

"Good girl."

Yep, my panties are soaked.

This is why I have a praise kink, because Logan called me a good girl a couple times ten years ago, and I liked it.

This is his fault. He can't judge me for something he created.

The book falls to the ground with a thud, and he moves so fast my breath leaves my lungs in a whoosh. With his hand on my back, his other hand reaches out, his fingers wrapping around my throat, and in two secure strides I'm pressed against the wall.

The panic doesn't come, and I can't remember what fear feels like, but there's a fire so hot in my belly, my hips instinctively rock.

"Relax," he orders, his nose grazing the shell of my ear.

I take a deep breath, and his fingers tighten—not enough to hurt, but the pressure has my eyes rolling in my head. My nipples pebble under my shirt. The friction against his chest shoots straight between my legs.

A soft moan escapes, but I'm too far gone to register that it comes from me.

His lips don't kiss my skin. Instead, they hardly touch me as he brushes them over my neck, all the way to my collarbone, along my jawline, over my cheek.

"Logan." His name comes out in a lust filled whisper.

"Fuck," he growls, his voice tight, and I find myself wondering what he sounds like when he comes. "I love when you say my name like that."

Yeah? Me too.

My dreams are going to be wild after this.

Nudging my legs apart with his knee, he says, "Tell me something?"

Anything.

"Are you wet?" he rasps.

My eyes bulge out of my head.

He did not just ask me that.

His hand tightens.

My legs weaken and heat unfurls between my thighs.

"Answer me."

I nod because my vocabulary is somewhere else.

"Use your words, Beth."

"Yes," I manage in a strangled cry.

"Such a good fucking girl," he whispers before his teeth nip my neck. It's not enough to mark me, but the contact is almost enough to make me come undone.

Towering over me, I'm caged against him when he finally looks at me. Fuck knows what he sees, but he looks feral.

And I love it.

I want more.

So much more.

Is this normal? Do neighbors always pin each other against a wall and choke the other until they're ready to explode?

But I should know better because Logan's presence has always whispered promises of so much more.

His thumb motions circles around my throat.

My eyes fall.

"Look. At. Me." When my eyes meet his, he releases his grip and guides his fingers over my parted mouth. "There's nothing wrong with wanting a man to possess you in the bedroom as long as he always protects you outside of it. The power is yours, baby. Never forget that."

He backs away, leaving only cold air in his wake.

"And Beth?" He smirks, but my body hasn't caught up yet, and I'm still spiraling. "I think you might be into it."

"You think?" I blurt, trying to even my breathing.

He leans in and presses a kiss to my forehead.

My heart stops beating.

"Glad I could be of service. What else are friends for?"

I glare at him.

I've never hated the word more.

"See you in a couple of days, pretty girl. Stay out of trouble." With a slow wink, he turns and walks away, leaving me on the verge of cardiac arrest and with a deep ache between my thighs.

I fall back against the wall and throw my head back.

What the fuck was that?

I stare after him, surprised when everything in me wants nothing more than for him to turn around and finish this.

His truck roars to life.

"Goodbye then," I mutter under my breath just as the water in the pot boils over.

THIRTY-FIVE

Cora: Girls are at your house with Maria. They had pasta and vegetables for dinner. Isabel napped for over an hour and did a number two. Hannah practiced her soccer most of the day. She's getting so good. Have a great night. LOL.

I don't know how many times I've told her that LOL doesn't mean lots of love, but she's committed.

Logan is out front working on his bike with his T-shirt tucked into the back pocket of his jeans when I return home.

Jesus.

I swallow, licking a dry tongue over my lips.

Thank you, Universe.

Giving myself a quick minute to appreciate him in all his glory, I watch—without the slightest ounce of shame—the bulge in his bicep, the cords in his neck straining, the tightening of his stomach muscles, and then I wipe my mouth because I'm pretty sure I'm drooling. He knows I'm here, but he hasn't looked up yet. I roll my shoulders back and palm my cheeks, trying to calm the blush I feel spreading.

Wiping the back of his hand across his forehead, he stands straight as I get out of the car and walk to him.

"You're back."

"Yeah." He breathes heavily in the late afternoon sun, tossing the dirty rag in his free back pocket. "Cindy had it covered. I have plans this evening."

"Oh really? And what plans were so important they dragged Logan King from his work?"

He smiles with that mischievous glint I've come to adore shining in his eyes. "I have a date."

My mouth falls open, and I can only hope I hide it fast enough, but the abrupt sting in my chest makes it impossible to speak. I chew my lip between my teeth harder than I should, but I need anything to distract me from the little green monster stomping around inside.

Of course he's going on a date. Why wouldn't he? I'm surprised he hasn't been on more since I moved in. Or maybe he has, and I've chosen to ignore it because acknowledging it means I would have to face the flutter of feelings I have for him.

No such luck tonight, because that flutter becomes a tsunami and washes over me until my eyes burn with unshed tears.

I'll soon need to get over this little infatuation because this is how it's going to be.

I just don't like it.

There'll be dates and women. There'll be that one woman who makes it impossible for all others to even have a chance.

It's stupid. Do I even want a chance?

No, because I swore I wouldn't do this to myself. The wounds are still too raw, yet knowing Logan is going on a date seems to be picking at a nerve that's been left open for a long time. A nerve I always buried, slapped a Band Aid on, and ignored. I'm just realizing it never fully healed.

Trying to keep my voice even, I force a smile and ask, "Who's the lucky girl?"

One slow but large stride forward and he's stealing the air from my lungs. My breath hitches, stuttering in my throat from his proximity. My eyes fall to the droplet of sweat falling over his broad chest and my fingers twitch with the want to reach out and trace it. When I look up again, that sexy smirk is curling on his lips.

He leans impossibly closer, and it takes all my power not to close my eyes and moan, dizzy from him. Gaze darkening, he brands me without ever touching me.

"You," he breathes. I feel it against my lips.

I'm still too hypnotized by him to remember what we were talking about.

"Excuse me?"

"You," he repeats, that beautiful smirk growing to a full-on grin that makes my heart race.

I point at my chest, confused. "Me?"

"Yes, you. I'm taking you on a date."

It takes a second for what he's saying to register. I fall back on my heels, but he reaches out and grabs my elbow, preventing me from moving back. I wish he wouldn't because I can't think straight and process what he's telling me when he's standing this close.

Closing my eyes, I take a deep breath because the ball of panic will come. I can't go on a date. "Logan—"

"Eyes on me."

When I do, I'm trapped again in jade pools, lost in the specs of earthy brown. He cups the side of my face, his thumb briefly brushing over my lower lip. The panic hasn't surfaced yet. I'm not sure if it's because I'm in shock or if Logan is chasing it away.

"It's me, pretty girl." Like I need the reminder. I know who he is, and I know what he isn't. I'm safe. "Let me take a beautiful woman on a date." He tips his chin. "As friends, of course. Maria's babysitting. The girls are happy. Take a night. Let me show you what it feels like."

There's a voice screaming in my head, *I don't want just friends*. And that's the only voice causing my fear.

I'm not supposed to want this. It's dangerous. My heart won't take it, and I'll break again.

Wordless, I shake my head, desperate to feel the guard coming down, to feel the foundation of a wall, anything to protect myself. Nothing comes. I'm left open to all the elements of Logan King. I grip his hand as it still traces circles on my face with his thumb.

"Let someone take care of you for a change. Let someone do it right. And fuck, just for tonight, I'm asking for you to let it be me."

There's a pleading in his voice. It doesn't have to be him to show me, but I want it to be.

My heart always did yearn for punishment.

Most of all, I want to. We spend most of our free nights together on the porch, but there's something about having a night with Logan, alone and away from home, that makes my insides somersault.

And like he said, it's as friends. Just two friends hanging out. But my stupid heart doesn't register it that way.

Feeling my lips tilt until my cheeks hurt, I agree with a nod. "Okay. For tonight, you can wine and dine me."

His laugh under his breath makes my skin tingle. "There she is."

"But Logan, it better be good. I have high expectations now."

He presses a chaste kiss to the top of my head and steps away, leaving only warm air in his wake. "Nothing but the best for you, baby."

Excitement builds in my chest until I'm giddy, but I smother it, not wanting to seem too enthusiastic. I haven't lost all dating etiquette. I'm not a teenager anymore. But fuck, I really want to stomp my feet and squeal like one.

He backs away towards his house. "You have an hour."

"If you're late you can't blame traffic," I joke, swaying on my feet because my limbs can't stay still anymore.

"An hour."

"Wait," I call after him. "What should I wear?"

His lips twitch with amusement. "Beth, wear a damn black sack, you'll still look beautiful."

I roll my eyes. "Save the compliments for later, King. Seriously, where are you taking me?"

He shrugs, taking another step back.

"Logan," I groan. "Give me a clue."

He shrugs again.

Infuriating.

"Fine, I'll wear something hideous and embarrass you." I'm on my way to find my sexiest outfit.

Another shrug. "You'll still be fucking breath-taking."

"Compliments for later, remember? And I'm going to need so many to make up for this."

Throwing my head back, I almost scream before stomping back to my house, but it's all an act because my stomach is in knots, anticipation making every nerve in my body tingle.

"Beth."

I spin around, smiling despite myself. With bated breath, I wait for him to tell me where we're going.

He wipes the threatening smile from his lips with his thumb, his eyes drinking me in head to toe and back again. "Nothing, pretty girl. Just looking."

I'm sitting on a mountain of clothes when Molly and Eden appear at the doorway of my bedroom. Concerned about the pathetic pile I've fallen into, they take in my disheveled state: hair neither up nor down because I couldn't decide, a dress pooling at my waist with a skirt underneath because, again, I couldn't decide, only one shoe on, and sweat forming on my brow. I'm an indecisive mess.

I blow out a breath as I look over at them. It's not below me to beg for help, but I don't need to. They're at my side and sitting in my clothes with me.

Molly crosses her legs under her and picks at the items of clothing. "We heard there's an emergency."

I don't ask, but I'm assuming Cora told Molly and the message was passed on. Being the friends they are, they knew I would need all the help I could get.

"It's hopeless. I don't date. Or at least I haven't in a really long time. And I never imagined going on one because I promised myself I wouldn't. I know we're going as friends so we're basically just hanging out. We do that all the time. But why won't my hair sit straight, and why do I suddenly have nothing to wear?"

Eden looks past me to Molly. "She's rambling. It's worse than I thought."

Molly nudges me playfully before standing and reaching out her hands to help me up. Forcing me to sit on the bed, she gets to work on taming my unruly hair. My hair is never unruly. It's the *I'm-going-on-a-date-with-Logan* nerves that's causing the static. And it's not just my hair. I've felt the static all over my body since he stood too close to me, and I needed to drag myself away from pressing up on my tiptoes and kissing him.

I attempt to fall back on the bed, defeated, but Molly pushes me back up to sit straight. She presses her palm against my cheek, smiling, her eyes soft. "You're going on a date."

I can't help but smile back.

I'm going on a date.

Baby steps.

Relaxing as she begins her work, the nervous energy swirling in my blood warms into something resembling excitement.

Eden is busy reorganizing my wardrobe as she assesses my options.

She scurries over and runs her hands along my bare legs. "At least buy me dinner first."

"You shaved," she deadpans.

"This morning." I didn't shave for a date.

"I really wish you hadn't."

"Why?"

"Those boys have a history of making women's underwear disappear," Molly explains. I look between them, bewildered. "Seriously. I think Archer got me pregnant by winking at me."

Not surprised.

"We're going as friends," I remind them, but my blood boils anyway at the thought.

Eden scoffs and ties her locks of red hair back from her face. She's getting to work. "Don't we all."

Nothing is happening between me and Logan.

Nothing.

Zilch.

My heart is beating out my chest and my body betrays me when he's near, but that's a crush, right?

Right.

Who the hell am I trying to fool?

It's not Molly and Eden. No, they're looking at me like I'm a moth about to come very close to a flame.

They know Logan. They know that if you have a pulse then you're not immune to him. Nobody is safe around that man.

Eden holds up a simple black dress, it's one every woman needs in their wardrobe. It's sexy and classy all in one. It's exactly what I should wear for a first date. But this isn't a real date. I'm going out with a friend. And right now, all I can see is how easily his hand can slip under it, or how I could hold it around my waist.

"No dresses," I blurt in a panic. "Jeans. Something with lots of buttons. A straitjacket might be appropriate."

Eden eyes the dress before understanding washes over her face. She slips it on the hanger and puts it back in the wardrobe where it belongs. "Honey, you are so fucked."

Molly laughs at my side. "Literally."

I blow out a long breath and fan my clammy skin with the collar of my sweater. Noticing my unease, Eden offers a warm smile and agrees, "Jeans and a straitjacket. I'm on it."

Those girls are miracle workers.

They left five minutes ago, and I feel like one of Molly's wedding cakes after she's done decorating it. She hugged me and wished me luck. Eden slapped my ass and told me I looked hot.

I'll take hot.

We couldn't find a straitjacket in my wardrobe, but at least I have dark blue jeans. Eden handed me a pair of high heels and I threw them back at her.

I'm not falling tonight.

Hannah joined my rescue mission at some stage and picked out the cream camisole I'm wearing under my brown leather jacket. The heeled ankle boots are gorgeous, but comfortable.

Molly sprayed something in my hair, then Eden took over and I thanked the heavens I have a hair stylist as a best friend because with some magic, my hair isn't poking out in all directions. Instead, loose curls fall over my shoulders.

With smoky eyes and glossed lips, I'm a put together, hyperventilating mess.

"You look beautiful, Mom."

Hannah lies on the bed, her feet kicked up behind her.

"Thanks, baby."

"Are you and Logan dating now?" she asks, and I swear I see the shimmer of hope in her eyes.

"No."

"But you're going on a date."

"As friends." I'm not sure if I'm trying to convince her or remind myself.

"It would be cool if you did. I love Logan. He's the best."

My heart expands in my chest.

I take a seat beside her at the edge of the bed. Her head falls onto my lap as I stroke my fingers through her hair.

"Thanks, I guess," I say slowly. "But you and Isabel are all I need."

She squints and her brows pull together. It's that look she gets when she morphs into an old woman with wisdom far beyond her years.

"You know someday I'm going to be a librarian and Isabel will run away to join the circus." I can't help the laugh because that might not be far from the truth. "But we're going to grow up, Mom. Someday we won't live here, and you'll need someone to cook for."

Tears burn the back of my eyes. No matter what, I will always need my girls, and even when they don't like hearing it, they will always need their mom. Part of me can't wait for the future she has planned and another part of me dreads it.

"How are you only eight?"

"Nine next month," she reminds me.

"Right." I kiss the top of her head. "I promise if I'm ever going to date someone, you'll be the first to know."

Her nose scrunches up like she's smelling something foul. "I didn't say anyone. Just Logan."

Hannah is team Logan.

Noted.

"You're the best thing that ever happened to me."

She smiles with teeth still too big for her mouth. It's adorable. "I know. You tell me every night before I go to sleep."

Because I mean it every night and she deserves to hear it.

A tap at the door has our heads snapping up from our bubble. It's Maria. "Logan is downstairs." She holds out a hand to Hannah. "Want to help me get your sister ready for bed?"

"Sure." She jumps off the bed and runs to Maria, but not without saying, "Love you, Mom."

"Love you too, baby girl."

Maria flashes me a familiar smile. "Have a good night."

And then they're gone.

I can't help but wish they weren't because now I have to go on a date with Logan.

"I can do this." I chant under my breath until I reach the top of the stairs.

And there he is.

Looking as gorgeous as ever, only tonight he's forgone the jeans and T-shirt for charcoal slacks and a white button down.

I'm drooling again. I know it.

As I reach the bottom step, he places a kiss on my cheek. "You are beautiful."

"Thank you." I eye the bouquet of flowers he's holding. "Flowers? Really?"

"I don't usually go the cheesy route, but you've never been on a real first date. I wanted to make it as cheesy as I could."

I take the flowers from him and inhale the scent. "Great start. You going to serenade me, too?"

He tuts. "That's third date behavior."

"I always thought third dates were about getting in each other's pants?"

"After the serenading."

"Of course. Sorry, my inexperience is showing."

"There's time to teach you."

After putting the flowers in a vase, I follow him outside where the damn motorcycle awaits.

"You can't ride a bike in what you're wearing."

He slips his arms into his leather jacket which he somehow makes work with slacks.

"Why not?"

Why not?

I don't know.

"You're really going to make me get on that thing, aren't you?"

He simply raises his eyebrows, his answer in the defiant grin he casts me.

I try to glare at him, but my cheeks are sore from smiling. "Fine," I huff, stepping forward to grab the helmet.

When he climbs on, I hold his shoulders and sit behind him.

In an instant, I go back in time. By how his body tenses, I know he's back there too.

He squeezes my hand when I wrap it around his waist. "Ready, pretty girl?"

"Ready."

THIRTY-SIX

Life has a twisted sense of humor.

This same woman was on the back of my bike ten years ago, and looking back, we were riding into an unknown future. Now here I am, taking her on a date. Even if I tell myself it's as her friend.

I've decided to write that word on a piece of paper later and burn it.

With her here, I can't help but wonder how things would have been if our timing was different.

I guess I'll never know.

Tonight, it doesn't matter because tonight I have her all to myself, and that's what matters.

Fuck everything else. Fuck the questions I'll never have the answers to.

Twenty minutes after leaving the house, we're on the peak of the mountain with the sun just setting in the distance. The violent torrent of the waterfalls makes it hard to hear my thoughts, but looking at Beth, I see the amazement in her eyes as we climb the steps to the restaurant.

"This place is incredible. How have I lived here for three months

261

and not known about it?"

"You haven't gone on a date."

She glares at me as I take her hand.

Inside the restaurant, the open-concept kitchen is partially visible, offering glimpses of skilled chefs preparing dishes of fresh, local ingredients. The bar features a polished concrete countertop. Reclaimed wood walls and floor-to-ceiling windows create a natural charm that has made it popular with tourists all year round.

But it's the artwork and portraits by local artists lining the walls that catches Beth's eye.

"Your photographs could be up there."

Her cheeks flush pink. "Not likely."

"Why not? I've seen your work."

She shakes her head, still focused on the art. "I haven't photographed anything but my children in a really long time. I still love to see other's work, though."

With a flash of sorrow in her eyes, I decide not to press the issue. Not yet at least.

A moment later, we're greeted by the hostess. "Welcome, Mr. King."

Beth nudges me and raises an eyebrow, intrigued by the attention we're receiving. "Mr. King? Do you come here often?"

I chuckle, escorting her through the restaurant. "You could say that."

Her face pales, and I immediately realize how it sounds. "I've never taken anyone else here on a date. It's not that."

Another flush of her cheeks and her eyes cast to the ground to hide it, but I catch it before she can.

We're led to the best table in the house, a prime spot overlooking the waterfalls. Beth's eyes widen as she takes in the breath-taking view, and she turns to me, her curiosity piqued. "It's incredible in here."

"You can thank Molly for the interior. She has a knack for those things."

It takes a moment before her mouth falls open. "Molly? Holy shit, you own this place?"

"Not just me. It's me and my brothers."

Her eyes scan the restaurant again.

"This is amazing. Anything else you own you want to tell me about?"

"Some." She shakes her head, imploring me to go on. "We've been lucky. About five years ago we set up King Industries and we've had some successful business ventures."

She leans back in her chair with a sigh. "What an impressive way to start a first date."

She remains a little wide-eyed and fascinated as we order our drinks. "You know, you're really taking the whole 'wide-eyed tourist' thing to the next level," I tease.

"Oh, come on. You can't blame me for being impressed. This place is amazing."

"I never said it wasn't. It cost enough," I reply with a smirk. "But try to act a little more nonchalant You're making me look bad."

She narrows her eyes, a smile playing at the corners of her mouth. "Alright, Mr. King. How's this for nonchalant?" She leans back in her seat, trying to look aloof but failing miserably as she nearly tips over.

Reaching out, I catch her before she falls. "You might want to work on that," I say, smirking. "You almost made a scene."

She laughs. "Well, it wouldn't be a proper date if I didn't embarrass myself at least once, right?"

"Pace yourself, woman. There's still plenty of time."

We fall into easy conversation just like we always do, but when the food arrives, I've lost her completely. Her eyes roll back in her head, and she makes noises I've only heard women moan when they're under me.

"Good?" I ask, unable to take my eyes off her.

Another groan of pleasure. "Too good."

And that's it.

That's all I get.

Conversation ceases until she's finished with what I can only describe as a food orgasm.

Life should be experienced how Beth is eating her food.

Sensing my eyes on her, her fork halts midway to her mouth.

"Please, continue. Watching you is fascinating."

She shakes her head with a smile.

The vibration of a plane flying over the restaurant is the only thing to distract her.

"Another plane?" she asks, her voice filled with curiosity as she watches it fly overhead.

"Private charters. It's a thing here."

"Interesting." She takes another bite, slowly savoring it. "Tell me something else."

"What do you want to know?"

"Tell me something that no one else knows."

I lean back, pressing my lips together as I ponder over her question. Deciding on something that won't have her running out of the restaurant, I keep it light. "Promise you won't laugh," I say, raising a brow at her.

She snorts in response, a small smile playing on her lips. "Promise."

"This confession comes with a disclaimer. When I tell you, please try to keep in mind that I was five years old."

Intrigued, she leans forward in her chair. "Noted."

I take a deep breath. "My mother was a ballerina before I was born, and she was obsessed with the ballet. When my father was gone… God knows where, probably prison, she used to play these video tapes of different ballets."

She squints at me. "That's not so bad."

"No, but I wanted to join the ballet… for a full year. Practiced every day in the living room."

For a moment, there's silence. Then, her soft snort turns into a full-on chuckle, her shoulders shaking as she tries to contain her laughter.

"I'm sorry," she wheezes out. "I just… you? Ballet?"

I try to keep a straight face but fail. "You said you wouldn't laugh."

She throws a napkin over her face. "I'm not." Her shaking body says otherwise. When she pulls the napkin away, there's a stream of tears on her cheeks. "I'm not laughing at you. It's just… It's surprising."

"Well, there you go. One fun fact nobody else knows."

"Wait, did you ever…?"

"God, no," I say quickly. "And if you ever tell anyone, I'll have to break out my leotard."

She's laughing so loud, people look over from their tables. I ignore them because fuck it, that laugh should be heard.

"Please tell me you actually have a leotard."

"Unfortunately, not."

She shrugs, her smile still wide. "Now I'm interested."

"Nobody wants to see that. Now, you, on the other hand… you in a leotard is definitely interesting."

She throws the napkin at me. "Shut up."

I close my eyes. "I don't know. I can see it."

She slaps my hand. "Stop picturing me in a leotard." Her hands are on her cheeks when I open my eyes. "My face hurts from laughing." Throwing her head back on the chair, she sighs. "Food and laughter, it's the best kind of stomach ache."

I feel my smile fade because the ache I feel is in my chest. I could sit here all night and watch her. I'm sure I would never get bored.

"Dessert?"

She lights up. "Yes, please."

THIRTY-SEVEN

BETH

Logan winks at me as the table is cleared. The setting sun highlights the angles of his face and my thirsty eyes drink in each one.

"Are you ready to go?" he asks, pulling me out of my musings. "I want to show you something."

I've eaten my weight in food. He will be lucky if he doesn't have to roll me out of here.

"You've got more surprises up your sleeve, Twinkle Toes?"

"Yes, and Beth? Don't ever call me Twinkle Toes again, or you'll find yourself over my knee."

Heat crawls its way up my neck. Not just because of his words, but the waiter is still clearing the table, and even he squirms.

When the waiter leaves and my heart climbs out of my throat, I raise an eyebrow. "Did you really have to say that?"

"Want me to do it here with everyone watching?"

I swallow. Hard. "I think they have enough of a view," I reply, getting to my feet before he makes good on his threat. "So, where are we headed?"

He reaches for my hand, lacing our fingers together. There's a softness in his gaze. It's endearing and somehow, incredibly sexy. It makes my heart race in a way nothing else can.

"Just a little farther," he says, guiding me towards the path that leads away from the restaurant. I can hear a waterfall in the distance, its rumble soothing, like a whispered lullaby. I know where we're going, but the anticipation is intoxicating.

As we walk, his fingers gently squeeze mine. It's a small gesture, but it sends a bolt of electricity through me.

He's clawing deeper under my skin. And the scariest part? I'm letting him. I'm not even putting up a fight.

As we continue walking, the sound of cascading water grows louder. My pulse quickens in tandem. Logan has an arm securely around my waist, guiding me towards the water's shimmering curtain.

I hear the murmur of other people around us, the distant sound of laughter and conversation. Yet, as we approach the waterfall, I feel like we've stepped into our own private corner of the world.

When I think we're just going to stand and watch, Logan takes another step.

"What are you... Wait, are we going behind it?" I ask, eyes wide. The waterfall, although beautiful, looks intense, and I'm not exactly dressed for a swim.

That look in his eyes tells me he's up to something. "Trust me?"

I nod.

Before I have the chance to voice any other reservations, he's guiding me towards the curtain of water. I gasp, close my eyes, and follow. The cold spray instantly chills my skin, but then he's pulling me through the veil, and surprisingly, we're not soaked.

Behind the waterfall, a cavernous space has been carved out by nature. The thunderous sound of water hitting water fills the air around us, creating a barrier that isolates us from the rest of the world.

In here, it's *our* world.

Our world is breathtaking.

When I've finished gawking and close my gaping mouth, Logan pulls me close. "What do you think?"

"I... it's amazing," I stammer, my words not doing it justice.

The enchantment of the space draws me in completely, but something on the other side catches my attention. My eyes are drawn to a photographer capturing a bride and groom on their wedding day. The scene is undoubtedly beautiful—the bride glowing, and the groom elated. It brings a pang of nostalgia, a memory of a life once lived. But there's something off.

"See that?" I point. "The photographer should change her angle. The light from the sun setting is better from the west."

He peers in the direction I'm pointing, a bemused smile playing on his lips. "I'll take your word for it." His hand squeezes mine gently, bringing my attention back to him. "Just saying... it could be you."

I try to hide the memories from playing so visibly on my face and shake my head with a smile. "Who? The photographer or the woman in the white dress?"

Teasing, he presses his fingers into the curve of my waist. "Jesus, Beth, you move fast. I mean, you haven't even let me feel you up yet." My laugh echoes around us, blending with the roar of the waterfall, his humor dispelling the wistful thoughts.

Despite his jest, his words reverberate in my head, creating ripples in the calm pool of my mind.

Both of those women... the one with the camera and the one in the beautiful dress feel like people from a different time in a very different life.

∞∞∞∞

The sun has long since set, and the stars above are brighter than the town lights we're overlooking from where Logan parked the bike. When we got here, we switched positions so I could sit up front with his legs on either side of me. He paled when I asked if I could ride the bike and instantly shot the idea down.

Someday.

His voice cuts through the gentle hum of the wind. "Your turn to tell me something no one else knows."

I lean back against his chest, my hands still gripping the handles as I take a steadying breath, or maybe I need the breath because the feel of his body against mine is warm and intimate.

Too intimate and not enough.

"Promise you won't laugh," I say, echoing his earlier condition.

"I'm not promising anything. You laughed at me. I'm going to laugh at you."

I roll my eyes, a smile pulling at the corners of my mouth despite the fluttering anxiety in my stomach. "Fair enough," I agree before

268

looking back at him from over my shoulder. "I want a tattoo."

He doesn't laugh. I'm not even sure he's breathing. Instead, he stiffens behind me.

The lack of response is more unnerving than the anticipated laughter. "You? You want a tattoo?"

I nod, well aware of the irony.

"Seriously?"

"I've been thinking about it for a while."

He blinks.

Then blinks again.

"What?"

"I'm waiting for the punchline here."

A little offended, I say, "There is none."

His silence stretches, the only sound between us being our rhythmic breathing. Then there's the slightest twitch of his lips before he runs his hand over his beard. "Where do you want it?"

I stand and put my foot on the seat before pushing the hem of my jeans past my ankle. The skin is no longer raised or red, but the scar is still visible. "Here."

He looks at me for a long second before reaching out and running his thumb along the marked flesh. Even that simple touch has my heart racing in my chest. A burn radiates from his touch like he's branding himself there.

His shoulders tense. "What happened?" he asks, his voice low.

I'm glad he doesn't look at me when I lie. "Childhood fall." The words leave a bitter taste on my tongue, but it's a wound I refuse to reopen.

Not tonight.

His thumb pauses its gentle tracing, but I still feel the tension coiling in his body.

"I know you're busy," I say, trying to inject a casual air into the conversation. "But do you think one of the guys could do it?"

Logan's grip tightens around my ankle, a silent, unspoken protest. The look he shoots me is one I've come to know, one of stubborn determination, a possessiveness I feel all the way to my core.

"There's nobody inking you but me," he says, his tone leaving no room for argument. His hold only leaves my ankle to wrap around my waist, guiding me to sit again. When I do, he gathers my hair in his hand and drapes it over my shoulder. His breath fans over my neck as his mouth grazes the shell of my ear. "Busy or not, pretty girl," he starts, his voice edging into a growl, "I don't give a damn. No one touches you but me. Especially not with a needle. Not Kyle, not anyone."

My breath catches in my throat as I shiver against his chest. Licking my dry lips, I bite down. Anything to stop me from squirming in his lap. No matter how hard I try, I can't dampen the flutter of excitement low in my stomach or the warmth spreading lower down.

"Understood?" His voice drops, filled with a tension that should frighten me, but it doesn't. It exhilarates me.

I swallow hard and manage to nod, my voice a mere whisper when I respond, "Understood. You're the only one I trust to do it."

There's a moment of silence before he speaks again. "Good because there's no one you don't trust marking your skin. That's a promise."

His grip around my waist tightens slightly, sending a wave of goosebumps over my skin.

The intensity of his statement leaves me breathless. My body leans into him instinctively, craving his protection, his calm.

When his chest vibrates at my back, I tip my head back to look at him. "Why are you laughing?"

"How long before you pass out?"

I think about it. "Thirty seconds, give or take a few."

He kisses the top of my head. "I should probably get you home."

I inhale the scent of leather and spice, and close my eyes, not wanting to leave his warmth just yet. "Five more minutes."

"Five more minutes," he agrees.

And it's in those five more minutes, right here, on this bike, surrounded in everything Logan, I feel a strange sense of home.

THIRTY-EIGHT

"Thanks for tonight." It's not enough, but it's all I have. "I didn't realize how badly I needed it."

When the wind picks up, my hair blows across my face. Like second nature, he reaches out and tucks it behind my ear.

"Thank you."

"What are you thanking me for?" I say, but my voice is shaky as his thumb brushes my cheek. His touch burns as if it's branded there.

"For allowing me to be the one to take you."

The air thickens and with it, my lungs set flame. My heart is about to break free of my chest, and my tongue is like sandpaper against the roof of my mouth. When I lick my lips, his heated stare follows.

What's happening?

I don't notice as he motions closer or how my eyes close when his scent invades every inch of me. I swallow it, allowing it to coat through my veins until my skin tingles with anticipation.

Oh God, he's going to kiss me.

And I'm going to let him.

Probably even going to kiss him back.

"Fucking beautiful," he whispers so close I feel his breath against my face.

There's a brief touch of his lips against mine and then it's gone, the moment short lived when I hear the familiar cry of a certain toddler.

It's like a bucket of ice water to my feverish skin.

Still dizzy, I steady myself and spin around.

Maria is standing at the door with Isabel in her arms. Her cheeks are red, and tears soak her cheeks.

"Beth, I'm so sorry. She just woke like this. I think she has a fever."

Logan is hot on my heels when I rush up the steps. Isabel's arms are already outstretched, and when she tucks her head in the crook of my neck, I feel exactly how warm she is.

"Hey, baby girl. It's okay. Momma's here. Let's get you some medicine and find out what's going on."

In a worn-out voice, she says, "Hi, Loggie."

He dries her cheeks. "Hey, Isabelly. You not feeling good?"

"Na uh." She shakes her head before resting it back on my shoulder.

Inside, Hannah appears at the top of the stairs. I swear she turns a darker shade of green with every step she takes.

"Mom, I don't feel too good."

"Come here, baby."

She reaches me just before she vomits… all over me.

"I'm sorry," she cries.

Maria gags.

Isabel screams again.

Logan has probably run away.

"You can go, Maria. Thanks so much for looking after them."

Her eyes are watering. "I'm sorry. I would offer to help, but my limit is vomit."

I laugh despite my soaked clothes. "It's fine, honestly. I can handle it."

She's grabbing her jacket and leaving in the next breath.

"Let's get cleaned up," I say, wiping the back of my hand against the sheen of sweat breaking out across my brow.

"Why don't you come over here, Isabelly?" Logan reaches for her, and she goes.

"You don't need to stay. This isn't included in date night."

"Sure it is." He runs a hand over the top of Hannah's head. "You two get cleaned up. I'll get a cool cloth for Isabel."

His offer of help is like a punch to the chest in the best way.

I blow out a breath, relief making my shoulders drop. "Thank you."

"Divide and conquer, pretty girl," he says as he disappears down the hall while rubbing Isabel's back.

I think she's already asleep.

Looking down at my stained clothes, I can't help but laugh.

I press a kiss to Hannah's forehead. "Come on, baby girl. Let's divide and conquer."

∞∞∞∞

After finally getting the girls' temperatures down, I changed from my vomit coated clothes into sleep shorts and a T-shirt.

I go downstairs, surprised to hear music floating from the kitchen.

He's still here, and it hits me that he never left us. The smile creeps to my lips before I can stop it.

It's not until I open the kitchen door that I realize my feet are planted on the floor.

The song.

The familiar melody brings instant tears to my eyes just as he turns with a smile of his own.

Nothing Can Change This Love by *Sam Cooke* floats from the speakers and straight to my chest like an arrow.

He takes a step toward me. "It's after midnight. Happy birthday, pretty girl."

Shit, I'm going to cry.

It's been ten years and he remembered what I told him about this song.

Not only did he remember, but there's a gift bag sitting on the counter.

"Who told you?" I ask, but it comes out choked.

That's a silly question. I know exactly who told him.

"I might have had a little girl whisper in my ear."

Another step and he takes my hand, pulling me into the center of the kitchen.

Closing my eyes, I let the music seep into my pores. "I don't want this song to end."

"I have it on repeat. Open your gift."

"You didn't need to do this. None of this. You didn't need to stay. I don't need birthday—"

He presses a finger over my mouth, keeping my words trapped in my throat.

Smiling so wide my face hurts, I cast him a weary gaze as I peek inside the gift bag.

"I'm no good at wrapping," he explains, his expression adorable and nothing like the man I spent a night having filthy thoughts about.

"It's perfect," I whisper, removing the lavender paper.

And there it sits in a box.

A camera.

Not just any camera.

The camera of my dreams.

"You deserve to live the dream."

"Logan," I breathe. Words won't do this justice, so I wrap my arms around his neck. A deep chuckle in my ear and his hands are on my waist, holding me against his chest. "Thank you."

"You're welcome."

After a long minute, he pulls away while never letting go of my hand.

The song plays again.

"I told you I was going to take you on a real date. Dance with me."

My skin zings with anticipation and my lungs burn for air, but I take that step toward him.

I leap.

I leap right into his arms because with him holding me I know nothing can touch me.

My eyes follow his hand as it caresses over my shoulder, down my arm until his fingers interlock with mine. His other hand holds me with a firm pressure on my lower back. A quiet gasp leaves me as he pulls me closer, my front flush with his, and he begins to move. I can't take my eyes off him when my hips sway against his hand.

"You're not stepping on my toes. You sure you didn't take those ballet classes?"

This man can dance.

He answers me with a smirk, as if the thought is absurd. He's just confident in everything he does.

His thumb slips under my T-shirt and motions circles on my lower back. My skin erupts in goosebumps, but I don't care. I can't deny the effect he has on me no more than I can ignore the sun rising in a matter of hours.

"You're blushing." He traces his thumb over my stained cheeks. "It's beautiful. I love how you can't hide what you're feeling."

When his thumb pulls my lip from the hold of my bite, I hold back a moan.

I want his lips on mine. I want to put an end to this curiosity. I want to know how he feels.

But I can't ignore the part of me that is screaming, "Please don't kiss me."

Do I want to know?

Do I want to know everything that could have been?

Reading my mind like Logan always does, he says, "We don't need to know. Not tonight."

He leans his head against mine and his hand returns to the base of my spine.

Disappointment makes my heart sink into my stomach, but it doesn't last long when he twirls me under his arm. A giddy laugh bursts from my chest before I'm back against the heat of his body. I rest my head on his shoulder and relax into the comfort his body gives.

I fit here like a jigsaw piece long missing.

The song ends.

Our dance doesn't.

A second of silence and the song repeats.

We remain trapped in this beautiful bubble, and I never want to leave.

I'm not sure how many times the song repeats, but he never lets me go.

It could be minutes. It could be hours. But the sun isn't far from rising when we finally part.

He leaves me with a kiss to the top of my head, and I go to bed with my fingers on my lips like he's engraved there without ever touching them.

THIRTY-NINE

"Beth, please don't die in my coffee shop. It will be terrible for business." Molly eyes me as I rest my head in my arms with a groan. Even that simple movement causes every joint to scream at me.

"I'm fine," I persist, my words muffled against my arms. "I got a cold from the girls. I won't die from a cold." I don't know if she hears me because I'm too busy trying to suppress a cough. I'm wheezing like I've run a marathon.

"How long have you been like this?"

All week, but it was easily disguised before today.

"A day or two."

"Liar."

Head colds can kiss my ass.

I managed to get through the morning rush in one piece, but now I have time to sit, I can't help but notice the excruciating burn across my back every time I take a deep breath, and my throat feels like I'm swallowing shards of glass. I clench my jaw shut, hoping she doesn't notice the sound of my teeth chattering.

"That's it." I raise my head just as she meets my watery eyes. "You're sick, and I'm making the call. Go home. You need to rest."

"I can't go home. It's not lunch time yet. I can't leave you on your own."

"I'll call Maria in. Besides, you're useless to me in your state. Having you drop dead while serving a chicken wrap isn't going to do my business any favors." She props her hand on her hip, but humor glistens in her eyes.

"Who knows, it might become a tourist attraction. Lots of people are into that kind of thing. You can tell them that my ghost haunts the place. And let's be honest, if I die while serving a chicken wrap, I'm going to haunt the place. I was hoping for my death to be more eventful."

She rolls her eyes before tossing the towel at me. "Go. Home."

I sigh, puffing my cheeks as the door opens and Logan, Archer, and Skip walk in.

"Fine," I agree. "After I get their order."

"Ladies," they dip their chin like a clone of each other. Logan and Archer might not be Skip's biological children, but he sure has done a good job of passing on his mannerisms. It's uncanny.

Archer leans over the counter and kisses Molly's cheek. She accepts it, but her eyes drop, and she immediately begins fidgeting. I can't be sure, but I swear there's a brief flash of hurt over Archer's features before he adjusts his mask to smile at me.

"Boys," I greet them.

"Morning," they say in unison.

Logan is the last to sit, and I don't miss the slight brush of his thumb along my lower back.

I smile at him and whisper, "Morning, Twinkle Toes."

The look he casts my way makes it clear that his threat of putting me over his knee was serious.

He doesn't miss it either as I shiver, and the heat rushing to my cheeks has nothing to do with how sick I feel. I glance at him over my shoulder before grabbing my order book from my apron.

I only have the order book to distract myself and hope he doesn't see a lone tear sliding down my cheek from my burning eyes. I already know what they're going to order.

These men are as predictable as they are gorgeous, but they look at the menu regardless. I place an inner bet. Which one will surprise me today?

Skip smiles at me, placing the menu back on the table. "I think it'll be the pancakes all round."

No surprises today, then.

"Coming right up."

I turn, almost escaping without one of them noticing the sweat

277

breaking out on my hairline, but Logan has been eyeing me since he walked in here.

"Beth?"

Shit.

I close my eyes before forcing my lips into a smile, praying my teeth don't start clacking again.

"Yep?" I spin around, ignoring the pain as I do.

"You good, pretty girl?"

"You don't look so good," Skip joins in.

Never. Not once in the history of time have men been so observant.

"I'm good," I chirp, feigning cheer, even as it dissipates and begins sweating through every pore.

Molly is right. I need to leave. My eyes are heavy, and a dull throb is beginning to bloom across the bridge of my nose.

"She's not okay," Molly says.

When I glare at her, she pokes her tongue out like a child.

"She's sick, but she won't go home."

Logan gets to his feet. "What the fuck, Beth?"

My head snaps back and forth between them like I'm watching a tennis match. "I was just taking your order, and I'm leaving. Relax."

But I'm not sure if they don't hear me or if I didn't speak loud enough because they're still talking over me. Then the call of my name rings in my ears, but my vision has suddenly blurred, and everything spins.

I think the ground is coming up to meet me, but an arm around my waist keeps me planted on my feet.

"You falling for me, pretty girl?"

I'm molded to his chest when my vision finally clears.

Logan's smile drops, his fingers digging into my waist.

Ouch.

Although, I don't think he's hurting me. I'm just so sore. Everywhere.

His jaw ticks. "You're hot."

I smile, holding my head back. God, it hurts so bad. "Am I? Thanks, Loggie."

"That's not what I meant, and you know it. You're burning up, woman. I'm getting you to a doctor."

Straightening my spine, I step away. "I'm not going to the doctor. It's the same cold the girls had."

His brows knit together.

I don't have the energy to argue with this man today.

"He's right." I think it's Archer. "You don't look good."

"I'm not going to the doctor," I persist, keeping my feet firm on the ground. I need to get my girls, give them dinner, bathe them, and maybe then I might fall into bed.

His shoulders slump as he runs a frustrated hand through his hair. "Fine, but you're going home."

"Fine," I agree with a grunt. "I was going home anyway."

He reaches around my waist, standing far too close. "Really? Have you ever heard of personal space? I'm burning up and you want a hug?"

Scowl still set in place, he stands back with my apron dangling from his hand.

"Oh."

He swaps my apron for my purse and grabs my hand. Delirious, and I'm pretty sure I'm on the brink of vomiting, I swallow and wave goodbye to everyone as Logan leads me out onto the street. He's still holding my hand as we cross over to the square and away from my car. I try to pull him back, but I don't have the energy.

"Hey, caveman, my car is back there."

"I'll get one of the guys to drop it off."

He must sense my hesitation when he spins around and faces me so abruptly, I stumble again. "I'm taking you home."

He eyes me head to toe. Without a word of warning, he lowers himself before wrapping one arm behind my knees and the other around my back.

I yelp.

It hurts.

"Logan," I grit, glaring at his clenched jaw.

What's he got to be angry about?

I'm the one flailing in his arms as he walks through the square with me towards his truck like I'm nothing more than a sack of potatoes.

"I'm not putting you down, so get comfortable for a minute." I try to kick again. "Fight me on it, baby. I dare you."

I groan into his neck, resting my head on his shoulder to avoid the awkward stares from everyone. Honestly, it feels good not to walk. I might not have made it.

"Logan?" It's Eden's voice but my eyes are already closing. "Is that Beth? Is she okay?"

He doesn't even stop and answers over his shoulder. "She's sick. It could be imminent death."

Fucking drama queen.

I find the strength to lift my head and look at her as my head bobs up and down. "Don't worry, Eden," I shout back at her. "I won't die because I'm sick. Logan here is making sure the only thing I die from today is embarrassment."

FORTY

Chest infection and a "touch of pneumonia". How anyone can have a touch of an illness, I'll never know, but that's what the doctor said. She didn't want to go to him, so I brought the doctor to her.

Cora is keeping the girls for the night. Beth didn't like it, and even shivering, she put up a fight. She eventually relented when the doctor demanded she stay in bed.

She passed out mid-protest. As soon as her head hit the pillow, her eyes fluttered closed, and her teeth finally stopped chattering.

She's a stubborn little thing, I'll give her that. No matter how many times I told her I was going to stay the night, she insisted she was fine. To prove it, she got up to make herself a cup of tea. It quickly resulted in her gasping for breath. How did she get through the day waiting tables in that state?

She wasn't fine. She looked like death warmed up.

Still beautiful as hell, even as she blew her nose for the hundredth time and coughed like her lungs were possessed.

She's not asleep long, maybe an hour, when I finally settle enough to do some work. With the TV on mute, I get to work on admin for the shop. Social media posts are the first to go out. I fucking hate it, but it works. I had someone to do it for me, but they always managed to make it tacky. In the end, I decided the only way to do it right was to do it myself.

Finishing up the last post, I hear a blood-curdling scream from upstairs. Jolting out of the chair, I run, taking two steps of the stairs at a time.

When I come barreling into her room, my heart is racing, heavy panting making my chest heave.

I expect to see her on the floor after a fall, but what I witness is much worse.

Her back arches on the bed before she kicks the sheets off her body with flailing legs.

Fever dreams.

But by the way her face contorts, the tears streaming from the corners of her eyes, and the pleas whispered from her lips, I know these dreams have haunted her before.

Her hands are balled tightly into fists, grabbing the sheets until her knuckles turn white.

I rush to her side, grabbing her by the arms and giving her a firm shake.

"Fuck. Beth, wake up."

Stilling, her body goes rigid, and I step away. The last thing she needs is a man standing over her in the dark.

Her eyes shoot open like repelling magnets, droplets of sweat forming on her hairline and streaking down her neck.

The fever broke, but she's trapped in her head.

Disoriented, she looks around and immediately sits back on the bed, her knees curled up to her chest.

And fuck, if it doesn't break my heart.

Where's the woman giving me sass in my truck just hours ago?

Her eyes are lifeless. Light brown pools search the room until they land on me.

I hold out a hand. "It's okay. It's me, pretty girl."

She seems to register the nickname, and a gut-wrenching sob comes from so deep in her chest, I feel it in my bones.

I want to reach out and hold her.

I want to tell her that nothing can touch her here.

But I don't think that's what she needs, and her body is so still it looks like it would be physically painful to unwind her.

Instead, I choose to take a tentative step forward, and when she doesn't react, I take another. Her body curls farther in on itself, but her shoulders relax back into the bed until I'm sitting on the edge.

Her lashes are dark and wet when she looks over at me, scrubbing the flesh of her palms across her cheeks. "I'm sorry. I must have had a nightmare."

No shit.

I thought people only had nightmares like that in the movies.

"Want to tell me about it?"

Hair stuck to a sweat clad forehead, she shakes her head and whispers, "No."

We stay silent for what seems like forever, allowing her time to catch her breath. Her legs finally straighten, and her next breath is shaky.

"It's stupid, isn't it?" She laughs, but her face soon falls as she glances around the room, her eyes anywhere but on me.

"What?" I ask softly, keeping my distance, but not wanting to.

"After everything, it's a nightmare that causes me to break down. I've been doing really good."

Her calf brushes against my arm so I move an inch closer. I raise my hand to wipe a tear from her cheek with my thumb. Her head tilts, her eyes closing as she relaxes into my touch. My heart drops before beating bruising rhythms against my chest. She doesn't pull away when her eyes open and meet mine.

"Logan," she whimpers, swallowing back her emotions, but a tear slips past her defenses. "I'm so sorry."

My fingers slide into her hair. "What? You think because you're crying tonight, you're weak? You think because a nightmare brings you back in time and you're struggling with it more today than you were yesterday that you're somehow weaker? That's bullshit. You're here. You're fighting. You've got air in your lungs. You do whatever you have to do just to get through the day. If anything, the days you have to fight a little harder are the days you show just how resilient you are. Your strength is unbreakable today just like it was yesterday. You're the fucking strongest person I've ever met. Don't let me hear you say that about yourself again. Do you hear me?"

I feel her body tremble against mine.

"Beth," I urge.

"Yes." She nods before another sob ruptures from her chest.

I can't hold it back anymore. I grab her arms and pull her onto my lap. Her arms lock around my neck like she'll evaporate and disappear if she lets go. "Goddammit, baby. I can't stand to see you hurting like this."

She's hot to the touch, and I know better than to hold her this close when she's sick. She needs to cool down, not my body heat, but her grip is so tight, I couldn't let her go if I wanted to.

And I just don't fucking want to.

After long minutes, my shoulder is wet from her tears, but her sobs have calmed. I run my fingers through her hair. She moans her comfort, relaxing in my arms as her breathing evens to a pace I'm sure she's fallen asleep again.

Her hair is tossed, curling around her shoulders and covering her face.

Her face should never be covered.

Gently, I pull back the curtain of hair so it falls down her back, and she's all but snoring.

Careful not to wake her, I wonder if she would be more comfortable if I just sat here all night with her in my arms because I still don't want to move, and it's the first time I've heard her breathe without a wheeze.

Holding her a little tighter because I can, my eyes drink in every feature. I can't see them, but I know those dimples are there, the curve of her nose, the captivating depths of her closed eyes, the bright brown orbs hidden as she sleeps.

"Hey," I whisper.

"Hmm?" she responds, keeping her eyes shut.

"Time for bed."

Standing, I pull back the blankets and lay her down.

I run my thumb over the outline of her cheekbone. "Goodnight."

Her hand falls and grabs mine as I begin to walk away. "Can you stay?"

My heart jumps into my throat.

I shouldn't.

It's a bad idea.

But my feet won't fucking move. They're like lead, weighed down and keeping me planted.

I can't see her having another nightmare. I might dig Rob from his grave just to piss on his corpse.

Too exhausted to open both her eyes, she peers at me through one. "Please."

How am I going to refuse that?

I dip my chin before kicking off my boots and laying down on the other side, careful to remain on top of the covers and keep the distance I don't want between us.

All I hear is her breath hitch as I rest my head on the pillow.

We don't speak, and I wait until I'm sure she's asleep to finally relax. My eyes grow heavy, but just before I fall into darkness, her finger hooks around mine. It's the smallest touch, but she might as well be everywhere from how my skin heats.

"Get some sleep, pretty girl. I'm not going anywhere."

She releases a long breath. "Thank you, Logan."

FORTY-ONE

BETH

"Babe, open the door."

My heart was pounding, sweat dripping from my temple as my legs gave way, and I sank to the cold tiles on the bathroom floor.

His voice was so calm.

"Open the door, Beth," he repeated, but I couldn't move.

I was frozen, waiting for my limbs to do as I wanted them to.

He was going to get in there. He wouldn't stop until he did. It would be easier if I just let him, but I couldn't fucking move.

With a loud bang, my body vibrated, and my heart felt like it was ready to explode. I wiped the trickle of sweat from my forehead only to realize it was blood.

His voice was getting louder, angrier, and I still couldn't move.

Why couldn't I move?

He was going to wake Hannah.

I needed to move.

"Open the fucking door, Beth. Now."

With a trembling, blood-soaked hand, I reached for the doorknob, but I was a second too slow, and he kicked it in.

Eyes as black as coal, he took a menacing step forward and gently closed the door behind him.

We didn't want to wake Hannah, after all.

I'd never been more thankful for this big house and how she was sleeping peacefully on the other side.

She couldn't hear from there.

I saw my future in his eyes. I saw a room with no doors. With no way out.

I did the only thing I could. I braced myself and stifled the sobs. I smothered the screams and went somewhere else. Somewhere where there wasn't pain. Where I was safe. Where Hannah was safe.

The anticipation always made the first blow the worst.

I was proud of myself when only a strangled moan escaped. Hannah wouldn't hear that.

I saw it on a tv show earlier that a good way to deal with trauma is to create a safe place in your mind. Somewhere you can go when it becomes too much. When you think everything is going to cave in, and you can't breathe. When you feel the least safe, you can dive into the depths of your mind, take a breath, and you're safe.

Just like that.

Magic.

Those people on the tv said it was good for anxiety, but I was willing to give it a try.

So, as I felt his breath on my face before he began another onslaught on my body, I closed my eyes, took a deep breath, and I searched. I searched for anything to make me forget the pain my body was being subjected to. I wanted to cling to an ounce of sanity as he beat me until I could smell blood and his knuckles crunched.

I saw my beautiful baby girl. I saw Hannah smiling, running towards me after picking daisies from the grass. I felt her arms around my neck.

Just the sight of her evened my breathing.

But it was my job to keep her safe, and I didn't want her image in my mind when her father was inflicting such a brutal punishment for a wrong answer.

Then I heard his belt buckle unclasp so I searched again, and I searched hard.

I sorted through my memories like a Rolodex and tried to remember the last time I felt safe.

I went to every corner of my mind, desperate for an answer.

I was close to giving up when there he was.

Emerald green eyes meeting mine, a warm smile under a dark beard. My fingers itched to feel it. His hand on my lower back as he moved me to safety and out of the way of the passing cars. His chuckle as he laughed at one my jokes I couldn't remember, but I was pretty sure it wasn't funny. The tingle I felt when he tucked a lock of hair behind my ear. The burn on my lips when I was desperate to feel him, to know what he tasted like.

I saw him.

I saw a stranger from all those years ago.

My safe place was the last time I felt truly safe.

He was my safety.

I wondered what he was doing. Was he married too? Did he have children? I bet he tucked them in every night and pressed kisses to his wife's forehead just because he could. I bet she didn't go to bed curled up in a ball to ease the pain of bruises or to hide the cascade of tears.

I bet she didn't choke on her sobs or flinch in fear when she heard her husband return from work.

I bet her skin wasn't marred with scars.

I bet she wasn't fearful of her every word.

I bet she was safe.

I bet she was loved.

I wished I was her.

Thinking of him worked.

The pain was there, but I was able to dull it.

Every time my husband hurt me from then on, I was going to think of my safety.

I was going to think of Logan King.

∞∞∞∞

"Beth."

Thump. Thump. Thump.

He's coming again.

"Hey, pretty girl. Wake up, won't you?"

With the sound of his voice, my eyes shoot open. When I wipe the trickle from my forehead, it's only sweat, and the pounding is the racing of my heart.

Even through the concern in those eyes, it doesn't take long to find what I was looking for.

My safety.

"Logan?"

He sits at the edge of the bed and rests a hand on my cheek. His touch is cold.

He's never cold which means I'm burning up.

"It was just a nightmare," he says.

Through the gap in the curtains, the sun shines a blinding ray of light.

He stayed through the night.

"The girls—"

"Are downstairs," he reassures, his touch never leaving. "You gonna take a deep breath for me?"

My teeth are chattering but I do as I'm told.

"I should make them something to eat." I attempt to pull the covers back, but he stops me.

"They're fine."

"I don't expect you to look after my kids. I've been sick before. I can do it."

"I know you can, but you should rest. Besides, if you interrupt Molly and Hannah's reading marathon, she might kill you."

"Molly's here?"

"And Eden. Isabel is educating her on potty training."

"Poor Eden."

I don't know if it's the fever or how much my heart is swelling but tears spring to my eyes.

"Kim said she's going to call by when she's finished her shift."

"Am I dying?"

He chuckles. "What?"

"Why is everyone here?"

"They heard you were sick and came to help out."

"That's it?"

He's looking at me like I've sprouted horns. "Does there need to be something else?"

"No," I breathe, fiddling with a loose thread in the blanket.

"That's how it's done around here. You need to get used to it. We look after our own."

I can see that.

And I'm one of their own.

God, it feels good.

"Now," he says, standing and pulling the covers back. "Move over." I stare up at him, unblinking, more confused than when I was waking from my dream. "Move your ass, Beth."

I don't know why, but I move, and stare at him as he climbs in next to me fully clothed. He wraps an arm around my shoulders and pulls me against his chest.

"Logan?"

"What?"

"What are you doing?"

"You sleep better this way."

I sit up, still staring, waiting for what he's saying to make sense. "What?"

"You wheeze if you lie too flat," he explains like this is no big deal. "I noticed you didn't wheeze last night when I sat up."

Holy fucking shit.

He stayed so I could sleep in his arms.

"Did you stay here all night?"

"Beth," he implores, and I know he isn't going to get into this with me. "Lie down. Get some sleep."

"And what about you? You must be exhausted."

He laughs under his breath. "I will sleep on a bed of nails. And I will sleep easier knowing you are."

All I can do is stare at him, my eyes stinging and my blood gushing hot in my veins. "You don't have to do this."

He smirks before pulling me back to his chest. "And here I am, doing it anyway." A soft press of his lips to the top of my head and he whispers, "Get some rest."

My body turns to putty in his hands before I give in and rest my head against his chest. It's hard, but the beat of his heart is comforting.

"Don't you have something more important to do?"

He scoffs. "Like what?"

"I don't know, maybe run a couple businesses."

"What businesses?"

I slap my hand against his shoulder, but it hurts, and I know he's right. I need sleep.

"Okay then, talk to me. That will put me to sleep," I tease, hiding my grin.

He only massages tense muscles in my back with no snide response which means he's been worried.

I look up at him, feeling my eyes getting heavy again as I relax into his arms. "I'm okay, you know?"

"You always are." He plucks his phone from his pocket. "Let me show you some of the designs I've been working on."

I smile even when it hurts. "Anyone I know?"

"You wouldn't believe it if I told you."

"Oh, come on."

"Sorry, pretty girl. Can't out the man running the country."

I shoot up again, or at least I try, but his grip on me is firm.

"The president of the—"

"I said the man running the country."

I'm confused, but don't press the matter. I know Logan will always be privy to information I don't need to know, and I know a lot of it has ties to The Kingsmen.

Dismantled motorcycle crew my ass.

I sigh against his chest. "Fair enough. Show me these designs."

I don't see his smile, but I can almost feel it as he takes his phone and slides through the designs. Some people he names. Others are ones I'll never know.

As the pictures skim past my vision, my lids grow heavy.

"Get some sleep, baby," I hear him whisper as I drift off.

FORTY-TWO

"Beth?"

"What?" I snap, trying to breathe through the panic attack ready to surface.

"You're going to break my hand."

Archer happened to drop by the shop to see Logan at the same time I'm getting this tattoo. There's a high possibility I could bolt so I grabbed his hand before Logan ever touched me with a needle. He still hasn't. He's only getting prepared, but I think I'm dying.

It took me three weeks to pluck up the courage to do this. I milked my glorified head cold for all it was worth just to get out of doing this.

Two of Logan's tattoo artists are here working on other customers, and they all seem to be enthralled with my nervous breakdown.

I should be embarrassed, but I don't have the mental ability to think about it.

"She's going to pass out, boss."

I only open my eyes to glare over at Kyle before shutting them again.

"I will not pass out." I'm determined. "I will not pass out," I repeat mostly to myself.

I don't know who I'm trying to convince.

I ease my grip on Archer, but only a fraction. "Talk to me. Distract me."

Logan barks a laugh.

"Shut up, Logan."

"Whatever you say, pretty girl. I'm just impressed you're not asleep."

"Shut. Up. Logan," I repeat which earns me a laugh from everyone.

"I remember my first tattoo," someone says. I don't open my eyes to see who it is. "I was nervous as hell."

"Really?" I ask.

"Yeah, but I was fourteen."

Great.

I'm being a baby.

Archer flinches when I squeeze his hand tighter. "It's just a small one on your ankle. It will be over before you know it." Bless his heart for trying to reassure me, but there's bile rising in my throat, and I'm sweating.

I almost leap off the bed when I feel something cold.

Logan grabs my ankle and soothes his thumb over my flesh. "Relax. I'm just cleaning the skin."

I blow out a breath in an attempt to ease the shaking, but it's no use. I'm close to vibrating right off this bed.

"Beth, you can open your eyes."

"I don't want to."

"What's the story with the scar?" Archer asks.

"What?"

"You want me to distract you. Tell me about the scar."

I finally open my eyes, only because I need to school my features when I say, "It's nothing. I broke a glass once."

Logan's grip slides from my leg and doesn't return.

When I look at him, his mouth is set into a hard line.

"You broke a glass?" The words drip from his lips like venom.

Shit. Shit. Shit.

I told him it was a childhood fall, and he saw my breakdown the night I broke the beer bottle. No matter how much I try to save face, his eyes burn a hole through me.

He sees it.

He sees the truth.

"Logan—"

He holds up a hand. "I need a minute," he says, clenching his jaw.

And then he's gone.

Archer looks to me like I should have the answer.

I do, but it's not one I can share.

"I need to talk to him."

I leave the warmth of the tattoo studio to find him pacing on the street.

"Logan?"

He stops, his head snapping back to look at me. The anger causing his brows to furrow is replaced with a clenched jaw.

"Go back inside. Kyle can do the tattoo."

I shake my head, taking a small step towards him. "I don't want him to do it. I came here for you to do it."

He runs a frustrated hand through his hair before blowing out a long breath. "I can't."

"Why?"

"Jesus, because I want to kill the bastard, but I can't. He's already dead."

I swallow the sticky lump in my throat, fighting the tears threatening to fall. "You don't need to be angry for me."

"But I am," he snaps.

Another step forward and I rest a trembling hand on his chest. His heart beats madly against my palm, sending a tingle across my skin.

Before I can look at him, his hands hold either side of my face, tilting my head back.

"You came here today to cover a scar he gave you. What the fuck did he do to you all those years?"

"It's not the only scar," I answer honestly. "Most of them you can't see. They're buried too deep." I shiver as his thumb traces over my bottom lip. "But I refuse to let him define who I am. I'm not what happened to me. I'm me. I'm Beth. And that scar only serves as a reminder." I grip tighter to the material of his T-shirt, feeling like the heat from his skin is the only thing keeping me planted to the ground. "He might have given it to me, but I want you to take it away. I'm trusting you with it."

His eyes widen before his head falls against mine and we're no longer standing on the street. I don't notice how we're probably blocking the path. I don't care. It's only me and him.

I'm safe.

"Okay," he relents.

Hope flutters in my chest. "Okay? As in you'll do it?"

Hands on my upper arms, he pulls away, and there's only

protectiveness in the heat of his stare. He nods, curling a finger under my chin. "I refuse to let that bastard have any more power over my girl. Let's do this."

∞∞∞

The sting on my ankle fades to a dull throb as Logan completes the last flourish of the intricate design. I didn't pass out, and I even let go of Archer's hand so he could return to work.

The hum of the tattoo gun falls silent, replaced by the heavy beat of my heart in my ears.

Swiveling on his stool, Logan takes a moment to study his work, the intensity in his eyes softening as he takes in the sight of the freshly inked daisy on my ankle. A symbol of new beginnings, concealing the painful past beneath it.

"Finished," he declares, carefully setting aside the tattoo gun and peeling off his gloves.

The reality of what just happened starts to sink in, a wave of emotion crashing over me. My fingers trace the contours of the daisy, the skin tender and sensitive to my touch. It's beautiful, and it's mine.

Logan picked the design, and I was too nervous to ask about it before he started. "Why a daisy?"

He looks at me, surprise etching his face. He hadn't expected me to question his choice, but then, there's always something unspoken between us, an understanding that runs deeper than words.

"There were daisies on your dress when we first met."

Ten years.

It's been ten years and he remembered that there were daisies on my dress.

Speechless, my mouth parts.

"All good?" he asks, his voice rough, but his gaze gentle as he looks at me.

"Better than good," I reply, unable to tear my gaze away from the new tattoo.

A satisfied smile pulls at the corners of his mouth, his fingers brushing a loose strand of hair away from my face. "I'm glad you like it."

Before I can respond, he's on his feet, telling me to wait as he goes to fetch something. I watch as he disappears into the back room, leaving me alone with my thoughts and the gentle hum of the air conditioning.

A moment later, he reappears, a small jar in hand. "This is some ointment you'll need to apply for the next few days," he explains, popping the lid open to reveal a thick, white cream. "I'll show you how to take care of it."

I feel the cool ointment on his fingers as he applies it gently to my skin, his touch surprisingly tender. There's something very personal in the way he treats this moment, as if acknowledging the weight of what this small piece of artwork means to me.

As he finishes, he leans in, pressing a soft, gentle kiss to the skin just above the daisy. It's a quiet, intimate gesture that sends a warm flush through my body. When he pulls back, his eyes meet mine, and the world seems to stand still.

The moment is broken by a burst of laughter from the main part of the shop, but for a minute, it was just us, a woman reclaiming her story and a man supporting her through it.

FORTY-THREE

"Beth, honey," Ms. Carter calls, waving me over to her booth. She's Hannah's teacher. She comes in here every Saturday morning.

I smile, taking my order book from my apron. "What can I get for you?"

She shakes her head and pats on the empty seat in her booth. "No, honey, I don't want another order. I wanted to speak to you about Hannah."

My body falls into the seat.

Not again.

Please don't say she's having a difficult time. I thought she would have told me.

Sensing my unease, she takes my hand. "You have nothing to worry about. She's a gem."

Pride swells in my chest.

"She's a beautiful girl, but she's more creative than she's letting on." She digs a hand into her bag and pulls out a sheet of paper. "I was going to wait until the parent teacher conferences to show you this, but I think you need to see it. I asked the kids to write a story about their favorite superhero, and every one of them wrote about the ones we already know. Batman, Spiderman, Wonder Woman, you name it. All but one child. I think you might want to see this."

She hands me the piece of paper with a drawing on top of the page.

Mom, Logan, Me, Isabel, and Missy.

We're all wearing capes.

In her words I find healing I never thought possible.

She thinks I'm a superhero.

And Logan... Logan is the protector of superheroes.

She describes how she asked him to protect me because even superhero moms need someone to look out for them.

"Can I keep this?" I ask, a stray tear slipping from my cheek.

"Of course."

I finally look at her, tears be damned. "I'm so proud of her."

She takes my hand with a gentle squeeze. "You should be."

The bell dings over the door, but I hardly notice as I look over Hannah's words. I don't think I've appreciated how much Logan has become a part of their lives until now. How much effort he made just to have Hannah have a little trust in him.

My brain is only barely registering the voices at the counter, but then there's something about the bass of the man's voice that has my head snapping back just as he says, "I'm hoping you can help me. I'm looking for a Beth Ellison. I've been told she works here."

The reporter.

He followed me.

Molly is quick when she answers. "Never heard of her."

I fold Hannah's paper and tuck it into my apron before going to the counter.

"It's okay, Molly. I've got this."

He smiles when I turn to him. I don't smile back.

"We can talk outside." He dips his chin and walks away. "Sorry, Molly. Is it okay if I take five minutes?"

"Sure, but is everything okay?"

I nod, trying to smile but it falters. "I'll deal with it."

Her gaze on me narrows, and I hope she can't read the panic seeping from every pore. "I'm calling Logan."

I almost dive across the counter when she reaches for her phone. "Don't." Heat rushes up my neck when people throw us curious glances. I lower my voice. "I'll deal with it. He'll get all caveman and make it worse. Please," I beg.

"Fine, but if he gives you any trouble, I won't think twice."

I try to thank her, but I can already feel the break bubbling in my throat so instead, I smile and hope it looks genuine. Heart hammering, I follow Benjamin outside.

I don't give him the chance to speak. "I told you I have nothing to say."

He shrugs, and credit to him, he looks remorseful as he holds out his hand. My eyes fall to the Polaroid gripped between his fingers, the date on the back written in my handwriting.

I try to control my breathing.

"What?" I snap, frustration bubbling in my gut.

"You told me to come back when I had proof."

No.

I want to scream it. I want to release the burn in my lungs, the panic creeping up my spine until my shoulders are so stiff, they hurt.

I don't take the picture, so he flips it over, and I swear the street starts crumbling in around me. But I need to stay standing. He can't see what's screaming at me from the inside.

I stand tall, rolling my shoulders. There's no face in the photo, just a badly captured picture of a back, painful bruises marring almost every inch of skin.

There's no tears either.

No lifeless eyes.

But I feel the hope draining anyway.

Keeping my eyes focused on the picture for one, two, three seconds, I lift my gaze again.

"What are you showing me?"

The wrinkles around his eyes deepen as he squints. "Are you telling me this isn't you?"

"I have no idea who that is." The answer comes too fast, and he knows it.

I want to steady my voice, stop my hands from trembling, but everything is on fire. All I really want to do is run and never look back.

I chew my bottom lip to hide how it's shaking.

"There's more," he informs me, sympathy dripping from every word.

I don't need his sympathy. I need him to leave me alone.

"It's not me," I repeat.

I want to ask where he got the picture, but all hope of him believing me will evaporate.

"I need you to leave me alone. I have nothing to say. I don't know who is in that picture but it's not me." I spin around as a single tear betrays me and streaks my cheek.

I close my eyes, begging the world to stop when his gentle touch presses to my elbow, keeping me frozen to one spot. "Just one comment."

I close my eyes, fighting more tears as they threaten to fall. "Please leave me alone." I'm almost begging because those pictures make everything come flooding back, like I'm in the ocean and sinking beneath the waves. Every second, I'm losing my footing more and more.

I'm drowning.

I can't breathe.

And I can smell him.

He's coming.

I just need to protect Hannah. When he strikes, I'll be quiet. I'll bite my lip until it bleeds so she doesn't wake.

"Please leave me alone," I beg again.

There's a roar in the distance and for a split second, I think it's Rob coming for me. But it's not his rasp. The gravel in his voice isn't the same. Then there's an expel of air as Benjamin's grip is yanked from my elbow.

"Did she tell you that you could put your hands on her?"

I spin around, tears spilling whether I want them to or not.

"Logan," I gasp, my voice getting trapped somewhere deep in my throat.

Benjamin's eyes turn to saucers as Logan keeps grip of his collar and pins him to the wall. Logan is taller, and Benjamin is on his tiptoes to keep from choking.

"Who the fuck are you?" Logan snarls.

"I… I… I'm a rep…"

"I don't have all day, buddy, so for your own sake, I'd spit it out."

"He's a reporter," I blurt. "Now let him go."

Logan tightens his grip, causing a strangled cry from Benjamin. "I knew I recognized you."

Like all the air is gravitating towards that goddamn photo, his eyes fall to the Polaroid still clinging between Benjamin's fingertips. He grabs it, and there's a brief moment of disgust before he lowers his face so close, they're almost touching.

"What the fuck is this?"

"Logan, will you let him go?" We're attracting quite the audience.

He doesn't even acknowledge that I'm speaking. It's no use. I don't think he can hear me.

"We're investigating Robert Ellison," Benjamin explains, his voice strained. "We wanted a comment from Beth."

"And this?" Logan holds the picture to his face.

I'm going to be sick.

I think I hear Molly exit the café, but I can't be sure because my heart is ringing in my ears.

"It's proof of what he did."

Logan slips the photo into his back pocket. "I don't give a shit what kind of proof you have or what you're investigating. Beth's name doesn't leave your mouth and appear in any newspaper. If you ever even breathe in her direction again, I guarantee it will be the last breath you take. Do you understand me?"

"Logan!"

Desperate, Benjamin's head bobs up and down before Logan pushes him and he scurries away from his hold, running back in whatever direction he came from.

He waits until Benjamin is out of sight before his gaze falls on me, and it's hardly a second before he grabs my hand, pulling me down the narrow alley beside the café and away from prying eyes.

"What the fuck was that?"

"I don't know how he got those pictures."

His brows furrow, his shoulders still vibrating with rage as he takes the photo from his pocket and examines it. I watch as it slowly sinks in. "This is you?"

Of course it's me.

I'd know those bruises anywhere.

"There's more." He freezes in his anger, so I continue. "Nobody was willing to prosecute Rob for what he did, and I knew the only way to stop him was with proof. I started documenting every injury with pictures, writing in a journal. I hid it away with Hannah's scrapbooks so he wouldn't notice. That journal was in the garage when the house burned down. I have no idea how anybody got them. I was told nothing was salvageable from the fire."

"And the reporter?"

"Is investigating how Rob got away with it for so long. How his father pulled strings for his son to walk free." I swallow the fear in my throat. "His father is Judge Ellison, but I'm sure you know that."

He backs away, his decision already made.

301

Archer is at his side. "What's going on?"

He's looking at me but is speaking to his brother. "I need you. Call Jaxson and get Ace on the phone."

Archer already has his phone in his hand as he walks away at Logan's side.

"Logan," I plead.

"Go home to the girls, Beth. This isn't fucking happening. Not to you. Go home."

"Wait." It's my last attempt before he gives me one final pained look over his shoulder.

Molly takes my hand. "Leave them to it, sweetie. They'll get it sorted."

I don't have a choice.

They're driving away before I can say another word.

FORTY-FOUR

LOGAN

"What do you need?" Ace asks, his voice sounding over the car speaker.

"Find something on Judge Ellison. Something he doesn't want to get out to the public."

"Any chance you'll tell me why?"

Usually, I wouldn't, but this man asked her on a date which means there's some feelings there. I need to put aside my own want to strangle him.

"It's for Beth. She was married to his son. Some reporter is trying to create a story about their marriage. Let's just say, he should've had a bullet in his head long before he put one in himself."

"Consider it done. Give me an hour. I'll find something. Is Beth okay?"

I grit my teeth. "I've got her."

"Of course. I'll call you."

When he ends the call, Archer looks at me. "Jaxson has a journalist friend at The Times. He's on it. Fuck. Ellison was her father-in-law? Does Beth know we have history with him?"

"She doesn't need to."

"Have you got a plan?"

"No. But I promise you, I'm not going back to her without this story being killed. Those photos came from someone. If the judge doesn't have them, he's about to realize real fast he needs to find out who does. And if he threatens my girls one more time, I'll fucking do time for his murder myself."

Even in the tense atmosphere, Archer gives a knowing laugh. "*Your* girls?"

There's nothing funny about the way I glare at him. "Yes, Archer. *My* girls."

His laugh trails off. The dip of his chin is nothing but understanding.

He gets it.

"In that case, she's family now, brother. No one fucks with family."

Exactly.

∞∞∞∞

"Judge," I cheer, pushing the door open to his office despite the protests of his secretary struggling to run after me in her heels.

Having Jaxson walk in here caused quite a stir. Between him and Archer's baby blues, the secretary was halfway to marriage with one of them before she noticed me sneak by.

It's a court day for our dear judge which made finding him that much easier.

His mouth is already hanging open, his tie draped over his shoulder as he enjoys his sandwich.

"Sorry to ruin lunch."

He remains seated in an office that smells too privileged.

"I'm sorry, Mr. Ellison." His secretary falls against the door, out of breath. "He got passed security."

I didn't. I was allowed to walk straight in.

Joe is head of security here. He's an old friend of Skip and a former member of The Kingsmen.

He's a good guy.

We even shared a wave when I walked into the courthouse.

I ignore her. "You remember me, judge? Logan King. I'm a little older since you last saw me, but that makes both of us. Let me take you down memory lane. You're the same man that let my father walk

304

free after he almost beat my mother to death. Raymond King, that's my father. As a matter of fact, I also happen to live next door to a woman who fell victim to another spineless bastard. His name sounds an awful lot like yours. Rob Ellison? Yes, that's it. Your son, right?"

Security is at my back. I don't need to look to know they're there. "Call off the dogs, judge. I need five minutes and you're going to give it to me."

His face pales. "Lia, you can leave us." He dismisses her with a wave of his hand.

When she leaves, he fists his hands against the desk.

It's a power move.

This poor bastard thinks he's already won.

"What do you want?" he snaps.

I grind my teeth and remind myself to keep my patience. Another second of staying in my head and I'll have his jugular.

"What do I want? I want you to stay away from Beth and her girls."

"I have no idea what you're talking about. I haven't seen them since they left."

Stepping into his office, I take a seat in his plush leather chairs.

"I have a reporter sniffing around Beth with evidence of what your son did to her."

Eyes murderous, his face turns red with nothing but fury. "That stupid bitch, I told her not to talk—"

He can't finish his sentence because his head just slammed onto his polished mahogany desk. Blood splatters from his nose, gurgling at the back of his throat. His scream is muffled as I press down.

I lean in, my voice a sinister whisper. "No, no, we don't do that, judge. That's not how we speak about her. Careful next time."

Yanking him upright by his collar, I brush off the drops of blood staining his pristine shirt and hand him the napkin from his barely touched sandwich. "You're making a mess on your desk. Sit the fuck down."

Wide, fear-stricken eyes stare back at me before his knees bend, and he sits.

"I know you tried to spin the story to fit your narrative. And as much as I would love the world to know what kind of scumbag you raised; Beth doesn't want it out there."

He opens his mouth to speak, but I hold up a finger. His mouth snaps shut again.

"That house was burned to the ground. After your son killed himself, you were declared his next of kin for all belongings not under Beth's name. Her name wasn't on the house, so whatever remained inside went to you and your wife."

How he managed that when Beth was Rob's wife, I'll never know.

I give him credit; he doesn't flinch.

"Get me the photographs, judge."

"I don't have the photographs."

He's bluffing. His mouth is twitching.

"You do. And I'll assume it's not you that's giving this information to The Times because you want this story buried as much as Beth. So that leaves me to believe you have a leak within whatever household staff you have. Maybe the young woman who cleans your dirty laundry or the gardener that keeps your rose bushes pristine but is probably fucking your wife, or maybe it's the recent contractor you had to renovate the dining room."

Nothing but a clenched jaw. "How do you know that?"

"It doesn't matter. I want those photographs. Now!"

He tips his chin in defiance. When he flashes me a smug smirk through the blood, I need to remind myself not to smash his head against his desk again.

"Or what?"

"I was hoping you'd ask that." I remove my phone from my pocket and press play on the video Ace sent me while I was driving here. "I'll give that reporter something better to write about. I know men who think they are powerful like to pay for sex, but judge, you are into some weird shit." I hold the video playing on my phone to his face. "And you like to record it. Come on, Ellison. I thought you would know better."

Any color in his fat, red stained cheeks drain in an instant.

"There's plenty more."

"Everything in those videos was consensual."

"Was it?"

"You can't do that. It can be proved."

"Proof, right. But by the time you get that proof, everything about you will already be pulled into question. You'll end up paying her off, but your reputation will be in tatters because guess what? Mud sticks. And that's only the beginning. She's only the tip of the iceberg. More women come forward. Prime time television with these women detailing how rough you could get, how possessive. Secrets come to light. That little pillow-talk you had with a woman you were paying suddenly isn't so innocent anymore." My eyes scan the room as if I'm following something. "See that." I point into thin air. "That's your Supreme Court nomination. Wave goodbye, judge. Now stop sitting there and looking at me. You're wasting my time. I asked for five minutes. There's two left, so I suggest you use those minutes to make whatever phone calls you need to have those photos appear in my hands."

He gulps, still holding his busted nose.

Patience lost, my fist slams down on his table. "Fucking move."

His back goes ramrod straight before finally, he picks up the phone.

A minute later, he hangs up and stares over at me. "My wife is on the way."

"Great." I smile, picking up his sandwich to examine it. "I fucking hate tuna." I put it back on the plate before leaning back and getting comfortable. "Please, continue with your lunch."

∞∞∞∞

"What's happening here?" The woman who must be Camilla Ellison strides into the office, her mouth falling open as she surveys her husband's bloodied face.

"Let me help with that." Effortlessly, I lift the box from her startled grasp and place it on the table, taking care not to smear it with blood.

It's filled with scrapbooks just as Beth said it would be.

Bile rises in my throat when I think of everything that's in there.

I just want to get home to her.

Clutching the box, I level a final look at the judge. "You might want to have a discussion with your wife. I'm sure you don't want her finding out about her husband's habits when she reads about it on the front-page tomorrow morning."

He points a trembling finger right in my face. I want to snap it in two. "You said—"

"Nothing. I said nothing."

That reporter was never going to kill the story without having something in exchange.

With a look of utter defeat, he sinks back into his chair.

"Mrs. Ellison," I address her with a curt nod, tucking the box under my arm and striding towards the door.

I'm leaving a ticking time bomb in my wake, and I hope it annihilates every last one of them.

FORTY-FIVE

BETH

When I spot Logan at the threshold, clutching a box that contains my most dreaded secrets, relief so strong washes over me, I sway on my feet.

But what's in the box isn't his focus. I am.

He discards it on the table and strides towards me. "Jesus, come here," he commands, pulling me into the safety of his embrace. "You look fucking petrified." His arms around me become a shield, his strength my fortress.

I was petrified, but it had very little to do with some photos. I spent the day pacing the floors, eyes pinned to the road, waiting to hear the familiar roar of his truck.

I wanted *him* back.

I didn't care what they printed.

I needed his warmth, his presence, his body against mine just to know he's there.

Feathering my palm along his cheek, his stubble pricks the flesh. I close my eyes, breathing him in. "Don't do that again." A tear slips down my cheek, but he soothes it away.

"Hey—"

"No, don't fucking do that to me. I was worried sick. You can't just leave like that."

Pressing my hand to his chest, I clutch at the material, unable to find purchase as my fingers glide over his shoulder.

And then something in the air shifts—an unspoken language lacing the space between us. His eyes are nothing but a blazing hunger, the need reflecting mine. We were both worried.

He cradles my face in his hands, his fingers massaging my scalp before a growl vibrates from his chest.

When he leans in, I don't back away.

I couldn't if I wanted to.

And I don't want to.

I'm sick of tiptoeing around this. Scared of what it will unleash, scared of my reaction.

His thumb pulls my bottom lip away from the hold of my bite.

And we both know—we just know this will answer so many questions… or leave us with more.

It's the briefest touch of his lips against mine at first. We don't move. I don't think I can. It's a taste, and I want more. It's only a grazing of skin when he pulls away. I don't dare open my eyes to look at him because I want to stay here.

"I've waited ten years. I'm not wasting another second." His lips are against my cheek. "Fuck it."

As his lips find mine again, the world as I know it grinds to a halt.

His kiss is potent, an intoxicating mix of gentleness and insatiable desire. When my mouth parts in a gasp, his tongue moves against mine, hot and skilled. It's a gentle coaxing, a slow exploration, a whispered promise all rolled into one searing contact. His taste is a heady blend of everything masculine, everything Logan, as his scent envelopes me like a second skin.

His hands on my body are a paradox, tender yet possessive. They glide over me with an intimate knowledge that's beyond time, mapping a path that feels both new and comfortably familiar. He swallows my moan with a growl rumbling in his chest as his fingers press into my waist, every point of contact igniting.

I slide my hand from his shoulders into his hair, the silky strands contrasting perfectly against the hard planes of his body. I can feel the controlled strength beneath the softness, the power he's holding back, but his grip is firm, pulling me closer, as if the space between us is a void he needs to eliminate.

"Fuck, you taste better than I imagined." I throw my head back as he leaves my lips, peppering kisses along my jawline, down my neck, each one a hot brand searing my skin, marking me as his. "How am I supposed to ever get enough of you now?"

I can barely breathe, let alone speak.

A small gasp escapes me as he kisses me again, proving his point.

My lips are probably bruised, but I don't care.

He's rooted himself in the marrow of my bones, a seismic shift that somehow has him embedded in my makeup.

Every sound, every gasp, is swallowed by the other. His breath mingles with mine, creating an air that's uniquely ours, flavored with an intensity that speaks of so many unsaid words. Each glide of his tongue against mine, each nibble, each suck, is a silent confession, an affirmation of his claim on me.

And I know, I'll never be able to belong to another.

As the kiss deepens, the world around us dissolves, replaced by the intoxicating taste of him. The force of his lips on mine, the rough scrape of his beard against my cheek, sends a wave of fiery heat coursing through my veins. The raw need in his every touch, every breath, sends my heart pounding, my senses spiraling.

Instinctively, he guides me backwards until I feel the edge of the table against my thighs. I'm vaguely aware of the cool surface under my palms as he lifts me up, settling me on the edge, his body pressing between my legs.

In my need to have him closer, I swipe my hand across the surface, not caring about what might break.

Then it happens. The box teeters precariously on the edge before tumbling over. I gasp as the contents spill onto the floor—the journal, its pages filled with haunting images, each a chilling testament of my past, lands open.

It's only one image. I can't even see it completely, but I see the bruises. I see the blood. And it's brutal.

I let out a strangled cry, breaking away from him and all but throwing myself off the table in a desperate scramble to close it. But it's too late. The damage is done.

As I whirl around, the journal clutched to my chest, my eyes meet his. He stands frozen in place, his eyes riveted to the spot where the journal had landed. His face is pale, the usual warmth in his eyes replaced by a horror I never wanted him to witness.

"Logan," I whisper, my voice catching on a sob. But he doesn't look at me. His gaze is glued to the floor, his expression one of shock and disbelief. My heart aches at the sight.

With a shaky breath, he finally looks at me. "By some fucking miracle, tell me that's not you." His voice is barely a whisper, but it echoes in the silence of the room, bouncing off the walls and stabbing me with each rebound.

But we both know it's me. I don't need to say it.

"Jesus Christ," he breathes out, his hands clenching into fists by his side.

"Don't look at me like that," I whisper, my voice shaking. I grip the journal tighter to my chest, as if the worn pages could shield me from his gaze, from his judgement. "Like I'm not the same woman you kissed a minute ago."

I see my words hit him like a punch to the gut, his entire body recoiling slightly. A moment of understanding flickers in his eyes before he blinks it away, replacing it with determination.

In two strides, he's in front of me, his hands lifting to wrap around the back of my neck. His fingers splay into my hair, gripping me gently but firmly as his thumbs tilt my chin upwards, forcing me to meet his gaze.

"I can't look at you differently," he says, his voice low and intense. "To me, you'll always be the same girl that walked into my tattoo studio ten years ago."

His eyes search mine, as though seeking to reassure me of his words. His fingers shift, stroking my hair in a soothing gesture.

A tear leaks from the corner of my eye and lands on his hand. "Isn't that the problem? I'm not her anymore."

I see nothing but pain in his features before he dips his chin in understanding.

"Listen to me, okay?" he murmurs, a new urgency to his voice. "We're going to get through this. Together. But right now, I need you to check if there are any photos missing. We need to know if they took anything."

He seems to sense my inner turmoil. His arms tighten around me, a silent promise of his unwavering support. With a soft sigh, he pulls away, just enough to capture my hand in his.

His gaze is intense as he lifts my hand, pressing a warm, lingering kiss to my palm. "I'm right here," he reassures, his voice a soothing murmur against my skin. His eyes never leave mine. "I'm right here, baby."

It could be five minutes or an hour, but he keeps his word and remains at my side. Silent, but a pillar of support I lean against.

This is what it has come down to.

Ten years in a journal. That's all that's left.

The corners aren't charred like I expected. There's no damage. It's exactly how I left it. This couldn't have been in the house when it burned down.

My gaze darts from the journal in my hands to the box it came in. It's filled with old scrapbooks, mostly of Hannah's. Her first steps, her first words, her toothless baby smiles—all captured and carefully preserved in these books. She's going to love them.

"Beth?" I don't realize there's tears streaming down my cheeks until Logan wipes one away with his thumb.

I don't want him to see more. Stepping away from him, I peel back the pages with trembling hands.

All color drains from my face as I see what's inside.

Pictures, so many pictures of a person I barely recognize. A woman battered and bruised, her spirit beaten out of her by the man who had vowed to love and cherish her. Each photo a stark reminder of a past I desperately want to forget. I stifle a sob with my hand as I continue to flip through the pages, my mind a whirl of emotions.

They're all there. But it's not the pictures or the words written in my shaky handwriting that truly terrify me. It's the red ink, the scarlet letters scrawled across some of the pages. Like a paper graded by a teacher, each page bears a mark of judgement.

"Whore," one page reads. The word is sharp, a brutal reminder of the cruelty I endured.

"Slut," it screams at me.

Page after page, each one tarnished with a vile word. "Worthless." "Useless." "Failure."

But I didn't write those words. They were added long after I was done with it.

They're *his* words.

With a gasp, I drop the journal as if it's on fire. The echoes of those words continue to bounce around my mind, but now they're muffled, muted by the deafening silence in the room.

Each breath is like inhaling broken glass, my chest tightening with a pain that doesn't have a physical origin. "He's dead," I echo, my own voice sounding distant to my ears, a hollow whisper that seems to reverberate around the room. "He's dead..."

Firm hands cradle my face, and Logan's intense eyes capture mine, grounding me, anchoring me to the present. "He's dead. You're safe."

The implications hit me like a freight train, staggering me back as the room spins, my hand reaching out blindly for support. My knees buckle, and I collapse against the counter, my heart thundering like a wild animal trapped in a cage. "Oh, God," I gasp, the reality too much, too painful, too raw.

Logan is there, a constant presence, a soothing balm against the storm of my emotions. "You need to talk to me."

The images haunt me, taunt me. The memory of Rob taking Hannah. The fire. His death. A tidal wave of guilt washes over me, threatening to pull me under with its relentless pull.

"He saw it," I whisper, each word a dagger to my heart. "He saw all the pictures."

Suddenly, it feels like I can't breathe.

"It's all my fault," I choke out, the words tasting like ashes in my mouth.

A look of shock flits across Logan's face, his eyebrows knitting together in confusion. "What are you talking about?"

A bitter laugh escapes my lips, and I press my hands against my temple, as if trying to contain the pain. "He found it, Logan. He found the journal. That's why he snapped. That's why he took Hannah from me."

His hand reaches out for me, as if he wants to pull me into his arms, to shield me from the horrors of my past. But I'm beyond the point of comfort now. As his touch lands on my shoulder, I feel my body rattle, my breath hitching in my throat. The world blurs around me, the edges of my vision fading into blackness.

"Fuck, baby, please don't flinch away from me."

"I need you to go. I just... I just need to deal with this on my own. Please, Logan. I just... I need a night."

The reality of my plea lands between us, heavy and palpable. I don't want him to go, but I need him to leave, and he recognizes it in the hard resolve in my eyes. This is something I have to confront alone.

The helplessness in his gaze tugs at something within me, but I force the feeling away, unable to afford any more heartache tonight.

His curt nod tells me he understands. He always does.

But he doesn't retreat immediately, not before he takes my face in his hands, pressing his forehead against mine. His voice is a whisper but strong. "None of this is your fucking fault. None of it. You're stronger than him. You always have been. Face whatever you need to face but come back to me." His thumb tenderly strokes my temple, soothing and grounding me. "Don't disappear in here. Stay with me, baby."

I want to promise him, but I can't. Not when I don't know if I can keep it.

"If you need me, I'm right here. You hear me?"

I manage to swallow past the lump in my throat. "Yes."

His fingers reluctantly slip away from my face, a torturous release, before he turns and walks away, his steps heavy, his frustration echoing in the curses he mutters under his breath.

With him gone, my gaze falls back to the journal discarded on the floor. I steel myself for the emotional turmoil that awaits.

I still feel Logan's lips on mine, and it's in that touch I take some strength.

It's time to spend a night with a ghost.

FORTY-SIX

Blood fell from my face, dripping into the sink and staining the porcelain until I washed it away with water. Hands trembling, I brought them to my nose and felt the sticky liquid smudge on the back of my hand. My heart was hammering too hard, my legs shaking until I was sure they would give out and I'd crumble.

I gripped the counter and inhaled a shaky breath before finally lifting my head to stare at myself in the mirror. I didn't recognize my reflection. He made sure of that. I was under there somewhere, under the swelling and the angry red marks that will be purple by morning.

I fucked up. Why couldn't I have kept my mouth shut?

Tears fell, stinging the cut on my bottom lip. My face needed ice, but I couldn't move my legs. I couldn't go back down there until he cooled off. But I needed to clean up. Hannah couldn't see me like this. A sob ruptured in my throat. It hurt, aggravating the skin marred by his fingerprints around my neck.

Grabbing a washcloth, I soaked it in warm water and pressed it to my face. At least my nose stopped bleeding.

My little girl is going to be so scared. She didn't hear. I always make sure she doesn't hear, but how do I explain my face? He rarely touches my face for that reason. It's too visible.

At least he didn't kick.

I rinsed the cloth, watching the blood swirl in faded pink as it mixed with the water and disappeared down the drain like it was never there. Erased.

I felt his presence before I saw him. Standing at the doorway, eyes glassy, tumbler in his hand before he took a drink and raked his eyes over my bruises. I'm not sure if he even saw them, if he saw what his hands created.

His dirty blonde hair was disheveled, tie loosened after a day at work. I wondered how he managed to get away without destroying his white shirt in blood. It was pristine. His knuckles weren't so lucky. They were cut and red, wrapped around the glass.

Hazel eyes locked with mine in the mirror, but I chose to see my daughter in those eyes, not the monster who was really staring back at me.

He's beautiful, my husband. Sharp jaw encases masculine features, shoulders broad and a waist he keeps lean by going to the gym every morning before dressing in a tailored suit.

It hides so much, that suit. He's the businessman with a family at home. I'm the envy of so many women, living a life of leisure in this big house. My husband's success affords me the luxury of staying at home with our daughter.

But this house is a prison and although I love being home with Hannah, it wasn't my choice. It was his. Every decision in my life that led me to this moment was made by him. I don't get choices. Choices are for people with freedom.

I shuddered when he stood at my side, towering over me. His eyes softened, but it was only on the surface.

Wordless, he wrapped his arms around my waist and rested his hands on my swollen belly. She kicked like she couldn't stand his touch either. Despite my nerves with him being that close, I let out a relieved breath. I had been waiting for her to kick. She did it again, reassuring me from the inside out.

"Oh, Beth." He shook his head.

As a hot tear slipped past my defenses, he gripped my jaw and turned my head to stare down at me.

"Rob—"

He brushed his thumb over my swollen cheek, cutting my words from my tongue. I tried not to wince, but even a touch meant to bring comfort caused more pain than his punches. Whiskey breath coated over me.

The corner of his mouth turned down. He looked... disappointed? "You're going to ruin that pretty face of yours."

And with that, he dropped his hand, drank the last of what was in his glass and walked away. Leaving me with nothing but more tears, a heart finally shattered after years of cracks, and the resolve I needed.

I guess this will be my last time writing in here, attaching these photos to the pages. I could take it with me, but if I don't get out and he finds me before I can, I fear he might kill me. I can't risk him finding this too.

If the worst happens, and someone else is reading this, please get Hannah out. My sister's address and phone number are at the back. Call her. She'll know what to do. Don't let them keep my girl. Don't let them poison her.

Either way, I guess this is goodbye because I'm taking Hannah, and I'm getting out of here... Tonight.

∞∞∞∞

Three years.

It's been almost three years since I left and tonight it feels like I'm trying to escape all over again.

The scared, shattered woman I used to be stares back at me from the pages I pour over while I battle to ignore the words he brandished me with... even in death.

Three years, and every inch of me is conflicted.

If he were still alive, peace would have remained a distant, unattainable dream. He would have hunted me down, his obsession knowing no bounds. I shudder at the thought. I don't even know if I would be alive, and chances are, I wouldn't have my girls.

Yet, a piece of my heart shrinks from the relief that floods me, relief borne from his death, from the knowledge that he can no longer reach out and hurt us.

Is it wrong? Is it reprehensible to feel an ounce of joy that the man who fathered my children is dead?

Perched on the edge of the porch, my gaze travels over the peaceful surface of the lake, the moonlight casting a mosaic of memories across the water.

I always knew how dark the blood ran in his veins, but I didn't realize until the day he took Hannah that it had penetrated his soul. He knew he was leaving this world, but not without inflicting one last blow to me.

If he was going, he was taking Hannah with him.

He wasn't successful. I know that. Everyone knows that.

When people hear my story, I get this look as if to say, "Aren't you so lucky?"

He took my child.

Her father. The man that was supposed to protect her with every fiber of his being.

If that's luck, I don't want it.

Each harsh word, each brutal blow, every cruel kick—I would take it all over again just to keep her safe. For her not to have those memories. For them not to grow up with the questions they're going to have.

How do I explain it to them when I find it hard to breathe?

The wind gathers strength, its touch cold against my skin. I close my eyes, taking a deep, steadying breath as I tilt my head back.

I don't forgive him, not entirely, not yet. But I've battled the storm for too long, and I, too, need absolution. I need to breathe freely again.

I don't know who I'm speaking to, but I need to say it out loud.

Blindly dismissing the tears tracing their way down my cheeks, my voice trembles. "I don't hate you anymore. I can't afford to because the energy it takes is a luxury I don't have. It robs me of moments with the beautiful children we brought into this world." Lifting my face, I draw in a lungful of cool night air. "Thank you for letting us go."

For the first time in what feels like forever, I draw a breath and there's no sting, no ache, no burn.

Just peace.

Standing on shaky legs, I don't go back inside. Instead, I take the steps to next door. His lights have remained on. A silent beacon, a reminder of his presence, of his promise.

I don't get the chance to knock before the door opens.

There's a form of agony I've never seen before until now, and it's in Logan's eyes—a thousand silenced words.

Somehow, we already know.

We don't need to speak.

Taking the final step toward me, he lifts me around his waist and carries me to his bed.

He doesn't kiss me again, but his hands remain constant on my body, grounding me, lending me strength.

Pressed against his chest, there's a part of me that finds its way back, to mend, to something resembling whole.

It's in his arms, a sleep free of nightmares comes to find me.

FORTY-SEVEN

"Beth, honey, I need a very large coffee." Eden comes traipsing into the café ten minutes before my shift ends. She pulls out a stool and slumps forward on the counter.

A burn radiates from the balls of my feet, reminding me the lunchtime rush just finished, and apart from an older couple and a young family, the only other people up front are me, Molly, and Eden.

"Sure." I smile, grateful for another distraction.

Being busy kept my mind from wandering to that kiss.

God, that kiss.

But I didn't want to think about it. No matter how much I could still feel the firm press of his lips on mine, the scratch of his beard I thought I'd hate but didn't and couldn't stop thinking of somewhere else. A shiver runs down my spine like it did when his hand went there, brushing the skin where my shirt lifted.

I've never moaned making coffee, but I'm close to it.

I dreaded my shift today, convinced people would see my cheeks still flushed, but now that it's finished, I wish there was another busy spell. It's too quiet. My thoughts love the quiet and everything in my head is overwhelming. Nothing makes sense anymore.

I peeled myself from his arms in the early hours before he woke.

Something shifted in me, in him, in us. Something in my foundation has cracked, and I need time. I need to make sense of all this before I face him again.

320

For now, I'll focus on the coffee.

Eden throws her head in her hands with a groan so loud, the remaining customers spin to see where it came from.

Molly appears from the kitchen with a fresh batch of cookies. "What's climbed up your ass today?"

"Remind me to never volunteer to organize a wedding again. She's my cousin and I love her, but she's Satan."

"Emily?" Molly questions.

An unexpected flame of jealousy burns in my belly.

Jesus, as if I don't have enough emotions to contend with today. I have zero right to be jealous.

She nods. "I can't blame her. The photographer she booked cancelled at the last minute. She planned her entire wedding around this guy."

"That's rough. I'm going to put an extra shot of espresso in your cup."

I swear she almost cries. "Bless you, Beth. I always knew you were going to be a good friend." She blows out a shaky breath as her shoulders round forward. "With two weeks to what she's calling, The Wedding of the Century, I need to find a photographer."

"It's wedding central here. Isn't there plenty of photographers?" I ask.

"You'd think. But she needs someone she can trust. She can't risk the photos being leaked right away. Her security is tighter than the secret service as it is."

"You sure coffee is going to be strong enough?"

"I went to the bar first," she confesses. "Archer wouldn't serve me. He said that I never drink this early and come back when his shift ends so he doesn't have to listen to me complain."

Molly rolls her eyes. "That's my husband, ladies. Archer King. The charmer."

"Please," Eden scoffs. "He hugged me while he said it. He's the only man capable of insulting me and comforting me at the same time." Her train of thought comes to an abrupt stop when she catches sight of Molly putting the cookies on display. "Are those gluten free?"

Me and Molly share a confused look. I'm pretty sure I served her a sandwich yesterday that was far from gluten free.

"Since when are you not eating gluten?" Molly asks.

"I happen to be very conscious about what I put into my body."

Molly places the tray on the counter and crosses her arms over her chest. "Really?"

"Always."

"Didn't you sleep with Jaxson?"

I almost drop the coffee cup. "What? How am I only finding this out now?"

"Don't encourage her, Beth," Eden whines, grimacing.

I pour the frothed milk into the cup and pass it to her over the counter. "I didn't know you and Jaxson were a thing."

The only King brother I have yet to meet... again.

"We weren't. It was brief and a long time ago. A mistake never to be repeated. I would rather gouge my eyes out and pour salt on the wounds."

"Wow."

Molly clicks her tongue against the roof of her mouth, disbelieving as she rests her hip against the counter and turns to face me, mischief dancing in her blue eyes. "The best orgasm she ever had."

Eden doesn't even flinch. She simply takes a large bite of the cookie and shrugs, mumbling something incoherent that sounds a lot like agreement. Then she holds up five fingers.

"Five?" My eyes go wide, and I lean over the counter like I'm half blind. "Five orgasms? What is he packing down there? A magic wand?"

I've forgotten what it even feels like.

She nods. "Close. I almost had to be hooked up to fluids after."

We all burst out laughing.

"I needed this," I trail off, ignoring their curious eyes.

Molly nudges me. "Everything okay?"

It's on the tip of my tongue to tell them about the kiss, but I'm not sure I can handle more opinions. Not when I can't make sense of my own just yet, so instead I shrug and say, "Just a restless night. I want to hear more about Eden and Jaxson."

There's a glint in her eye I recognize. It's memories. The ocean of secrets women keep. They're hers, and she wants to hold onto them.

"That's all there is to tell. He always manages to get on my last nerve, but even I'm not stupid enough to deny that those King men have something special." She tilts her head toward Molly. "You should know."

She doesn't respond, instead choosing to refill the already full napkin holders as her eyes glaze over, the ghost of a sad smile curling down on her mouth.

They've walked through the depts of hell together. I can't imagine it's been easy. Honestly, I admire her for being here and having a normal conversation.

She scratches at her neck nervously, so I revert the subject. "Logan says Jaxson is thinking of moving back to Pine Falls."

He did. He told me last week.

Now both women look at me with wide eyes. Though I'm sure the color is only draining from Eden.

"This day keeps getting worse." Clearing her throat, her gaze darts to Molly. "He wouldn't, would he? Jaxson back in Pine Falls?" She doesn't give us an opportunity to answer. "Never."

"Apparently, the band are taking a break."

"It makes sense," Molly adds. "He did mention it a couple of times during Evie's funeral, but I assumed it was wanting to be around family at a time like that. I don't think he's had the same love for the road since."

"Did Archer not say anything to you about Jax coming home?"

"Ah, that would involve speaking to each other." She tries to laugh off the comment as she brushes imaginary wrinkles from her apron. She lifts her gaze to stare out onto the square.

"Moll?" Eden reaches for her hand as I wrap an arm around her shoulder.

"It's a rough patch. We'll get through it. We always do."

"Of course you will. You're the strongest couple I've ever met," Eden says, casting a worried frown my way.

"We're here if you need us," I offer.

"Thanks, you two. I appreciate it." She smiles and opens her mouth to continue but the bell rings over the door, signaling another customer. I silently curse the interruption.

"Oh, fuck," Eden curses. "Satan is following me."

Ah, Emily.

White blonde hair styled in a straight bob cut, high cheek bones, and crystal blue eyes, she's practically a Victoria's Secret model.

No, wait, she *is* a Victoria's Secret model.

Her eyes immediately fall on Eden, who is trying to hide behind the menu.

"There you are." Emily slaps the menu from Eden's hands. She stuffs the cookie in her mouth before wiping the crumbs from her lap.

"I promise I'm just eating this and I'm going to find you a photographer for your big day."

"Where are you going to find a photographer with less than two weeks to a wedding?"

"Um..."

Molly quickly steps in to save her friend, distracting Emily by throwing me into the lion's den. "Emily, have you met Beth?"

As she spins around, I'm met with a scowl so deep it causes an indent of a line between her brows. As she lets out a breath, her features soften considerably, and my shoulders relax.

"Beth? Oh, Logan's neighbor."

That's my identity now.

Logan's neighbor.

My shekels instantly rise, but when her lips lift, her smile is warm. "It's so lovely to finally meet you."

Eden takes a gulp of her coffee to wash down the rest of the cookie before mumbling, "Or if we're feeling fancy, we like to call her Bethany Rose."

She's worse than Kim because she knows how much that name grates at my last nerve.

Emily stills midway through shaking my hand, and I feel the tension as she squeezes my knuckles so much it almost hurts. Then her hand falls, slapping against the counter.

"Bethany Rose?" The use of my full name and the way she whispers it makes me uneasy.

I shift under the weight of her stare. She's scanning me like she's recognizing me from somewhere, but she can't place it.

"You don't happen to be a photographer, do you?"

"You can't just ask a stranger—" Eden tries to interrupt, but Emily slices her hand through the air to stop her.

"Are you?"

"Um..." I stutter as my tongue gets tangled around the words. Why am I suddenly nervous around this woman?

"She is. She took pictures for one of our charity events."

Thanks, Molly.

I peel my dry tongue from the roof of my mouth. "I haven't done it in years."

"But Logan bought you a camera for your birthday."

I glare at her.

324

Shut up, Molly.

Emily falls back into the stool. "Holy shit," she breathes, still staring at me. "He did it."

"Who did what?" I whisper back. I don't know why.

"Logan. He found you."

I laugh but it comes out strained and more like a screech.

What did she just say?

"Excuse me?"

"I'm not sure if you're aware, but Logan and I were engaged. It was a mistake on both our parts. We were friends for years and should have stayed that way. That man had no interest in a marriage, and even less interest in organizing a wedding. So, I was over the moon when he wanted to book the photographer. The thing is, he was so picky. I never got it. I'd never heard of the photographer he was looking for. And he insisted on this particular one."

The rush of blood behind my ears makes it hard to hear anything she's saying because I know what's going to come out of her mouth, and I don't want to hear it.

My heart stops as she smiles at me, and there's no bitterness there. I wish there was.

Don't say it.

Christ, don't say it.

"He was looking for you, Bethany Rose."

She stands and taps her long fingers against the counter like she didn't just tip my world off balance, like the earth isn't spinning at lightning speed around me.

"Now, I'm not one to let some misplaced jealously get in the way of the wedding I'm supposed to have with the man I'm destined to marry. And if Logan thought you were good, then you must be amazing. So, I'd really love if you could join us in two weeks and take some pictures of our day. We shouldn't let all of Logan's work in finding you go to waste."

My mouth simply flaps open and shut. My thoughts are too many and my words too few.

I don't know how she reads the shock on my face as agreement, but I don't argue with her when she says, "Great. Wow, that's a relief. I'll see you in two weeks."

And with that, she simply waves and leaves, taking the world I thought I knew with her.

My eyes sting but no tears fall, my hands simply rattle at my sides.

"Beth?" I flinch as Molly's warm hand rests on my shoulder. Eden is at my side now, too. When did she move?

"He looked for me?" Emotion clogs my throat, making my voice thick. "When were they supposed to get married?" I finally ask.

"Three years ago."

I think I stumble because Eden grabs my elbow. "We had no idea."

"Why? Why did he look for me?"

They both share a look before flying into action. One tosses my hair, or maybe she's trying to tame it, while the other pulls my apron from around my waist.

Molly grabs either arm, giving me a small shake. "Don't ask us. Go and talk to him."

Eden giggles. "I've got goosebumps everywhere."

They're right. I need to talk to him.

He looked for me.

He looked for me three fucking years ago.

We've wasted enough time.

I nod before grabbing my purse from under the counter. I'm out of the coffee shop and marching across the square toward the tattoo studio in the next breath.

"Damn you, Logan," I whisper as a single tear streaks my cheek. "What have you done?"

FORTY-EIGHT

LOGAN

"Is Logan here?" Beth's voice is muffled on the other side of the door.

"He's in the office, but I think he might be busy," Kyle says. "Beth, you can't... Shit."

Ignoring his protest, she's already swinging the door open before stepping inside and slamming it shut. The sight of her tear coated cheeks has my heart dropping to my stomach and my legs turning to lead until I'm standing.

"Beth?" I round the table and step towards her, desperate to close the distance between us and erase the moisture from her face.

"You looked for me," she gasps, her breaths shallow as her chest rises and falls.

I stop in my tracks. "What?"

Closing her eyes, twin tears fall as she clenches her fists and leans her head against the door. "Did you look for me?"

Fuck.

My head falls between my shoulders as I pinch the bridge of my nose to ease the headache blooming behind my eyes. There's only one person who could have known that, and even she wouldn't have known the meaning behind it.

"You spoke to Emily?"

Her eyes widen to saucers, chocolate orbs swimming behind a sea of tears. She was waiting for me to confirm what she already knew but couldn't believe.

She stutters, her hand coming up to stifle a sob. "When?"

My mind filters through the times I've thought about her enough over the years to do a quick Google search or seek her out on social media. I never found anything.

I wouldn't, would I? Especially when I was looking for Bethany Rose. Not Beth.

Bethany Rose disappeared that night, leaving me wondering if I had dreamed her up.

What started out as a simple curiosity for the woman I spent a weekend with, somewhere along the way turned into a fantasy. And I could never put my finger on why. She crossed my mind a lot after she left. Just a passing thought. As the years went by the thoughts became a little less. She began to fade. But then there were those days, the days when a brief memory would flood my mind, and it set something off in my head. A switch was flipped, and I would spend the entire day thinking about her.

Until she came back into my life, I didn't know why.

Beth isn't a woman you forget about. Her memory embedded itself in me and festered throughout the years. In one weekend, I felt more connected to her than any woman I've been with since, including the woman I was willing to marry. Which is fucked up, I know. Emily deserved more of me.

Did I end my engagement because of Beth? No.

Knowing what I know now, did she have a part to play? Maybe.

Which doesn't make sense. None of this makes sense.

My connection with other women ended when they left my bed.

Until her.

I'll never know how, in such a short period of time, she was more. Beth was always more. Even if I didn't fully understand it.

Truth is, I still don't.

Maybe I don't have to understand it.

"Why?" She looks pained, like I've garnished a dagger and driven it straight through her chest.

Scrubbing my hand over my face, I give her honesty, and I don't know how much that will do. "I wish I had a straight answer for you.

Fuck, I really do, but I don't know. You were just there. Somehow, you stayed with me."

With the answer, her breathing calms. I find myself taking a steady breath with her.

Looking down at the floor, she wipes mascara-soaked tears with the flesh of her palms.

My chest constricts until it's painful to breathe because knowing her now, knowing what's she's been through, a knot of guilt burns in my stomach.

I didn't look for her hard enough.

Unable to take another minute without having her in my arms, I walk towards her, but she holds a trembling hand out to stop me.

And fuck if it doesn't hurt.

"I need to get something from my car. Just give me a minute."

Before I can stop her, she opens the door and leaves through the shop, ignoring the sets of eyes following her and then back to me.

"Everything all right in there, boss man?" Kyle asks.

"Get back to work," I bark.

I'm not in the mood.

Giving Beth what she asked for, I wait exactly one minute before moving, but she's back before I even have a chance to leave the office. Shutting the door, she resumes her position with her back against it. Only this time she has that fucking journal clutched to her chest.

"I need you to understand something," she starts, meeting my eyes and trapping me. She tucks her blonde waves behind her ears as she gathers herself. "In one night, ten years ago, you knew me as well as anyone because there wasn't all that much to me. Nothing eventful had happened in my life up until that point. I didn't have crazy stories to tell. I was average, living an average life." I grit my teeth so hard I'm surprised I don't crack a molar. She never was, and is not now, average. "There wasn't much to me. What you saw is what you got."

Endless tears stream like a river as she pounds a closed fist against her rib cage, a fractured sob echoing around the office.

Thump.

Thump.

Thump.

"I didn't have this fucking pain."

My chest cracks wide open because it's exactly how she looks. Agony seeps from every tear and every word.

There's a silence before she speaks again, and I feel every second like the countdown to a nuclear bomb. "For the most part, you know me now. But you didn't know me for ten years." She looks down at the journal and whispers, "You didn't know her. You only know what that time made of me, and I feel like there's this massive part of me missing when you look at me. Like I'm broken, and the pieces are scattered and buried beneath the weight of my past."

She's looking at me, but I can't help feeling like she's looking through me, too lost in her own memories to realize. Her eyes are lifeless, and I fucking despise it. I want to take that journal and burn it for good this time.

"I need closure. I needed to see it again," she says, reading the murderous expression on my face. "At first, I thought it might be good evidence for when I finally found the opportunity to leave. In the end, it became something I hoped someone would find after his fist hit one too many times."

Christ, she thought he was going to kill her.

Her fear is palpable, her body rattling, and I want to go to her, but I'm too afraid of my reaction if she flinches. Instead, it's her that takes a step toward me, and the relief is visible. But she's still too far away. I want to take her in my arms and carry her the fuck away from here.

"Logan, I'll understand if you don't look at this. I promise it doesn't change anything. It's just sometimes, I think you look at me in search of a missing part of me." Her head drops so I grab her chin and tilt her head.

I see you.

She smiles, but it falters.

"There are things in here I will never speak of out loud. But the woman you're searching for is in there. She explains a lot." She rests the journal on my desk, her entire body relaxing when it's out of her arms.

But it takes all my oxygen because I know if I open it, I'll want to commit murder, and the only bastard I want to kill is already dead.

Pressing up on her toes, she places a devastating kiss to my cheek. When she turns to walk away, I know I should let her go, but fuck that. I can't. Not without holding her first. I reach out and grab her wrist, gently pulling her back. She falls against my chest and ruptures, soundless sobs scraping against her throat.

Her legs give up. I just hold her a little tighter. "Hold on, baby. I've got you."

It's minutes, but not long enough because I don't want to let her go. She straightens, running a hand through her hair.

Her mask is back on.

Cupping her face, I dry her cheeks with my thumbs.

"I'll try." It's the closest thing I can offer.

With an understanding nod, she says, "I should go and get the girls. I promise, whatever you do, it's completely up to you. I don't expect anything."

But I do because I know how difficult it must have been for her to hand it over. And she's trusting me with it. It's Beth's way of opening up about a time in her life she fights so desperately to run from.

Her hand stills on the doorknob before fully opening it. She looks at me over her shoulder. "Logan, you were never a man I had an almost date with ten years ago. To me, you were so much more. If you read it, you'll understand. You were always just... more."

FORTY-NINE

Ten years ago

Beth

"I thought we were going for tacos," I say, my voice barely audible over the deluge falling around us. My clothes are sticking to my skin, my hair is plastered to my forehead and neck, and my feet are sloshing in my drenched boots. The chill setting in my bones is doing little to dampen the mood. I'm still mad at him, although I'm madder at myself for reacting.

Have at it?

What the hell does he think I am? Leftover dinner meat?

Though there would be a part of me lying if I said his jealousy when he saw me dancing with Ace at the bar didn't spark a fire in my belly.

He must notice my features change because he smirks at me. And damn him for looking that good while soaking wet. His black hair clings to his forehead, and it takes effort to stop from reaching out to put it back in place.

He cocks a brow, fighting a full smile. "You still mad at me?"

"I would be less mad at you if you would finally bring me for these tacos you promised."

"We are," he replies, seemingly unfazed by the storm. Passing the tattoo studio, he leads me down a narrow alley, sidestepping puddles. We stop in front of a nondescript door, nestled between the studio and a garage. After fishing a set of keys from his pocket, he unlocks it.

Inside, we ascend two flights of stairs. Halfway up, I realize I've been holding Logan's hand since we left the bar.

Now that I think of it, I've been practically plastered to his side since we danced, and he almost brought me to orgasm by brushing against me.

His grip is firm and comforting, his hand warm against mine. I halt mid-step, pulling on his hand to stop him. I look into his eyes, their depth framed by the dim light filtering in from a nearby window.

"Are you going to murder me?" I blurt out, my words echoing in the tight space between us. I hardly know this man.

He doesn't miss a beat. "Depends. You going to behave yourself and maybe smile?" he counters, his voice smooth as silk and just as unnerving. There's a challenge in his eyes, a glint of mischief that wasn't there before.

"Behave myself? I told you I'm not a little girl."

"No, you're definitely not," he replies, his gaze intensifying. It seems to draw me in, locking me in place. "But that doesn't mean you can't be punished all the same."

My mouth goes dry as the heat in his stare sizzles me head to foot. I swear I could dry off with just that look alone. A shiver runs down my spine that has nothing to do with the chill of my wet clothes.

I lick my lips. His eyes drop.

"Punish me for what?"

"Oh, I'm sure we can find something."

He tugs at my hand, clearly intending to carry on, but I pull him back. The question spills from my lips before I can think it through. "Like what?"

Shaking his head, a slow devilish smirk graces his features. "Don't worry, I won't corrupt you."

Something akin to disappointment takes root, blossoming with a sting of regret. Part of me—the rebellious young woman wanting to take a chance—wants him to corrupt me. There's an allure in his confident demeanor, his cocky attitude, and the mystery that shrouds him. My heart thumps against my chest, the rhythm wild and untamed, matching the restless stirrings inside me.

I want to see what lies beyond his eyes. I want to know what kind of corruption he's capable of and—perhaps even more terrifying—I want to know if I'm capable of letting him.

Swallowing the knot of anticipation, I force a weak laugh, hoping it will dispel the sudden tension as we finally begin to move again.

At the top, Logan opens another door, revealing his loft.

"You live here?"

It's amazing. The city lights drift in from the large, steel-framed windows, lining the brick walls. The ceilings are high, with exposed wooden beams. He goes ahead, switching on a lamp in the living room.

It's a bachelor pad, but there's photos on the walls, a desk littered with papers, and his scent lingers in the air, making it homely and essentially Logan.

The open floor plan gives the loft an even more spacious feel, with the kitchen flowing seamlessly into a living area.

"You should get dried off," Logan suggests, snapping me out of my stupor. He disappears into what I assume is his bedroom. When he doesn't return, I tentatively follow.

He hands me a black T-shirt that I'm sure will fall to my knees. "Here. I'll dry your clothes. Bathroom is right in there."

I take the offered shirt with a mumbled thanks, feeling oddly self-conscious. I disappear into the bathroom, and when I emerge with my damp clothes bundled in my arms, he's already changed into a fresh white T-shirt and black jeans.

He's mouth-watering.

Handing over my soaked clothes, I can't help but follow him curiously with my gaze as he takes them, disappearing briefly into another room before returning. By the time he's back, his hands are empty, and the faint hum of a dryer resonates from the room, accompanied by the soft warmth that wafts into the open loft.

Logan goes straight to the fridge, pulling out ingredients before getting to work on chopping.

"You're making the tacos?"

He grins at me over his shoulder, a glint of satisfaction in his eyes. "I told you I knew a place with great tacos."

Of course he can cook.

"You're quite sure of yourself."

He does nothing but wink at me in response.

I take the opportunity to explore his apartment, curiosity guiding my steps. The loft is big, an artist's sanctuary, and somehow, I feel like an intruder tiptoeing around his world.

As I inspect the photos lining the walls, my gaze is drawn to one picture in particular. It's a stunning woman with a radiant smile. The eyes are familiar because they match that of the man cooking like a professional behind me.

"She's beautiful. Who is she?" I ask, unable to look away from the picture.

Logan pauses, following my gaze to the photo. "My mother. She passed away when I was fourteen. My aunt and uncle practically raised me."

He leaves it at that, offering no further explanation. There's a raw vulnerability in his admission, and it's clear he doesn't like to talk about it. I decide to respect his silence.

My exploration takes me to his desk, littered with sketches that showcase a skill and talent beyond tattoos. I run my fingers over the pages until I skim across another photo printed on a sheet of paper.

"What is this?"

I hold up the picture of two identical houses side by side, obviously in need of restoration with overgrown grass and secluded in forestry. Even in their dilapidated state, the scenery is heaven.

"A project," he simply answers.

I roll my eyes.

"You flip houses?"

"No."

I hold my hands out and squint at him, imploring him to go further. I almost miss the satisfied smirk on the corner of his mouth as he lowers his head and gets back to cooking.

"I bought the houses a couple of years ago. I'll get to it someday."

It looks like an amazing place to raise a family. I hide my smile and the warmth in my chest. He hasn't shown that side of him until now—the side planning for a future.

"You should add blossom trees." I love blossom trees.

He dips his chin. "Noted. Why don't you pick the music?"

"You sure?"

He finally meets my eyes as he rests his hands on the counter and leans in. "Have at it."

I glare at him with so much intensity, I feel the burn. "Asshole," I mutter under my breath, ignoring his quiet laugh.

His record collection is a surprise. Old school vinyl's, a collection that would make any music enthusiast green with envy. My fingers trail over the worn covers, lingering over each title until one familiar record stops me in my tracks.

Nothing Can Change This Love by *Sam Cooke*. I pull it out, placing it onto the player.

The soulful melody fills the loft, and I can't help but sway to the rhythm, a soft smile on my lips as the familiar tune washes over me. His brows lift, a silent appreciation in his gaze.

He doesn't ask, but I tell him, "My father used to play this every year on my birthday."

He keeps his gaze on me but allows me to remain in the music. I sway my hips, acutely aware of Logan's watchful eye. It's not oppressive, nor is it uncomfortable. It's a silent appreciation, a curiosity, a desire. Even as he focuses on preparing the *World's Greatest Tacos*, I feel the heat of his lingering stare, a tangible connection between us that sets my nerves on fire.

Unable to resist, I find myself moving toward him. Approaching from behind, I peer over his shoulder, curiosity getting the better of me. His muscles tense slightly, but he doesn't stop, not until he sets the knife down and turns to look at me with an unreadable expression.

Without a word, he wraps a strong hand around my waist, lifting me with surprising ease, and placing me on the edge of the kitchen counter. The sudden shift from standing to sitting stuns me for a moment, my thighs becoming exposed as the T-shirt rides up. I quickly tug it back down, cheeks burning.

He traces his thumb along my chin. "If you're going to watch, you might as well have a front row seat."

∞∞∞∞

As the taste of spicy beef, fresh cilantro, and tangy lime hit my palate, I can't help but close my eyes, savoring the flavors.

This wasn't the plan. I intended on telling him it tasted like shit just to get him back for his earlier statement, but I can't. There's an orgasm happening on my tongue, and I'm practically salivating.

"Okay, I can admit, these are amazing," I mumble between bites.

A triumphant smirk plays on his lips. I want to slap it off, but that would mean leaving my food, and wild horses wouldn't have a hope of doing that.

"Didn't realize you were a man of many talents."

He winks at me, and I melt all the way to my curling toes.

"Do you always cook for women you barely know?" I ask. "Because Logan, you bought me dinner—"

"Breakfast."

"Breakfast, whatever. I've met your family, you danced with me, and you cooked for me. I should let you know; this feels like a date."

He shakes his head with a laugh under his breath and chooses not to enlighten me with a response to this being a date. "I only cook for the ones I find interesting."

"What makes me interesting?"

He takes a moment to study me. "I'm usually pretty good at reading people. You... you're a bit of a puzzle."

"I don't know if that's a compliment, but I'm going to take it as one."

"Good for you."

He ignores my responding glare.

The conversation shifts to my photography. He's curious about my work, asks about the places I've been, the people I've photographed. The warmth in his gaze as I speak, the interest in his voice, it's flattering. I tell him how I'm going to miss my random shoots around the city, and how I regret not doing it one last time before I leave.

"Leave? You running again?"

"No. I'm going to London tomorrow. I have an internship there," I admit, watching his face for a reaction.

"Tomorrow?" I swear I see a hint of disappointment before it's gone.

I nod.

"An internship? For photography?"

"No, for law."

The shock on his face is priceless. "You are not going to be a lawyer."

"Why not?"

"You don't look like the lawyer type. Don't suit you." Mouth slightly agape, he keeps going before I can respond. "How does someone like you end up wanting to spend her life in a courtroom?"

Choosing honesty, I tell him, "My father was a lawyer. I promised him before he died."

Logan's face softens, the playful glint in his eyes replaced with a deep understanding. "And is that what you want?"

The silence that follows is heavy, filled with the unspoken thoughts and feelings that I've been avoiding for so long, but my answer is resolute. "I made a promise." The tension in the room dissipates slightly. "I like law. There's a sense of order to it. There's black and white, it's about finding right and wrong."

"Ah," he hums, finishing the last of his taco. He leans back on his chair, studying me like he did earlier. I shift in my seat. "You're a good girl."

Another flutter low in my tummy battles with the defensive roll of my shoulders. "What's that supposed to mean?"

"What I mean is that you live by the rules. You follow the plan. You do the right thing. Even when it might not be what you really want."

"What's wrong with that?"

"For most people, nothing." He shakes his head, presses his elbows on the table, and leans in. I find myself doing the same. "For you, it's a fucking shame. Life doesn't happen in the black and white. Life happens in the color."

I roll my eyes, ignoring how intense his stare is and how it's pulling truths out of me I haven't faced yet, or how easily he can read me when we hardly know each other.

And who the hell does he think he is telling me what I want?

Catching me off guard, a slight blush creeps to my cheeks. I'm slightly offended, a retort on the tip of my tongue, but before I can voice my thoughts, he interrupts. "Will you stop doing that?"

I put my taco down. "Doing what?"

"Biting your tongue," he answers smoothly. "Say what's on your mind."

His statement throws me off balance, and for a moment, I'm at a loss for words. I'm used to holding back, used to choosing my battles. I'm not confrontational. Ever. But Logan's open challenge is as intoxicating as it is frightening.

The flame of frustration flickers inside me, stoked with every word. "I think you're arrogant, presumptuous, and…" I pause, searching for the right term, and when I find it, I spit it out with an acrid bitterness, "And insufferably self-righteous!"

I expect anger. I expect another scowl. Anything but how he throws his head back and laughs.

Bastard.

"Now we're getting somewhere."

But he's back to studying me and pinning me to my seat. There's a different intensity in his gaze now. One that sends a thrilling chill down my spine.

"Fine." I cross my arms over my chest. "As we're choosing honesty. I want to know what you think about me."

His lips curl into a half-smile. "Ah, the tables have turned." He seems to ponder over his words for a moment before continuing. "I think you're scared. Scared of living outside the lines, of following your passion instead of your obligations."

See. Bastard.

His words hit me, yet I can't deny the truth of them.

"I think you're stronger than you believe you are. You've got fire in you. Don't ever let anyone put it out because in this world someone will fucking try. I think you're naïve in thinking everything is simply right and wrong, black and white. Maybe that's to be expected. You're young. But life is so much more... And you're beautiful. So fucking beautiful, especially when you're mad."

There are many things I could say, but I can't because my face is on fire and my words are tangled in my throat.

He pushes my plate toward me. "Eat. You need something to fill the gaping hole in your face."

I'm too hungry and they're too delicious to care about my wounded pride. "Jerk," I mumble around a mouthful of food.

After minutes of charged silence, he gets up and returns with my dry clothes before throwing them on the table.

I raise an eyebrow at him, my curiosity piqued. "What now? If you're throwing me out, you can wait until I finish my food."

He tosses a leather jacket at me. I catch it, surprised by the weight. "We're going for a ride."

"But it's late," I protest, albeit weakly.

He grins. "You want to go crazy with that camera before you leave tomorrow?"

My head bobs up and down, excitement fluttering low in my belly.

"Then get your ass up and get dressed."

I don't argue with him.

True to his word, he takes me on a tour of the city. We visit spots I'd never thought to explore. He shows me hidden gems, places where the city's soul is bared, where beauty springs from the most unexpected corners. He introduces me to people from all walks of life. Everyone knows him, it's crazy.

And I capture it all, my camera clicking away as Logan stands guard, watching me with an intensity that stirs something deep within me.

I think he might be all mush on the inside, despite his exterior. Every time we're on the sidewalk, he always places his hand on my lower back and moves me to the inside, away from the passing cars.

It's uncharacteristically sweet.

On our final spin, he lets the bike roar on the open road. Fear seeps away, and I throw my head back, spreading my arms out wide.

Freedom.

When he parks up, we're overlooking the city skyline, a sea of sparkling lights against the black canvas of the night sky. It's breathtaking, and my fingers itch to capture it, to freeze this moment in time. But Logan takes my camera from me, the edges of his lips tugging upward in a smirk.

"Your turn," he says, his tone soft yet commanding.

He gestures for me to stand, the cityscape serving as my backdrop.

I protest, but he ignores my complaints, his fingers dancing over the camera with an uncanny familiarity. He captures me in all my vulnerability, his eyes soft behind the lens as he clicks away.

When he looks at me and says, "I think you've got a flight to catch," my heart drops into my stomach.

I find myself mourning the idea of leaving him.

The journey back to my apartment on Logan's motorcycle is a sensory overload. The roar of the engine vibrates through me, while the rain-slicked city streaks past in a kaleidoscope of neon and shadow. The cold wind nips at my cheeks, but Logan's warmth seeping through the leather jacket he lent me keeps the chill at bay.

Every red light, he takes the opportunity to reach down and grab my ankles, like he can't help himself from touching me.

I'm acutely aware of him, his solid presence against my chest, the firm grip I keep around his waist as we navigate the labyrinthine city streets. His cologne, mingled with the rain-soaked city, intoxicates me.

Despite the whirlwind of sensations, an uncanny silence envelope us, a bubble in the midst of the city's cacophony. It's the kind of silence filled with unvoiced thoughts and burgeoning feelings.

Once we reach my apartment building, he parks the motorcycle, the engine's purr dying down to a quiet hum. He swings his leg off the bike, his boots echoing against the pavement. As I follow suit, pulling off my helmet and shaking my hair free, I feel him step up behind me, his presence comforting in the cool predawn drizzle.

As I turn, his hands cradle my face, his thumbs gently brushing the wet strands of hair sticking to my cheeks. He leans in, his breath warm against my skin, causing a shiver to ripple through me.

"God help London. Give um hell," he murmurs.

A laugh bubbles up from my chest. His fingers gently caress my cheeks as we both instinctively move closer.

My lips burn, wishing I could feel him there.

"Fuck do I want to, but I'm not going to kiss you," he whispers, his voice barely audible over the soft patter of rain.

"Why not?" I ask, my heart hammering against my ribcage.

"Because it won't be nearly enough. If I taste you, I'll want all of you. And something tells me I'll want it over and over again."

My breath catches in my throat, and the flicker of his desire in his eyes brands me where they land.

He's right. Kissing him wouldn't be enough for me either.

He smiles and my chest tightens. "When you're back... if you ever want a tattoo, or the best tacos, you know where to find me."

"And if you want a photographer, you can look for me."

He dips his chin.

It's too final.

I really hate goodbyes.

"A photographer? I thought you were set on living in the black and white?"

I shrug, "Maybe I'll give some color a try." I don't want to, but I step away with an understanding nod and walk toward my apartment. Turning around before I reach the steps, I can't help myself when I say, "You're probably right not to kiss me."

"Why's that?" he asks, humoring me.

"What if it's life changing?" I look up at the sky, feeling the fresh drops of rain on my face before resting my eyes back on him with a shake of my head. "I'm far too young for life changing."

FIFTY

Present day

BETH

Wine.

It's the only solution to get me through tonight.

Since giving Logan that journal, I've regretted it. My stomach is tying itself in knots, and I've thought about being sick more than once.

What was I thinking?

He's going to take one look at those pictures and never see *me* again. He'll only ever see my bruises, the scars no number of tattoos can cover.

But isn't that the reason I gave it to him? To see the part of me he missed out on. To fill in the gaps.

The house suddenly feels too small, too claustrophobic. I open the back doors, letting the cool breeze sweep over my clammy skin.

His truck and bike are parked out front, so I know he's home, but I don't see any lights on. I want to go over there just to check. I want to see the look in his eyes when he sees me.

Or maybe he didn't look at it.

At this point I don't know what I wish for more: for him to have read it or not.

I step away from the doors, choosing to leave them open as I pour the first glass of wine.

It's almost midnight: a ridiculous time to start drinking, but my blood needs the kick of alcohol to remain pumping.

I switch off the lights, wanting to be in darkness like the house next door.

I always feared the darkness until I moved here. And if I were anywhere else, I wouldn't leave my doors wide open, but no matter what Logan thinks of what's in that journal, I know he's there. The thought alone wraps around me like a warm blanket.

Nothing can touch me here.

Nothing but his dark eyes.

My breath is knocked from my lungs as he appears at the open doors, hands gripping the frame, breathing heavy.

"What the fuck are you doing with the doors open?"

I cling to the counter like it can keep me planted to the ground. "I always leave them open when you're home." There's no point in lying to him. That's the truth.

He steps inside, and the oxygen in the house gets sucked out. His chest is heaving, the muscles in his arms straining, making the veins protrude.

He read it.

And I'm not sure if he's drunk or mad.

"Have you been drinking?"

"No," he answers honestly as he takes another step forward.

Mad it is.

"Logan?"

My mouth goes dry as my legs meet the stool and I sit.

He's still so far away, yet not far enough because I don't know what's going to come next.

"How many times did you walk past the studio?"

"What?"

"Goddammit, answer me."

I put everything in that journal. Including the days my feet lead me to King Tattoo Studio. It wasn't to see him exactly. I wanted to know he was still there, that I didn't imagine it all.

My safety.

Hands balling into fists at his side, his nostrils flare, but he doesn't move.

Is he angry with me?

A lump forms in my throat, and I fight to swallow it before it makes my voice break.

Biting my lip, I place the wineglass on the counter before standing and putting more space between us. With every second, I feel the frustration bubbling under my skin. "I don't know, Logan, about as many times as you thought about looking for me." The second the words are out of my mouth, I want to suck them back in.

I watch as his shoulders rear back like he's shielding his body from a blow, and it breaks my heart.

"I didn't look for you hard enough," he mutters mostly to himself.

We're both angry and confused without knowing how to fix it.

I take a step forward, but quickly halt when his words pin me.

"I can't move. I can't fucking breathe without thinking about what he did to you. To *you*, Beth. *You!*" He throws out his arms. "I grew up with his shit. I helped women as I got older, and it tore me apart. But what I saw tonight... that wasn't abuse, that was torture. TO YOU!" he shouts. "Fuck. Just thinking of another man resting a hand on you tears me apart."

I could go to him. Comfort him. But it's not what he needs, and it's not what he wants.

I said my piece in the journal.

He needs space to tell me what he's thinking.

So, I stand, and I wait.

I wait for the blows.

But they never come.

"You, baby... So, I can't describe this feeling when I think of him putting his hands on you. Not just to touch you but to hurt you. I can't fucking breathe. And now I've seen it... I don't know what you were trying to do by showing me, but if it was to turn me away, it didn't work." My chest rises and falls with his, both of our bodies falling in sync. "Nobody will touch you without your say again, do you understand me? Not without getting through me first, and I guarantee, it won't fucking happen."

Wordless, I nod, trying to swallow the lump in my throat.

"He hurt you." It's not a question. "Really fucking hurt you."

I nod again.

He's seen the pictures. I can't deny it now, and I'm done defending

344

a man that doesn't deserve it.

"He did, but I'm still here." I stop myself because there's a fire beginning to build in my belly. It's a flame I long suppressed, a rage I never put my energy into because it doesn't make sense. But none of this makes sense.

I refuse to meet his eyes because I know I'll never get it out if I do. "Logan, I need you to understand something... I love my girls. I breathe for my babies." I bite down on my lip, scrubbing a hand over my face to dry the threatening tears. "And I would do it all over again just to have them. I would take the hurtful words, bruises, and broken bones just to have those girls in my arms." My lungs are desperate for air, but I need to get this out because if I don't, I'll drown in it.

The wind picks up through the doors, blowing my hair onto my face, but I take the moment to inhale a steadying breath. "Then you happened, and I was starting to see parts of a girl I thought was dead. Like a fucked-up crime scene where you were the last one to see her alive. And that girl... she's so fucking angry at you."

He flinches but remains steady on his feet.

"You kissed me, and it was like..." I try to find the words.

"Everything made sense," he finishes for me because he gets it.

Of course he does.

Trembling, I finally ask, "Why didn't you kiss me? That night, all those years ago, why didn't you kiss me?"

Everything would have been different.

And maybe not.

But I'm sinking into the possibilities of the unknown, and I'm suffocating in it.

I expect him to step away.

He doesn't.

His pain is so raw, he's practically bleeding out in front of me.

I meet his eyes, letting the tears fall as I finally admit out loud, "It should have been you."

Jaw set, he stalks towards me with determined strides, roughly taking my face in his hands and pressing his head against mine.

"Oh, baby, I wish I had kissed you. If I could go back, I would kiss you a thousand times over so when he looked at you, you wouldn't see it because all you would feel is my touch."

My heart breaks all over again.

I want him.

Probably more than I've wanted anything in a very long time, but I can't if there's a risk this isn't everything I've dreamed it to be.

"You get to walk away at any time. I don't think I can risk that. Not with the girls." Because as much as everything in my body is screaming at me to give in, they will always be my priority.

Head raised, his eyes are dark, and I see nothing but fear. "You act like I haven't been tethered to you in some way for ten years. You act like those girls haven't become the center of my universe since you moved here. I'm risking too, because if I lose you and those girls, you can take my fucking heart from my chest and stomp all over it."

I try to say his name, but it leaves my lips in a tortured whisper.

"Somewhere along the way, I fell in love with you, and make no mistake, Beth, I'm crazy in love with you. It's the type of love that will drive me insane. The one that keeps me up at night, but the one I don't think I can breathe without anymore. You consume me, and everything around me. I don't belong to myself anymore. You made sure of it."

The fracturing of my heart takes me by surprise, an unexpected ache so profound it leaves me breathless. Yet, there's a beauty to it, a unique tenderness that permeates each crack, each fissure. It's as though my heart seeks to reshape itself, contorting and mending into a shape that's meant to fit only him.

He doesn't stop, even as I stand here, unblinking, desperate for his touch.

"But I didn't just fall in love with one woman. I fell in love with three. I'm not their father. I wish I had, but I didn't create them with you. But this feeling in here..." He thumps his fist against his chest. "This love for those crazy, beautiful girls, that's got to be how a father feels. It can't be more because I swear, I'm about to burst."

He's right. I think he fell in love with my children before he ever allowed himself to fall in love with me.

There they go... all those walls I spent so long creating simply crumble. My legs give way and a sob ruptures from my chest.

But this time, I'm not alone in my pain. His is just as raw.

I've never seen a man break completely until this moment when Logan's knees buckle and bend.

He doesn't let go.

Not once.

If anything, he only holds me tighter.

I hear "I'm sorry" against my head over and over again. But he has nothing to be sorry for.

I look up, tears streaking my cheeks, and press my palm against his face. He wipes the tears away with his thumb. "I'm sorry too. Even when we shouldn't have to say it, I'm still sorry."

His hands continue their tour of my face, like he's trying to commit every inch to memory. "You'll always be safe here, you know that, right?"

A weak smile curls on my lips. "I've always known that."

"I need to kiss you. I need to know this is real."

I can't answer because my heart is in my throat, but I nod and keep nodding until his mouth crashes against mine.

It happens again.

The world stills.

Everything makes sense.

A groan vibrates against his chest. His hands are in my hair. Mine are tugging at his T-shirt.

When a small gasp fills my lungs, his tongue dives into my mouth. Each movement I meet with equal vigor, and before I know it his hands wrap around the back of my thighs, lifting me against his waist as my back meets the wall. Tongues dueling, his dominance is overpowering, and I willingly submit. He's somehow greedy and giving in his kiss. I take everything he's giving, drinking him in as he swallows the moans escaping my throat.

My legs lock around his back, pinning him to me. He's hard between my legs, and with an animalistic flick of his hips, my core burns hot, and my head falls back against the wall.

"Fuck, baby, you need to tell me to stop."

If he stops, I will die.

His eyes meet mine. There's a question there.

Mouth so close I can taste him, I whisper, "I trust you."

His eyes turn dark, ripping me of flesh and leaving me raw beneath him.

In my next breath, his mouth collides with mine, my body melts into his, and I give him everything.

It's his.

I wouldn't ask for it back if I could.

And my dreams didn't do this man justice. Just a kiss puts every dream to shame.

The moment he backs off, I grit out, "God damn it, Lo—"

He doesn't let me finish. My protest is permission enough.

Still wrapped around him, he carries me upstairs. I expect the nerves to come, but we're both still clothed, and my instincts take hold as I grind against him. For a minute, I wonder if we'll make it to my bed when a string of curses spew from his lips.

In my bedroom, he sets me on my feet. I'm surprised they still hold me upright.

His eyes no longer show me reservation as they scan my body.

I'm done with waiting.

I've waited ten years.

Holding the hem of my shirt, I lift it over my head, leaving me in my black bra.

I want it over with, this awkward stage of taking off our clothes but he doesn't allow it. He stills my hand when I try to remove my jeans. He grabs my wrist, his other hand dancing over my collarbone, before lowering to the valley of my cleavage. My breathing is stuttered when his thumb motions circles over my hardened nipples and my breath comes in harsh pants.

"You said you trust me?"

"I do." And I mean it a hundred times over.

"You trust me with your body?"

"Yes."

"You trust me to make it mine? Because I promise, Beth, once I'm inside you, you'll be nothing but mine."

It's the easiest answer I've ever given. "Yes."

I bite my lip, but he pulls it away with his thumb. "That's mine. Stop biting it."

I think I'm only capable of moving my head up and down now.

With my nod, my bra is on the floor.

I didn't even feel his hand reach around my back. "You're good at that."

His expression remains the same, as if he's trying to keep himself from devouring me. It's nothing but invigorating.

It's a long second of staring before he snaps… and he turns feral. His hand wraps around my throat, yanking me to him, while his other hand keeps me close with his palm spread against my lower body. It climbs by back, over my shoulder blades, until his fingers are in my hair, and in one swift tug, he forces my head back to swipe his tongue along my neck.

Holy shit.

I've died and gone to heaven.

With the anticipation climbing to a fever pitch, a shiver dances along my spine.

I feel him smile against my skin.

He knows exactly what he's doing.

Just as I imagined he would.

When he kisses me again, it's bruising, and I melt into him, desperate for more.

He pulls away, leaving me dizzy as he kneels, unbuttons my jeans, and slides them down my legs, leaving me in nothing but black lace panties.

Always trust a woman's intuition because these panties are usually bigger, but today I felt like something a little sexy.

Thank Christ for that.

A growl vibrates from his chest as he hits the sensitive flesh between my legs. He has hardly touched me, and I can already feel the slickness between my thighs.

Almost leaping off the floor when his finger glides along the lace, a jolt of heat unfurls between my legs as he pushes the material aside until his skin is on mine.

"Fucking perfect."

And, oh, sweet lord.

His tongue.

My head falls back. "Oh my God."

"You forgetting my name already, baby?" I think that's what he says, but I can't be sure because the blood is pounding behind my ears... and everywhere else.

"Jesus," I gasp, grabbing the dresser to steady myself.

"Still wrong." He somehow laughs while his tongue motions circles on my clit.

"Shut up, Logan."

His fingers press into my thighs and pull me closer. "Finally."

With his mouth, he works me into a frenzy while somehow keeping me steady with his hands on my thighs.

A sensation long since forgotten roots itself at the base of my spine. I swear my legs are about to give in, but not before he pulls away, staring up at me as he trails kisses up my body.

I'm transfixed watching his tongue dart out to lick the skin only to blow cool air over the moisture his mouth left. I shiver, sure I'm on the precipice of combustion.

He stands tall, towering over me in a way I've learned to love, and I'm suddenly all too aware of how naked I am while he is still dressed.

Heart stuttering in my chest, I do my best to cover myself with my arms.

I don't get a chance.

As if reading my mind, he grabs my wrists, raising them above my head and pinning me to the wall.

"You don't hide from me. Ever." When I don't answer, he implores, "Beth?"

I nod, unable to find the words trapped in my throat.

He places a soft kiss to my lips before molten eyes find mine.

"You're not a possession. I don't want to own you in that way. I want to adore you." A soft kiss. "You're mine to cherish." Another kiss sends tingles down my neck, and I lose my breath. "Mine to love." Another press of his lips against mine. "You're just... mine." He maintains his grip on my wrist, guiding it to his chest. Through his shirt, I feel the pounding of his heart. "And I'm entirely yours. From the moment you stepped into my studio, I've been yours."

Tears sting the back of my eyes, but I don't let them fall.

Not now.

Not tonight.

Right now, it's just us and I want to keep it that way. I want to stay in this moment and make it last.

Arm secured around my waist, he walks me backward. When my knees hit the bed, they bend, and I sit.

"Lie back and spread your legs. I want to look at you."

Swallowing hard, I nod, but obey with every inch of me trembling under the pressure of his touch.

In his eyes, I hear words he never needs to speak.

Here, I'm safe.

Here, in his arms, nothing can touch me.

His fingers trace over the curves of my body, dancing lower on my stomach, and I'm suddenly consumed by all the flaws I have. I feel every stretch mark and a pouch from carrying two healthy children.

"Beth," he growls close to my ear. "Open your eyes and spread your legs because you're fucking perfect." My breath comes in heavy pants as I feel his hands brush my inner thigh. "I don't know where you go when you close those beautiful eyes of yours, but I want you here." He kisses the sensitive spot below my ear. "I want your eyes on me when I make you come on my fingers."

My body goes lax, nothing but putty in his hold as my legs fall open and I feel the slip of his fingers between my folds. Eyes wide, my head falls back as he applies the slightest pressure to my clit and presses a firm kiss to my throat before I feel a thick finger slip inside me. Then another. I fist the bed sheets, afraid if I don't hold on, I'll simply melt into the fabric. As my head tilts back, he captures my chin between his fingers and lowers it, so my gaze is locked with his again. "I told you to look at me."

I try. For a long second, I try to keep my eyes open, but Christ, it's been so long. And I've never, not once, had a man touch me like this. A loud moan escapes, and this time, I don't notice my eyes flutter closed.

"Pretty girl," he whispers in a husky warning. "If I have to tell you again to open your eyes, I'll put you over my knee and spank you until you're raw. Do you hear me?"

I nod frantically as I feel the heat swarm in my belly. "Logan," I cry, arching my back. "I think..." I don't know what I think because I know I won't have a coherent thought for days.

"I know, baby," he says against my mouth, never losing his rhythm as his fingers slide in and out of me. "Come for me."

A tidal wave of pleasure is building, so intense I feel dizzy. It's a race against time now, a battle between the discipline Logan demands and the sheer force of my own impending release. The coiled heat in my lower belly is unbearable, and my body instinctively starts to quake in anticipation.

A breathless sob slips from my lips, and I clench my teeth as the raw waves of pleasure threaten to overtake me. The promise of Logan's punishment if I disobey has an unexpected effect, only adding fuel to the fire, making my arousal spike, even more, flooding me with a kind of intoxicating, rebellious thrill.

"Good girl," he murmurs, his hot breath against my ear sending shivers down my spine, pushing me even further to the edge. "That's it, let it go. Let me feel you come apart."

It's all too much, too intense, and I surrender to the onslaught of sensations. My entire world narrows down to this moment, to the feel

351

of Logan's body against mine, to the intoxicating blend of pleasure and pain as I fall apart under his touch.

With one last, keening cry, I surrender completely, a starburst of ecstasy ripping through me. It's all-encompassing, all-consuming, washing over me in powerful waves that leave me breathless and spent. Through it all, Logan's voice in my ear, his touch on my skin, anchors me, a strong and steady presence in the whirlwind of sensations.

Slowly, as the pleasure begins to ebb away, I become aware of the world around me again. My heartbeat is erratic, my body heavy and sated, curled against Logan's comforting warmth. I'm a woman transformed, awakened, and there's no going back now.

In a split second, he grabs my hands and I'm on shaky legs before he spins me around. His lips meet the nape of my neck, as if he wants to taste every inch of me before he goes farther, but he stills, and I know exactly why.

My body doesn't just bear small scars. I'm a walking reminder of the cruelty another's hands can inflict.

I feel his breath on my back as I tense. There's nothing for long seconds until his fingers trace the outline of the marks on my skin.

My husband liked to punish, and usually his belt was the nearest thing to hand.

The silence stretches between us, thick and heavy, and all I can do is wait. Wait for him to break the quiet, wait for him to turn away. But he doesn't. Instead, I feel his lips, soft and reverent, pressing a kiss against the first scar, then another and another, each one a silent pledge.

His movements are slow, as if he's trying to memorize every line, every curve of my body. My breath hitches when he reaches the lower scars, the ones that always seemed to hurt the most. But as his lips press against them, any lingering pain seems to evaporate, replaced with a warmth that seeps into my bones.

Then he's moving down, lower and lower until he's on his knees. His lips never leave my skin, each kiss a reminder of his acceptance, of his love. I can't help the tears that prick my eyes, overwhelmed by the tenderness of his actions. I've never felt so seen, so cherished.

He rises again, trailing kisses up my spine, until he's standing at his full height. I feel his strong hands on my shoulders, turning me around to face him. I meet his eyes, seeing my own vulnerability reflected back at me. But there's something else too—a fierce protectiveness that takes my breath away.

Without a word, he pulls me into his arms, his lips meeting mine in a searing kiss. It's a kiss that speaks of acceptance, of healing, of love. It's a kiss that says, 'I see you, all of you, and you are beautiful.' It's a kiss that I will remember for the rest of my life, a kiss that marks the beginning of something new, something beautiful.

His grip is gentle, yet firm, the surety in his hold a silent promise. He lays me down with a tenderness that sends a shiver through me, our bodies still flush against each other.

Eyes locked, he straightens, pulling his shirt over his head and tossing it aside. The sight of his bare chest, the lines and contours of his muscles glistening under the dim light, sends heat pooling low in my belly. I watch, breathless, as he unbuttons his jeans, letting them drop to the floor.

"Logan..." I squirm, doing everything to hold back a gasp. I hadn't quite been prepared for the sheer size of him, his impressive girth filling my hand as I reach out and run my thumb over the tip.

"Fuck." He groans, the sound a low rumble in his chest as he throws his head back.

I bite my lip, eyes wide as I take in the sight of him, fully naked. My body responds instinctively, a shiver of anticipation running down my spine. "That... that's not going to..."

Anticipating my reaction, he says, "It'll fit."

Okay, then.

I guess there's worse ways to die.

Goodbye, World.

Naked, he crawls back onto the bed, hovering above me. His hands trace the outline of my body as he leans in, his lips pressing against mine. I can taste the promise in it, the passion, the raw desire.

My teeth nip the flesh on his shoulder just before he grips my hips and flips us over so I'm straddling him. I clench my thighs, feeling his erection between my legs.

What is he doing?

"You take control here. Now lift your hips for me."

On instinct, I'm already doing it.

"Atta girl."

The cry that comes from my throat is nothing short of animalistic as he sheaths himself inside me. The sting is quickly replaced with blinding heat. His large grip is still on my hips and guiding me every step of the way, but it doesn't take long before I find my own rhythm.

"Good girl. Ride my cock. Take what's yours."

I still for a minute because I need to see him. He's giving me back the control. He wants me to know that whatever happens tonight, the power is in my hands.

I lower to meet his lips as his hand skims my waist, and he whispers against my lips, "I might possess you in this bedroom, but you'll always have the greater power over me."

He kisses away the response on the tip of my tongue, meeting me thrust for thrust until my head is falling back and I'm crying his name from my lips again. I'm so close, the edges of my vision turn black.

"Fuck, baby. I can feel you coming. Come for me."

With his words, the tension in my body unwinds, sending me spiraling until I'm sure I'm floating.

As my body shudders, riding the wave of pleasure, he grips my hips even tighter, his fingers pressing into my skin.

"That's my girl," he grunts, his voice thick with desire. "The way you come around my cock... it's fucking perfect."

He pulls me closer, burying his face in the crook of my neck. His breath comes in ragged, heated pants against my skin as I continue to move above him, my body still pulsing from the orgasm.

His hand slips between my breast, along my stomach, then finding my clit again as he starts rubbing in tight circles. The sensation has me whimpering and squirming, sensitive from the orgasm he just brought me through.

"I'm not done with you yet," he murmurs against my skin.

I gasp, as with one swift move, he flips us over, pinning me beneath him.

He's done letting me have control, and so am I.

The image of his body over me, the muscular arms caging me in at either side, it's almost enough to send me over the edge again.

As he lowers himself, my nails rake down his back, a desperate attempt to pull him closer. He hisses at the contact, his body tensing above me.

"Oh, baby," he says with a dark chuckle. I don't even notice him grabbing my wrists and pinning them above my head until it's too late. "You looking to be punished?"

I clench around him.

Yes. Yes. Yes.

And with a smile so devilish, I shiver, he drives into me. It's both unforgiving and sweet bliss.

He lowers, never losing his rhythm, and takes my nipple in his mouth, sucking and licking before taking it between his teeth. The sensation is intense. My back arches, desperate for more. He bites down enough for it to hurt, but just enough for it to mix with the pleasure coursing through my veins.

His pace is relentless, the sounds of our bodies colliding echoing in the room. Sweat glistens on his skin, his muscles flexing with each movement, a sight that only fuels me.

"Logan…" His name slips from my lips in a plea, my body winding tighter with each thrust. He only smirks, knowing exactly the effect he's having.

Jesus, what is this man made of?

And then, in one deep push of his hips, I feel the shock root itself at the base of my spine, warmth engulfing me once more. I bite my lips together, knowing if I open my mouth, the sounds that come out will be nothing short of animalistic.

Watching me, his eyes turn dark, before he takes his free hand, grabs my face between his fingers and squeezes, forcing my lips to part. I know I'll feel his touch long after it's gone. He's branded there now.

"Fucking scream, baby," he demands.

I do.

I scream his name, my body convulsing beneath his as my release washes over me in waves. He doesn't slow, riding out my orgasm, prolonging the pleasure until I'm a trembling mess beneath him.

"That's my girl… Fuck. You feel so fucking good."

His movements become erratic, his grip on me tightens. I can feel him throb inside me as his orgasm takes hold, each pulse of pleasure drawing a rumble from deep in his chest. He holds me tight against him, as if anchoring himself to me.

His thrusts become uneven, more desperate.

It's in the next breath, he stiffens, and I feel the warmth of his release fill me.

A shuddering sigh ripples through him as he breathes my name against my skin, his heart pounding in rhythm with mine. The grip he has on me doesn't lessen, and I understand he's grounding himself in this moment, in me.

His eyes lock with mine, both of us covered in a sheen of sweat, and breathing like we can't catch enough air.

Pressing a soft kiss to my swollen lips, he says, "I should have known you were going to be too perfect."

FIFTY-ONE

With dawn's first light stealing through the slats of the blinds, I find myself watching her sleep like a fucking creep, yet I can't stop. My free hand traces patterns on her back, relishing in the fact that she's here with me.

Somewhere on this long path of darkness, I managed to find her. A beacon. A force so strong she's impossible to stay away from. She's my guiding light. She casts away the shadows while fighting her own.

In loving her, she taught me my most important lesson. I thought she was my weakness, but a man's greatest weakness isn't a woman. A man's greatest weakness is underestimating the strength of one.

The world is quiet except for the soft exhale of her breath, each one a warm puff against my skin. She's draped over me, her head resting on my chest.

Her hair, splayed over her face in a wild mess, and her cheeks flush with sleep... she's breathtaking, even in sleep.

Her eyelashes flutter, the first signs of her waking, but before her eyes can fully open, I lean in, pressing my lips to her ear. "Morning, pretty girl." Her breath hitches before she relaxes into me with a sigh. "You snore," I whisper, a teasing grin tugging at the corners of my mouth.

Her eyes snap open, a sudden look of indignation replacing the sleep-filled confusion. "I do not," she retorts, sitting up to better glare at me.

My grin widens. "Like a chainsaw. You woke the neighbors."

She nudges me. "Our nearest neighbors are at least a mile away."

"Exactly."

"You're the worst," she huffs, flopping back down on the bed.

She gingerly lifts the sheets to peek underneath.

"We're naked." A blush creeps up her neck to her cheeks as she quickly covers herself again.

I've been hard since I woke and found her in my arms. It took all my strength not to wake her, but it was the middle of the night before we finally fell in a tangled heap and found sleep.

My hand roams the plane of her back, journeying down until I find the curve of her ass, giving it a light squeeze.

"And I plan on keeping you that way."

There's a spark of anticipation in her gaze.

Her brows knit together, a playful defiance in her eyes as she challenges, "Oh, really? You decided that, did you?"

With a low chuckle, I roll us over, pinning her beneath me.

"I did. I'm a god, remember? You called out to me over and over and over last night." I trail my fingers along the sensitive skin of her inner arm, drawing a gasp from her lips.

She swats my chest. "In your dreams, King."

Hands skimming over my shoulders, her fingers trace my tattoos as if she's committing them to memory. It's a simple touch, but it makes my heart thunder in my chest. It stirs in my blood in ways I never thought possible.

Leaning down, I capture her lips in a gentle kiss, pouring every ounce of my feelings into it. When I pull back, she's looking up at me with soft, doe eyes, and I'm hit with a wave of something akin to devotion. To think, this woman, with all her strength and resilience, chose me. And damn it, I plan to prove to her every day that she made the right choice.

Her thigh slides up my waist as she bites her lips together to stop from smiling, but the grooves of her dimples give her away.

"In my dreams? Really?"

"Uh huh."

I graze my lips against hers. "You're the dream."

As if on cue, her body responds beneath me, each curve calling out for my touch, my exploration. My hand finds her waist, pulling her closer.

"Think I can't make a decision, sweetheart?" I roll my hips. The sudden motion causes her breath to hitch.

"Meh, I'm still not convinced," she says through the heavy pants of her breathing.

We both feel it when the air in the room shifts. I watch her, studying her reactions, drinking in the intoxicating sight of her beneath me, bare and trusting.

Slowly, I slide my hand between her legs, and groan when I feel her already soaked.

It's close to torture when I lower my body onto hers. With one swift movement, I push into her, drunk on how her mouth falls open and her eyes roll.

"Fuck, baby," I rasp, sure I'll never get sick of the way she grips my cock.

Her nails graze my skin, a fiery trail in their wake that only fuels every thrust. I lean down, claiming her mouth, our bodies moving together in a rhythm that is becoming dangerously addictive.

I remember her challenge from earlier and can't help but smirk against her lips. She's too far gone to notice. "Still think I can't make a decision?" I punctuate every word with a purposeful roll of my hips that elicits a moan from deep in her throat.

Wrapping her legs around my waist, she pulls me deeper.

"Logan…" she breathes out, the rest of her words getting lost when I slam into her.

Our bodies are slick with sweat, the air in the room heavy with the scent of us. She arches beneath me, her body tightening around mine.

Pressing up on my knees, I run my thumb over her taut nipples, down the smooth skin of her stomach until I pressure it against her clit.

From here, I get to watch her.

All of her.

"Oh, God," she cries out. Her head falls back, a soft gasp escaping her lips as pleasure overtakes her.

"Let go, baby."

"God, Logan, don't stop," she pleads, her voice shaky.

I watch her, the sight of her surrendering is enough to push me to the edge. But I hold back, letting her ride the wave of her climax. It's a sight I'll never get tired of.

I feel her pulse around my cock, her body tightening under me until she comes undone.

Fucking addicting.

Leaning over her, my hand slips down her spine, resting at the small of her back and pressing her tighter to my chest. She whimpers, her body twitching in anticipation.

"You feel that, baby? How well we fit together?"

Her gasp is music to my ears.

I nip and suck at her nipples, tasting every inch of her and it's still not enough. I'm close to branding her when she stutters out between ragged breaths, "I-I'm yours, Logan."

The words coming from her mouth make me nothing short of primal. My need for her is already bordering on obsession.

She belongs to me, and I belong to her.

A renewed fervor takes over as I move, the room filled with the intoxicating sound of our bodies coming together. It's raw, and perfectly us. I claim her lips. Her hands clutch at me, pulling me impossibly closer as I lose myself in her.

Our shared release is a crashing wave, leaving us both breathless.

Later, with her head tucked comfortably against my chest, I feel her fingers trailing over my skin. I don't know how long we lie there, simply enjoying the peace of each other, but the rest of the world doesn't seem to matter.

Eventually, her exploration leads her to the array of tattoos covering my skin, each one a token of my past. One by one, her fingers trace the designs as if she's reading a language only she understands.

She pauses, her fingers outlining the inked contours of a lone wolf howling against a full moon, its face upturned and fierce. "What's the story with this one?" she asks, her eyes never leaving the ink.

I gaze down at the tattoo, the stark black now faded slightly. It's one of my older ones, a symbol of my youth, my rebellion, and my solitude.

"This one," I begin, my fingers joining hers to trace the tattoo, "Is a testament to an old life. To the times I thought I had to face the world alone, like a lone wolf." I laugh lightly at the memory of my younger, much more naïve self. "I got it when I was just a young punk, convinced that solitary was the way to survive."

Resting her chin on my chest, she looks up at me. "Do you still think that?"

"No."

"Why not?"

Because she owns me, body and soul.

I take her hand and press a kiss to each of her fingers. "I met you, and I learned that even a lone wolf can find its pack, its family, its home."

Understanding washes over her features. She raises to her knees, moving herself to straddle me before she lets the blanket drop and pool around her waist, leaving herself bare and exposed... for me.

Wordless, she leans forward and presses her lips to mine, spilling her agreement into her kiss.

In the journal of her darkest memories, Beth called me her safety. But this woman... this woman is my home.

FIFTY-TWO

BETH

Bare-chested and humming a tune under his breath, Logan maneuvers around the kitchen with surprising grace for a man his size. He's effortlessly flipping pancakes and sizzling bacon on the stovetop while I sit perched on the counter, my legs dangling off the edge.

"I can't believe you're cooking." I'm gawking at him, but I don't care. He deserves to be gawked at. The sight of him in nothing but his jeans, cooking breakfast, is enough to make my heart flutter and my thighs clench. It's with that movement I feel the sting and remember why my body is so stiff.

"Only for you, pretty girl. You're going to need your energy," he retorts, flashing me a roguish grin.

He sidles up to the counter and lifts me by my waist, setting me down on the cool granite. I giggle, swatting his chest lightly as he leans in for a kiss. His lips press against mine, all warmth and tenderness, making my stomach flutter.

"OH MY GOD!"

Our eyes snap open.

It's true, I've called for God more times than I can count in the last twelve hours, but that one didn't come from me.

We both turn to see Kim standing at the doorway, two kids in tow. Her gaze finds us, eyes widening at the sight of us wrapped around each other.

Hannah strolls in after her aunt, unfazed by the scene she walks into. She merely scrunches up her nose and mumbles, "Gross," before making a beeline for the fridge.

A hot blush creeps up my neck as I hastily hop off the counter, tugging Logan's oversized sweater down. He doesn't seem to be the least bit bothered. Instead, he merely chuckles, flipping another pancake onto a waiting plate.

"Morning, Kim," he greets casually, grinning like the cat that got the cream.

Kim's eyes widen comically, taking in the sight of her sister's half-dressed lover in her kitchen. "Morning? That's all you have to say?" she sputters before staring at me and mouthing, *It's about time.* "I text you about dropping the girls off early, but you were obviously... indisposed. There's a toddler running around, you know," Kim continues.

"Speaking of which..." Logan trails off as Isabel totters into the kitchen, a mess of curly hair and morning sleepiness. She holds her arms up, babbling something unintelligible as she toddles towards Logan.

Bending down, he swoops Isabel into his arms, pressing a kiss to her chubby cheek. "Good morning, Isabelly," he coos, making her giggle.

I'm still trying to find words. I think Logan swallowed all of them.

I need pants for this conversation.

Without a word, I hold up a finger and rush to the other room, grabbing a pair of clean shorts from the laundry before slipping them on.

Hannah is pouring herself a glass of juice when I return, and Kim... Well, I think my sister has gone into shock. Not completely sure it has anything to do with the scene she walked in on because she's too busy ogling Logan's chest.

Hannah levels him with a gaze that has more calculation than any nine-year-old should have. "Do you live here now?"

I swear, I'm close to passing out. This is not how this was supposed to go. Me and Logan were going to take things slow, and when we felt truly ready, I would tell the girls. That plan has gone up in smoke.

Running my fingers through my tossed hair, I manage a flustered, "No, honey," but my eyes dart to Logan. His smirk is nothing short of sinful, and his eyes are twinkling with amusement as he mutters low, "Not yet," just loud enough for me to hear. I shoot him a glare that I hope is intimidating, but all it does is deepen his amusement.

The interrogation continues with Hannah. "But you're dating?"

How do I explain to a nine-year-old the delicate, unspoken dance Logan and I are participating in?

"Um... I guess so?" I respond, my gaze pleading for Logan to chime in. But no, he's enjoying this way too much, leaning back with a smug smile and watching the scene unfold.

Fortunately, Hannah seems to take my admission in stride. With a casual shrug, she says, "That's cool." I nearly sigh in relief, thinking that the worst of the interrogation is over, but then Hannah adds, "Do we get to keep Missy?"

Logan finally decides to join the conversation, wrapping an arm around Hannah and pulling her into a hug. "Her, you can keep."

In the next breath, Kim is at my back, squeezing the air from my lungs in a hug. I hear her sniffle and spin around. "Are you... crying?"

She wipes her face. "You're happy."

I am.

She swats Logan's chest. I think she just wants to touch it. "And you make her happy... Holy shit." She looks at her hand. "That hurt." She palms his chest again, looking at me. I swear, she has zero shame. "Is he real?"

"Still not sure."

Taking Isabel from his arms, Kim rolls her eyes. "Put a shirt on, King. You're distracting the women."

I throw my head in my hands and laugh, feeling Logan plant a kiss on the back of my head as he leaves to do as he's told.

Ugh, family.

∞∞∞∞

I settle into the chair at the breakfast table, pulling Isabel onto my lap as Logan brings over the plate of pancakes. At least his bare chest isn't a distraction anymore, especially when he's wearing a triumphant grin. Across the table, Hannah is watching him, her eyes full of awe.

I catch Logan's eye, and we share a moment, an unspoken bond that fills my heart with warmth.

Hannah, ever the negotiator, puts down her fork, her serious gaze turning to me. "Mom, can we have ice-cream for dinner?"

Her question catches me off guard, and I shake my head, chuckling. "No, ice-cream is a dessert, not dinner. And you're eating breakfast."

"But Mom—" she tries to protest, but I shake my head again.

"Don't even try it, baby girl."

She rolls her eyes.

Watching this unfold is like a roller coaster of emotions, and I don't expect the casual yet poignant question from Hannah, "If you're dating my mom, does that mean you're our dad now?"

I sense a shift in Logan's demeanor as his playful smile fades and his gaze softens.

I'm on the verge of intervening, but before I can form any coherent words, Logan stands. He walks over to Hannah and crouches down to her level, meeting her gaze straight on. His eyes are filled with such sincerity it's almost heart-wrenching.

"I'll be whatever you need me to be. You want me to be your friend, I'll be your friend. You want me to be an annoying kind of uncle, I can do that too. You don't ever need to feel pressured. I'm not here to replace anyone, but if it's okay with you, I'd be honored to love you like a daughter."

His words hang heavy in the air, but the brightening smile on Hannah's face dissipates any tension. "When I started school, a boy made fun of me because I didn't have a dad." Her confession is a sharp pang in my heart.

Logan's face is all softness and warmth as he asks, "And what did you say?"

"I said it's okay because I have a mom… and a Logan. I think you would make a cool dad."

Overwhelmed, I swipe at the tears that have managed to escape as Logan pulls Hannah from her chair and into his arms. Over her head, he locks eyes with me. His voice is a silent apology as he whispers in my direction, "I'm sorry."

Sorry?

For what?

But before I can even fathom a response, he's turning back to Hannah, the playful glint returning to his eyes. "Now, what flavor ice-cream do you want for dinner?"

FIFTY-THREE

I'm not sure how long I've been standing here, staring at myself in the mirror, the tube of red lipstick shaking in my hand.

It shouldn't be this difficult to apply some damn lipstick. I've attempted to apply it too many times to count, but right before it reaches skin, I feel his touch there instead.

My heart pounds in my chest as my inner argument causes a sweat to break out along my hairline.

A part of me just wants another piece of control back.

It's stupid.

It's lipstick.

Yet, I can't press it to my lips without wanting to be sick.

With every second, my eyes become more hollow, every ounce of life lost in the memories—his fingers touching my chin in a bruising grip, parting my lips as his soft thumb smudges the red along my cheeks. Tears blister in my eyes, falling over the smears.

His voice echoes there, ringing around my head until my lungs constrict and the air leaving my mouth is shaky.

"Hey, pretty girl." And just like that, a monster's voice is replaced with Logans.

I flinch, dragged back to reality with a bang, but my shoulders slump forward as I grip the edge of the sink.

"Where did you go, baby?" he asks softly, taking a tentative step towards me. Our eyes meet in the mirror.

"Just getting ready for our *real* first date." I try to smile but it falters.

I relax into his hold as his hands press lightly to my shoulders and he spins me around to face him. I drop my gaze, afraid he'll see the ghosts replaying in my eyes.

"No, I mean where did you go?" He curls his fingers under my chin, tipping my head back. Goosebumps erupt as his fingers trace an imaginary line from my neck to my temple. "Where did you go in here?"

How long was he standing there?

Sometimes I hate it when he can read me so well.

I open my mouth to explain but the lump is so thick in my throat it threatens to choke me.

The same hand drops from my face and lightly brushes my arm until his hand wraps around mine to remove the red lipstick. His brows pull together as he feels the tremble in my fingers.

"Did you get in an argument with your makeup?" He takes the lipstick from my hand and places it on the counter, not once taking his eyes off me, and I'm pulled into him like always.

He doesn't ask why I'm shaking, and I don't tell him, but I think he knows. My memories play so easily on my face.

"My dad had a girlfriend when I was little. I don't think they lasted long, but she was kind to me." I have no idea why that's the explanation I come out with, but it's the first place my mind went, and I can never think straight when he's so close. "She was beautiful. Glamorous. And she always wore red lipstick. I loved wearing it too, but..." The words get trapped in my throat.

With a reassuring squeeze of his hand, I know I don't need to explain.

He understands.

He read the journal.

His fingers are still dancing over my skin, his gaze attentive to every word.

"Do you trust me?"

A small smile curls on my mouth. I wasn't expecting him to ask that, but the answer screams at me as I press my hand to his chest. "Yes."

I never thought I would see the day when I could answer that honestly to another man.

He places a chaste kiss to my forehead. "Good. Can I try

something?"

Confused, I shift on my feet, but agree with a nod.

He wraps a strong arm around my waist and in one swoop he places me on the vanity. My dress crawls up my thighs, but I don't dare move. Not when he's looking at me like the rest of the world doesn't exist. Heat flushes over my body. It's hard not to squirm under the weight of his stare, but I'm pinned. I don't think I could move if I wanted to.

With his eyes still locked with mine, he grabs the lipstick and removes the cap.

"You see," he starts, positioning himself between my legs. My breath catches with the friction. "Anyone with eyes can see that you're beautiful. You don't need red lipstick to prove that, but you want it. And what do I always say you have?"

"The power," I breathe.

"Exactly, baby. And a powerful woman should get what she wants. Lesser men will feel threatened by it which is why they will try to break you. Poor bastards." He chuckles but it's dark, full of sin, and my thighs clench around his waist. "No one can break you."

My heart stops when he pinches my chin between his fingers, tilting my head back as he parts my mouth just like Rob did before he called me a whore and smudged red all over my face, but Logan's touch burns for another reason, and suddenly the touch before doesn't matter. It goes up in smoke.

"You've taken back the power of all the big things in your life, and I'm so fucking proud of you. But that doesn't mean you shouldn't have the power over the little things."

Like red lipstick.

A split second before he presses the stick to my lips, he kisses me like he wants one taste before the lipstick stains my mouth and I change. Like he's convinced I won't be the same woman after.

The man who relies on a steady hand for a living is suddenly shaking as he presses the lipstick to my mouth. His gaze darts from my lips to my eyes, and then he spreads the red. And like the flip of a switch, the air becomes thick. His chest heaves, and I think my breathing is non-existent.

Trembling, I reach out and press my palm to his chest where his heart beats bruising rhythms against my touch.

He halts his movements before blowing out a long breath and continuing.

"Your heart is racing," I murmur with him still holding my chin.

"It always does around you."

He pulls away, but only an inch to inspect his work with a satisfied grin. "Still beautiful."

I almost don't want him to stop. I want to stay here in this moment, with my face in his hands and believing I can take on the world when he looks at me that way.

He finally puts the lipstick down before he holds either side of my head, and the look in his eyes is enough to knock whatever air I have left from my lungs. Tears sting my eyes, but for a different reason than when I walked in here.

This man is fighting to pull all the strength hidden in my body just so he can hold it and hand it back to me.

I feel strong.

Over some stupid lipstick.

It's ridiculous if I think about it long enough so I don't. I stay here, in the moment with Logan.

"Your beauty isn't what makes you powerful. It's your fight. Your spirit. And no one can break your spirit but you, baby. The power is yours." He tucks my hair behind my ear, leaving a shiver in the wake of his touch. "You can easily bring any man to his knees, and for you, I'd happily spend the rest of my life kneeling."

It's what all of this has been about. He wants me to feel the power I have.

My spine stiffens and the familiar warmth pools between my legs.

My power.

My power over him.

I have the control.

"You would?" I ask, my voice so husky with need I hardly recognize it.

"Every day, and I'd thank you for it."

I claw at his chest, gaining a satisfied hiss against my mouth. "Prove it."

He smirks, the same one that sends a zing over my skin. It's a beat before his hands fall to my hips in a bruising grip.

"That's my fucking girl."

His eyes grow dark, and the beast is unleashed. He yanks me forward, sliding my dress past my thighs so it pools around my waist.

My head falls back, a sting burning across my flesh as he rips my panties and discards the material.

Goodbye, lovely underwear.

We're going to have to discuss his obsession with ripping my underwear. I'll have none left.

All thoughts drift away as his lips sooth over the burn.

And just like he said he would, he kneels between my legs, hiking my foot on his shoulder.

A devilish smirk pulls on his mouth as he takes one final glance my way.

I'm glad I'm sitting because everything in me has turned to jelly, and it takes all my power to stay upright.

I don't remember my dress feeling so clingy when I put it on.

Christ, he hasn't even touched me yet.

The heaviness in my pelvis is too much and on instinct, I try to shut my legs, but his hand clamps down on my knee.

"Be a good girl and spread those pretty thighs for me."

I nod and do as he says, desperate for more friction to release the tension building in my body.

Everything in me goes lax.

With the first sweep of his tongue on my clit, I almost come undone. A loud moan escapes, echoing against the walls but all I can focus on is his eyes and the expert tongue against my core.

The heels of my feet dig into his shoulders, and his groan vibrates against my already sensitive flesh.

He inserts two fingers, fucking me as his tongue delivers the most delicious punishment, and I shamelessly grind against his face. His fingers curl, beating gentle rhythms against the exact spot that makes my back bow. He works me with expertise, knowing my body like he's spent a lifetime studying it.

A firm grip of his other hand on my hip keeps me pinned to the counter.

"Logan," I moan, feeling heat deep in my stomach.

"I can't hear you. You're going to need to scream my name."

He rolls his tongue in circles. My eyes flutter closed as my legs begin to quiver.

"Logan," I cry, hardly hearing it as my heart thrums all over my body.

"Louder, baby," he insists on a growl, yanking me even closer.

The print of his fingers will be on my body by morning, and fuck,

I hope they are. For once, I want to see bruises on my body and quiver in all the best ways.

"Say my name when you come, Beth."

I want to throw my head back, but watching him between my legs, working my body like it's commanding him, I can't help but stare. His eyes meet mine. There's a demand there, a warning.

My next moan is too breathy.

Not enough for him.

He begins to suck on my clit, drawing screams from me I've never heard before.

Stars begin to cloud the corners of my vision as heat unfurls between my legs. I fill my greedy lungs, and only release air again when the orgasm racks so deeply in my bones, I don't think I'll ever stop shaking.

"That's it, baby. I want to feel you come on my tongue."

I moan over and over again as he eases me back to earth, slowing his strokes and drawing the orgasm out of me so slowly I'm not sure if it's too much or if I don't want it to stop.

With both our chests heaving, he stands and presses a hard kiss to my lips. I can taste my arousal on his mouth, and I moan into his dizzying kiss.

He pulls away too soon, leaving me breathless and wondering what the hell just happened.

Gently, he grabs my hand and helps me to stand, steadying me when my knees lock. His grin is filled with both smug satisfaction and awe when he spins me around to look in the mirror.

I hardly recognize myself. Flushed cheeks, hooded gaze, and lips as red as a blazing fire.

Panic doesn't settle in. I don't want to wash it off or scrub my lips until they're raw. Instead, I roll my shoulders back, stare at the woman looking back at me, and think of the man who painted my lips just moments ago.

He slips my hair away from my shoulder and kisses my neck. "You are stunning."

Our eyes meet in the mirror.

I wonder if I look different to him now.

Can he see it too?

"I'll wait downstairs." Before he leaves, he taps his knuckles against the door frame. "Don't forget that lipstick."

When he disappears, I stare down at the tube, expecting memories to surface.

They're there, but they're not as potent.

Now I see Logan's hand as he brought the lipstick to my mouth, his racing heart, and how he worshipped me on his knees.

Tears spring to my eyes.

He's replacing memories.

He's teaching me that I have the power to do that.

I might not ever replace the old memories. They might always haunt me. But I can always make new ones.

The power is mine.

FIFTY-FOUR

Logan: Meet me in the studio at three.

Me: Why? I'm not getting another tattoo.

Logan: I'm not a big believer in miracles. Just get your ass over here and stop asking questions.

I've been staring at that text for half the day, wondering why he won't tell me why he wants to meet me. I mean, we live feet away from each other.

I glance up at the clock. I've got five minutes, but the curiosity has me itching to leave.

Molly pushes her way from the kitchen, catching me checking the damn phone again. "You should finish up. It's quiet. I've got things under control here."

Usually, I would refuse the offer, but I'm about to combust.

"You're sure?"

"Of course."

I don't waste another second. As I'm packing up, Molly calls out to me, a strange glint in her eyes. "I'm going to miss you."

My brows furrow. "I'm only going across the street."

Her grin widens as she waves me off, "Yes. Yes, you are."

She knows something, but I know even if I ask, she won't tell me.

The air is crisp as I cross the street to Logan's studio, autumn well settled into the streets of Pine Falls. I push open the door, the soft chime of the bell echoing. It's quiet in here, too.

Venturing further, I find Logan waiting for me, Hannah and Isabel on either side of him.

"What are you two doing here?" I ask, taken aback by the sight of them.

Hannah bounces on her toes, barely containing her excitement. "We have a surprise for you!"

"You do?"

Logan only sends me a slow wink and I melt all the way to my feet, the chill from outside quickly forgotten.

I look between them. "A surprise, huh? Does it have anything to do with why I'm here?"

Logan just chuckles, ruffling Hannah's hair. "Maybe it does, maybe it doesn't. You'll just have to wait and see."

Impenetrable.

Isabel giggles from her spot beside him, her little hands covering her mouth as if she's guarding a secret.

They herd me out of the tattoo studio, and I let myself be led, my curiosity fully piqued now. We stop in front of the building next door.

Logan hands me a key, a teasing smirk playing on his lips. "Go ahead."

Confused but eager to know what's going on, I insert the key into the lock, turning it with a click. The door swings open, revealing a flight of stairs. Hannah and Isabel grab my hands, pulling me forward with infectious excitement.

"What's going on?" I ask, glancing back at Logan who only nods for me to continue.

I let them lead me up the stairs, and the sight that greets me at the top leaves me stunned. It's a fully equipped photography studio.

The studio is an impressive blend of design and functionality. Natural light filters through vast windows, illuminating the room in a gentle glow. Neutral walls serve as a blank canvas, ready to highlight any color palette, while an array of backdrops in various hues and textures are set in one corner.

Lighting equipment—soft boxes, umbrellas, beauty dishes, ring lights—are scattered around, a spectrum of tools to achieve the perfect lighting.

In the room's heart, a large desk laden with high-resolution computer monitors sits as the creative command center. A top-tier printer waits patiently nearby to materialize digital art into tangible prints.

Two doors branch off to other rooms, likely housing a treasure trove of lenses, tripods, and more, the stuff photographers dream of.

It's like Logan walked into a store and asked for one of everything a photographer could ever need or dream of.

It's absolutely perfect.

I whirl around to face him, my mouth hanging open in shock. "What is this?"

He crosses his arms, leaning against the door frame with a satisfied smile. "It's yours."

I blink at him, speechless. "Mine?" My brain is struggling to catch up. "Logan, this must have cost a fortune."

His brows pull together like I'm speaking a language he doesn't understand. "And? You need studio space."

Just like that.

"Why? Why did you do this?"

He simply smiles and takes my face in his hands. "Because you shot Emily's wedding last week," he replies, his eyes twinkling with pride and a hint of mischief. I gawk at him, the pieces not quite coming together in my head.

I was proud of that shoot. It turned out incredible, but when you're taking pictures of a runway model, it doesn't take much work.

"Your photos are about to be featured in just about every magazine in the country," he adds.

The room starts to sway, but he keeps me steady.

"How do you know that?"

"Emily called me this morning," he confesses. "She thought I might like to be the one to tell you."

I blink at him, trying to process what he's saying, what he's done. It feels like I'm standing at the edge of a dream, on the precipice of something wonderful and life changing.

"Everyone is about to see just how amazing you are," he whispers, his voice laced with admiration and a deep, unwavering affection. "And I'm so fucking proud of you. You're about to live the dream, baby. Live life in color. Though, you might want to give Molly your notice because you're going global."

I glance around, my mouth still on the floor. The girls are looking up at me with so much pride, my heart is about to burst out of my chest.

"You did all of this in one day?"

"No." He takes Isabel in his arms when she practically climbs up his leg. All of this, me, the girls, it's second nature to him. "We've been working on it since you told me you were the photographer for Emily's wedding."

"You knew?" I say, swallowing the lump in my throat, even as tears fall.

"Knew what?"

"You knew it was going to be a success."

He eyes me, offended. "I always knew."

"I...I don't know what to say.".

"Say yes," he whispers, a plea hidden in his voice.

Suddenly, a chorus of tiny voices fills the room as the girls join in. "Say it. Say it. Say it." Their enthusiasm is infectious, and I can't help but feel the corners of my mouth tug upwards.

But it's not what I say. I don't say yes. Not yet.

Heart ready to explode, I turn to him, and I know.

I've always known, I just didn't say it before because I've been too busy basking in *his* love. And Logan's love is all consuming. It holds you together when you think you might break. It heals when the scars of the past become a little raw.

My voice sounds strong despite the tremble in my hands when I say, "I love you."

I can't pinpoint since when or how long ago, but I know I've fallen too far to ever find a way out. I know I'll keep falling because that's the thing with loving someone like I love this man—a love like this is like falling without ever hitting the ground.

There's no shock on his face, only the flash of a smile. The one that makes my breath catch in my throat.

He knew.

He knew I loved him all along.

Curling his fingers under my chin, he tilts my head back and presses a soft kiss to my lips.

Hannah gags and Isabel giggles.

We both laugh against each other.

The room is suddenly filled with the soft murmur of Logan's voice, all attention trained on him.

"And I love you. More than I ever thought it was possible to love someone," he starts, his gaze never leaving mine. "You have no idea how much you've changed my life. From the moment you stepped foot into it, you gave it meaning."

He then looks at Hannah and Isabel, his smile gentle, full of love. "And you two… You two own my entire heart."

He takes a deep breath then, pulling back to look at me once more. There's a certain look in his eyes, a promise of the future, of the lifetime we're about to spend together. "Now say it, baby. Say yes. I need to hear what it sounds like, because I plan on making you say it again someday soon."

I smile through the tears flowing down my cheeks.

Taking a deep breath, I look at Logan, my eyes darting between him and the girls, this new life he's offering me. I think about my dreams, my passions, my future. My heart swells at the thought. At the opportunity. At him. And then, with a smile that threatens to split my face in half, I let the answer roll from my mouth.

"Yes."

FIFTY-FIVE

Three months later…

I asked Logan to come to the studio before he leaves for the evening. I'm usually home by now with the girls, but if I don't do this, I'll chicken out and it'll swarm around in my head until it drives me crazy.

The studio is set up and ready to go. My camera stands on the tripod in between two box lights, illuminating a simple white background. I have no idea how this is going to turn out, and I have a feeling it's going to wreck me emotionally more than frustrate me if it doesn't turn out right. I check the lighting one more time, already knowing it's perfect, but the nerves have begun to bounce around in my stomach until I'm nauseous.

Shifting from my heels to toes, I go into the back to check my phone again. Maybe he can't make it. I expected him to be finished forty minutes ago.

I hardly have time to second guess it when I hear my name. Exiting the back room, my stomach flips when I set eyes on him. That smirk zings across my skin.

"Sorry, I got held up with a customer," he explains before his eyes ping-pong from the studio setup to me and back again.

"That's okay." I try to take a step, but my feet remain stuck to the floor beneath me.

His eyes fall to my bare feet, lifting along the length of my body before settling on my face. I cross my arms to hide the tremble in my hands.

"What's going on?"

What if he doesn't agree? What if he thinks this is a crazy idea?

I'm unable to find a coherent thought while he searches my face. I cast my eyes to the floor, as if the answers will magically appear there.

This was so stupid.

Four slow but determined strides and he's so close he robs my next breath.

"First of all…" He slips off his jacket and drapes it over the chair before grabbing my chin between his fingers and forcing me to look at him. "You're too fucking far away."

I try to smile but even my cheeks shake. He presses his lips to the corner of my mouth, then the other side before finally capturing me in a kiss so gentle yet so invigorating, I forget why I'm scared. He pulls away too soon, leaving a dizzy fog in his wake.

"You're nervous." It's not a question.

I nod, feeling the back of my throat prickle with emotion.

"What do you need from me?"

Not what's wrong? What do I need? Because truthfully, there's nothing wrong.

"I'm going to go crazy if you don't speak to me, pretty girl. Do I need to kill someone? Help you bury a body?"

I burst out laughing but only because there's no humor in his tone. He's ready to go to war because I'm nervous.

"No body. Not tonight anyway." I swallow the fear-soaked lump. "I need your hands."

He cocks a brow, the ghost of a satisfied smirk curling on his mouth. I yelp when he grabs my ass and presses me flush against his chest. "They're all yours."

"Horn ball," I tease, slapping his chest and stepping out of his hold. I don't want to, but if I remain in his arms, I'll never get this done.

"I want to take some photos." I fiddle with the supplies on the table, heat rushing up my neck before straightening his jacket. Anything but look at him. "Don't worry, our faces won't be in it. I just want to try something. I don't even know how it will turn out, and you can say no, it was just an idea."

With a firm grip on my waist, he spins me around, making me

swallow the rest of my ramblings. "I'm all yours."

No questions.

That's it.

I need him.

He's mine.

"Thank you."

He dips his chin before I take his hand and guide him in front of the camera, positioning him so he's center.

Lighting looks good.

But I'm sure even in the worst lighting Logan looks good.

He watches me intently as I make some minor adjustments with the angle, toning down the lights a fraction.

"I need you to take off your T-shirt." Another arch of his brow before he fists the material at the nape of his neck and pulls it off in one swoop, discarding it out of view. Behind the lights, where he probably can't see me, I take a moment to ogle him. This is how he should always be. The man was made to be put in front of a camera, even if he'd scowl at me if I told him that.

Inhaling a steadying breath, I set the timer and join him on the other side. This side of the camera isn't my comfort zone, but with him, I can do it.

Heated eyes warm me as I remove my sweater. I hear him groan when I slip my jeans down my legs and throw them to the other side, leaving me in nothing but a black bra and panties.

Not daring to look at him because I don't want to see what he thinks, I press my hands on his shoulders, turning him so his back is to the camera.

The camera flashes.

With a cleansing breath, I close my eyes and I remember. I let myself go back in time, feel fresh bruises and warm blood on my skin, and another piece of my heart shatter. I need to bleed one more time so I can stitch up the wounds.

In my head, I scan the pictures stored away inside, long before I began putting them in a journal.

The first bruise was on my shoulder.

It takes a long minute before I bring a trembling hand to his, interlocking our fingers. He squeezes, sending me strength without ever having to speak.

What must be think?

The camera keeps flashing.

The memories keep coming.

I press his hand to my shoulder.

The camera flashes.

Then I guide it to my stomach. The time keeps ticking, the camera keeps flashing, and I reel out of control.

Shaking like a leaf, I let his hand rest on my hip.

It's when I attempt to move his hand again, he becomes rigid, his hold on me tightening until I finally open my eyes and stare up at him. And for the first time heavy tears leak out.

He sees it.

Like I've punched the air from his lungs, his mouth sets into a hard line.

He's seen the photographs.

He's touching me everywhere I've been hurt.

I'm not sure what I was expecting to see, but in there, he's furious, protective. He schools his features until all that's left is adoration.

This amazing man has no clue what I'm doing, yet somehow, he still understands it.

He understands me.

"Eyes on me, baby," he demands quietly, his own voice cracking. "It's just me, pretty girl."

His hands move on their own accord now as the camera continues to capture the journey, and I don't take my eyes off him for a second.

Strong and warm, his hand spreads out over my collarbone until his fingers dance past my neck and his thumb brushes my lower lip. A lip that has been busted more times than I can remember.

With a tortured groan, he cups either side of my face and presses his forehead to mine, all the while gently soothing away non-existent bruises from my cheek bones, around my eyes, my temples.

I already know how a man's hands can inflict pain. Logan taught me that they can also heal the wounds.

"You're beautiful," he whispers. With his words, a sob ruptures from deep in my chest, and all the touches before his drift away as if they've been washed away with the threatening storm outside this studio. "You're perfect." His breath sweeps across my neck as his lips touch the shell of my ear, and his next words take root in the depths of my soul. "You're safe." His hand glides down my arm, leaving goosebumps prickle the flesh as his thumb motions in circles around my wrist. "You're mine."

He tours my body, his fingers the needle, thread, and stitch, healing open wounds he didn't create.

Dizzy from him, my eyes fall closed as he continues whispering in my ear. "You drive me crazy in the best way, and I'm in love with every inch of you."

Eyes locked, that familiar energy charges in the air around us.

Pressing on my toes, my lips graze his as I whisper, "I need you."

Grabbing the back of my neck, he takes two steps and pins me against the wall, his eyes searing into mine. I see a wildfire there, uncontrolled and insatiable, licking my skin with white hot flames.

His kiss elicits a moan from me that echoes in our intertwined breaths.

In an effortless movement, he lifts me, my legs instinctively coiling around his waist, our bodies perfectly aligned against the cold, unforgiving wall. With a swift yank, my panties are off, the sound of ripping fabric only spurs him on.

His jeans follow, discarded in a heap at our feet.

I feel him against me, hard and ready, and the anticipation has me gasping for breath. Then, in one deliciously agonizing motion, he pushes into me.

The familiar stretch draws a cry from my lips, both from pleasure and sweet, sweet pain. He fills me completely, never loosening his grip.

With my eyes falling shut and my hands clutching his broad shoulders, I retreat into the sensations taking hold.

"Keep your eyes on me," he orders gruffly. My eyelids flutter open, meeting his intense gaze.

It's enough to send me over the edge.

He thrusts again and again, this time with a fervor that steals my breath away. It's raw, it's unyielding, yet so achingly right. Our locked gazes are the only anchor in this whirlpool of desire.

When his gaze shifts from me, drifting down to where our bodies connect, there's an audible hitch in his breath, a stammering heartbeat that echoes my own. His hand, hot and steady, guides mine to join his gaze.

"Look, baby," he implores, voice a throaty rumble. His words dance on the edge of a whisper and a plea. "See where you belong, how good you look on me."

An overwhelming surge of pleasure mounts, growing with each

devastating trust of his hips. His grip around my waist tightens as he continues to drive into me with abandon. It's almost too much—the intense stimulation, the exhilarating sensation of begin held up against the wall so effortlessly by him. But I can't, I don't want to look away.

Logan's muscles tense, his eyes darkening with the same impending release that threatens to unravel me. A guttural groan rumbles in his chest, matching the rapid rhythm of our entwined bodies. I feel his body tremble, his controlled movements becoming erratic as he succumbs to the inevitable.

And then it hits me. A white-hot, all-consuming wave of pleasure that sweeps over me with such force it wrenches a strangled cry from my throat. The sight of us, lost in our shared ecstasy reflected back at us, only serves to intensify the sensation.

"God, Beth..." His voice is strained, choked out between clenched teeth. He buries his face in the crook of my neck, breaths ragged against my skin as he follows me over the edge. His body shudders violently against mine, each pulsating wave of his release matching my own.

Even as our movements still, his arms remain firm around me, holding me with a strength that belies the aftershocks that continue to rock his body. His breath, hot and uneven, tickles my ear, and I know in this moment, I've never felt more cherished, more loved.

FIFTY-SIX

"Beth, you ready, baby?" Logan's voice floats in from the living room.

"Almost," I shout back, grabbing my heels.

For one night, and one night only, we're back in the city. I already can't wait to get home. But we've been locked in Logan's loft most of the day, which has made it easier.

From the bathroom, I give a quick nod at my reflection. In a year, there's so many changes and my dress reflects as much. Instead of the black satin I wore last year, this is a cream off-the-shoulder that hugs my waist. The slit is a little higher than I'm comfortable with, but I'll live.

I take a deep breath, summoning my courage, and then I step out of the bathroom.

When I walk into the living room, Logan's back is to me. He's wearing a tailored tux, and his broad shoulders fill the suit jacket perfectly. The trousers fit him like a glove, hugging the hard lines of his legs and making me think about how it feels when those muscles press against me.

At the sound of my footsteps, he spins around, and his eyes lock onto mine. When he sees me, there's a fire in his eyes that makes my heart race. He stands frozen for a moment, the intensity in his gaze making me feel like the only woman in the world.

There's something about a man in a well-tailored suit that can make a woman weak in the knees. Seeing Logan in a tux, looking so debonair and dangerous at the same time, sends a thrill of excitement through me. My mouth goes dry, and I have to remind myself to breathe.

He's a sight to behold, a dream in the flesh, and he's all mine.

"You look... unbelievable," he says, his voice rough.

His eyes travel the length of my body before meeting my gaze. His expression is intense, making heat pool in my stomach.

"Christ," he breathes, and I'm acutely aware of the effect I have on him.

His feet carry him across the room, until he stands inches from me. His strong arms encircle my waist, pulling me close to him.

"How do you feel about being late?"

His fingers dance lightly along the curve of my waist, making me gasp. I can see the smug grin that plays on his lips, knowing the effect he has on me. His lips hover over mine, so close yet so far, teasing, promising.

"You're a menace. It's the charity art exhibition. Jake and Claire are going to kill us," I say, but my voice lacks conviction, and he knows it. His grin widens before his lips finally meet mine in a searing kiss. A kiss that promises more, a kiss that promises a night of love, and a kiss that, I know, will definitely make us late.

His hands roam my body, igniting a trail of fire wherever they touch. My fingers clutch onto his shirt, pulling him closer. "We can be a little late."

∞∞∞

Stepping out of the car, my fingers are entwined tightly with Logan's as we make our way to the grand entrance. Underneath the bold archway, warm light spills out onto the cobblestone path, illuminating the vibrant floral arrangements lining the doorway. The excited murmur of voices and soft strains of music reach us from inside.

Squeezing my trembling hand, he leans in. "Nervous?"

"Just a little," I admit, a light flush creeping onto my cheeks.

"We don't have to go in there."

"Of course we do."

"I'm serious. I'm willing to double my donation just to get you home again."

I blow out a breath, still feeling the throb of having him between my legs just moments ago. "You're insatiable."

Nothing but a wink, but it helps to settle my nerves. The scent of his cologne washes over me, grounding me.

As we make our way inside, my heart is pounding with nerves.

Logan never releases my hand, his thumb rubbing circles on the back of it, his touch reassuring, even as he's stopped every few seconds by someone he knows. His confidence is infectious, and it helps me relax, pushing the nerves to the back of my mind.

My heart is ready to explode out of my chest when we turn a corner and he stops in his tracks, his grip on my hand tightening. I follow his gaze to a large canvas hanging on the wall.

"Beth?"

The room hushes around us—or at least it seems that way.

Wordless, he looks at me. I don't know what he's thinking and it's killing me. He doesn't speak as he takes the steps toward the canvas, pulling me along with him.

His jaw ticks, the muscles tense, and even in these shadows I see tears well in his eyes.

I'm making Logan cry.

I'm not sure whether to feel accomplished or guilty.

As we take the final step, I see my name, and emblazoned at the bottom of the canvas is the title of the piece: "Healing Hands."

The piece is made up of the photos I took during the darkest period of my life, pictures from the secret journal I kept when I was married to Rob. The images don't reveal my face, but they capture the marks, the bruises that were hidden beneath clothing and makeup.

But overlaying those stark black-and-white images are other photos, ones in color. They're images that represent my new life, my new love. It's the photos of Logan and me in the studio, although nobody knows but us because our faces aren't shown. He's touching me, caring for me, in all the places where I was once hurt. It's past pain and present healing.

After my photography took off, Claire called me and demanded I donate a piece for the auction. I doubted myself but knew I couldn't refuse. The shelter saved me. And I knew it was time to tell my story… for me. I had the power to do it and do it how I wanted, tell it the way I wanted it to be told. I didn't tell my story with words. I've never been much good with those. But I could tell it in snapshots of time.

Logan's entire body tenses at my side, and his hand on mine becomes a vice. The jovial atmosphere around us seems to fade as he steps towards the canvas. His eyes, always so filled with life and mischief, harden into ice.

For a long moment, he's silent.

I'm on the precipice, laid bare before him. I had been excited for him to see, but now, I'm petrified at what he might say, how he might react.

Finally, he turns to me.

"I know...I know it's a lot to..." I begin, but he cups my face in his hands, his touch firm but tender, and pulls me into his gaze.

"I look at this," he says, gesturing towards the canvas, "And I don't see what he did to you. I see your strength, your resilience, your heart. I see the woman I fell in love with." His voice breaks, but he continues, his grip on my face tightening. "I see a woman who took her pain and turned it into art. A woman who survived.

"I want you to know something." His thumb gently wipes away a tear that escapes my eye. "I am so damn proud to stand beside you. I am honored to be a part of your life. I am in awe of you, and I am so fucking in love with you."

And in this moment, I know that he sees me—all of me—and he loves me. In spite of it all, because of it all. He loves me.

He silences my response with a kiss, a kiss that speaks of love and promise, a kiss that says I am his and he is mine.

Surrounded by beautiful art, I realize that we are the masterpiece.

"I love you," I whisper against his lips, my heart soaring.

His lips curve into a smile, his hands dropping from my face to wrap around my waist, pulling me closer to him. "That's all I needed to hear," he murmurs, his eyes softening with love. "That's all I ever need to hear."

"There's more," I admit, pulling an envelope from my bag.

"More?"

I extend the envelope, but the second he moves to open it, panic surges through me. I quickly grasp his wrist, stopping him.

"No! Don't look at those here," I insist, my eyes darting around to make sure no one is watching us too closely.

He raises a brow at me, a knowing grin starting to form. "What's in there?"

My cheeks flush and I lean in, my lips grazing his ear as I whisper, "The camera was on a timer. It captured... everything. And I mean everything."

Frozen, his eyes widen in surprise before a familiar spark of heat flashes across them, a wicked grin curving his lips.

"Is that so?" he says, his voice dropping. The timbre sends a shiver of anticipation down my spine.

"Yes," I say, pulling back to meet his gaze. I can't suppress the mischievous smile that creeps onto my lips, watching as his eyes darken with a mixture of shock and unmistakable desire.

"Sounds like we have some viewing to do later," he murmurs, tucking the envelope securely into his jacket pocket.

"Pervert."

He squeezes my waist and silences me with another kiss.

"How about you get me something to drink. You're making me sweat." I give him a faux stern look, but my amusement bleeds through. "I'm going to find Claire."

He concedes with a grin, pressing a brief kiss to my forehead before slipping into the crowd.

I turn to leave, but after just a few steps, I hear him call my name. Puzzled, I turn back around, meeting his eyes across the room. He's watching me, a soft smile playing on his lips.

"Yes?" I call back, tilting my head in question.

"Nothing, pretty girl," he answers, his smile growing wider, "Just looking."

EPILOGUE

Two years later…

LOGAN

"Please help me in welcoming Mr. and Mrs. King!" The announcement vibrates through the hotel suite, rolling in like distant thunder from the celebration below.

Beth's cheeks are flushed, pressed into the white sheets, her brown eyes fluttering. "I think they're looking for us," she murmurs, her voice low and breathless.

I growl in response, my hips rolling against hers as I thrust into her once more. "Let them wait."

"But—" she begins to argue, the rest of her words dissolving into a moan as I bury myself deeper.

"They can wait," I repeat, reaching between us to tease the bundle of nerves at her core.

As she starts to protest again, I cut her off, thrusting into her harder. She tightens around me, her body trembling as she clenches, a stifled whimper escaping her lips.

"Do you still want to leave?" I tease her, smirking as I meet her gaze.

"No," she gasps, her back arching off the bed, the pool of white silk that is her wedding dress gathered at her waist. Her fingers dig into the muscles of my biceps, the sting of her nails drawing a hiss from me.

Reaching down, I grab her discarded veil from the floor. "What are you doing?" she asks, a note of anticipation creeping into her voice.

I capture her wrists in one hand and tie them together with the delicate material. "Preventing my wife from tearing me apart," I tell her, my voice hoarse with need.

Her eyes widen, and a sultry smile dances on her lips as she tests the restraint. The sight of her, bound and writhing beneath me, is enough to make me forget the crowd waiting below. The lust in her eyes mirrors my own desire, raw and unrestrained, as she revels in the position I've put her in.

I take her again, harder this time. Each thrust a promise, each gasp a testament. She's mine. Just as I am hers. And I relish in the privilege of making her mine in every way possible. Her body tightens, her moans rising in intensity, filling the room with a symphony of pleasure.

I keep my pace, moving in rhythm with her, the pleasure building. Her breath hitches, her body tensing beneath me as she reaches her climax. I follow soon after, our names echoing off the walls in shared ecstasy.

Our panting breaths are the only sounds as we come down from our highs. I gently untie her wrists, pressing kisses to the slight red marks left behind by the veil.

With a groan, I roll off her, pulling her to my side. I press a soft kiss to her temple, my thumb tracing lazy circles on her bare hip.

"We really should get downstairs," she whispers, her voice barely audible.

I pull her closer, pressing another kiss to her forehead. "In a minute."

After all, we have a lifetime of minutes to spare.

Despite the clamoring crowd below, despite our absence from our own wedding reception, I find myself cherishing this moment of quiet intimacy, the calm in the storm. It's our first moment as husband and wife. And as I hold her in my arms, I realize, it's only the beginning of our shared journey.

I can feel her smile against my chest, her heart matching mine beat for beat.

For a moment, we lay there, tangled in the white sheets, her in the remnants of her wedding dress, me, bare and basking in the afterglow. This is the kind of tranquility I crave, an intimate hush just between us.

"But seriously, we can't keep them waiting any longer," she breaks the silence, her voice laced with amusement and an undercurrent of mischief.

I press my lips to her forehead, pulling her tighter against me. "Maybe we should give them a reason to really celebrate."

She swats at my chest. "You are incorrigible."

"Only for you," I retort with a grin, pressing a lingering kiss on her lips.

Reluctantly, I get up from the bed, offering her my hand. She takes it with a shy smile, our fingers intertwining naturally. She's beautiful, a sight to behold, her hair a wild mess, lips swollen, her skin still flush from our earlier activities.

As we prepare ourselves, stealing glances and sharing soft kisses, I know that every second with Beth is worth more than any applause waiting downstairs. This woman is my world, my universe.

We descend the stairs hand in hand, met with applause and cheers that echo throughout the hotel. Our girls are here somewhere, busy playing and oblivious to our absence. The room is filled with the people we love, but all I can see is her, the woman who stole my heart and healed it, the woman who is now my wife.

As the crowd toasts to our happiness, I pull her close, whispering into her ear. "To forever, Mrs. King."

BONUS EPILOGUE

BETH

"Look, Daddy, I got the ball." Isabel stands still, beaming up at Logan with pride. It's very short-lived pride when a kid from the opposing team takes the opportunity to steal the ball back.

Isabel growls, sprinting away with determination.

Please don't bite anyone.

"Go get 'em, baby!" Logan's voice echoes across the soccer field, his enthusiasm reverberating as he cheers.

Hannah rolls her eyes, a flush of embarrassment staining her cheeks. She turns to me, a pleading look in her eyes. "He's going to give himself a heart attack, Mom," she complains, sinking into her chair.

I nudge her. "Aren't you used to this yet?"

"No." She crosses her arms over her chest. "And he's going to stop doing that at my games now, right? I'm thirteen."

From beside us, Logan overhears her comment and barks out a laugh, a grin splitting his face. "Not a chance, kid," he retorts, catching his breath.

Hannah sighs, but I see the corners of her mouth twitching. For all her teenage embarrassment, I know she adores him. She gets up and wraps her arms around his waist.

"You'll always be my little girl," he tells her, kissing the top of her head.

"Happy Father's Day, Dad," she murmurs into his chest.

A tenderness washes over Logan's face as he wraps an arm around her, pulling her closer.

When the crowd erupts into cheers, we all whip our heads around to see Isabel dribbling the ball toward the goal. Her eyes are alight with determination, her tiny form a streak of energy.

"Go, Isabel!" I cheer, my voice joining Logan's. His hand finds mine and he gives it a squeeze. We're both on our feet now, hearts hammering in our chests as we watch her give it everything.

And then, as if in slow motion, we see Isabel's foot connect with the ball, sending it flying. It sails through the air, a perfect arc, and lands right into the net. The crowd roars in approval, applause rings out across the field. Our little girl just scored her first goal.

The joy on Isabel's face is priceless. She turns to us, her arms raised in triumph.

Hannah is the first to break free, rushing onto the field to scoop up her little sister in her arms. Logan follows suit. I hang back, my heart swelling as I watch them, my family.

As I watch Logan holding the girls, love spilling from his eyes and warm affection coloring his voice, my mind wanders back through the years, marveling at how we've evolved, how we've grown into this beautiful family.

For Isabel, it was natural to see Logan as her father. She was so young when he came into our lives, her memories of a time before him fading into a blurry past. He has been there for all her firsts since.

Hannah, on the other hand... I'm not sure exactly when that transition happened. When he'd promised to always be there, he'd meant it, and he'd followed through in ways that still surprise me. There was a certainty in his voice, a promise that he'd kept, faithfully.

He was there for every milestone, every victory, and every challenge. We were a team. Parent-teacher conferences, illnesses, homework sessions, tantrums, tears—Logan was there through it all. More than that, he was usually the one who could put a smile back on their faces.

One day, the word "Dad" slipped from Hannah's mouth. It was so natural, so unforced that it caught us both by surprise. There was a moment of silence, and then a smile stretched across Logan's face, before he excused himself. He said he didn't, but I know he was crying like a baby. Since then, it became a title he wore with pride.

Watching him now, surrounded by the love of our daughters, the enormity of it all hits me. The man who promised to always be there for them had gone above and beyond to keep that promise. He hadn't just filled a void; he'd given us all a whole new dimension of love and family.

Witnessing this scene, I'm overwhelmed with love, for the father he has become, for the family we have built. I've never been more certain about anything in my life—Logan was meant to be a part of our lives.

"Dad" isn't just a title. It's a promise. It's a commitment. It's love. And Logan—well, he's the best Dad I could ever have hoped for our girls.

∞∞∞∞

The air is cooler, the taste of Springtime fresh on the breeze. I'm standing on our porch, leaning against the wooden railing. The rhythmic pulse of distant crickets and Missy's quiet snores are the only sounds echoing in the calm darkness. The comfort of solitude wraps around me like a blanket.

When we decided to live together, we knew that we wanted something that was truly ours—a place that symbolized our unity, our combined dreams and hopes for the future. So, we built a house together. A labor of love that, brick by brick, reflected our joint effort, our shared vision.

It wasn't just a house; it was a home. A place where we laughed, cried, and loved. A place that saw us through our best and worst days. A place where we grew together, not just as individuals, but as a family.

Without needing to turn, I know he's there. Like always, I can sense him, his presence, his warmth. He moves behind me, an unseen smile curving his lips.

"Is Isabel finally asleep?"

He yawns, a soft exhale of breath against the nape of my neck. "That fifth reading of *We're Going on A Bear Hunt* really did the trick," he replies, his voice low and husky with tired satisfaction.

His strong hand slips around my waist, anchoring me against him.

He's warm, a constant source of heat in the chill of the night. His other hand lifts my hair from my neck, his fingers cool against my heated skin. His lips descend on the curve of my neck, setting my nerves alight. Each kiss he presses is a sweet torture, a delicious assault on my senses. I arch into him, a soft moan breaking the silence.

Secure in his arms, I close my eyes. I'm awash in the feel of him, the scent of him.

After a long minute, I ask what I always ask. "What's the dream?"

His hold tightens around me, pulling me closer still. He buries his face in my hair, a deep breath ruffling the strands.

A heartbeat of silence passes before he answers, "You, pretty girl. You've always been the dream." Pressing another kiss to the sensitive spot below my ear, he says, "Come on, I want a shower."

I eye him over my shoulder. "Have at it."

He digs his fingers into my waist and tickles before his words hit my ear in a growl. "With my wife."

The promise in his voice ignites a spark in me. His gaze is warm, filled with an intensity that has my pulse fluttering.

With a crooked smile, he extends his hand. "Ready?"

I thread my fingers through his. "Ready."

The End

We love hearing your thoughts.
If you enjoyed It Should Have Been You, please consider leaving a
review on Amazon or Goodreads.

WANT TO READ MORE BY
LAURA ASHLEY GALLAGHER?

CHECK OUT *THE WHAT WILL BE SERIES*

GET IN TOUCH

You can reach me on my website. I would love to see you there.
www.lauraashleygallagher.com

You will also find me on Facebook, Instagram, and TikTok.

ACKNOWLEDGMENTS

First and foremost, I want to express my profound gratitude to the woman to whom this book is dedicated – my sister. Your unwavering support and love have been the beacon guiding me through this journey. Thank you for being my cheerleader, my confidante, and my best friend.

To my wonderful husband, thank you for being my rock, my safe harbor, and my biggest fan. Your encouragement and belief in me have been a constant source of strength. And to our son, who brings so much joy, love, and laughter into our lives every day, you are the light of my world.

To my parents, thank you for fostering a love for stories and the written word in me from an early age. Your unfaltering love and belief in me have been my pillars of strength, and I am forever grateful.

This past year has presented some unique challenges. Being diagnosed with MS was a hurdle I never expected to encounter, but life often throws us curves when we least expect them. Writing this book was my solace, my escape. Beth and Logan, their story, their struggles and triumphs, became my companions through some of the toughest moments. The journey was longer than any of my previous books, but it was also the most rewarding.

My heartfelt thanks to Joanne Campbell, my editor. Your remarkable patience, wisdom, and invaluable feedback have been indispensable in shaping this book into what it is. I couldn't have done it without you.

To Josh, for always being at the other end of the phone with answers. For that, I'm eternally grateful.

To my incredible team of ARC readers, thank you for your invaluable input and unyielding support. Your insights and encouragement have been invaluable, and I'm grateful to each one of you.

And finally, to all of my readers, thank you for taking this journey with me. Your support, your messages, your reviews, they all mean more to me than I can ever express in words. You breathe life into my stories, and I am so grateful for each and every one of you. Thank you for allowing me to share my dreams with you.

Thank you all from the bottom of my heart. Here's to many more stories to come.

Made in the USA
Monee, IL
04 August 2025

22597664R00236